CONNECTION

GIFTED BOOK TWO

R.L. MERRILL

Published By: Celie Bay Publications, LLC
Edited By: Kelli Collins – Edit Me This
Cover Design: Elizabeth Mackey

❦ Created with Vellum

For my bestie, the real Cassidy. Thank you for believing in me as much as you've always believed in yourself. I love you.

PROLOGUE - GODFORSAKEN PLACE

Prologue - Godforsaken Place

Irene

Fall

Irene counted and recounted the items in the supply closet of her makeshift clinic over and over, taking solace in things she had control over.

Ten rolls of gauze

Three tubes of Bacitracin ointment

Two bottles of Calamine lotion

One box of syringes

Twelve doses of penicillin

Denise had to choose this place. Why, Denise?

Three boxes of Band-Aids

God, I hope snakes don't get in here. I hate snakes.

"Have you finished taking inventory of the infirmary? If you need more supplies, the men are going into town tomorrow, so just leave a list with Lance."

Matt's voice tore her from her guarded thoughts and caused her to jump.

"Yes, sir," answered Irene. Matt was the lieutenant of the man they called The Second, the son of the pastor in charge of The Maker's Plan Community.

Matt glanced around the room as if he too were cataloguing its contents. "That's good."

Irene focused on her list, not letting her thoughts stray from the items she'd meticulously written down, especially with Matt in the room.

"Is that all, Irene? Is there something else?"

She pressed her lips together. She needed to do a better job of keeping her mind clear. He could be reading her right now. Nothing good would come from pleading with him. He was a dedicated member of the community, one who believed the teachings of the pastor, Gerald Rains—or as they'd been instructed to call him, His Right Hand.

"Yes, sir. I'll finish my list of needs." She shoved her hands in her pockets and poked herself with the paperclip she'd stashed there. It helped her focus.

Matt looked around once more…perhaps looking for anything that she might use as a weapon. He tilted his head to the side and appraised her once more. Then he nodded and stepped out of the small shack. The screen door slammed closed behind him, bouncing once against the wooden frame, leaving Irene alone with her thoughts. Thoughts that sent her heart into palpitations.

She spent most of her time in the infirmary to avoid interacting with the others in the "community," as they called it. She had made a small bedroom for herself in one of the two supply closets and rigged a lock on the inside. It would at least slow someone down, but wouldn't likely keep anyone out.

The few medical supplies the community possessed were in the larger closet. They didn't even take up half of the shelf space. There wasn't nearly enough of anything for the amount of people gathered here deep in the Florida Everglades.

The snakebites and insect stings were bad enough, but if something tragic occurred, Irene knew the community would likely perish.

If only Denise had come to her senses and we'd left like I've been begging her to do, we wouldn't be stuck in this godforsaken place!

Irene didn't allow herself to dwell on her worries, let alone speak her thoughts out loud. She was terrified of anyone hearing her. Any negative thoughts, if sensed by one of the readers at their compound, could lead to pain and suffering, worse than what she'd already suffered in this place. Mosquito bites, extreme heat, dehydration. Hunger. They were lucky they didn't all have malaria. Or worse.

For the past six months, she and her daughter had been living among people who had outrageous beliefs about God and the end of the world. It was certainly not how she'd pictured her life when she turned forty-five. But being a mother meant caring for your child from the womb to the tomb. She just hoped that the tomb wasn't their reality sooner rather than later.

The screen door was yanked open once more and Irene cleared her mind, though her hands were still shaking.

"Good morning, Mom. I came to see if you needed any help."

Denise bounced happily into the room. Her work assignment was in the kitchen and since she'd finished preparing breakfast, she was free until her supper shift. The lieutenants had the entire camp on rations, so they were down to two meals a day. Irene was managing, but others were increasingly unhappy. Though no one dared say anything, nor did they show any discomfort outwardly.

Irene turned to her daughter and, yet again, whispered, "Denise, I'm begging you, please, can't we just leave this place? We're not safe here. I have a bad feeling."

Denise's cheery disposition faded and she narrowed her eyes at her mother. "That is no way to talk. His Right Hand has spoken. We are here to do His work. You mustn't have selfish or negative thoughts or His Plan will not come to fruition. Haven't you paying attention at service?"

Irene sagged. For so long, she'd thought maybe she could get through to her daughter...but with each new day, her suspicions were confirmed.

Her daughter was lost to her, completely enraptured by the man she'd followed here.

"You're right, Denise. I'm sorry. I must be tired."

Denise was happy once again. "You'll see, Mom. When Our

Maker comes, we will be ready, and we'll be his Chosen. Then all of this will seem like just a distant struggle and our path will be clear before us."

Denise embraced her mother tightly, and Irene swallowed back tears.

She had a decision to make: either join without reservation or attempt to leave. Leaving might mean she met her end before the others. It would also mean abandoning her daughter.

The lieutenant returned minutes later.

"Prepare for a patient. We have an emergency!" He let the screen door slam as he ran back out and down the steps.

Denise and Irene jumped into action, working as a team, and had the room prepared just as Matt returned. Two men dragged in a third in oversized clothes, his head hanging forward and his arms pulled over their shoulders. They carried him to the bed and lay him down as gently as possible.

"His Right Hand!" Denise gasped, covering her mouth with her hands. "What happened?"

"He was on the brink of death when we found him," one of the men, Earl, explained. "We were tracking the ones who took his daughter and he confronted them in Shreveport, but something went wrong. The authorities transported him to the hospital there and we... picked him up. It's a miracle he survived. One of the signs."

The men exchanged looks that led Irene to suspect that wasn't the whole story.

His Right Hand moaned, and Irene grabbed her blood pressure cuff and stethoscope. She took his vitals and instructed Denise to take his temperature.

"Temp 103, BP 200 over 120... He needs to be in a hospital."

His Right Hand grabbed Irene's arm with a surprisingly strong grip.

"You will heal me." His voice was hoarse and his mouth moved as though he'd been stranded in the desert and was completely dehydrated.

"I'll do what I can, but—"

"We will pray for you, sir."

His Right Hand turned his head toward Denise. She took his other hand and bowed her head.

"Bless you, child," he said, and his cracked lips split into a smile. He let go of her hand...and placed it lovingly on Denise's abdomen. His eyes fluttered closed and he seemed to lose consciousness.

Irene's stomach turned. *God, no.*

Denise had met Gerry—His Right Hand—when she was nineteen, and was immediately taken with him and his ministry. Now, two years later, she'd helped The Second and Gerry build this community and was the latter's trusted assistant.

Denise had always been passionate about things; animals, the homeless, boys... She would throw herself into causes until she got tired of them and moved on to the next crusade. This time, though, she believed she'd met her true calling. She was attending church near their home in Coral Gables, a town between Ft. Lauderdale and Miami, when she'd met Gerry. He was a visiting pastor at the church, and she was immediately infatuated with both him and his message.

He was an older man, but still fairly youthful in appearance, if not plain. He traveled a lot with his ministry, and each time he'd returned to Coral Gables, he'd brought "brethren" with him. After a few weeks, he started talking to Denise about her calling. He said he was called upon by "Our Maker" to bring together His followers in preparation for His Plan.

Denise had told her mother all about it, asking her to come and be a part of their new community of brethren. They had rented a large house in Coral Gables and people were showing up weekly to join their cause.

Concerned for her daughter's safety, Irene had gone down immediately and tried to talk some sense into her daughter. Denise had already given Pastor Gerry all of the money she'd had in savings bonds, and she had it in her head that she was going to be elevated to a leadership position.

Soon, the house wasn't big enough, so they moved out to the swamp. Now Gerry was called His Right Hand, and Denise did his bidding.

Irene cringed, now realizing just how dire Denise's situation was.

She'd seen the way Gerry looked at her daughter, knew there was more than a working relationship between them. Irene had feared the worst. With Denise's baggy clothes, it was difficult to tell, but now… she knew it was true.

It disgusted her to think of her daughter lying with a man older than Irene herself, but Denise had always been a force of nature, a willful child who'd grown into a bold woman. Irene never could exert any sort of control over her daughter, especially after her father had left them.

Now Irene was stuck. There was no way she could leave now, especially if a grandchild was on the way.

She had a terrible feeling that things were going to go from bad to worse.

CHAPTER 1
RESTLESS

Jackson
Winter

"Mr. Howe, can you come take a look at my painting? I'm not sure if I should add more color."

I crossed the room to see what Matteo had created this time. The kid was an art prodigy, and all because of a series of heart-wrenching tragedies.

Teaching art to child victims of trauma meant being prepared for any type of response, especially for the students at Havenhart Academy. They were all here because they had a little something...extra about them, and Matteo's gift was exceptional.

"Matteo, that is incredible. Que bueno."

His latest work featured a beautiful brick courtyard draped with delicate palm fronds and various species of ferns. In the corner was a woman cloaked in white, kneeling next to a fountain. Only the side quarter of her profile was visible but it was enough to see that she was smiling softly to herself as her fingers grazed the surface of the water.

I placed a hand on Matteo's shoulder. "Your mama would be so very proud of you."

Matteo had joined Havenhart Academy in the fall and had excelled in all of his subjects. His English was improving, he kept Skye Livorna—the academy's science teacher—on her toes with his wild experiments in the lab...but it was in the art studio, where he spent most of his time, that he'd really opened up.

I asked him frequently why he wasn't hanging out with the other students, and he would always respond, "Mr. Howe, if I don't get these images out of my head, no me puede dormir. I can't sleep. And if my drawings can help another person, no me quiero falta. I don't want to be late again."

Matteo's family was killed in separate terrorist attacks in Spain. He started drawing pictures at a young age of explosions and other terrible tragedies, which sadly seemed to correspond with actual events. When the headmaster of the academy, Nigel Hart, went to visit him, he was astounded by the images Matteo had been drawing in his sketchbooks, and only wished he'd found him sooner.

I felt for the kid. I knew what it was like to be powerless to change the events that played out in my head, and I'd been much older than him when my "curse" took root.

Matteo helped me close up the studio for the evening and we walked together back to the boys' dormitory.

"Señor Howe? Does it ever get easier? What you see?"

Not really, no. I was pretty raw tonight, but I knew the kid needed to talk. He knew the minimum about my past. The other kids knew, as well, but I didn't go out of my way to give them details.

"It does. Most of the time, I can at least recognize it for what it is." I didn't want to tell him that I had nightmares most nights, that I saw shit happening I wished was *only* a nightmare, but knew in my heart to be true. I saw suffering on a daily basis. The things that helped the most were art and music...though on days when I was in particularly bad shape, I had other ways of dealing with it. Which I would be doing as soon as I dropped him off at the dorm.

"I just hope I can learn how to use what I see to help people, tú conóces? Then at least I'm giving people a chance."

"Si, claro. Of course. Now hit the bunk and get some shut-eye. Can't help anyone when you're dead on your feet."

"Yes, sir," he said, rolling his eyes. The kids laughed when I went all Ranger on them. They had no idea. If they thought *this* was rough...

But then, I had to remember that the structure of military life—the life I'd spent the previous twenty years living—likely *would* be a cake walk for these kids, who'd experienced so much trauma.

I waved to him as he walked into the lobby of the dorm before I headed over to the front gate.

"Vincent, I'm taking the truck. I need to head into town."

Vincent was the academy's driver and head of security. He spoke little and liked being out of the spotlight, but his presence kept those on campus feeling safe. This was crucial, given the clientele we served.

Havenhart Academy took in broken and damaged kids from around the world who'd been touched by tragedy, and who possessed certain gifts that either enhanced or hindered their lives. Headmaster Nigel Hart brought them here by whatever means necessary to help heal them and watch them flourish. He staffed the school with only the most brilliant and gifted people who could meet the needs of the students, with skills ranging from physical and emotional healing to manipulation of the elements.

Staff members also possessed a wide range of Sight, meaning they were able to See events occurring elsewhere, people in danger or pain or, in some cases, things that have yet to happen. Some were incredibly powerful, while others were only just learning how to use their skills to help the students.

Delaney Frost, for example, the new counselor, never knew that her ability to make others feel safe enough to share their personal stories— including bringing big, burly men to tears when they'd never shed them before—was more than just good active listening techniques.

Dr. Damien Preston, the Director of Students, had interviewed her the previous spring, and was so impressed that he'd brought her to Havenhart this year. Then he'd proceeded to seduce her—which I'd *hated* at the time. But now it made sense.

As for me? I made Connections with certain people, though I had no idea why fate chose the particular people I Connected with.

I rubbed the back of my neck as I drove into town. I was so tired.

Tired of being alone, tired of faking happiness for others when inside I was a fucking mess. I'd thought my prayers had been answered when Nigel hired Delaney this past summer. Ever since meeting her back in college and Connecting with her, I'd wondered if we'd one day have a chance together, if that was maybe the *reason* I Connected with her. When she arrived here at Havenhart, it was quickly apparent that she was meant to soothe the pain of someone else.

At first it royally sucked, but Damien was a good guy, and Delaney was so happy with him. Not to mention, there hadn't been the spark between us that I was expecting. I knew it was better this way. I wasn't exactly a catch.

That didn't keep me from thinking of Cassidy.

Delaney's best friend.

My most recent Connection—and the strongest I'd ever experienced.

As I turned onto the main street in Blue Spring, Arkansas, the small town closest to Havenhart, I was assaulted by memories of the events that occurred the day we met…

———

It all happened so fast. One minute we were gathering ingredients for making s'mores, the next, our worst nightmare was coming true…

The evil presence had once again gotten past our wards and technology, and was gunning for our friend.

We couldn't lose Delaney. She was too important.

She took off running into the woods, with Damien hot on her heels.

"Delaney!" Cassidy darted forward, but I grabbed her hand.

"Go back to the kitchen and tell whoever you see that Delaney's in trouble. Send them our way. Please! Then stay inside."

I hoped like hell Cassidy would listen. I feared for her safety. If Rains knew she was equally important, she'd become another target.

I pushed my body forward, running at a pace I shouldn't due to the fact I was still healing from a gunshot wound. I ran for all I was worth, becoming winded quickly. I heard Damien calling out to

Delaney just ahead. Every breath stabbed me in the gut, but I pushed on, trying to catch up to them, until my legs gave out and I nearly fell. I bent over and held my side, trying desperately to catch my breath, when all of a sudden the woods filled with light—and I heard a gunshot.

Delaney.

I took off again, scrambling to find them, when Damien's screams ripped through the woods. I found them in the clearing the school used as a campfire pit. Damien was holding a bleeding, unconscious Delaney, begging and pleading with her to breathe.

I had a choice to make: stay and administer aid to her, or go after Rains. If he got away again, who knew how long this nightmare would continue? And I knew Damien was a powerful healer.

"Where'd he go, Preston?"

Damien gestured with his head, indicating the direction of the assailant. I took off running again.

Former Marine and medic George—and Delaney's cousin, security expert James—caught up to me, and I pointed them in the direction I thought Rain's had gone, but I couldn't speak. I ran for another hundred yards before my lungs seized up. I dropped to my knees, light-headed, and had to fight to remain conscious. I reached deep within myself to draw on my intuition, listening in the darkness for the intruder. I feared I was too late.

I heard nothing for several minutes, until the crash of boots to my left let me know that James and George hadn't found the assailant.

"Son of a bitch!" James fought to catch his breath as well. "He somehow managed to scale the wall and made it to the road back there. I heard a car taking off."

I cursed under my breath. I'd been cocky, thinking we could handle anything this guy threw at us. I wouldn't underestimate him again.

"Howe, are you wounded?"

Still unable to speak, I shook my head. James offered me a hand and I allowed him to pull me up, gasping when I was back on my feet.

"Shit. You probably tore that wound. Let's get back. I need to see Delaney."

Somehow, I knew she would be okay, though our Connection was faint. She was far away, I could barely sense her, but she was still with us.

Damien had carried Delaney into the infirmary and was still beside her, trying to use his healing powers.

My God.

Delaney was so pale. They were both covered with blood.

Nigel, Grace and Morgan fussed around her, hooking her up to various pieces of medical equipment, when Damien abruptly collapsed on the floor next to the bed. George lifted him effortlessly and placed him on another bed. Even unconscious, his head was turned toward her.

More of his hair had turned white. There was a new chunk at his temple to join the previous two.

My heart went out to them both. They'd only just found each other. Their bond was so strong, they had to be okay.

Cassidy.

I Saw her in my mind as she stood alone in the hallway outside Delaney's room, silent tears streaming down her face. I sensed her worry and frustration that she didn't know what was happening and couldn't help. She looked vulnerable there, her shoulders hunched and her hands wringing, nothing to occupy them. I gathered she didn't do well with idleness.

Cassidy shivered as I approached, and instinctively I put an arm around her, though I should have asked.

She leaned into me and let out a stuttering breath. "I can't believe this is happening."

Her pain overwhelmed me at our contact and I cursed. "I shouldn't have *allowed* this to happen."

She patted my chest. "You can't control the actions of a madman. Don't blame yourself."

I couldn't explain to her why I should have been able to stop this, and why I should have known it was going to happen. There was no logical or rational explanation, and Cassidy was a logical and rational person. She'd never believe me, and the last thing we needed was her thinking Delaney wasn't safe or getting the best care.

"Why don't you two get some rest?" Grace stood in the doorway with a sad smile. "I'll call you when they wake."

Cassidy wiped at her tears and shook out her hands.

"Hey, she's going to be okay," I said, pulling her closer. She turned into my chest and let out a shaky breath. I wrapped her in my arms and held her close, as though I'd known her forever.

And I did. I *knew* her. From the moment I'd shaken her hand the previous day, flashes of her life had played out in my mind like a movie montage. Vivid, emotional, revealing, and visceral.

The Connections could be helpful from time to time, like tonight, when I needed to locate Delaney. But my gift was mostly awkward, especially when it was with an incredible woman like Cassidy.

And if I told her anything about my stupid curse, she'd think I was crazy and that would be the end of it.

Cassidy's breathing grew steady and I tried to quiet her with soothing words, even as my insides were screaming over our proximity. Random images of her life continued to flow through my mind. Her as a young girl with pigtails in a pink dress with a white collar, then as a gawky teen with her pet rat perched on her shoulder, and then at her wedding.

That Sight sliced through me like shrapnel.

Her feelings and sensations in each of the scenes were so raw. She was heading into a divorce, and it was such a disconnect, seeing her happiest memories but feeling the anguish over fresh hurts at the same time. Especially those involving Delaney. Understandable, of course. She'd just seen her best friend near death.

I shut my eyes tightly and fought to bear the emotional onslaught...

———

I parked the truck and rested my head against the steering wheel. My chest ached, my muscles felt weak, and breathing was a chore. After a few moments, I looked up to see that I'd made it to Shenanigans, the dive bar we hung out in sometimes when we needed some "grown-up time." Being the Head Resident of the boys' dorm meant I had very little time to relax and let go of the tension. I didn't keep alcohol or any other illicit substances in my place, to avoid temptation, both mine and the kids'. But I intended to tie one on tonight.

I'd either grab a room at the inn or sleep in the truck; I wasn't *that* stupid.

I stepped out of the truck into the cool winter night and shivered. All of my battered bits screamed angrily about the temperature drop, another reason for my foul mood. *Just a few more steps, Howe, and you can forget all about it.*

I bellied up to the bar and ordered a bourbon straight. And another. And another. It was so good to feel the alcohol shutting down most of my neurotransmitters and the ensuing fog was somewhat peaceful.

When the bar started to get a little more crowded—Thursdays were Nacho Night—I shifted clumsily to a booth in the corner. My hope was that the fog would envelop me and allow for a complete numb-out. Every once in a while I needed it. Problem was, when the numbness came on, I lost a bit of my control over what I Saw.

CHAPTER 2
CHAOS

Cassidy

The life of a pilot runs like organized chaos. Five to six days on, three or four days off. Fly at night, fly during the day, go to bed in the afternoon, wake up in the middle of the night. I loved my job and didn't usually mind the chaos, but it gave me time to think. A lot of time. Too much to think and reflect. And lately I'd been thinking a lot about my best friend, Delaney, and the last time I'd been to see her back in the fall...and the fact that I still didn't completely understand what had happened. I was due for a visit, and frankly, I was motivated to visit for several reasons.

When I'd hopped a flight to Arkansas to visit her four months ago, I'd needed a hug, a good time, and a distraction from my problems. I never thought I'd watch her almost die.

Watching Damien carry Delaney into the infirmary proved to be a reminder of our mortality, and had me questioning so many things in my life.

I'd been a mess when I arrived, fleeing divorce and a close call with potential financial ruin. I'd run to the one person in my life who I knew could help me get my head on straight, who'd suddenly needed me to be strong for *her*. Which I'd done willingly.

I hadn't expected to walk into the middle of a dangerous situation, and I definitely hadn't thought I'd find myself standing in the arms of a man I'd just met who felt eerily familiar to me for some reason. I'd needed his sturdy frame for just a few moments, to get myself together and try to clear my head of what I'd witnessed.

Delaney was fine now, and her new love interest was as well. The whole situation had left me in shock at the time, and it wasn't until later that I questioned things...like why hadn't anyone called an ambulance? I'd seen with my own eyes that she was receiving excellent medical care from Grace, who they explained was a trauma nurse, and her husband George, who'd been a medic in the Marines. Delaney's boyfriend Damien was a doctor as well, although he had seemed quite pale himself.

But there was something about the school, the situation, that was sort of...odd. I couldn't put my finger on what it was, however.

And though she'd been seriously injured, somehow I knew at the time that Delaney would be okay. At least, that's what I told myself when I stood in the hallway in Jackson's embrace...

———

I inhaled deeply, aware of Jackson's cologne, as well as hints of sweat and medicine, when he suddenly seemed to weaken for a moment and stumbled.

I caught his weight against me. "Hey, you aren't okay either. Let's sit you down."

He was trembling and looking at me like he'd seen a ghost. I was a strong woman, but if he was going down, I couldn't handle his full weight. I guided him over to a couch in the lobby at the end of the hallway outside the infirmary.

"You need to sit. Let me get you some water."

He watched me like a wounded animal as I dug in my pocket for change, hurried over to the vending machine, and bought a bottle of water. I returned and knelt in front of him. I tried to hand him the water, but he didn't take it.

I opened the bottle and held it up to his lips. "You need to drink this."

"Thank you." He took the water from me, brushing his fingers against mine, then drank deeply. His green-brown eyes were as dark as the entrance to a deep cavern. I pressed my hand to his cheek, waiting for his coloring to come back, and he closed his eyes, leaning into my touch with a relieved sigh.

Just as I was about to pull my hand away, his eyes flew open and he sat up straight, that dazed expression gone.

"I'm so sorry you had to see all of this," he said, his voice hoarse.

"What happened out there?"

Jackson shook his head. "By the time I got there, she was already down. I ran in the direction of the shooter but..." He paused. "Did Delaney tell you anything about what happened here a couple of weeks ago?"

"No. I knew something wasn't right before I got here, but now I know she hasn't been telling me everything."

I'd always been able to tell when people weren't being completely truthful, but I'd let myself grow complacent during my marriage and shut down that part of myself out of a need for self-preservation. I couldn't reconcile my love for my husband and the doubts I had about him. I should never have let my guard down, but I had. Knowing he was lying to me regularly—which made me physically sick—became too much to bear, and I'd had to block out my intuition in order to function.

Jackson nodded sadly. "We've got a nutjob after one of our students. Her father. He's been trying to get to her through us. He's very...persuasive. He's been able to convince people to do his dirty work. I'm assuming that's who was here tonight. What I don't understand is how he got through our security." He frowned, and I could tell he was sizing me up, determining how much he should tell me, how much I could handle.

"The last time we had a run-in with his people, I took a bullet to the gut. I've been feeling much better, but my body didn't appreciate me trying to fly through the woods." He barked out a humorless laugh. "Guess I'm not Superman after all."

I tried to process what he said. A gunshot wound? *A couple of weeks ago?* I'd watched him take off at a full sprint. There had been nothing impairing him then. "You expect me to believe you were shot just two weeks ago?"

He fidgeted in his seat and frowned. "I'm a quick healer? I've been shot before. This wasn't even the worst—"

"Let me see it." I knew deep down that he was telling me the truth, but I needed to see it. I didn't trust myself to believe him without seeing.

He blanched at that. "Somehow I don't think showing you is going to make you believe me."

"I'll know if you're lying." I stood and crossed my arms over my chest. "Come on, Superman. Well, you can't be Superman if you've been shot. That would mean you're not faster than a speeding bullet."

He laughed again, but this time winced and pressed a hand to the left side of his stomach.

"Come on," I said, seriously now. "Let me see, Jackson. Maybe you need to see the nurse too."

"Fuck that. George just likes to stick me with his big needle."

I snorted. "Does he now?"

He rolled his eyes. "Fine."

Jackson sat back and lifted his gray sweatshirt and white tee shirt.

What I noticed first was his incredibly sculpted abdomen. My breath caught in my chest and I looked up into his eyes.

His long dark-blond hair fell in big curls around his face, past his shoulders. I had a fleeting thought that I'd like to feel those curls against my skin, but I chased it away before it had time to really take root in my psyche. The last thing I needed was to be lusting after Jackson. I didn't know what kind of guy he was, only what Delaney had told me, but I didn't need *any* guy right now.

I cleared my throat and looked to where he pointed with his pinky at a small, puckered, reddish welt a few inches below his ribs. I couldn't put together a gunshot wound with what I was seeing. I reached out, tentatively, and touched his warm skin. This scar looked much older than two weeks.

When I glanced up, he had a resigned look on his face.

"See? Quick healer."

"Yeah, okay, Superman." I waited for my bullshit meter to go off, but it remained silent. Maybe it was broken? Maybe *I* was broken.

"Hey, it's a secret," he said, bringing a finger to his lips. "Can't have everyone knowing my true identity."

His smile was infectious, even though I could see the pain behind it. He was joking to lessen the gravity of what had just happened, and I appreciated that.

Maybe he was a superhero after all.

———

Even months later, I ran through the events that took place over and over. I hadn't been able to stop thinking about that place—or Jackson—ever since.

CHAPTER 3
NUMB BEFORE THE STORM

Jackson

"You gonna need a bib there, soldier? Cuz I ain't wiping up your drool."

My solitude was interrupted by my latest Jiminy Cricket. Delaney's cousin James had come to Havenhart to help out last fall, when a situation got critical with one of our high-profile students, and he'd been kept on to help out with security. He'd even started teaching self-defense, archery, and marksmanship classes to interested students. The two of us hit it off well, despite the fact that our military service had been in rival branches.

"The only assistance I'd take from you, Squid, is another bourbon. Otherwise you can leave me to my drunken stupor." I wasn't really drunk yet. I had a pretty high tolerance for alcohol.

James cocked an eyebrow, recognizing a fellow soldier's need for inebriation. "Depends on how many you've had tonight, Ground Pounder, and what you plan on doing after."

I snorted at his words, louder than I'd intended, leading me to the conclusion that I was a bit more trashed than I'd thought. "I felt no need to keep track. I just needed a break, man."

I drained the rest of my glass while James motioned to the bartender for refills. "I hear you. Far be it from me to play dad. Anything in particular you needed a break from?"

I groaned. I was so not in a sharing mood tonight. Besides, how did you get across to someone that you were tired of Seeing and feeling other peoples' pain, as well as your own, and just didn't want to feel *anything* for a little while?

"Nah. Everything, nothing. Just tired. How about you, what brings you here tonight?"

"Same shit. Wanted to take off my upstanding citizen face and replace it with one a little less squeaky-clean, dig?"

I laughed at that and smiled appreciatively at the dour-faced barmaid approaching our table. She was dressed in a spaghetti-strapped bra top with cutoff denim shorts and wedge heels. Her hair was dyed black and rolled up in a pinup style. Her makeup, perfectly donned, made her dour face look even more severe.

"Darcy, my love, how wonderful of you to grace us with your warmth and compassion."

"Bite me, Howe. The last thing I need tonight is another shit-faced asshole confessing his undying love to my rack."

"No worries here," James said. "Our devotion is solely to your quick wit and dry sense of humor, as well as the haste with which you serve us our liver-killing beverages."

We were rewarded with a curl of her lip and an exaggerated eye roll, but she kept us in drinks steadily for the next hour.

"How do you people do it, dude?" James continued. "I mean, I love kids and shit, but being all proper and dressed up is really starting to chap my ass. Every morning I look longingly at my Levi's. They miss me, you know? They're the only thing that's going to cup my ass lovingly these days, that's for sure." We clinked glasses at that.

"I hear you. Sometimes I feel like I've joined a monastery. Then again, at least we get to take a break and enjoy less sophisticated activities, like tonight. Just without female companionship, it seems."

"Monastery," he frowned. "Shit. More like back in boot camp, feel me? At least there's some eye candy, but damn. Not that I want to do anything other than look right now."

"You're full of shit, Morton."

"Okay, some touching might be exceptional. But seriously, I have no desire for anything else. Women just suck the life out of you, then they leave you a rotting shell of a man. I got no time or energy for that anymore."

Delaney told me that James' ex-wife had taken off with his daughters and he'd been unsuccessful in his attempts to reconnect with them. I wasn't sure how long it had been, but it was still obviously raw for him.

"I feel you." I finished another bourbon and sat back, resting my head on the booth wall. "Sometimes I just need to get away from being responsible. These kids look at you, man, and they just *need*. I don't know how much more I have to give."

"Yeah well, these kids are lucky. Not everyone gets someone in their life to actually give a shit about them."

James spoke those words as if from experience. I didn't know much about the man and was thankful tonight that I hadn't made a Connection with him. Then I'd know the absolute truth.

We sat there without talking for a while, just watching the other pub-goers. Some folks were trying their hand at karaoke, unsuccessfully. Darcy brought us a couple more rounds and we fell into telling war stories.

"Yeah, dude. My father was a top Navy recruiter and served in Vietnam. I fought entering the service, I really did. I made it my life's purpose to piss dear old Dad off."

"And what did that look like?"

James grinned. "I followed the Grateful Dead, got into fights, spent time in rehab. It wasn't until I decided I was ready to get away from home, far away from home, that I went ahead and joined the Navy. Once I was in, I wanted to get as deep into it as I could. I found several things I excelled at. I made the SEALs and spent several years abroad, in and out of some heavy shit." James finished off his beer and gestured to Darcy for another.

"My parents were both in the Army, they met in R.O.T.C. training. Mom was among the first women admitted after the Army opened up most of its positions to women. We moved around a lot, as you do, and I was usually without one of my parents for a length of time. They were good to me, but not necessarily toward each other, so their frequent deployments were actually for the best. Dad suffered serious PTSD after Vietnam."

Why I was talking about this topic, I had no idea, other than the fact that I knew James would get it.

"Same. Dear old Dad had some hairy nightmares. Pulled a gun on me once when he caught me sneaking in, and it took a minute for him to stop screaming at me in Vietnamese."

"Yeah, my dad had episodes where he would break down crying, screaming, or even go catatonic. I didn't know what to do when that happened because we never talked about it. Dad tried to take care of me the best he could, for as long as he could."

It should have been easier to talk about it after all these years, but my stomach still churned. I could blame it on the alcohol, but even stone-cold sober, I still got sick thinking about it.

"Your dad still with you?"

I could tell James hated to ask the question, but we were at that part of the conversation.

"Committed suicide when I was seventeen. Left me with the memories and my fucking curse."

It had been so damned hard to deal with, but I actually took comfort in the notion that my father was no longer suffering.

"Your curse, you mean that thing you do—"

"Yeah." I didn't need him to go into details.

"I'm sorry, man." He held up his beer. "We've lost way too many."

We toasted the fallen and sat quietly in remembrance for several beats. When it got weird, I continued my tale.

"I joined the Army after high school for two years, then went to Graceland while in the reserves."

"Ah. Where you met Cousin Frost."

"Indeed," I said. "Briefly."

He rolled his eyes. "Thank God Preston isn't a shit stain. Del didn't have the best track record."

I snorted. "We all have our shit stains, James. At least she learned."

James grumbled and took his beer from Darcy.

"You guys want some food to soak up that booze?"

I smiled at her. "Aw, it's like you care."

"I care for the tips, Howe. I'll bring you something. It's not like you're picky."

I blew her a kiss and she flipped me off.

"So art, huh?"

"I always loved art. It was my best friend when I was yet again the new kid in school, and the art community at Graceland was really supportive. Then when I graduated, the Army came calling once again and I ended up joining the Rangers."

"Ah, let me guess. Special training, dangerous missions in the Middle East and Eastern Europe, body beat to shit."

"You got that right," I said, rubbing my knee under the table. Dammit, this booze was not doing its trick. "I got a medical discharge after an IED sprayed me with shrapnel and sliced the shit out of several muscles and tendons in my legs. Physical therapy got me back in working order, but cold weather sucks ass."

"Hear-fucking-hear. Some days it's a bitch to wipe my own ass."

James was a little less forthcoming about his internal battle scars, leaving me to ponder whether he had ever acknowledged them.

Darcy brought us appetizers, which we graciously accepted with assurances we would tip her grandly.

"Yeah, well, it's just to keep your sorry asses from passing out in my section."

The food soaked up some of the alcohol and kept me from my goal of totally numbing out, but the fog was fairly effective in getting me to a more relaxed state than I'd been in since the fall. And the company was doing a lot to improve my mood.

We got silly as the night wore on. James had me in stitches with a story about losing his clothes at a Dead show, when Delaney and Damien walked in. The glow around them was almost tangible. It was comforting to see such a strong bond between two very deserving people. It kind of gave me hope.

Guess I was feeling better, or was just really hammered.

James, on the other hand, was doing his best to appear sober and trying to hide just how many empties sat on his side of the table.

Damien shook our hands, while Delaney just shook her head.

"Boys," she said in her counselor voice.

I squinted to keep from seeing two of her. "You have the exact raised eyebrow that James had when he found me at the bar earlier. Y'all got some strong family traits."

"Good evening, Miss Frost," James whined in a nasally schoolboy voice.

"I see you've been imbibing a considerable amount. Is that a good idea on a school night?" Her arms were crossed over her chest, and if I looked down, besides falling on my face, I'd probably see her foot tapping. That image put me in hysterics, which made James laugh, which made me laugh even harder.

Delaney's expression was all schoolmarm-y, but when she looked at James, she appeared genuinely concerned.

"What, you gonna give us detention now?" James answered her with a smirk. "We're just a couple of lone wolves seeking companionship with Jim Beam. No harm, no foul. What about you, out late on a school night?"

Damien chuckled, and she turned to give him the evil eye.

"It's true, we're just as guilty as these two. We were out for a ride and…er, we seemed to have developed a bit of an appetite."

"Yeah," I said. I tried to copy Delaney's eyebrow look and failed spectacularly, so I used my finger to push my eyebrow up.

She rolled her eyes at me. "Fine. It's late for all of us. We should all be getting back to campus, don't you think?" She glanced up at Damien and the two lovebirds made googly eyes at each other. I hated it.

No, I didn't. Not really.

"Man, can you guys do that somewhere else? I'm kinda sick here," James groaned.

"That could be the Beam, my brother," I whispered loudly.

"Oh yeah. That." James finished his beer and set it down hard, catching the plate on the way down. The bottle was empty, however, so there was no spill, only the clink of glass as the bottle fell over and rolled into his lap. He put it on the bench with the others, making quite a racket, and then folded his hands and smiled at his cousin.

"Right," Delaney said. "Is there room for us with all those bottles?" She slid into the booth next to James, who reluctantly took his bottles and set them back on the table. There were seven.

"You lot have made a nice dent tonight," Damien said as he sat on the bench next to me. I slid over to make room.

"Those are his." I pointed at James. "I've only had bourbon, and I lost count about an hour ago."

Damien took Delaney's hands on top of the table, and I sighed. I loved seeing them so happy, I did, but it made me feel emptier inside.

I zoned out for a moment, looking at the clock above the bar—then found myself gazing at a different clock. This one was on the metal wall inside of an airplane hangar. Under the clock was a window, and I caught my reflection, only instead of my goofy mug, I was looking at a feminine figure in a navy-blue uniform who was checking over some pages on a clipboard. I heard muffled voices in the background and the figure turned to speak to someone on the other side of the glass.

A wave of auburn hair brushed the cheek of the woman in the reflection and grazed her delicate neck. My gaze followed along a slender jawline and up to a radiant smile. Twinkling blue eyes looked amused as she laughed at something someone said to her. She ran a hand through her hair and looked down at her clipboard again—

"Yo, Jackson, you with me?" James' face came into my line of sight as sound came rushing back from the bar.

"Cassidy," I said. And I immediately realized my mistake. None of my gathered friends knew of my latest Connection, and I'd hoped to keep it that way.

"Cassidy?" Delaney asked, glancing at Damien.

The table fell silent, and I wasn't about to offer an explanation.

Damien eventually stood and broke the awkwardness. "All right, kids! Who wants a ride home?"

There was some grumbling, mostly from James, who didn't want to leave his bike.

"I'll take yours back and leave mine. Delaney will drive you two gentlemen back to campus in the truck we saw outside."

James never let anyone ride his bike, but even he knew when he was busted.

"Alright, Jackson, time to go home and hit the hay." Delaney stood and took my hand and tugged me out of my seat. I reluctantly slid over to the edge of the booth and got to my feet, and then I promptly swayed toward her.

"Whoa there." Delaney tried to catch me but I was too heavy. Before we crashed to the floor, Damien reached over and caught me by the waist. He slung my arm around his shoulders.

"Now now, my tipsy friend, let's not impair our counselor. We need to get you to bed."

"Hang on, I need to get the check."

"I got you, Howe," James said, tossing some large bills on the table.

Delaney seemed pleased that James was in better condition than me and had already gotten himself mobile.

"Don't give me that look, Favorite Cousin. I'm bigger'n you, and I can still put you over my knee."

Delaney just shook her head and put her arm around his waist. "Don't I know it. Although if Mom were here, we'd both be running from her wooden spoon."

He kissed the top of her head and we went out to the truck. James crawled in the back of the cab and Damien loaded me in front with Delaney. All I could do at this point was groan.

"You should just put me out of my misery now, Counselor."

"Okay, you big baby. You'll feel better in the morning," she said.

And with that, I promptly passed out.

CHAPTER 4
EVERYTHING'S FINE

Cassidy

"You can keep the truck, Cassidy. I'm tired of arguing with you. I'm dead anyway."

I let my ex-husband carry on with his dramatic tirade when I should have just hung up on him. I was so exhausted by this argument we'd been having since I'd him served with the divorce papers.

"Robert, I don't know how many times I have to tell you. I'm done. *We're* done. The company is never going to happen. There is no way in hell I'll invest one more penny in your damn schemes. Isn't it enough that we've lost the plane *and* our house? If you owe people money, that's on you. It. Is. Over. Don't call me again. If you have anything else to say to me, call my attorney. Goodbye, Robert."

I hung up and swallowed the last tear I ever wanted to shed for that man.

Since returning to Los Angeles after visiting my best friend Delaney at Havenhart Academy, I'd been working on turning over a new leaf. I was a woman in control of my own destiny. My divorce from Robert Crane was finally done. We'd been separated for over a year now, and after consulting with a lawyer, I discovered that he had ruined us financially. He owed so much money to "prospective clients" that he'd taken out liens against our townhome, our hangar, and even our Cessna, which we were going to use to start a small flight-training company.

Like an idiot, I'd let it happen. Let him handle the finances since I was on such an unpredictable schedule, and now I was going to pay for it for a very long time.

My credit report was thoroughly trashed. I was staying in a "crash pad" with six other commuting pilots and flight attendants while trying to decide where to go or what to do next. I loved my job at the charter company, and they had been extremely accommodating, given my situation. My supervisor assured me that I could transfer wherever they had a hub. My clients gave me excellent marks for service—many specifically requested me for their trips—and I was highly regarded by the other pilots I flew with.

Whatever I decided, I was going to put a lot of distance between me and Robert.

He was still begging me to continue with the company. His pilot license had been suspended a year ago—another thing he'd kept from me—and he needed me to help him out of a jam with his prospective clients.

His delusions knew no bounds. There was no way I would ever work with him, not after he'd betrayed me. True, our courtship had been quick and our marriage was often a struggle, but when I learned the true depths of his deception, I left him without looking back. I'd had a sick feeling about things for a long time, but I told myself I was being silly. I knew better and chose to ignore my instincts.

Now I would trust that feeling no matter what the consequences. I'd always trusted it before. Look what happened when I tried to ignore it?

The crash pad was in Hollywood, not too far from any of the Southern California airports. I loved the city but there really was nothing left here for me. I just wasn't sure where I wanted to start over, and for now it was easier to focus on work rather than sorting out my drama.

Delaney and I had always wanted to live close to each other again, and the headmaster at Delaney's new school had offered me a position there as his private pilot, complete with housing. It was tempting. I'd teased Delaney about dealing with the bugs and weather extremes in Arkansas, and I wasn't sure I could handle them either. Could I actually move to the South?

The scenery there was amazing, that was for sure. Including one very tall, very blond, very serious Jackson Howe...

He was not at all the typical guy I went for, but I found myself picturing him whenever I needed a pick-me-up. His long lashes and dark brown-green eyes had looked so haunted when he spoke to me about the troubles the academy had experienced, but there was nothing cold about him. When he showed me his scar, and I touched him, I'd felt more than just his smooth skin. I'd felt a jolt that started a slow burn in my psyche. One that had me wondering how it would feel to get closer...

I knew better than to find a pretty face just to keep my mind off my troubles. Problem was, he was more than a pretty face, and I knew it. He was intense, calm in horrific situations, and intuitive about those around him.

"These kids are all here for a reason, Cassidy. We do what we can to protect them. Most are victims of trauma and they need a lot of support to move on from what they've experienced."

I'd listened, turning on my inner bullshit detector, and I knew there was more.

Delaney and I talked often, and I was happy that she and Damien were fine, but I still had questions. I hadn't been able to get back there because of my schedule, and I didn't want to ask Delaney a bunch of questions over the phone.

They're fine. And I'm so not fine. I was taking care of business but my heart was hollow, like it was meant to be doing something more meaningful than just moving blood around my body. I'd put off making decisions, hoping for a sign of where I was meant to be or what I was meant to be doing.

Ugh. Unlike Dorothy, I couldn't click my heels and be swept home. I *had* no home, only a temporary shared space. I wanted to be someplace where I was valued, where I was allowed to live my life the way I chose.

No closer to making a decision, I decided the best way to get through the rest of the night was a hot bath, a good book, and a restful night's sleep.

CHAPTER 5
THE Q WORD

Jackson

"Why? Why must the day begin so bright? Why are the drapes open?" I squinted and made out Delaney's cat, Ramses, staring at me from the windowsill of—

"Why am I in *Delaney's bedroom*?"

I rolled out of said bed onto my ass and looked around, confused. The morning light coming in the window blinded me and something had obviously died in my mouth last night.

"Hey, keep it down in there, Howe. Some of us are trying to heal a hangover." James was standing in the doorway in his boxers, drinking orange juice out of the carton. "And my cousin doesn't have any beer. Fuck. Everyone knows beer is essential in curing a hangover." He rubbed his hand over his barely there hair. He kept it trimmed to his skull, and his goatee more than made up for his lack of hair up top. It fell to about six inches below his chin, full and thick.

I was still confused. "Why am I in Delaney's room? And where did you sleep?"

"Well, my friend, you took it upon yourself to become

completely inebriated, zoned out and then passed out. I dumped your hairy ass on the bed and I crashed on the couch for fear of you getting over-amorous in your unconscious state."

I ran a hand through my tangled mop of curls. "I don't remember anything. That doesn't happen to me, dude." Seriously, all I could remember was sitting in the booth with James crashing my pity party, Darcy bringing us food, and then—

"Cassidy," I whispered.

"You said that. Last night. What about her?" James stared at me. It was one thing for us to get chatty when we were drunk, but I didn't need him poking around in my bullshit

"I don't know. Forget it. I gotta get back to my place." I looked at the clock. "Damn, my class starts in a half hour." No time for breakfast in the commons, barely time to change, brush my teeth and try to get my shit together.

"I'll close up here, no worries. You should get something to eat." James pulled on his jeans and shirt. "I'm gonna go check on my bike, make sure that damn Limey didn't put a scratch on my baby. I don't care what kind of ride he's got, he ain't a Harley guy. Gotta take special care."

"Yeah, see you later," I said as I rushed out the door. I squinted at the bright sunlight as I stepped off Delaney's porch and once more regretted my decision to cozy up to Jim the night before. *Ugh.* For sure, Delaney was pissed and probably thought I was an idiot. And who knew what I'd told James in my drunken state? I was a fairly private person. It was important to keep my mouth shut, especially considering the amount of other peoples' secrets I kept.

My gift. More like a bloody curse.

Usually it was no more than a few images from someone else's life, kind of like a commercial break between scenes in the soap opera that was my own. Some of the Connections brought me the pain and suffering of others, but I was forced to learn in the service to clear my mind, and once I came to Havenhart, I learned how to control it. Most of the time, I kept the random feelings and thoughts at bay. Those skills were failing me at present.

I'd tried walking my life's path alone to avoid making Connections, but I was an extrovert at heart. I needed the energy I got from being with others. Whether it was the Army, in college or here at Havenhart, I'd surrounded myself with people, but still tried to keep a reasonable perimeter—keep people at a safe distance—to lessen the chances of Seeing things. But as hard as I tried, it still happened.

Loneliness threatened to swallow me up sometimes, like it did last night. It wasn't like me to get so wasted I didn't remember anything. Numb, yes. Oblivious, never.

However, I did recall one important detail. I remembered seeing Cassidy in a hangar. Her smile was like the sunshine. It hurt my eyes, it was so intense, but it did wonders to warm my wretched soul. Her dark auburn hair and adorable freckles intrigued me, sensual and innocent at the same time. But her eyes, blue with a constant sparkle, were ultimately what captivated me. The moment she'd turned them on me and shook my hand last fall, she'd taken my breath away, even before I realized I'd made a Connection with her. She was one of those women who exuded mischievous intentions, and man was I drawn to that.

I'd tried to get her out of my head since that weekend, and I'd thought I'd done a good job. Things had been quiet. Until last night.

I got to my class two minutes late, cursing under my breath the whole way.

"Mr. Howe? You okay?"

Matteo. Bless the little guy. I was too raw to get into it with him, so I just winked and unlocked the door.

The kids were riled up, I could tell from the moment they entered the studio. Normally I didn't mind, but I was feeling a bit prickly. Could have been the hangover, could have been something else.

"Alright, my little budding artists, simmer down. Today we're going to attempt to do a sketch from memory. For some of you this will come easier, as you're clearly able to visualize a person's face or their likeness. The point is not to have the most accurate representation, rather it's just for you to bring out your own perception. This is an exercise, folks. You can use pencil, pens, pastels...whatever you like. Let's see what you've got."

The ten students in my beginners drawing class ranged from new arrivals at age twelve to seasoned academy dwellers who were nearing eighteen. As I strolled around the room after giving them time to get started, I took note of their moods. Keeping my finger on the pulse of their emotional states helped me guide their learning and artistic expression, and also helped curtail the occasional meltdown.

Some of the young ladies were giggling in the corner and when I got to their easels, they turned several shades of pink.

"Well, you've certainly nailed his hair," I joked as I saw all three had chosen to draw Harry Styles. "The dresses are smashing."

They giggled, and I shook my head as I moved on to the next ones.

Matteo was in the corner, and he was working on a beautiful portrait of his sister. Matteo often drew portraits of his family members as if it were the only way he could get the visions of their deaths out of his mind. I gathered that somehow he felt they were still close to him, close to his heart.

"Que bonita," I said to him, giving his shoulder a squeeze. He kept at it, only looking up at me to nod before getting lost in his work.

My next stop was behind the lovely Joanna Rains. The girl was a goddamned superhero. The shit she'd been through. I'd met Rangers who didn't have the guts she did.

Joanna was drawing what appeared to be a self-portrait, but it was abstract, almost like a Picasso. I watched how she picked different blues and held them up to the eyes, seemingly dissatisfied with each one.

"You don't have to add color," I told her. "It's brilliant as it is."

She shook her head. "I can't remember the color of my mother's eyes."

She said it so matter-of-factly, the poor girl. No one knew what had happened to her mother, but it was assumed her father murdered her. She held her pencil so tightly her knuckles were white ,and the vein in her forehead, visible underneath her pale skin, seemed pronounced, as though she were concentrating on a life-or-death issue. *These poor kids.*

A chill ran through me and I rubbed at my arms, warding off the goose bumps.

"Were they like yours?"

She tilted her head to the side. "Maybe? But darker, I think." She turned to look up at me, and I could see her mind working. "I can't see her anymore."

For a girl who could See so much—what had happened already, what was going to happen—this was alarming to hear, and I could tell she was disturbed by it as well, when she was usually fairly matter of fact about the trauma she'd been through. I'd have to talk to Delaney about her. Maybe they needed a check-in.

I squeezed her shoulder and reached over to pull out a navy blue that was a shade darker than her eyes. I'd grown pretty close with Joanna. She often stayed after class to talk about art, which I recognized as her being uncomfortable with her peers. Delaney and I had talked about it and agreed that we could give her a little push toward other kids after she'd settled in a bit more. It had only been a few months since her father had nearly died trying to kill Delaney and Damien. She had a lot to deal with, including an ability to See that went beyond the strongest gifts I'd ever witnessed in our students.

I thought maybe I could do an Internet search, see if I could find any pictures of her mother, but then, I didn't know if I wanted to bring up the pain that might come along with them.

"Wanna try this one?"

She took it and looked up at me. "It's okay, you know. I know she's in a better place."

Joanna turned with the pastel and began carefully adding color to the eyes while I tried to compose myself. I wanted to scream. So much had been taken from her and the other kids here at Havenhart, and now she couldn't recall the color of her mother's eyes? So unfair.

"Mr. Howe, I am sticking."

I frowned and walked over to where Sergei, a young man from Russia, was crumbling up his drawing paper. "I am sticking, I cannot get a start."

"Ah, translation time, Sergei. You are *stuck*. Understandable, you haven't much experience with this. Let me demonstrate."

I put up a clean sheet of drawing paper and reached for my leather-wrapped charcoals. I drew a jawline and hair framing the side of a face. The collar of a uniform came next, and then a clipboard…

"Wow. Mr. Howe, she is really beautiful. Can I take her number?"

I was too busy staring at what I'd drawn to correct him. It was Cassidy's likeness, how I remembered it from the vision I'd had last night. I finished sketching the lines of her face, even trying to catch the sparkle in her eyes. Students crowded around to see what I'd drawn and some of the gasps behind me were clearly audible.

She *was* stunning.

And so very out of my league.

"Hi guys, what's going on? Mr. Howe, I was hoping to talk to you about—"

Delaney had come in behind me and caught me in the act.

"Oh, my. Jackson, it's beautiful!" She looked down at me sadly.

I gave her an apologetic smile and said, "I had a beautiful subject to work with."

She rested a hand on my shoulder and the students began moving back toward their easels.

I let out a deep breath. "I'm sorry. I swear I've been trying not to," I said in a low voice.

She shook her head. "It's fine, Jackson. I know you can't always turn it off. And truly, you did such a nice job, I feel like I'm looking over her shoulder." Then her face turned serious and she lowered her voice to a whisper. "I was worried about you last night. You need anything? Like a swift kick in the ass?"

I chuckled and pulled her in for a hug. Delaney gave a surprised yelp—probably surprised by the intensity—but she held on. I appreciated the comfort. A moment later, I felt warmth radiating from her, and I laughed. She was sending some "feel goodness," what I often called her gift.

"Thanks, Counselor. Guess I should have just asked for *that* instead of tying one on last night."

"You think?" She ruffled my hair. "Remember that next time, ya big goober. I'm just glad we ran into you guys." She looked at the drawing of Cassidy again and frowned. "I should really give her a call. It's been too long since I checked in with her." She gave me a wicked glance and winked. "Shall I tell her you said hello?"

"Not unless you want her to think I'm a stalker. On second thought, yes. Tell her I said hello and that I'd love to fly with her sometime. Wait, don't say that. Just tell her hey... Gawd, I really am a mess." I ran a hand down my face. "No wonder I'm perpetually single. With this kind of defect, it's lucky for me I have any female friends."

"There, there, big guy. She'll be back to visit soon and then you can say 'hey' to her yourself."

I glanced around to be sure the kids were otherwise occupied. "She doesn't know anything, does she?"

"No," Delaney said, looking down at her feet. She kicked at the stool in front of her. "After everything that happened...I probably should tell her, but Cassidy is suspicious by nature. She's been manipulated before, most recently by that asshole husband of hers. I don't know how to tell her in a way that she won't think it's bullshit."

"Probably a good call. And it's not the kind of conversation best had over the phone. Or email."

"Not if I ever want her to come back here," she said with a laugh. "Cassidy is tough and she knows when people aren't telling her the truth. Well, usually. I think that's what hit her so hard about her ex. She seems to have a blind spot where men she cares about are concerned."

I knew there was more to that story, but in front of the kids was not the place to have this talk. "You think she will? Come back here?"

Delaney grinned. "Definitely. And I'm hoping for good. The headmaster offered her a job and I'm hoping she'll take it." She took one last look at the drawing with her head tilted. "Beautiful. You take care, Jackson." She waved goodbye to the students, giving a couple of kids hugs on her way out, and left the room.

I let out a slow breath. That went better than expected. I'd worried Delaney would freak out, but I should have known better. She'd become a true friend and she understood better than anyone how difficult my Connections were for me.

The rest of my classes went by uneventfully and at the end of the day, Matteo and Sergei came in to help clean up the stations. We chatted about their latest video game obsession, Team Fortress Two, and then I closed up the studio. I felt restless on this late-February evening. The chill would soon be gone and then I'd be able to spend more time outdoors. Arkansas winters, for the most part, were mild. Spring was beautiful, and getting out to do some paintings of wildflowers would make me feel better. Eventually.

I trudged slowly back to my apartment on the ground floor of the boys' dorm. Being the Head Resident fit right in to my standard operating procedure of caretaker. My whole life, I'd tried to care for others, first my father and then my fellow Rangers. It gave me fulfillment and made me feel wanted, needed. Someday, though, I'd like someone to take care of *me*, and not like Delaney's counselor routine. I wanted a woman to be my friend and partner, everything my parents were missing in their relationship.

I was so deep in my thoughts, I nearly collided with someone I truly didn't want to see while in my current state.

"You better watch where you're going, Jackson. You just might unintentionally take someone out."

Morgan's mocking tone was the last thing I needed today.

Fiery-haired maven of the media center and the academy's resident mystic, she was ever so blunt. She was also very powerful, and her work was extremely important to the school. She often found students in need through her own sort of pain network. She described it almost like a radio broadcast. Whenever she received those kinds of messages, she'd work to nail down where they were coming from. If it was a child Nigel felt the academy could help, he would go and offer them a spot. There was no charge for the academy and damn if I knew how the school stayed afloat. Nigel must really be rolling in it.

Anyway, given her importance, I figured I should behave.

"You're right, Morgan. I'm sorry." We were standing just outside the boys' dorm. She was obviously on her way back from the commons to the library. "Just preoccupied I guess."

She crossed her arms and kicked out a hip.

Awesome. I was in for it now.

"That seems to happen to you a lot lately. I hope it's not affecting your work." She raised an eyebrow and, gods love her, I didn't have the energy for this exchange.

"I'm keeping it together." I couldn't resist sarcastically adding, "Thanks so much for your concern." I knew she meant well, but damn. Sometimes it felt like folks at this place were hovering, just waiting for me to fuck up.

"Do we need to have a session? I've got time this weekend."

A session? Morgan's sessions drew on all kinds of woo-woo magic that I'd never been a hundred percent comfortable with. Not that I thought it was anything bad, just outside my parameters of copacetic. They often turned out to be painful, embarrassing, and usually left me feeling like piranhas were swimming around my insides.

"I'll pass, Morgan. Thanks, really, but I don't need anyone else getting in my head right now. Its murky depths are nothing to trifle with, milady." My attempt at Pythonesque humor was lost on her as that eyebrow arched even farther.

"If you change your mind—and you should—I'll be here." She narrowed her eyes at me and lifted her chin, continuing on her way.

"Can't wait." I exhaled and shook my head. I was fine. If folks would leave me alone to do my job, everything would be peachy, but alone time was a luxury I didn't get to experience often.

Besides, my Connection with Cassidy was not something a spell could cure. I couldn't go to therapy and heal, nor would a pill make it go away. It was a bond, an open communication channel that tethered me to her, and I'd learned over time that Connections were permanent. Like a "till death do we part" sort of thing, and for whatever reason, I couldn't push this particular Connection to the back of my mind where it would merely hum like a generator or ring in my ears like tinnitus.

I opened the door to the boys' side of the dorm and went inside, thinking perhaps I could sneak in a nap before dinner. The lobby of the dorm was fairly empty with the exception of a few kids who were heading over to the commons early for dinner. They waved as I entered my apartment, and thankfully I got inside without being needed for anything. I pulled off my shirt and flopped down on the couch, rubbing my temples. I'd had a headache for most of the day, a remnant from the previous night's excursion.

No one would miss me much if I skipped dinner, and I wasn't on duty for any activities tonight. A little shut-eye would do wonders.

I let sleep claim me right there on the couch.

And dreamed of Cassidy.

CHAPTER 6
BEST LAID FLIGHT PLANS

Cassidy

"Hey Bestie!"

Delaney FaceTimed me and it was much-needed medicine for my weary soul, seeing her smiling face. "It's so good to see you! I only have a second, though. I'm just about to board a flight."

I so wanted to talk to Delaney, it had been too long—at least two weeks—since last we'd chatted. But duty called.

"Of course! I'm sorry. Going anyplace fun?"

"Probably not. I'm so ready for this trip to be over."

"Aw. I wish you could come visit. I hate going this long without seeing you."

"I knowwwwuh."

She giggled at my reaction. Then her eyes flared. "Oh, and I happened to be in the art classroom today. Jackson said to say hello." She wiggled her eyebrows at me, and I laughed.

Jackson. *Hmmm.* Now there was a face I'd love to see again. I'd only spent a short time with him, but something about our interaction stayed with me, and I'd be lying if I said returning to Havenhart Academy would be only to see my best friend. I was aching to put my divorce behind me and move on. If that meant spending time with a nice guy...

"How is Mr. Howe?"

Delaney looked away from her screen and then back. "Good. Lonely maybe, but good."

"Where are you?" I asked as she seemed to be on a covert operation.

"I'm trying to sneak out of the administration building and get to Damien's without being seen by any— Oh, hi sweetie! I'll see you tomorrow." She waved to someone and then the phone got really close to her face. "They're everywhere. Hold on, I'm going to hide in the conference room." She opened and shut a door. "There. So when are you coming?"

"Cassidy, are you ready to check over the flight plan?"

Janet Dunn, my first officer, was helping me do the last-minute flight checks before I flew the company jet to pick up my next client. It was day four of a five-day trip, and I was so ready for a break. If I had to fly one more whiny snow bunny to Aspen or Jackson Hole, I was going to throw up.

I bit back my hostility, grateful I had a job these days. After everything I'd been through this past year, it was all I could count on. That and my best friend.

"Thanks, Janet. I'll be right there." I pouted at my phone and Delaney laughed at me. "I promise, I'll look at my schedule and make a plan with you as soon as I get home. I love you, friend. I'll call you later."

Delaney wished me a safe flight and we hung up. I walked over to Janet and frowned when I saw the flight plan.

"Ft. Lauderdale, eh? Guess it's time."

"Yeah, spring break excursions usually start later in March, though. Who knows? Maybe it's business."

"At least we aren't going back to the snow."

We finished our pre-flight check and rounded the plane to wait for our clients.

Two women—both with long hair pulled back from their faces, neat-looking plain cardigans, and long black skirts—walked out onto the tarmac with a small bag each. One walked a little in front of the other, also clutching a leather-bound book to her chest.

I smiled professionally and looked down to make sure my uniform was on straight. I tucked a stray piece of hair behind my ear and waited for them to approach.

"Good afternoon, I'm your captain, Cassidy Mackenzie. Can I get your bags for you?"

"That won't be necessary," said the first woman. She wore no makeup and had a smile that didn't reach her eyes. No, her gaze was intense and trained on me. The woman with her glanced around, taking interest in Janet and what was going on in the hangar.

A dull ache took up residence just below my navel, and my stomach lurched as if my lunch hadn't settled well. I hoped I wasn't getting sick, although this sort of pain didn't feel like the flu.

"How long will the flight take?" the first woman asked. "We are returning to our community's headquarters and we'd love to make it in time for evening fellowship."

I tried to keep the smile pasted on my face as they handed Janet their IDs and confirmations for her to run through our additional security.

"We should land in Fort Lauderdale at seventeen-hundred hours," I said.

"Wonderful," the woman said, nodding to her companion. "We should have plenty of time to reach the camp by then. Our services are quite moving. Captain Mackenzie, have you had the opportunity to join in fellowship with other believers recently? We would love for you to join our flock for some much-needed worship time."

The other woman nodded at Janet then pulled out a flip phone, stepping a few feet away to make a call. The phone seemed odd in her possession, since she was dressed as if she were from an older time. It was subtle, but she didn't seem comfortable with the device.

"Oh, thank you for the offer, but we're on a tight schedule." I glanced at Janet, who gave me a closed-lipped smile. She knew exactly how I felt about religious folks. We'd had to fly a few in our past trips together, and even though I'd done my best to be professional, my feelings were obvious to Janet. "Once we takeoff, if there's anything you need, don't hesitate to ask our first officer, Janet Dunn."

The second woman was still on the phone, but the other nodded at me. "Fine. When do we take off?"

"We should be finished with our pre-flight checks and ready to take off in about ten minutes. Why don't you two climb aboard and get comfortable. We'll be with you shortly."

They exchanged another look and then one of them turned and climbed the steps to the cabin while the other continued her phone conversation in a hushed voice, even cupping her hand over the receiver.

Janet elbowed me, a worried look on her face.

"What do you make of them?"

My stomach continued to ache, feeling increasingly tied in knots, but I didn't want to worry Janet. When I'd had this kind of reaction in the past, it usually meant that the person I was dealing with wasn't being truthful, but these women seemed straightforward enough. I had no reason to suspect them of anything other than possibly being hypocrites, but my gut wouldn't stop its spasms.

I took a minute to walk a few steps away and try to breathe through what I hoped were the last of the cramps and I went back over the flight plan. The women's names were Rachael Smith and Sophie Jones. The names didn't ring a bell, and there had been no hits when Janet ran them through security. The company who'd chartered their flight was a religious group called Maker's Plan. Folks like these women, who oozed religious fervor, poked at my deepest source of irritation. Having grown up sheltered by devout Christians, I had little tolerance for people who were driven by fanatical dogma. I needed to suck it up and get them to their destination, though, whether I liked it or not.

"Okay, Janet, you ready?"

Janet smiled and stood close to me. "Amen, sister."

I rolled my eyes and snorted. "I know, I'm terrible."

"No," she said, placing a hand on my arm. "You have your reasons. I know you've been through a lot with your parents."

I sighed. "Yes, well, who knows? Perhaps these women truly are good people out to make a difference."

She hip bumped me. "I'm going back into the office to grab my bag. I'll meet you onboard. Need anything?"

"Nope. Well, some more emergency chocolate?"

"You got it."

Time to put on my big girl panties and do my job. It wasn't fair to distrust people just because of my past.

I walked past the woman on the phone and she glanced up at me once before turning away. I reached the steps—and the dull ache roared to life, strong enough that it made me stop to catch my breath. *Shit.* I really hoped this wasn't going to be a problem. I knew if I got in trouble on the flight, Janet could take over, and it was a short flight, but I was one cramp away from calling for a replacement. I hated to do it for several reasons, but mostly because I needed the money, and it was inconvenient for my supervisor to get another pilot out here.

"Get it together, Cassidy."

I climbed the rest of the steps and the pain in my gut eased enough that I figured I was in the clear.

Until I stepped through the door—and my passenger grabbed me by the biceps and shoved my face into the wall of the plane.

She used more force than I'd have thought her capable of as she pressed the barrel of a gun into my side. Hard. I felt her lips near my ear as she spoke.

"Don't struggle. If you cooperate, you won't be hurt."

She breathed down my neck as my whole body tensed, debating my options. She wasn't that much taller than me, but she was strong—way stronger than I would have thought possible under her unthreatening clothes.

I ran through my training, preparing to act, but then the other woman entered the plane with another gun pointed at me, shutting the door behind her.

"You are going to fly this plane alone, Cassidy," the first said, clearly the leader here. "This is your new flight plan."

The quiet one handed me a paper with new coordinates and I

looked at her in disbelief. "The flight plan was already cleared. You can't just—"

"It's already done," the leader interrupted.

"What about my copilot?"

"She won't be coming with us." The creepy smile on her face made my gut clench once more and my skin crawl. What had they done to Janet?

"We work for a powerful man, and his will is *always* done. You will fly us to these coordinates or not only will we kill *you*, but your parents in Fremont, California, will die as well. We have an associate outside their house right now."

My gut told me she was telling the truth. These women were seriously dangerous, regardless of how shockingly harmless they'd seemed moments ago. I knew they wouldn't hesitate to hurt me or anyone else.

I wrenched my arm away from my captor and walked over to the cockpit. I started to close the door when she stopped it with her hand.

"This stays open, and my partner will be sitting up front with you."

I blew out a quiet breath and slid into my seat. I put on my headset and spoke in a clear voice. "Tower, this is F646 requesting permission to taxi."

Within minutes, I was taxiing down the runway at the busy Houston airport and given clearance to take off. I cringed at how smoothly this was going, and I worried about Janet. Did they...hurt her? Kill her?

I waited until the intruder in my cockpit wasn't looking and entered the emergency code—7500 for Unlawful Interference—and then we took off.

"Which one of you is Smith and who is Jones?"

"I am Rachael," the leader said as she returned to the cockpit. "And all will be well if you do as you're commanded. His Right Hand has foreseen this. Our Maker has plans for you, Cassidy Mackenzie."

Her smile should have given her evil intentions away, or would have if I was paying attention to my gut.

I had no choice but to remain calm while my mind ran through scenarios. I didn't get this far in my career without keeping a cool head under pressure, but I was nervous. Dammit, I should have trusted my gut the minute it started with the aches. If this was five years ago, before I met Robert, maybe I would have acted on my concern.

There was nothing I could do now but fly. The old Cassidy would never have let this happen, but new Cassidy apparently no longer trusted her intuition. Now I was headed to who knows where with these women who'd made it clear I had no choice if I wanted to live.

CHAPTER 7
WHERE THERE'S SMOKE

Jackson

I woke suddenly, completely disoriented, my heart banging around in my chest. The banging I heard grew louder and more frantic until I realized it was the door. I stumbled over and buttoned up my pants before opening the door. Outside was Joanna Rains and Marcia, the girls' dorm head resident. Joanna, a frail young girl with long black hair and piercing silver-blue eyes, looked frightened and even paler than usual—and I knew whatever she had to tell me was awful. She'd experienced so much trauma and usually took everything in stride. But not now.

"Jackson, I'm sorry to bother you, but Joanna said she has to speak with you."

I nodded and crouched my 6'4" frame so I was eye-to-eye with the small girl.

"Joanna, what's wrong?"

She was shaking, her lower lip quivering. "Mr. Howe, I Saw something, but I don't know what it means."

I ushered them into my apartment. It wasn't much, a one-bedroom unit with a great room, including a small kitchenette that I rarely used. The furnishings were tones of tan and brown and the walls were covered with student artwork. I guided them to the couch and I sat on the coffee table facing Joanna.

"It's okay, honey. Tell me what you remember."

She nodded and rubbed her little hands on her thighs. "Green everywhere, hot and wet with slithery sounds. Loud engines and a scream. Raised voices. And..." She trailed off, hugged herself and lowered her head. "And I Saw my father. He's alive."

My stomach dropped at the mention of the man who'd wreaked havoc on us all several months ago. The man was powerful, but he'd been severely incapacitated by Delaney at a hotel in Shreveport and taken to the hospital, where he'd been pronounced dead. Though none of us had fully believed that to be true. Still, we'd all breathed a tentative sigh of relief, hoping we were in the clear. Joanna hadn't had any visions of her father since, slowly growing more comfortable within our community. We'd all thought better days were ahead.

This vision put that happy reality to the test.

"Do you have a sense of what it means? Any landmarks or voices that you recognize?"

Joanna shook her head. "I'm sorry, that's all I know."

"Can I give you a hug?" I asked her.

She nodded and fell into my arms, crying softly.

"It's alright. Thank you for telling me. I had a bad dream too," I said, giving Marcia a knowing look. "We'll figure it out. You're safe. Okay?"

"I know, but I think someone else is *not* safe."

"You might be right." Something was very wrong. I felt it too. "You just go back to your room, okay? We'll figure it out. What time is it, anyway?"

"It's five o'clock. Joanna was headed to dinner when it happened."

"Oh, man. You caught me napping." I smiled like the guilty one I was and covered my mouth, which made Joanna laugh.

"Thanks for seeing us," Marcia said. "I'll take her to eat."

I walked them to the door, and Joanna turned to face me.

"Mr. Howe, please tell Headmaster that all is not as it seems and he should trust his intuition."

"Thanks, Joanna. I will."

Well, that made it official. Cautiously happy days were definitely gone.

I plopped down on the couch with my head in my hands. The nightmare I mentioned to Joanna? It was about Cassidy, and I couldn't shake the sick feeling that something was horribly wrong. I threw on a sweatshirt and decided this news couldn't wait until the morning.

I stepped into the evening air and it did wonders to clear my head. I walked toward Delaney's bungalow, thinking again about Cassidy—

Suddenly, my vision was full of lush greenery and the smell of rotting vegetation filled my sinuses. And blood. My skin was damp with a layer of sweat, courtesy of suffocating humidity. The sky was dark but there were lights in front of me. I stepped forward and felt asphalt under my feet, still hot. The lights wavered and I realized why.

There was fire, and a lot of it.

Smoke filled my nostrils and my chest was tight from the combination of heavy air and acrid soot. My eyes and chest burned. I couldn't get enough oxygen. My legs gave out and I hit the ground hard. Glass shattered in front of me and I shouted when the shards hit me in the face.

"Jackson! Oh my God!"

"Delaney? Is that you? I can't see!"

"Damien! Help me get him inside."

Delaney attempted to drag my 200-pound ass into her bungalow without much success. Damien gave his assistance and between the two of them, they were able to get me up the steps and onto a soft surface .

"Dear God, he smells like smoke. What the hell happened?"

Damien placed his hands on my chest. The smell grew stronger and filled up the room, causing Delaney to wheeze.

"Is he burned anywhere? What happened?"

I heard the puff of her inhaler and I winced, frustrated that I'd brought this to her door. "Delaney, I'm sorry."

"Are you alright, love?" Damien asked her.

"I'm fine, I'm fine. Jackson, can you tell us what happened?"

"It burns," I cried. "The fire…my skin!"

"Help me get these clothes off him."

My sweatshirt was yanked over my head. Cool air brushed my skin like shards of glass, but then it was a relief. Smaller hands, probably Delaney's, went to work on my jeans and when they had me down to my boxers, I started to cough.

"Grab some water. He's going to need it. His skin feels warm to the touch but I don't see any burns."

"I'm tossing these clothes outside," Delaney said, then I heard the fridge open and close. Damien propped me up and a bottle was lifted to my lips. I took a tentative sip and coughed some more.

"His skin is cooling," Damien said. "What the hell happened? Where have you been?"

"My apartment. Joanna had a vision. She came to tell me and I… and I feel like I just *lived* it. I was coming to tell you." I blinked a few times. Thankfully my vision started to return.

"What did she say?" Delaney asked.

"She Saw something. It was a plane crash." I knew my next words were going to crush her. "Delaney—it's Cassidy."

CHAPTER 8
THERE'S FIRE

Cassidy

I'd never felt such pain and heat in my life. If this was a nightmare, it was the most vivid one I'd ever had. My ears rang and my head pounded as though I'd been through an explosion. I couldn't open my eyes no matter how hard I tried, which made me believe I was dreaming.

I tried to move but my limbs ached and my muscles wouldn't cooperate. I started to panic. I knew I needed to slow my breathing or I'd pass out. Without sight or hearing, nor the cooperation of my nervous system, breathing was all I had control over. I reached back in my mind to try to recall my last waking memory. Janet talking to me at the hangar, a sick feeling in my stomach, women with insincere smiles...

Fucking hell. The two seemingly innocent women and their guns. The hijacking.

I'd followed their instructions and prayed the tower picked up my distress call. When we got to Florida, however, I attempted to thwart their plans by landing at an airfield I knew of where I'd be able to get help. Sophie knew just enough about flying and the instruments on the plane to catch me in the act, and her swift backhand had split my lip and caused my ear to start ringing. I was furious as I followed her coordinates…and terrified when I realized they wanted to land in the heart of the swampy Everglades.

"Are you two complete morons?" I balked. "There's no place to land here!"

Sophie wordlessly pointed out a dilapidated landing strip that had been hacked out of the thick greenery.

I guided the plane in that direction, said a quick prayer, and prepared for landing.

It was rough. I did the best I could, but it wasn't enough to save the plane.

We hit hard and skidded into the trees.

Rachael was thrown into the back of the plane just as the fuselage split in half. An explosion sent the front half of the plane lurching farther ahead.

Sophie held on for dear life as I tried to steer the plane through the vegetation. What was left of the cabin erupted in flames. Glass shattered as the windshield was impaled by a tree branch.

My face was struck by flying glass but I knew I had to keep it together.

As the plane's carcass finally slowed its momentum, I unhooked my safety belt. I was running on pure adrenaline, my limbs moving on instinct as I scrambled to get out of my seat. Flames curled up the walls and I choked on the smell of burning metal.

Sophie wasn't moving in the copilot's chair. I momentarily debated trying to pull her to safety but it appeared the only way out was through the broken front windscreen. I climbed onto the instrument panel and turned for one last look.

Bile rose in my throat when I saw that the branch that had come through the front of the plane had actually gone through her chest, pinning her to the chair like a scene out of some horror movie. She was dead, and I would be soon if I didn't get out. The smell of burning fabric hit me as her body was consumed by the fire.

Turning quickly, I placed my hands on the edges of the now-destroyed windshield, cutting my palms on the jagged glass. I heaved myself up and through the glass, then slid down the front of the plane and fell to the ground below. I dragged myself as far away from the plane as I could before I collapsed and lost consciousness.

When I came to, I was being lifted, and I moaned. The pain was more than I'd thought any human could actually survive. I couldn't hear anything but a high-pitched squeal ringing in my ears. I was carried jarringly for a while and when the movement stopped, I was laid out on a hard, uneven surface. Hands stripped off my clothes, and I desperately wished I could open my eyes to see if the hands were there to help or if the nightmare continued.

As the potential saviors continued to work on me, I felt stings and aches wherever they touched. When they moved my left arm, a flash of searing pain ripped through me and I screamed.

The next memory I had included voices reaching over the ringing in my ears. I heard the words "burns...risk of infection...concussion..." I tried desperately to hear what else they were saying but the ringing increased. I focused my energy on moving something. A toe wiggled, a leg bent, and I held onto the hope that I wasn't completely broken.

When I tried my arm, though, I discovered, excruciatingly, where my limits were. My shoulder was damaged somehow. Even trying to wiggle my left-hand fingers hurt. My right side worked but felt heavy. I managed to reach up and touch my face, discovering finally why I wasn't able to see. My eyes were bandaged heavily, as was my head. I had a moment of paralyzing fear but I refused to let it take over. I needed to keep it together so I could figure out where I was and how to get help.

Someone was touching me again, sticking a thermometer under my tongue and replacing bandages. I couldn't tell if the person was talking to me or not as the ringing was still very loud. I had no idea how long I'd been in this condition, and my last thought was the hope that my sensory deprivation would be over soon.

The next time I woke, I was aware of others near me and discovered that the ringing was now only in my right ear. Sophie had probably busted my eardrum when she hit me. I had a fleeting thought about Rachel and figured if she wasn't dead, she was probably in worse shape than me. That brought me some satisfaction. But then I was being moved again. It was smoother this time, like maybe I was on something solid, maybe a stretcher?

"Get her settled in the infirmary and then we'll let Mr. Rains know she should be coming around soon."

Rains. I'd heard that name before. My mind raced, trying to remember why I should know that name. Delaney's co-worker Jackson's face came to me. He'd said that name after Delaney was shot...

Terror gripped me. How this could be happening? He was supposed to be dead. Did his menace reach from beyond the grave?

"How is our little patient?" A man's voice, soft-spoken with a Southern accent. The ache was back in my gut, much stronger, and every nerve ending in my body seemed primed to fire. A dread filled my chest. Wherever I was, I was not in a hospital, which meant I could be at the mercy of...unsavory characters.

"Her IV needs to be changed in thirty minutes and I'll need to remove the bandages on her eyes later tonight. Then we'll know just how much damage was done. This was a terrible idea. She should be in a hospital." A woman's voice. No-nonsense. Hopefully a nurse.

"Do you dare to question him? I would think you of all people should know better. What about your child? If he learns that you are not fully committed, do you know what he'll do?"

The man's voice, so soft before, now sounded as if he were spitting venom from within clenched jaws. He laughed, a twisted, humorless sound. "Yes, of course you do. I see you trembling in fear. Let that thought be your guide, your motivation." His voice was coming from farther away now; thankfully it wasn't his hands I felt on me. Something touched my left arm, and I felt the sting of a needle in the back of my hand.

"Of course I know what he'll do. I'm not stupid. But if she dies, I hope he knows I did the best I could with what I was given. That's all."

Die? I refused to die like this, at the hands of a lunatic. I hadn't come this far in my life, gotten away from my husband and all the drama, just to see it end like this.

"As long as you're working to the best of your ability, that's all the Maker will expect of you. Keep me posted on her condition."

Footsteps echoed on a wood floor and a door squealed before slamming shut.

"Well young lady, whoever you are, you'd better wake up soon. I'm so sorry they hurt you." The woman's voice was sincere. I turned my head toward the woman and tried to speak but all that came out was a croak.

"Oh, oh! Shhhh. Let me get you some water." Hurried footsteps. A water faucet turned on. A moment later, a hand lifted the back of my head and the rim of a cup touched my lips. I winced, trying to form my lip to the cup, and I remembered the blow I'd received on the plane. I grunted and tried again, determined to get some water into me so I could speak to this woman.

"Easy, easy, young lady. Drink slowly. Your body has been through a lot." Her tone was low, almost a whisper. I wondered if she was trying to be quiet on purpose. The cold water in my mouth was heavenly and I fought back the urge to take in big gulps. The woman pulled the cup away too soon. "That's enough, dear. Not too much or you might be sick. Can you hear me?"

I nodded, my head weighing much more than usual.

"My name is Irene and I'm a nurse. You've been out for the past twelve hours. Do you remember what happened?"

I nodded again and tried to speak, my voice raspy. "Where am I?"

The nurse squeezed my hand and spoke in even more hushed tones.

"You're at the compound of the Maker's Plan community. Your plane crashed in the swamp and they brought you here. You're lucky to be alive. The two women you flew with didn't make it out."

I swallowed, which was much more painful without the cool water. I knew just how close to death I'd come.

"Why am I here? What is this place?"

The nurse put a gentle finger to my lips. "You mustn't speak, it's better if they think you aren't awake yet. You need to rest and gather your strength. You're going to need it, I'm afraid."

"Does anyone know I'm here?"

"I don't know. We're in a remote spot in the Everglades. It could take time before someone comes looking for you."

It was hard to believe that in the United States, there was a place so remote. I'd flown over the Everglades before. They went on forever. We could be anywhere. I wanted to ask more but as I struggled to form a coherent thought, I drifted back into the void.

CHAPTER 9
DEPLOYMENT

I SAT IMPATIENTLY in the headmaster's parlor with Delaney, Damien, Morgan and Joanna, waiting for his sources to get back to him with any news.

"She was hijacked in Houston. Her first officer, Janet Dunn, claims two women arrived for their flight minutes they were scheduled to leave. Their names were Smith and Jones, and some group called Maker's Plan was on the invoice. Cassidy led one of the women onto the plane, and the copilot saw the other on the phone. Miss Dunn had returned to the hangar to call the company, because Cassidy had a bad feeling. Someone tased her and when she came to, the plane was gone and security was there. Cassidy managed to get off a distress signal just after takeoff. Miss Dunn says they were scheduled for Ft. Lauderdale, but there's no record of the flight arriving and, according to the copilot, the flight should have landed around seventeen-hundred hours."

"That was hours ago, Nigel! No one has heard from her? I can't get her on her cell. Oh my God, Cassidy!"

Damien held Delaney as she fought back tears.

Joanna and I both had the same pained expression.

"As for Rains, the medical staff at the Shreveport hospital claim his body was released to family two days after the incident at the hotel. A trip to the hospital wouldn't be a bad idea. Damien, I need you to fly there tomorrow and see what you can find out. You and Delaney are the only two who have seen him in person, and I'm guessing the staff has been manipulated. He's escaped before using his Influence. Who's to say he didn't convince them he was deceased?"

"I shall prepare to leave first thing. But what of Delaney?"

"I'll be fine. I want to stay here with Joanna and wait for news of Cassidy. James will stay with me."

He pulled her close and kissed the top of her head. She reluctantly stepped back from him and quickly typed on her cell, probably texting James.

I'd already decided on my course of action. "I'm going to Florida. She's somewhere in the Everglades. She's still alive. I can feel it."

Only Delaney and Damien knew that I had Connected with Cassidy on her visit. Morgan looked at me as if I'd grown a second head. Nigel nodded as though my pronouncement was just par for the course with my impulsiveness.

What none of them knew was that, to me, it was more than a Connection. I was drawn to her in a way that was…different. My visions of her, including the fire she'd experienced, were far more intense than any I'd had. I experienced what she sent through with all of my senses, not merely seeing what happened as if I were watching a screen. It made this Connection so much more powerful—and I intended to use that power. I had the best chance of finding her by tapping into her consciousness through our Connection.

"I'll go and pack. Nigel, see if your contacts can find out any more details. Radar had to have picked up where the plane went down. Morgan, I need you to help me try to go back and See what happened just before they left."

Morgan nodded and stood. "I'll go make the necessary arrangements and inform Elijah. I'll need him too."

I looked around at the others. They all seemed somewhat confused by my behavior, how I knew so much, except Delaney. She didn't totally understand, but she was able to convey with one look that she trusted me and wanted me to bring her best friend home.

"I'll find her. I promise. I have to." I refused to consider any other alternative.

Damien spoke. "I'll be in touch as soon as I've conferred with the authorities in Louisiana, but I think we all know what I'm going to find there."

"Yes, of course," Nigel said. "We shall go forth with the impression that we are once again dealing with Rains."

A forceful knock at the door announced James' arrival. He entered the parlor and stood beside his cousin.

"Delaney filled me in a bit. Besides staying with her, which is a given, how can I help? I do have some connections in Florida."

"Thanks, man. I've got a Ranger buddy in the park service in the Everglades." I'd call Ryder as soon as we were done here and let him know I was coming. "I'll take whatever intel you've got."

James assured me he'd set me up, then added, "You sure you want to do this alone? This dude means business."

"I'll be more difficult to detect if I'm alone. If I get in a jam, I'll send word to Morgan. She and I, uh, kinda work that way when we need to."

James looked confused but nodded.

"I'll make arrangements for you both," Nigel said. "Damien will take the private jet, and Jackson, I'll have you fly commercial. Use your military ID. Rains may not have access to that level of clearance. I'll also get in touch with my network in Florida and see what I can find out about this Maker's Plan." He turned to a wide-eyed Joanna. "Do you know anything about a camp?"

She shook her head. "He had meetings with people in our hotel rooms. He was gone a lot, sometimes for a few days. Sometimes weeks. I know he talked about supplies all the time, and the money he'd taken from people was going somewhere, certainly not to buy anything for ourselves."

I remembered when she joined us, she was in bad shape. Malnourished, dressed in rags...poor thing. She was the strongest kid I'd ever met.

"If he's gathered followers, has numbers to follow his commands, we're in more trouble than we're currently prepared for," I said. "And with Damien and I leaving, you need to call in reinforcements to provide security.

"I'll reach out to my contacts. I'm going to assign a female security agent to be with Joanna at all times. I have a special lady in mind, a former student who would come at a moment's notice. She has experience with this sort of thing."

Delaney pressed her hand to her chest. "I feel much better knowing that she'll be protected." She reached for Joanna's hand and gave it a squeeze.

Nigel left to make his phone calls and the rest of us put our extraordinary talents to work.

Joanna was able to give names and descriptions of some of the visitors her father had at their hotels, and I took notes. I let her know that if she thought of anything else, to speak to Morgan. Morgan would be able to pass any additional information along to me once I'd left. We'd developed a sort of information chain. Morgan's talents allowed her to manipulate my visions, which would be crucial for us once I left.

"I spoke to Charisse and she said she'll arrive in the morning. For tonight, I've asked Marcia to keep Joanna in her apartment." The headmaster appeared…shaken. There was no other way to describe it

It was creeping up on midnight, and I still needed to work with Morgan and Elijah. I said my goodbyes to those gathered at Nigel's and jogged to the media center, mentally preparing myself for Morgan's magical invasion. I'd blown her off earlier, but I knew that I needed her if I was going to look for Cassidy.

Through a brief trance, I was able to Connect with Cassidy and See the moments before the plane took off. I flinched when I saw the women subdue her. They were armed and clearly trained. I felt Cassidy's heart speed up when she realized it as well. I drew sketches of them, thanked Morgan and Elijah, and then went back to my apartment to grab a couple hours of sleep. Fitful sleep. Images of the plane crash filled my senses, sending me into a coughing fit. The acrid smoke burned my lungs and my skin was so sensitive, I threw off all of my bedcovers, hating the feel of anything against me.

I was tired, and I knew I needed rest, but I had to try to reach her.

I gasped when I found her. Normally, I'd see what she saw…but everything was black. I felt her breathing and her heart beating, so I knew she was alive, but she was terrified. She was alone. She was in pain.

And dammit, I needed to get to her.

I woke after a few hours of tossing and turning and went across the lobby to Marcia's apartment. I wanted to speak to Joanna before I left. I showed her the sketches I'd drawn after my work with Morgan, and she recognized the women.

"I never talked to them, but I've seen them. There was one man who was kind," she said. "A Black man named Lance, with gray hair." She gave me a sad smile. "He brought me sweets and a doll once. My father wouldn't let me keep the doll, but I knew this man had children of his own."

"Thanks, sweetie." I hugged her tight. "If you think of anything else, you can tell Morgan and she'll let me know."

Joanna pulled back and placed her frail hands on my cheeks. Her pupils expanded and her body slumped. "Cassidy is with a non-believer. She tells Cassidy not to show she's awake. She is a friend. You can trust her." She turned ghostly pale and pressed hard against my cheeks once more. Joanna spoke in a shaky voice. "Cassidy will know the truth when others around her can't see it. She is his tool, he needs her for his plan."

I took her hands in mine and squeezed. "I promise, I'll bring Miss Mackenzie back safely."

"You must," she said, blinking her eyes. Her pupils returned to their normal size. "She's very important. To Miss Frost, to this school. And to you, Mr. Howe."

"I know," I whispered.

I left the dorm with only a backpack. It held all I'd need to get through the Everglades and bring Cassidy back, hopefully in one piece. I ran out to the gatehouse so Vincent could take Damien and I into Fayetteville to catch our flights.

Damien looked even less rested than I did.

"Dude, tell me you at least got some sleep?"

He yawned and rubbed his stubbled chin. He was normally so put together that his unkempt appearance worried me. "Not much rest for me, I'm afraid. Delaney had nightmares so I didn't sleep much. I hope this time they were just dreams...but I have a terrible feeling."

"Damn. We can't afford to have terrible feelings. What did she dream?" Knowledge was power, true. But in this case, I wasn't sure how much more bad news I could take. I was already worried about what I was going to find in Florida.

"She saw Rains speaking to a group of people. He was preaching to them and they were all in his thrall." He shook his head, his face gaunt from lack of sleep and worry. "She couldn't make out what he was saying but the people looked completely devoted. Were you able to learn anything from your visit with Morgan?"

"Just about the two women who took Cassidy. Joanna recognized them from my sketches but she didn't know anything about them."

Damien grunted and then clapped me on the shoulder. "My friend, be careful. Do not hesitate to call for help and we'll be there as soon as possible. I certainly don't want to lose Delaney's best friend, but losing you would be an equally painful outcome."

Damien and I had certainly been to hell and back. I'd taken a bullet for him, and though his relationship with Delaney had been tough for me to accept at first, he was truly the most honorable man I'd ever met. We shook hands, and I tried to convey my appreciation and admiration to him without getting sappy.

When we arrived in Fayetteville, Vincent dropped me off at the terminal and he and Damien continued to the private hangars. I slung my backpack over one shoulder and melted into the crowd. My military ID allowed me to bypass security, and my clearance level allowed me to travel armed. Once seated, I tried to relax and see if I could get a read on Cassidy. I closed my eyes and tried to focus on my breathing.

The air around me grew smoky and humid. Not a good combination. Cassidy's head was pounding and her eyes stung as she fought to regain consciousness. I sifted through her memories and found pictures of what happened. My anger burned as hot as the fires in the plane wreckage.

The women had forced her to redirect their flight into a remote area of the Everglades, just outside the park boundaries. The landing strip was old and definitely not meant for a jet the size she was flying.

Flashes of the plane crashing through the green filled me with her terror and my heart beat faster. Sweat beaded on my forehead. The flames licked at me, singing my hair. Broken glass sliced into my hands as I climbed through the hole in the windshield.

Dear God, Cassidy. What hell have you been through?

Even in that last moment, Cassidy considered saving her kidnapper, but she was already dead. Her strength amazed me. I was determined to get to her as soon as humanly possible.

A flight attendant shook me gently to let me know we were preparing for landing. I must have been tired because I rarely slept on airplanes. I thanked the woman, and she lingered, looking concerned, before heading to the jump seat. I returned my own seat to the upright position, running through plans in my head. The landing was rough, and once again I was reminded of Cassidy's horrifying ordeal...

"Sir, are you all right? Can I get you some water or something?"

The flight attendant was back, leaning over me—and the plane was mostly empty now.

Shit. I'd nodded off again! I stood quickly, smacking my head on the overhead bin.

"Sir! Oh my, you're not well."

She motioned to another attendant.

"I'm fine, I assure you." I pulled as much wattage as I possibly could into my smile. "Rough night last night. My—"

Daughter?

Why had that term come into my head? With an image of Joanna?

Forgive me, Joanna, for this little fib.

"Your...?" The two flight attendants watched me cautiously.

"My daughter had nightmares last night. She kept me awake."

Their faces softened into that *awww* kind of thing women did over babies. I didn't miss the one woman's subtle glance at my naked left ring finger.

"How old is she?"

"She's..."

Fourteen.

"Uh, fourteen. Teenager. Smart girl."

I was hearing Joanna's voice in my head! How the heck was she communicating with me? I knew she had the Sight, but no one mentioned any telepathy.

Elijah and Morgan taught me how. Now focus or they'll think you're hearing voices.

"Are you sure you're okay?"

I got my backpack out of the overhead compartment and gave them another Jackson Howe High-Wattage Smile. Did a little hair toss, too. It seemed to work with the ladies. "Absolutely. Just clumsy. I'll down some water and grab a good meal and then I'll be fine."

Their smiles shifted from concerned to flirtatious with the toss of my curls.

"You do that. If you need any recommendations..." One of them slipped me a business card, and the other gaped at her associate's boldness.

"Thank you. I appreciate that." I gave her a wink and a wave. "Travel safely, ladies."

They waved at me as I hurried off the plane,

I strolled through the Miami airport, looking for the nearest exit with a taxi stand. The attendant hailed a cab and I tipped him generously. I told the cab driver to head out of the city and I'd give him directions soon. I had two voice mails waiting. The first message was from Damien.

"Hospital staff were very confused when I asked questions about Rains. They could find no official death certificate nor a receipt of transfer. Officials are looking into the disappearance of Cassidy's plane, and they've pinpointed the crash site near Big Cypress National Park, but the roads are impassable due to flooding, so rescue efforts are taking some time."

Big Cypress jogged my memory. My old friend from my Ranger unit, Ryder Simms, had gone to work for the Park Service after we'd been discharged, and I recalled talking to him about the place. I searched my contacts and found his number.

"Jesus Christ, Howe. What the hell are you doing way out here?"

"Figured it was time I saw gator country."

"Right. You just up and decided, did you?"

"Sure. Let's call it that. Where are you?"

Ryder gave me directions to the Big Cypress Visitor Center, and I shared them with the cab driver.

"I don't usually come out this far," he said to me, a frown marring his forehead.

"I've got cash, don't worry. I'll make it worth your while."

The man grumbled, but thankfully kept driving.

I could have rented a car, but I didn't want to leave a paper trail. I hated being so isolated out here, but I knew I'd be in good hands with Ryder.

Ryder Simms was an excellent soldier and an even better friend. He always respected me and never questioned me when I would seemingly space out. We went through Ranger school together in Ft. Benning, served a tour in Iraq, and when I was injured during our unit's takeover of an airbase, Ryder pulled me to safety and stayed with me until a medevac unit was available. A Florida native, he'd had grown up fishing and hunting the swamps, and after his time in the service, he came back and led tours with his uncles until he eventually got hired by the National Park Service. I'd kept in touch with him the entire time, but we hadn't gotten together like we'd always planned. Time gets away from you like that.

Ryder was waiting for me outside the visitor center, standing next to a ginormous 4x4 truck with fog lights, a winch on the front and a gun rack in the back window. The man himself stood a mere 5'9" and his black hair was still buzzed as though he'd never left the service. His build also hadn't changed since his military days. Then again, he'd come from a military family, just like me. When he wasn't working for the Park Service, he still ran tours through the giant Cypress-filled swamps with his uncles, and he was a volunteer firefighter in his hometown of Ochopee. Ryder wasn't one to slow down and coast.

His lips slipped into a mischievous grin as I climbed out of the cab and stretched my arms and back. All the sitting on the plane and in the car had my legs stiff, and I was feeling every one of my battle scars. I paid the cab driver a hefty sum, limped over to my old friend, and we embraced jovially.

"Good to see you in your element here. You look good, buddy!"

Ryder laughed and pulled on a lock of my hair. "Can't say the same about you. Damn, ain't they got barber shops near that place you're working?"

"You wound me, Simms." I clutched my chest in mock pain and Ryder rolled his eyes, used to my theatrics.

"Yeah, yeah. Save the drama. Talk to me. What's got you coming out here to the swamp after all these years, cuz I know it ain't for no pleasure cruise." Ryder frowned. "And if you tell me it's about a woman, I'll knock your ass into next week."

I barked out a laugh, though Ryder would soon realize there was nothing funny about my purpose here. "There *is* a woman involved, but it's not what you think." Might as well jump right in. Ryder was not one for bullshit, and I knew implicitly that I could trust him. "You hear anything about a private jet going down in these parts?"

Ryder scratched at the back of his neck and frowned. "I heard. What's goin' on?"

I'd never spoken of my Connections with Ryder before, but I knew he suspected something wasn't quite normal about me. As I was trying to determine the best way to approach this situation, he spit on the ground, giving me a look.

"This about how you *know* shit?"

Guess he knew more than I thought.

"A friend of my colleague is a pilot for a charter company, and her flight was hijacked out of Houston. They were headed to Ft. Lauderdale, but crash-landed on an old airstrip in the Glades. I need to get there. From what you've told me, you know this place like the back of your hand. So I'm here asking for help."

Ryder studying me for a long few seconds, then blew out a slow breath, planting his hands on his hips. "I heard there were no survivors, Howe."

"She's alive."

With another look, Ryder nodded and led me inside. "Let me make some calls."

The visitor center had a simple office in the back room for the park rangers, with a radio and computer. Ryder made himself right at home.

"I'll also check with the aerial tour guys and see what I can find." He glanced over his shoulder at me, letting me know not to hover, and

I took a step back. "You look like shit, man. Why don't you go over to the shop and get something to eat? This might take a bit, you know how these good ol' boys operate. They might be out patrolling or taking their afternoon naps or some shit like that. I'll come get you." He raised an eyebrow.

"It's crucial that I find her. She's important."

"I can see that."

Ryder got me. He had a clear understanding of my objective without me having to say anything: get Cassidy back alive.

"Now get out of here and go get some chow. I'll find you." Ryder turned back to the phone and started to make a call. I knew I could count on him to do everything in his power to help me find Cassidy.

It was now coming up on 24 hours since she'd gone missing, and I was buzzing with nerves. I hadn't Seen anything from her, everything was still black, but if I reached out, I could still feel her. I was sure she was alive, just not sure what kind of shape she was in.

I walked back down the hall, noticing for the first time that my stomach was growling. A small cafe sat on the opposite side of the building from the office. I grabbed a pre-made sandwich and a root beer, paid the cashier, and sat down at a table by a large window that presented a view of the pristine Cypress groves.

Where are you, Cassidy? Give me something to go on.

I finished the sandwich and root beer in record time...and as I stood to throw my trash in the bin, my vision blurred and I lurched forward, grabbing onto the wall to stop my fall.

Pain.

It ran down my left side, and my skin stung like a serious sunburn. My lips were cracked and my mouth was dry. I heard moaning and tried to speak but I couldn't get my throat to work.

Then I heard a woman's voice. "It's better if they think you're still out, so try not to move. I'll care for you. You just keep quiet."

I was experiencing what Cassidy was, but I still couldn't see anything. The woman's words sounded like it was coming through an earful of cotton. I took a deep breath and tried to keep the Connection going.

"The Second said His Right Hand believes you're important, but that worries me. He's not a good man. You just be still as long as you can."

Cassidy's heart thundered but she remained still and quiet.

Fucking Rains. Gods knew how he'd faked his death or how long he'd been building up this so-called community. He could have dozens of followers...hundreds. I needed to get to her *now*. Before her situation went from awful to tragic.

CHAPTER 10
GOOD TO HAVE FRIENDS

Jackson

"Howe, what the fuck? What the hell's going on with you?"

Ryder's hands on my shoulders woke me out of my fugue. I leaned into him, and he led me over to a bench. My legs collapsed under me and I sat down hard. I had no idea where I was.

"Jesus, you're white as a fucking ghost"

I couldn't see anything but shapes and my hearing was just coming back online.

"Water, please," I croaked out and started coughing. I tasted and smelled smoke. A cup was pushed to my mouth and I gulped it down, choking but unable to stop myself. My vision started to come back, blurry at first, and the harsh fluorescent lights stung my eyes. I finally stopped coughing and looked up at Ryder, whose eyes were wide.

When he spoke, his voice was quiet. "I'm thinking there's more going on than just a missing plane. You better start talking before I kick your ass."

"Like you could ever kick my ass." I chuckled but it fell flat. "You're right, though. I think it's time I told you a little story."

Ryder leaned against the wall and crossed his arms. "'Bout fucking time."

I sucked in a breath and took another drink of water before I started. The building seemed deserted, so I wasn't worried about anyone eavesdropping.

"So, you know I lived with my father, that he served in Vietnam."

Ryder nodded.

"Mom and Dad were together, but Mom was deployed a lot. Dad was unstable and not much of a parent." Ryder knew part of this story already. He'd relaxed his stance a bit and was listening intently.

"One day I was at school, sitting in my ceramics class, and my vision blurred. Suddenly I was standing in his living room, only…I was my dad. I felt the weight of a pistol in my hand and the motion of my arm being raised to my head as if I were actually doing it. When the trigger was pulled, I fell out of my seat. Everyone laughed at me but I was too messed up to make a joke. I scrambled up and ran for the door. My teacher tried to stop me, but I pushed past him and ran home. Where I found my dad."

"Jesus, Howe."

I had to keep going. It was actually a relief to finally tell him. "The next thing I knew, there were police cars and an ambulance in front of the house. Mom showed up, held on to me tightly, not shedding a tear, just trembling."

I stopped talking for a moment and took another drink of water. I ran a hand through my hair and sucked in a breath, finally not feeling like I'd cough my lungs out. Then I continued.

"After that I was, well…different. I had strange feelings and saw things, and I had no idea why. There was a lady…" Fuck, I was *not* going into the time I'd been working as a bartender and saved a woman from a beating, only for her to OD in our bar bathroom. Yeah, I saw the latter happen like I was her, while I was miles away at home. "Anyway, I tried to ignore it, terrified of going crazy like I'd seen my father do."

Ryder stared at me for a few moments and then stepped closer. "That wasn't the last time that happened to you, was it? That freaky shit you used to pull when we were on duty, that kid you kept trying to find in Nasiriyah? That's all part of it, huh?"

I nodded, glad to have it off my chest but concerned as to whether my old friend might have me committed. "Yeah, like that. When I handed him that candy bar and he touched me, it was just like that. I would See him, See what happened to him...I can't control it, dude. It just happens sometimes, and I don't know why or who it's going to happen with."

Ryder was quiet for a bit, and I thought, *Huh, well, he's either going to kick me out of his truck in the middle of the swamp or drive me straight to the psych ward.* I wouldn't have blamed him for either.

"So, when you see this stuff, what, like, happens?"

"I experience whatever they're experiencing like I'm them."

He frowned a little deeper and cleared his throat. "And with your dad?"

That one was easier to talk about now, honestly. "Let's just say I know what it feels like to get shot in the head."

"Fuck. Okay. And that eau de burning vegetation I'm smelling?"

"Yeah, it's me," I said.

"For real? Like, the wheels-turning kind of smoke?"

"Not exactly. Whatever went on out there," I said, gesturing to the expanse of green around the building, "whatever happened to Cassidy, it's like it keeps happening to me. The crash, the fire. I've got aches and pains that I can't explain. My vision and hearing go out. And the smoke..."

"Weird." He nodded. "Well, all right. You've got me convinced. My friend Geoff, well...he don't believe much in what he can't see, feel, or shoot, you get what I'm saying? But he's a solid dude."

My turn to clear my throat. "And you? Do you...can you even take me seriously after all that?"

"Howe, it don't matter to me. You've always had my back. I trust you with my life, always have. You tell me you're the Easter Bunny and I'm likely to believe you."

"Fucker," I said, relieved and only a little bit disappointed about the Easter Bunny shit. He didn't need to completely believe me to help me, and I knew he'd help. "I'm not the Easter Bunny."

"Fair enough," he said with a smile. "But is there any rhyme or reason? Anything solid?"

"For the life of me, I can't find a pattern. The last person it happened with was a few months ago at Havenhart Academy, the school where I work, with the very woman I'm looking for. Her name is Cassidy Mackenzie, and this time, well, it's different. It's stronger than ever and..."

"Yeah, I get it. She's important."

Good old Ryder. I was grateful he hadn't written me off, and now I was ready to get active. I'd had enough of the baring-my-soul shit. "Did you find anything?"

Ryder scowled and crossed his beefy arms over his chest. "I got a hit. Sheriffs were called to assist an FBI investigation into a plane crash. It was in an area that's uninhabited and, according to the feds, there were no survivors, like I said."

My teeth were going to shatter if I clenched my jaw any tighter. "She's *alive*."

Ryder held up his hands. "Geoff'll take us out there in his swamp buggy and check it out. He said he'd come with us if we need backup. If the FBI are out there, though, they might not let you get close." Ryder waited for a response.

"I'd rather not get anyone else embroiled in this, unless you think we need him." I knew I had to tell him what we were dealing with. "Before we go any further, I need to tell you about the people that I think are involved."

Ryder nodded. "All right. Why don't we talk on the way?"

He started to walk outside and I reached for his arm.

"This is some heavy shit, Simms. You want nothing to do with it, I'll understand."

He looked down at my hand and up at me pointedly. "*Anyway*, Geoff is waiting."

We headed outside to Ryder's truck. "We don't know much about what's going on here in Florida," I started, "but the guy in charge? Straight-up killer. Has lots of dangerous people working for him. Beat the shit out of his kid. He's also able to get folks to do his bidding, no matter how depraved."

Ryder clicked his key fob and the truck chirped as the locks popped. "Then we need Geoff," he said, looking at me over the bed of the truck. "He knows the spot and can get us there. He's ex-Marine, he's tight. A bit of a backwoods boy, but solid. And he knows the people around here."

"More backwoods than you?" We climbed into the cab and I shut my door, looking around at the decked-out interior. "Do you even own anything that's not hunter camo?"

Ryder laughed and slugged me in the shoulder. It seemed we were both ready for lighter discourse. "Sorry, there's no Abercrombie and fuckin' Fitch out here, girlie man."

I looked down at my strategically distressed Levi's and pastel blue button-down shirt. "Hey, I don't mall shop, ass. I've got to dress appropriate for the kids, and I kinda like not looking like a bum some of the time."

Ryder rolled his eyes at me.

"Besides, there's a tailor in the town near the school. She's pretty hot and good with her hands. She's a genius with slacks."

I needed some levity at this moment.

"Yeah, getting felt up by some slick-dressed chick might be worth wearing pansy shit like that. Better than sandy BDUs, feel me?"

I shuddered, recalling how gross our uniforms got out there in the desert, the heat, the filth. I took showers every day when I returned, sometimes more than one, just to make up for the years I'd lived in my own nastiness. "Don't even remind me. Sometimes I get grit in my clothes from working in the ceramics lab and I get the heebie-jeebies."

"So that's what you're doing at that school, right? Teaching art? They treat you good?"

"Absolutely. The headmaster lets me do whatever I think is best for the kids, and they're great, truly. They all just want someone to believe in them, you know? Someone who accepts them for who they are. I can relate."

"I bet," Ryder answered. "You know, I never asked you about all that stuff because I figured you were dealing with some heavy shit. The other guys asked me, and I'd just tell them to fuck off. You were solid. You pulled your weight." He drifted off for a minute. "But I worried about you, man. I've *been* worried about you. Didn't want to find out, you know..."

"Like my old man, right? I was worried too. But when the head-master, Mr. Hart, came to see me at Walter Reed? He told me things... and he knew about me. He knew what happened to me, knew people who could help."

Ryder was a quiet dude when he got emotional. His voice lowered and he couldn't make eye contact. Now, he looked out the windshield and nodded. "I'm glad, man."

I appreciated that he'd been concerned about me. I firmly accepted that the more people believe in something, the more power that belief is given. Which could go either way. The more folks who believed I should be worried about, the more possible the *need* to worry.

It was why I was so concerned about this Maker's Plan business. This was some serious Jim Jones shit here, and I was terrified about Cassidy being in their clutches. I wasn't sure what would have been better, if she'd been rescued by some hillbilly in the Glades, about to be gator food, or kidnapped by Rains' community.

My mind was spinning with the possible scenarios. I was glad I'd hooked up with Ryder and that he knew this place well, even more pleased he had a friend we could count on, but the thought of anyone else being hurt because of fucking Rains had me on high alert. He'd caused enough damage.

Ryder's truck was outfitted like the damn vehicles we drove in Iraq. Satellite phone, laptop, navigation system, all kinds of gadgets that would make our lives easier. I was sure it wasn't standard gear for a park ranger.

"Geoff will meet us at his dock, we'll head toward the crash site, and then we'll see what's what."

"Ryder," I started, knowing full well what his answer was going to be. "I'm fully prepared to do this on my own from there. I appreciate everything you're doing for me, but if this is what I think it is—"

"Yeah, yeah, yeah, spare me the Lone Ranger bullshit, Howe. The more dangerous this might be," he said in a snarky tone, "the more I ain't letting your ass out of this truck without backup."

"I'm armed, I can handle—"

"If there's hinky shit going on in my swamp, it's my business. If you hadn't noticed," he pointed at the patch on his uniform sleeve, "I represent the Man out here. End of discussion."

I snorted. "The Man, huh? More like the reptile or the fish, maybe."

He punched me in the arm again and I laughed.

"I'll have you know there're more armed whack jobs out here running around than in Fallujah, you got it? These hillbilly folk ain't no joke."

"Aw, and now you're a poet."

The late-winter morning was wet and gray, but outside the massive truck, the world was alive. The lush foliage of the Big Cypress Reserve seemed to fold in on itself, creating what seemed like an impenetrable wall. I hadn't spent much time in terrain like this since my early training days, but survival tips and tricks ran through my head from my time in Ranger school. I'd been out of the service for close to three years, but that knowledge never leaves you.

We pulled up to the dock and a big guy with greasy light brown hair and ruddy cheeks was waiting for us. He had deep-set brown eyes that tracked our movements as we got out of the truck, and a lopsided grin that made him appear more approachable than he probably was, knowing the kind of dudes who lived and worked out here.

"Who you got here, Simms? Another one of them pansy Rangers?"

Ryder spit on the ground. "Call it what you want, maggot, but this Ranger's dealt with some of the hairiest situations I ever saw, and I trust him completely."

Geoff raised an eyebrow and chuckled. "I'm just messin' with you. Geoff Clements," he said, sticking out his hand. "Damn glad to meet you. Now, about this plane crash?"

If Ryder trusted the guy, I'd have to do the same. "Friend of mine was hijacked out of Houston. Charter flight. Authorities claim there are no survivors, but I've got a lead that she escaped, only to be recaptured by some folks who have a religious compound out here."

Geoff cocked his head and frowned. "That's some serious shit."

"These people who took her are lethal. They've been involved with previous kidnappings and attempted murders. Not sure what their endgame is, but I have to know. My friend...she's important." How did I define who Cassidy was to me? She wasn't a friend, really. She was more. She was vital. Crucial.

I'd find her and bring her home. Then I'd figure out just who she was to me.

"All right. I'll take y'all out there and we'll see what's what."

As we climbed into the swamp boat, its massive fan whirring to life, Geoff put on a straw hat and tightened the strap below his chin.

"Ladies, fasten your seat belts and keep your belongings inside the boat at all times. Some croc takes off with your dick, it stays behind."

I laughed but it was lost as I was slammed back against my seat. Geoff was about to give us a helluva ride, and if it were under any other circumstances, I'd be enjoying myself.

But Cassidy was of the highest importance. There was no alternative. I'd find her and bring her home no matter what.

CHAPTER 11
SEE NO EVIL

Cassidy

"Please. Tell me."

Not being able to see the shape I was in had me borderline paranoid. This woman's voice was my lifeline right now, and I still didn't know if I could trust her. I had no idea of the time of day and I was disoriented not being able to use my sight, my most important faculty. It took all of my strength to remain calm.

"You're incredibly lucky that you weren't burned worse. Seriously. From what I saw at the crash site, I thought for sure... The others were burned."

"I climbed out," I said softly. "I remember I climbed through the window before the flames took over."

"That's good. You have a couple of spots that are second-degree burns on your arm, but those'll heal up like a bad sunburn. The glass, however, was not kind. You had it in your eyelids and forehead. I was able to get it all out, and I didn't see any in your eyes. Your cuts aren't infected, so that's a plus. I had to use steri-strips on a couple of spots on your arm." She touched my left shoulder and I sucked in a breath. "You dislocated it when you fell, I think. I put it back to rights, but there may be other damage. I can't tell a lot without an MRI or even X-rays."

"It's okay. Thank you, so much, for taking care of me, but is there any way—"

She pressed a hand to my good arm and squeezed, our signal to be quiet.

Apparently the nurse, Irene, didn't trust most of the people here. She'd explained to me that we were in a religious community. She thought my eyes just needed some healing before we unwrapped the bandages and saw what we were dealing with, but we had to be careful, and the longer the community leaders thought I was out of commission, the better.

"You don't want to see him," she whispered. "He's evil. His son isn't as bad, but he's just as dangerous."

I remained still and tried to calm my breathing as someone entered the room. Wherever we were, the door sounded like a squeaky wood-framed screen door on rusty hinges. It creaked and rattled when it was opened and, most of the time, slammed shut with a bang and a follow up, softer impact, anytime someone came or went.

"Hello, Miss Irene. How's our patient?"

The cheerful man sounded like he was in his twenties...young but not a teenager. I pictured him smiling, not necessarily in a genuine way, but pleasant. He'd been here before—there had been several voices besides Irene's—and I tried to listen carefully to how she responded to each of them to get an idea of who might be trustworthy.

Irene was definitely afraid of this man.

The nurturing tone she took with me when she talked about my injuries and when she changed my bandages was gone. She stammered when she greeted him.

"Sir. How may I help you?"

"Bless you, Miss Irene. You are doing all of the heavy lifting with our guest. I thought I would check and see if you needed any help."

"We're fine," Irene answered in clipped words. "Sir. She's in and out of consciousness and hasn't said much that sounded coherent."

She was lying to this man. My bullshit meter sparked to life, but Irene was clear that most people here were not to be trusted. The nurse hadn't done anything previously to set off my inner alarm, and this man was either really good at hiding his ill intentions, or he was genuinely trying to be helpful. But he wasn't to be trusted. I'd have to rely on Irene, to trust her. A woman I'd never laid eyes on, because it might be some time before I could see again. *If* I could see again.

"That's unfortunate. We'll keep her in our community prayers. Speaking of, we sure have missed you at the nightly meetings."

"I can't leave her," Irene said. "I don't want her to wake up alone. With the bandages, she can't see, and I'm worried she'll pull them off and injure herself."

The visitor made a thoughtful sound. "Very well. I'll let my father know. Perhaps your daughter can relieve you this evening so you can join us. Prayer is good for the soul, Miss Irene." I heard footsteps move toward the direction of the door and then they stopped. "I'll send Denise over after supper. She could use a prenatal checkup, don't you think? His Right Hand wants her treated like the queen she was meant to be." There was a pause before the door slammed and footsteps pounded down the steps outside. "Have a blessed day," he called out distantly as he walked away.

I heard a sob, and Irene pressed against my arm.

"He has your daughter?" I asked, my throat straining with the effort. Irene's fear seemed reasonable now. Something was very wrong in this place, and I was completely at the mercy of a nurse held hostage here in terror.

"Yes. She's thirty-four weeks pregnant. His Right Hand...Gerry... he slept with her. She's carrying The Third. His birth will be...well, I don't know."

I listened to what she wasn't saying. The future was bleak for this woman and she feared for her daughter and grandchild.

"Irene," I croaked. "My company will be looking for me. The hijackers tried to destroy the transponder somewhere over the Gulf before we crashed." I hesitated. Suddenly, I felt a sense of calm, as though everything would be okay. Somehow. "Help will come," I said before my hearing got fuzzy and I knew I was likely to pass out again.

"Just hang on," Irene whispered. "I'll do whatever I can to help you. It's all I can do."

The sorrow in her voice led me to suspect her powerlessness to save her daughter from her current fate made her want to help me. Whatever her reasons, I was grateful.

The zealous overtones in the man's voice had made my skin crawl. I'd had my share of that type of dogma. As a child, my parents attended a church that leaned toward the oppressive side of Christianity. I never felt comfortable going there, especially after the church fire that nearly killed my best friend Delaney. My parents took the church's teachings too far and blamed me for all of the strife in our house. It caused a rift between us. My younger brother was stuck in the middle of our frequent battles, ruining my relationship with him as well.

I had a strong dislike for any religious institution by the time I reached eighteen and struck out on my own. I had a tenuous relationship with my parents now, but I hadn't stepped foot in a church for over twenty years.

And now I'd crash landed in a religious stronghold. I wasn't above using what I knew to survive, and I would do all I could for Irene and her family. If I could see.

If I couldn't. Well. I'd be at the mercy of strangers.

I allowed myself to fall into sleep. I knew my body needed it to heal, and it gave me a reprieve from the persistent feeling that I might not make it out of here alive. Or whole.

"Wake up."

A voice that was not Irene's woke me. A man's voice. I felt hands on my arms and I jerked.

"Now, don't fuss." I was lifted to a sitting position and all of the jostling was murder on my shoulder. "Boss says we gotta take these bandages off."

"Irene?" I started to panic.

"Oh, it's okay," said a younger woman's voice. "I'm Denise. Irene's daughter. You're in good hands. Esai and I are just going to get these bothersome bandages off for you. Don't you want to try to see?"

Not if it's worse here than what I'm already imagining.

"Now don't move," Denise said. "These scissors are sharp. You don't want me to cut you."

I remained as still as possible, wondering if I'd heard a subtle threat in her words. The man's hands were huge and he held me with a firm grip. The skin of his palms felt like sandpaper against mine.

I heard the *snip snip* of the scissors, wondering if I'd have any hair left as she cut, and then she unwound the strips, relieving some of the pressure on my face. The humid air was not a balm on my cuts. I was covered in sweat and sticky under the loose sheet, and whatever Irene had dressed me in didn't breathe.

"Oh, my," Denise said as the bandages were gone. "You poor thing. Can you open your eyes?"

I paused as if I were trying before giving a small shake of my head. "I don't think so."

I wasn't sure I wanted to. All I felt was pain. I wanted the bandages back, to continue to hide from the possibility that not only was I now disfigured, but that I may never see again.

"Well, that's too bad. We'll just leave these off, then, and after prayer service, my mother can redo them if she thinks they need to be replaced."

It was bizarre that I had no idea what the damage looked like—and I had no desire to have this woman describe it to me. Yet, I wanted to know how bad it was. But maybe I didn't.

"Come on," the man said, before he yanked me forward with enough force that I cried out in pain.

"Esai, be careful, now. His Right Hand wants to see her for himself. He needs her functional. Don't hurt her worse."

"Sorry, ma'am."

He reached underneath me and lifted me from the bed. I fought to keep from crying and kicking and screaming for him to put me down like a little girl. The two of them carried on a conversation using some kind of code; at least I thought so, because I had no idea what they were talking about. She spoke in a slow, thick accent, thicker than her mother's. She seemed to be placating him. His tone was gruff and impatient. He walked in jerky movements, almost as if I was too heavy for him, which jarred my shoulder with every step.

I fought the tears, because the first wave of salty liquid stung like hell. I tried to focus on taking steady breaths through my sore nose, which felt swollen, as though it had sustained an impact as well. It was difficult to get any air in. It was a good thing I wasn't a vain woman because I was sure I looked like hell.

Denise sang a long-forgotten hymn as we walked. Lights flickered of and on behind my eyelids, as though we were passing through a wooded area and the sun was trying desperately to shine on us, darting around the leafy barrier. At least that's what I pictured in my mind. She sang off-key, which gave a haunting quality to the tune, and dread welled up within me until I thought for sure I'd vomit from the unease.

"Prayer should start soon," Esai said. "Can you walk, ma'am?"

I didn't trust that if I opened my mouth I wouldn't scream.

He paused to wait for my answer and when I didn't speak, he lowered me to the ground. My stomach lurched as my feet hit the ground. I staggered but Esai caught me hard around the waist.

"Lean on me. I'll guide you. We've got some steps ahead."

"Wonderful," Denise said. "He'll be so pleased."

"Here we go."

Stairs were probably not the best idea for my first steps, but I wasn't going to criticize the man. I'd gone to the bathroom in the infirmary with Irene helping me, but stairs were a whole different scenario. I attempted to open my eyes for self-preservation, but they were so swollen and the pain was unreal. I fought the urge to run my fingers over the area, knowing that could lead to infection. Irene had used a salve to help, but I didn't want to end up worse off—

"Careful," Esai said in a gruff voice. Someone came around my other side, Denise maybe? The person was shorter than me and had small hands. When she began humming the tune again, I knew it was her.

We ascended the remaining steps, and if I was less panicky I might have counted them. I wouldn't dare try to run away without being able to see, but I knew I needed to start paying attention to details like that if I was ever going to escape.

They weren't likely to let me go. Not after all this.

I heard another creaky screen door open, and then I heard gasps.

"Ladies and gentlemen…what a blessing we have this evening." It sounded like the younger man who'd spoken to Irene earlier, the one who'd encouraged her to come to the prayer meeting.

My guides led me forward and while I wanted to drag my feet, I needed to focus on not tripping and faceplanting.

There were hushed voices all around me. It sounded like a lot of them, but I had no way of knowing. My shoulder throbbed but thankfully it wasn't the excruciating pain I'd originally felt.

"Please welcome Miss Cassidy Mackenzie, our special guest. She's blessed to be alive. If it hadn't been for the quick actions of Esai and our lovely Nurse Irene, she would have perished."

Murmurs of "praise Him" rose up around me and my guides turned me around.

"Oh, her face," I heard someone say.

"Poor thing."

"How did she survive?"

"She survived…" a different voice boomed out, silencing the room. I was immediately covered in goose bumps and if I'd been able to see, I'm sure it would have made me want to look away. It was a terrifying voice, one that was just as frightening when he spoke low as when he raised the volume. He was somewhere to my left and in front of me.

"She survived, because Our Maker allowed it. Our Maker is a truly benevolent and all-powerful being. Only He can bestow His mercy upon those in peril. The fact that Miss Mackenzie survived is testament to the glory and grace of Our Maker. Her continued recovery will depend upon this community's strength in prayer and faith. We have been tasked with caring for her on her road to recovery."

The next time he spoke, he was right next to me. He placed a hand on my good shoulder. "Then we will welcome her into our community with open arms."

There was applause and shouts of joy and someone began playing a guitar. The congregation began singing the hymn Denise sang on the way here and it was even more unsettling coming from many mouths at once. The words were about blood and sacrifice, definitely not an uplifting tune.

Another pair of hands rested on my waist, and I jumped, sending a jolt of pain through my left side.

"It's me," Irene whispered close to my ear. "I'm so sorry. Are you all right?"

I placed my hand over hers and squeezed twice for no. I was terrified and thought at any moment my legs would give out.

"I'll get you back to the infirmary as soon as I—"

"Mother, go sit down."

Irene's hands were yanked away, and I heard her gasp.

"Please join the congregation, Irene." The man who apparently led this group was so close, I could feel his breath on my cheek.

"But sir, she's unsteady. She hasn't walked much."

"She will gain strength from the group. Have faith."

Denise pulled me tighter to her when I started to lean. A strong arm came around my lower back, probably Esai's. He smelled of oil and gasoline, as though he'd been working on some sort of car or machine.

The hymn wrapped up and I heard footsteps move away from me. We were standing on some sort of wood flooring that creaked and scraped with each step.

"Please bow your heads in prayer to Your Maker."

His words sent icy chills through my limbs. They took me back to a time and place I'd never wanted to revisit.

"Our Heavenly Maker, whose strength and power blesses this community, we thank you for bringing us into your flock. We bow to your will and pledge our loyalty to your cause, for you are our purpose for being, your plan our purpose for existing, and your generous love shines down upon our work. We thank you for the bounty you have bestowed and we praise you, Maker, and ask for your glory to rain down upon us."

He shouted this last part, and as he did, thunder rolled through the sky, rattling the building. A hard rain began to fall, pelting the roof, which must have been made of metal. The sound was deafening, but his voice could be heard above the din as he laughed and continued his strange prayer.

"And Our Maker shall bring about a new world for His repentant followers and our community shall be lifted up in His holiness. In His name we pray."

A communal "amen" was spoken and the rain continued to pound.

"The waters flow down upon us to wash away our sins. Go forth and cleanse yourselves, my brethren. Cleanse your bodies of pride and give of yourselves to Our Maker's Plan."

Chairs scraped the floor and the crowd chattered excitedly as they ran, presumedly, for the door.

"Her bandages weren't ready to come off," Irene said, approaching us.

"He wanted to see the damage for himself," Esai said.

"Fine, but we need to keep those wounds covered to keep infection from setting in. Now, let me take her back to the infirmary."

"Mother, I believe you should go and cleanse yourself first."

Denise's sharp words gave me pause. No wonder Irene was so frightened. If her own daughter had turned against her, she was now on her own in a dangerous situation.

"But I need—"

"We'll bring her back. You can take care of it when you're finished." Esai sounded gruff as he scooped me up and began carrying me at a quick pace through the pouring rain. I kept my head tucked down, afraid of water and whatever else getting into my cuts. He climbed the steps and deposited me on my feet as I heard the screen door slam behind us.

"You'll need to take off those wet clothes," he said.

I froze. No way was I stripping in front of him.

"I can wait for the nurse." My voice sounded raspy but it didn't hurt as much as it had. I shivered, it was March in Florida, the temperatures already balmy, but no way I was removing my clothes in front of a strange man.

"Take them off."

"No."

As he grabbed my arm, the door opened.

"I'll take care of her, Esai," Denise said in an authoritative tone. I hadn't thought I'd ever be happy to hear her voice.

He squeezed once more then let go. "I'll be outside."

"Thank you," Denise said, and I heard his footsteps and the door slamming.

"Here are some fresh clothes," she said, and I felt her press something against my stomach. "I'll walk you to the bathroom."

"Thank you," I said. I had no idea what else to say. I was completely at the mercy of these people, and as much as I didn't trust her, I needed her as a buffer, at least for now.

"Esai is intense, but he's a decent man. All of the men in our community are good in their hearts. And if they're not, well, they won't go against His Right Hand or The Second. Their orders come from the Maker. No one will disobey them or they'll feel His wrath." I heard her pull the chain for the light in the bathroom and then she guided me to the counter. I knew the toilet was to the right of the sink. "Here you go. You may shower and dress in these clothes. My mother will be back soon, and she'll take care of your bandages."

"Why did you remove them? Your mother said they needed to stay on." I was curious as to whether it was her idea or if she'd been ordered. I'd know one way or the other.

"It was his will. His Right Hand. He wants the community to see you as the miracle you are. You survived a plane crash. You were meant to be with us. It's one of the signs."

That sounded ominous.

"Denise?" Irene called out and then I heard the door slam behind her. "Are you here? Where is— Oh, thank Heavens."

"Thank The Maker."

There was a pregnant pause in their exchange, and I stood holding the bundle of clothes, waiting for more.

"I'll just shut the door for you," Denise said, and I heard the click of the bathroom door.

I lowered myself to the toilet and concentrated on trying to hear them speak. I couldn't make out any words, though. Only hushed voices. I stripped and felt my way around to the shower. Irene had shown me how to tell by touch where things were in the stall, and I was grateful I'd paid attention. My shoulder-length hair felt disgusting. She hadn't been able to wash my hair with the bandages on my face.

I tolerated the cold water that poured from a spout above me, grateful for running water period. I knew there wasn't a lot of it, so I didn't waste time. I washed the best I could, wincing every time I bumped a scrape on my arms. I kept my face out of the water, however, as I knew there were areas Irene had used steri-strips to hold deeper cuts together. Once I finished, I dried as best I could before putting on the soft clothes Denise had given me. They turned out to be a pair of scrubs, or at least that's what I assumed by how they felt.

There was a knock at the door. "Cassidy? It's me. They've gone."

I breathed a sigh of relief and opened the door.

"I'm so sorry," she said as she guided me back to the bed where I'd been the past couple of days. How many? I couldn't remember.

"It's okay," I whispered. "I know you're in a terrible situation here and I appreciate all you've done for me."

Irene let out a sob. "I just wanted to come here and convince her to leave with me, but I was too late. I had no idea that he would...keep her. Make her pregnant. Now he won't let her go. And she doesn't want to leave. She says she loves him and believes in his teachings."

I reached for her and squeezed her arm. "Once a person sets their mind on a course of action, it's very difficult for them to change, especially when it comes to faith. I'm sorry. I hope she's able to see for herself before it's too late."

"I'm sorry you were dragged into this. I think..." She trailed off and I heard her moving around the room.

"Irene?"

"Sorry, I'm going to clean your face and replace the bandages. Unless... Were you able to open your eyes? Do you want to try?"

"I don't know," I admitted with a humorless laugh. "What do you think?"

"Well, I didn't see any objects in your actual eye. The glass was in your eyelids and I'm pretty sure I got it all out. Nothing looks infected. It really was fortunate that your eyes were closed when you were hit with the glass. But without the proper equipment...and I'm not an eye specialist. I did the best I could—"

"I know you did, and I'm grateful. I seriously can't thank you enough."

"I just wish I could have convinced them to take you to a hospital, but The Second said his father insisted you were brought to us for a reason. That your coming was a sign."

I'll bet he said that. "I know you did what you could. You're not here voluntarily either," I said, patting her hand. "Okay, let's give this a shot."

Now or never. I slowly worked my eyes open to just a slit.

And sat there. Devastated.

"Well?"

"It's blurry. I can see lights and shadows, but I can't make anything out."

"That's okay, it's…okay. You may have detached your retina when you fell, but I can't tell. I think it will continue to get better, though. I do. And when you get out of here, you can see a real doctor."

The tears burned my eyes again and I blinked them hard, which hurt like hell.

"Oh, don't cry, sweetie. We'll get you well. Here, let's put some more of this salve on and I'll wrap you back up. The swelling will keep going down and you'll improve. We have to have faith."

"Faith. Maybe that's not the best word to use."

She snickered. "You're probably right. Listen, I'm a Catholic. Lapsed, but Catholic. Denise was raised in the church, did her communion and everything. But she stopped going in high school, thought it was a waste of time. I never thought she'd fall for something like this."

"Oh. I understand," I said, my throat growing dry as memories assaulted me. "I've seen it happen."

"I guess where there's a vacuum, manipulative people find a way."

"You're so right."

Irene tucked me in and we talked for a bit longer, until my voice gave out.

"Get some rest. You're going to need it."

I knew she was right and that did nothing to relax me. I drifted in and out of sleep and though I couldn't see anything, I knew that someone was watching me. Someone other than Irene. I felt it with a certainty. Whether they had good or bad intentions, I had no clue.

CHAPTER 12
WRECKAGE

Jackson

Geoff brought the speedboat to a halt suddenly, and I nearly fell out of my chair.

"Right up here's where I saw some feds gathering earlier today. We can't take the boat in that far, though, so we gotta hump it."

"Shouldn't be a problem for you, Marine," Ryder said to Geoff. I loved their banter back and forth. I'd missed the camaraderie that comes along with having guys at your back no matter what. I loved my co-workers at the academy, don't get me wrong, but it was a different situation. Although having James around was nice. He understood.

We grabbed water bottles out of an ice chest on Geoff's boat and set off on foot through the sludge.

"We've only got about an hour left of daylight, so let's do this."

"Anybody living out here?" I asked.

Ryder unfastened his holster for quicker access. I noticed Geoff was carrying, too. I'd slid my 9mm into the holster attached to my belt and I had a .22 strapped to my ankle just in case. I also had my trusty knife in a sheath and a flashlight in my pocket. I hadn't geared up like this in years. But I had no idea what I was walking into and I wanted to be prepared.

"A few families have hunting cabins scattered around out here," Ryder said. "There are some small communities, but not many folks at all."

Geoff told stories about his tour business as we walked, but I needed to focus on my surroundings. The vegetation certainly looked similar to what I'd seen when Cassidy's plane crashed. In some places it was thick and impassable, in others it was just soggy marsh grass with a few trees and shrubs sprinkled throughout. At one point, I saw large movement at ground level consistent with an alligator slipping into the water, and I remembered I needed to step with care. There were several things that could kill you in the swamp, and only a few of them carried guns.

"It's just another couple hundred yards," Geoff said, and that's when I smelled it, the acrid smoke and rotten leaves. It burned my nostrils first, then continued to spread through my limbs until I started coughing. I was reliving the accident again. The heat was so intense I had to stop walking and pull off my button-down shirt, ready to strip down to my white tank undershirt. I bent over and coughed violently, causing Ryder and Geoff to come to my side.

"Howe, you good man?"

"You smell it?" I croaked out.

"Smell what, boss? What's going on?"

Ryder placed his hand on my arm and yanked it back. "Jesus, Howe. You're on fire!"

It's not real. It's not happening. It's over. Get it together, Howe. Cassidy needs you.

I coughed a few more times and then stood upright. I slid my arms back into my shirt but didn't button it. I poured the rest of my water over my head and tried to breathe deeply without coughing.

"I'm okay." I shot Ryder a look and his eyes widened. I'd explained to him what was going on, but I wasn't ready to trust this Geoff guy with sensitive intel.

"You sure? You good? We can go back—"

"No. Please. I need to see it."

We walked another hundred yards and then paused before entering a clearing with an asphalt path.

"Holy shit," Geoff said when we saw the wreckage and a couple of FBI agents milling around.

"Holy shit is right. This is the old county landing strip. Used to be you could land prop engines here. We've used it for helicopter landings in emergencies, but no one's used it to land a prop—much less a whole-ass jet—in years," Ryder said in a low voice. "I'll run interference with the authorities. Do what you need to do."

I moved swiftly toward what was left of Cassidy's jet as Ryder and Geoff walked straight up to the FBI agents on the scene.

There had been a fire, but the plane's fuel tanks hadn't exploded. I walked around the plane with my hand on my weapon, my hackles on high alert. I wasn't taking any chances. Rains' people could be hanging around.

Eventually, I caught up to Geoff and Ryder with the FBI folks.

"This is Jackson Howe, and he's been hired by the family to search for Miss Mackenzie."

I schooled my expression and shook hands with the agent in charge.

"Mr. Howe. I'm Agent Noffsinger. I'll need to get clearance from the field office—"

I knew he would get it, as Nigel had connections everywhere. "Absolutely. Once you receive that clearance, I'm going to need access to the plane. I'm assuming nothing has been moved?"

Noffsinger shook his head. "Not yet. We had a helluva time getting out here at all, and our technicians weren't able to get their equipment in. Only myself and Agent Barnes have been inside."

"Very well."

Noffsinger's phone buzzed and he stepped away to answer it.

"You think that clearance will come through?" Ryder asked me.

"No doubt." Nigel's reach never ceased to amaze me. I was confident he'd get me what I needed.

Sure enough, Noffsinger returned a few moments later. He was an older Southern-bred guy with a slight drawl and a smile that bordered on suspicious at all times. His skin was weathered from too much time in the Florida sun, and his thinning hair barely covered his dome. Noffsinger was likely a career agent near retirement, who could either present a problem or be an easy obstacle to surpass.

"That was my field office supervisor. I've been instructed to give you whatever intel we have." He seemed surprised by the phone call, but nevertheless he led me to the wreckage and started sharing the little information they knew.

"We haven't been able to get into the cockpit yet. We're waiting on a ladder, but we did find one of the hijackers in the rear portion, and we're assuming the other and, uh, Miss Mackenzie are located in the cockpit."

I eyed the wing's height and knew I could get up there with no problem.

"Thank you," I said. "We'll be taking a look then. Don't worry, we won't compromise the scene."

The agent started to protest before Ryder pulled him aside. I climbed up the broken fuselage and prepared myself for the worst.

I pulled out my flashlight and looked inside. The first casualty was bent backward over a row of seats. A piece of the ceiling rested across its torso. I couldn't see the head, but the skirt looked familiar from the visions I'd had.

I climbed back down. "Help me up here," I asked Geoff, and he boosted me to climb into the forward portion of the fuselage several yards away. Once inside, I reached down and helped him up. The plane was stable, it didn't shift under our weight, so I moved toward the cockpit, my heart in my throat.

The smell that hit me when the door opened made me retch.

"Jesus Christ on a cracker," Geoff said, reaching for his handkerchief. "Eau de bar-b-cued corpse."

I found casualty number two impaled by a tree branch in the copilot's seat.

And no Cassidy.

Thank the gods.

Even though I knew she wasn't there, every once in a while I doubted my curse was real, wished it wasn't and would convince myself I was imagining things. I was grateful I hadn't imagined that she'd survived. I looked out the broken windshield and saw blood smeared on the nose of the plane and two red handprints, probably Cassidy's where she'd climbed out.

I'd seen it all in the visions, but being here, seeing the devastation, I was desperate to find her. My current state of mind meant I wasn't likely to make good decisions. Thankfully Ryder was good at handling the feds so I could do what I needed to do.

"Howe," Ryder called from the ground. "Come see this."

I climbed down from the broken plane after Geoff and landed with a little pain in the knees on the ground. I took a second to clear my head and feel the relief that I hadn't found Cassidy before joining them. Ryder and Geoff were kneeling next to a spot under the nose of the plane.

"The indent here makes me think someone lay here for a bit before they were found." There was a small flattened area, which could have been the size of a body curled on its side. There was also more blood and what looked like a clump of hair. Hair the color of Cassidy's.

"There're two sets of boot prints in the mud at the edge of the clearing over there," Ryder said, pointing northeast of the plane's nose. "And the grass is flattened like they dragged something out of here. Maybe they brought a stretcher and carried her out?"

"Sounds likely," I muttered. "But who is *they*?"

We both turned to Geoff.

"The nearest inhabitants are a community of church folks. They took over an old collection of hunting cabins. Call themselves Maker's Mark or some shit. They burn trash sometimes out in these parts, which my uncles bitch about."

I grabbed Ryder's arm. "Maker's Plan. Geoff, what do you know about those people?"

He rose to his full height, stepped back and crossed his arms over his chest. "Not much. Don't seem to be no drugs going in and out, nothing illegal, so we haven't bothered with 'em much." He tipped his chin at Ryder. "You hear anything?"

"There're some guys living out this way who make the local gun show circuit. We've seen 'em bringing truckloads of supplies through a few times. They've got a big swamp truck and a couple of boats. Could be they've got weapons."

I stood and towered over them both. I needed to get my anger under control, but I also needed them to know what we were dealing with.

"Maker's Plan is a religious organization associated with a guy named Gerald Rains. Rains is a con artist and violent offender. He's suspected to have murdered his wife and possibly her father, and he beat his own daughter so bad, he put her in the hospital." I didn't want to tell them about Joanna. I knew I could trust Ryder, but the fewer people who knew about her, the better.

The men looked at each other and frowned. "When you say religious organization, you're talking more like a cult, that right?" Geoff said.

"Absolutely. We don't know much about the group here, but we know enough about Rains. He's manipulated churches around the country as a 'guest minister' and gotten countless people to give up their financial assets to him. That's how he's been able to start this community, I'm guessing. We had a run-in with his people that got me shot, and then he showed up himself and shot a friend of mine, who thankfully made it. Now he's targeted Cassidy, had his people hijack her plane—Maker's Plan was the client on the flight manifest."

"Damn, Howe, what the hell you messed up in? I thought you were an art teacher?"

I shrugged and gave him my most innocent smile. "I am."

"Uh-huh." Ryder shook his head and I knew he wanted to ask more, but we had a task at hand. "State police and FBI will deal with the crime scene. I'll see what I can find out."

"Good. Geoff, how far is it to where the community might be located—"

"Whoa, Howe, you're not going in alone." Ryder put a hand on my chest and frowned at me. I appreciated his concern but I'd been patient too long.

"I've got to get to Cassidy," I said, ready to throw down if Ryder thought he was going to stop me.

"Hold up," Geoff said to Ryder. "From what I know of the folks who live out here, they do so for a reason. If they hijacked a plane to get this woman, I don't think traipsing into their commune with a peashooter and goldilocks over here is gonna go over too well."

"Then we wait for the rest of the feds," Ryder said, and I knew whatever I said next he'd argue with. We shared the rank of captain when we finally left the Rangers, and that meant an impasse. Not that ranks mattered anymore, but they kinda did.

"Fine. We'll get more information. Then I'm going in—alone. I need to get her out alive. We can't take a crew of law enforcement into that community. People will get hurt."

Ryder appraised me, and I could see his wheels turning. "Call your people," he said finally, handing me the SAT phone. "Find out what they know. I'll deal with Noffsinger."

"Thank you," I said, and I hoped he knew I meant it. I hated that I'd dropped this mess on his front porch, but I also knew him well enough to know he'd want this mess dealt with, and would hate it if more people were hurt just *outside* his front porch.

I stepped away and called Damien on the SAT phone.

"Preston."

"It's Howe."

"What did you find?"

I exhaled harshly. "Wreckage. Two corpses. No Cassidy."

Damien huffed. "No doubt. Any sign of her?"

"Evidence points to something like a body being carried away. Not sure of her status, but Damien...I—"

"You know she's alive. Joanna said she Sees her. And Rains is most definitely there in Florida. He's not dead, as we presumed."

"How the hell are we going to deal with this man? No place can hold him."

Damien sighed. "Hart apparently has a solution, *if* we are able to locate him."

"I've got a lead on the location of a community calling themselves Maker's Plan. Sounds like Rains."

"That it does. What is your next move?"

I looked around and saw more uniformed officers and dudes in windbreakers and slacks entering the clearing with the last bit of sunlight, just as I heard a helicopter nearing us.

"More authorities just arrived. I'm going to talk to whomever is in charge and work out a plan. I know Rains. If uniformed officers go in after Cassidy, it will be a bloodbath. But if I go in—"

"Jackson, no. He knows you."

"I'll change my appearance. And I can block him psychically. Morgan's taught me a thing or two. If I can get in there and get the lay of the land, I can get intel out and they can move in, hopefully without anyone getting hurt."

"I don't like it. Delaney will *hate* it."

I chuckled. "Delaney wants her best friend back, and I'm the man for the job."

"You're also the man to care for our children here at the academy. You are invaluable to us, Jackson. Don't forget that."

I swallowed hard. "I won't forget it. But Damien, you know I'm right. If we don't handle this well, Rains will kill Cassidy and keep coming at us until he gets Joanna back. I won't let that happen."

"You're correct. Fine. I'll speak to Nigel and you touch base with me before you make any moves. I'm assuming you'd be going in without any method of communication?"

"Most likely."

He cursed, and I laughed. "Always great to hear the uptight Brit cussing like a true American."

"Sod off, Howe. Keep yourself safe and keep me posted."

He hung up on me and I closed my eyes.

There was no alternative. I had to do this. I'd have to go in after her myself. I'd do whatever it took to get Cassidy out alive, save as many innocents as I could, and hog-tie Rains until Nigel can figure out how to take him out of commission. No problem.

"Hey Howe?"

Ryder waved me over. The helicopter had landed and he was talking to another guy in an FBI windbreaker. "This is Special Agent Todd Barringer. Agent, this is Retired Captain Jackson Howe of the 75th Army Ranger Division. We served together. Captain Howe is here at the request of Mackenzie's family." He turned to me. "Howe, Special

Agent Barringer is assigned to the field office in Miami. He's been in touch with Cassidy's company. He's taking the lead from here."

I shook hands with the younger agent, sizing him up a little. Guy looked like he could handle his shit, but we'd see.

"As of now, her company has not received any ransom demands—"

"And there likely won't be any. They don't want her for monetary purposes."

Barringer frowned at me, the crease between his dark eyebrows severe. "Then why the hell would these people go to all this trouble?"

I glanced at Ryder, figuring I better share what I knew. The trick would be telling them what they needed to know while protecting the kids at the academy. We had protocols. This wasn't the first time.

"Leverage. The leader of this group? Gerald Rains. We have his daughter. The headmaster of the academy where I work has guardianship. Rains is a multistate fugitive—"

"I know exactly who Gerald Rains is. Or *was*. He's dead."

"He's alive and well in Florida, and likely leading a group of religious zealots who will do his bidding."

Barringer rested his hands on his hips. "I know there's a lot more you're not telling me, but for now, locating Miss Mackenzie is priority one."

"Absolutely." I appreciated this guy's sense of urgency.

Barringer gave me a once-over. "We've got local police and state troopers involved, we're going to start a search of the area in the morning. There's not much that can be done tonight."

"Agent Barringer, my colleague, Geoff Clements, and his people know where this religious community is staying." Ryder waved Geoff over. "However, there are complications."

"Complications?"

"They're most likely heavily armed," I said. "And Rains is willing to sacrifice his flock for his endgame. I think a better option is infiltration. With your help, I can enter the camp as a new recruit. Your people can set up surveillance. I'll get you info as I can and we can come up with a safe plan to get the innocents out."

Barringer blew out a breath. He stared me down, likely thinking about how much trouble this situation was going to get him into. "Suppose you've had undercover experience?"

I smirked. "It's classified, but yeah. And I'm close with his daughter. I can get details from *her* that will make my entry believable."

"Well then," he sighed, "let's get you back to Miami and debrief the situation. Simms, you and your colleague care to join us? I could use your knowledge of the area."

Ryder looked between us and spit on the ground. "I'll help. On one condition."

"What's that?" Barringer asked.

Ryder grinned at me. "I get to shave off that hippie hair."

CHAPTER 13
CAPTIVITY

Cassidy

Remaining in bed was a way to hide from the reality of my kidnapping, but I was getting restless. I decided it was time to confront my captors and find out their intentions. I'd lost track of the days, but I figured it had been at least three days. We'd removed the bandages yesterday and my vision was cloudy, but I could at least see shapes beyond five feet. Nearer than that, things were still blurry but I could make them out. I was grateful for that much. I was less dependent now, could dress myself and do minimal tasks around the infirmary to help Irene.

Who knew what the future held for me? My sight could be permanently damaged, or I could continue to improve. Only time would tell.

I'd been with Irene the whole time, with the exception of the prayer service her daughter had forced me to attend, and I knew I wouldn't be able to hide much longer.

When Irene brought me breakfast, I could tell by her expression that my reprieve was up.

"He wants you."

I accepted the bowl of oatmeal and sighed.

"I'm supposed to bring you to him after breakfast."

"What does he want me for, do you think?"

She shrugged. "Hopefully just to talk. Either His Right Hand or The Second spends alone time with every community member when they first join. It could be that..." She trailed off, and I shuddered at the thought of what else he would do with me alone.

I shoveled the oatmeal in for strength and tried to formulate a plan. If I played dumb, pretended like I didn't know what was going on and he figured me out...

"What do you think I should do?"

"Be honest. He'll know. He reads people. And be wary. He can make you...do things. Feel things. Believe in things that aren't true or right."

That was a big no for me on the last part. I could always tell when someone was being dishonest with me. Well, except for my ex-husband. With Robert, well, I knew he'd loved me. I also knew he made impulsive decisions and that he'd been careless with his money before we got together, but I assumed incorrectly that if I was handling the books, we'd be safe. Unfortunately by the time I'd discovered his betrayal, his whole personality had changed.

It was weird; it hadn't been gradual, it was as if overnight he became this desperate monster with no self-preservation and certainly no consideration for me. Something had happened to make him change, but he'd never told me. Then it was too late, and I lost all respect for him. I'd be all the more cautious in the future. If I even had an inkling someone wasn't being totally honest with me, I'd never let them get close. I couldn't. I wouldn't.

But from what Irene was saying, I might not have a choice in this case. This man could allegedly take whatever he wanted from me, and that thought made bile rise in my throat. "Did he ever hurt you?"

She shook her head. "Only by taking my daughter and turning her against me. Since she's joined with him, he's not been open about sleeping with other women, though I suspect he does, and she likely knows about it. He treats her like a queen, so I suppose she ignores his indiscretions. The Second, however, is supposed to choose a wife, or so I've heard."

"The Second is his son, correct?"

"Yes." Irene's voice shook on the word.

"I'll keep that in mind. Maybe they'll see me as too old or damaged goods."

Irene shook her head. "You're very beautiful, Cassidy. And you're special. You're brave. You survived a terrible accident, and he's using that in his teaching. He's told his community that your survival constitutes a miracle, maybe even the one they've been waiting for."

Great. This was moving into prophecy territory. I'd been around people like this before.

"Thank you. For everything, Irene. No matter what happens, I'll always appreciate you for taking care of me." *And protecting me.* At least three times in the past couple days, men had entered the infirmary and attempted to claim they were fetching me for His Right Hand. Irene shooed them all away, thankfully. I did my best to memorize something about each of them, to alert me if I came in contact with them again. Their smells, their voices... Something that would remind me they weren't safe people to be around.

I helped Irene clean up and made my bed with fresh sheets.

"Will I be coming back here?"

"I don't know what they're going to do with you, Cassidy. I'm sorry. I'm not in the know, and Denise basically won't speak to me any longer except about the baby."

I squeezed her hand and took a deep breath.

"Okay. Maybe you can help me figure out the best way back here... in case I have the opportunity to see you."

"I will." Irene took my hand and placed it in the crook of her arm. "You've been a bright spot for me, Cassidy. I'm sorry we met under these circumstances, but...I'm *not* sorry."

"Me neither."

I squeezed her hand and began to count steps as we went outside. I saw a lot of green surrounding us, so dense it appeared to be a solid wall. I counted twelve cabins, all about the same size, and also painted green. The roofs seemed misshapen. I started to ask Irene when she spoke.

"They cover the roofs with branches and vines so they're not as visible from the air. There's the pavilion where we eat together, and where we hold evening prayer meetings and Sunday service."

"How many people are here?" I asked. I could see person-sized shapes in my peripheral vision, but had no sense of the population.

"Maybe forty of us now? That are here. There are some followers who come and stay and then leave for weeks at a time."

"How do you survive out here? It's not like this is prime farming territory."

She glanced around. "On the level, there are folks who do day work in Everglades City, a few who work for the oil company. His Right Hand and The Second travel and gather donations and supplies that are then brought back for the group. Lance, who's one of the elders, runs the day-to-day camp operations. Matt's in charge of security and the workers who go out and take day labor. Esai is his lieutenant, and in charge whenever father and son aren't here. The others cook, clean, watch the children... One of the reasons many of the folks stay is because they have people to watch their kids while they work, and they like the fellowship. There's a school and everything."

"Interesting. So no industry or production, but services. Okay. I get it."

"And everyone has to share their skills with His Right Hand. He sends people out on tasks to prove their loyalty."

I'd counted over a hundred and fifty steps from the infirmary to the pavilion's edge, and then another fifty steps to a set of stairs. Irene led me up the steps, which felt much more solid than those of the infirmary. This building seemed to be a very nice log cabin-style home. It made sense that His Right Hand...Rains...lived here.

"Hello, Mother," Denise said as she opened the door. As we grew closer, I saw that her belly was indeed swollen with child. She was petite and appeared to have a massive beach ball under her knit sundress. "He's expecting you, Miss Mackenzie."

Irene didn't make a move to enter the home. She gave my hand a squeeze and backed away as if she dreaded what was on the other side of the door.

"Here," Denise said. "Take my hand. I will lead you through to his study." Irene had explained to the others that I had profound vision loss. She'd made it out to be much worse than it was. For my protection.

"Thank you."

The inside was a large space, simply decorated with functional furniture and a wood table large enough to seat numerous people.

"His Right Hand spends his days in prayer and working for the community in his study," she said. "He's asked me to bring you to him so you can become better acquainted with our ways. Once he's completed your induction, he'll direct you to your new living quarters and your work assignment. Everyone works here, even those with…disabilities."

"Of course," I said, then cleared my throat. She led me through a kitchen toward the back of the house. There was an upstairs level, and the size of the building seemed to indicate there were likely more rooms on the first floor. It was huge for being in the middle of the Everglades.

"Watch your step," she said as she led me up two steps to a hallway. It seemed as though this part of the house wasn't as solid, as if it were a non-permitted addition. The hallway was dark and I found myself reaching out to avoid walking into something. It wasn't an act; I was genuinely worried.

"Here we are," Denise said. She knocked on a door in front of us and we waited.

The door opened and there was dim light behind the figure who appeared, but I couldn't make out anything about the person.

"Hello, wife. Thank you for bringing our guest to see me."

The booming voice made my skin crawl.

"Yes, sir. As you requested."

Denise took my hand from her arm and a moment later, I felt a larger, rougher hand take mine gently.

"Thank you. Close the door behind you."

I heard the tiniest pause before Denise said, "Yes, sir," in a less enthusiastic voice.

"Please come in," the man said to me. His voice reverberated, like a car with way too much bass that rattles the items inside your house as it drives by. I fought to keep my composure. I was glad I couldn't see his face clearly. I was terrified that I would run screaming or cry or beg for mercy.

He led me ten more steps into the room and I heard the door close. We turned slightly and I felt something behind my calves.

"You may sit here," he said.

I dropped my right hand to my side and lowered myself slowly until I felt the cushion of a couch. The material was some sort of scratchy fabric and the cushions were lumpy, as though it were an old piece of furniture.

"I thought we should get acquainted," he said as he lowered himself to my left on the couch. I desperately wanted to put distance between us but I feared any move like that would fuel his anger, and I still had no idea what he wanted me for.

"I wanted to thank you and your people for caring for me after my accident."

I placed my hands on my knees, and I felt him pat my left hand.

"Of course, Miss Mackenzie. Our community believes in caring for our fellow man and woman, and shelters those in peril. My men were out in the field and they witnessed the plane crash. They radioed that they'd found you, so I ordered them to bring you here. I believe it is nothing short of a miracle that you survived, and that you landed so close to us."

"I'm glad to be alive," I said, unsure how to tell him he should have called the fucking cops and let an ambulance take me to a hospital. He had more of a role in this than just ordering his men to rescue me, I could feel it.

"It is His will. Part of our glorious Maker's Plan. The sole purpose of our community here is to serve Our Maker and do His bidding. Bringing you into our flock was part of His plan."

I swallowed back bile as he launched into his preacher tone. I'd spent enough time in my life being subjected to religious zealots.

"I wanted to ask you," I said, bracing myself for his ire, "if there is any way for me to get in contact with my company? I'm sure they'd be willing to provide transportation for me."

I held my breath waiting for his answer, which would tell me whether or not I was truly a captive.

"I've already been in contact with your company," he said matter-of-factly. "We were able to retrieve your credentials from the cockpit, and we let them know we found you and that you'd asked that they call off the search, that you had chosen to stay with our community. They asked me to pass along good tidings and assured me that you would not be held accountable for the faulty aircraft."

No. No, there's no way they would believe that. They can't. They have to come for me. Someone...

I suddenly recalled what Irene had said, about Rains making people believe things. Was that what he'd done? Was that even possible?

"It's procedure for them to investigate any crash site," I said. "They'll need to send a representative out. Perhaps I could meet with them, as I'd like to clear my name."

"That will be unnecessary, Cassidy." He attempted to use a soothing tone, like an anesthesiologist telling you to count back from a hundred before you slide into darkness. "You've already submitted your resignation. Your roommates at your temporary housing in Los Angeles have been notified you will not be returning. No one will be looking for you."

I felt a squeeze inside my skull, like the change in cabin pressure.

"You and I both know that's not true," I said, trying to keep the fury out of my voice. "The authorities—"

"Do not come out this way. We have an understanding with local law enforcement. They leave us alone." His hand tightened painfully over mine. "*No one* will be looking for you," he repeated. "You belong to the community now."

I sucked in a shaky breath. Playtime was over.

"And just what do you intend to do with me, now that you're clearly planning to continue holding me against my will?"

He sighed. "It doesn't have to be that way, Cassidy."

I felt tiny tendrils of cold around my neck, slithering up my throat and seeking entrance into my body. For a moment it was so intense, I felt paralyzed. He used a finger to turn my chin, trying to force me to look at him, but I could only see darkness where his face should be, a faint glow where his eyes were located. He was doing...something to my senses. I fought to see even the limited amount I usually could, but whatever was happening took over.

"You were meant to be here, for multiple purposes, and you will find that you belong with us if you will just...let...me...in."

I panted and squeezed my eyes shut, swallowing hard. It felt as though the tendrils instantly popped off the surface of my skin.

I heard a faint growl of disapproval, and then the tendrils were back. "Cassidy, *let me in.*" The icy tentacles surrounded me, squeezing my torso until it hurt to breathe.

I tightened every muscle in my body and screamed *no* in my head. I refused to be controlled by this man.

"You..." he said, sounding out of breath. "You surprise me."

"I'm not easily duped," I said.

"But you are a child of The Maker. You have studied the scripture. You must know it is the End of Days."

"What? Like Revelations?" Was he really keeping these people captivated by horror stories from the Bible?

"And he who was seated on the throne said, *'Behold, I am making all things new.' Also he said, 'Write this down, for these words are trustworthy and true.'* Revelations 21:5."

"They also talk about monsters and devils in Revelations. It's just stories."

"So you are not easily influenced, and you are a lapsed Christian."

"I don't believe blindly in a book written by men that has done more harm than good in this world."

He chuckled and patted my knee again. This time his hand lingered.

"It is a work of power, of truth. At least, the truth I need to serve my purposes. My congregation will follow my guidance until His will is carried out. I have worked hard to bring this all to fruition, and we are so very close to completing the task given us." He sounded

proud. Power hungry. He wouldn't succeed in making a sheep out of me.

"You can't keep me here," I whispered.

"My people know that you were a victim of a plane crash and nothing more. They will believe anything I tell them, and I've told them to welcome you as a gift from The Maker. Your survival of a horrible accident was exactly as I've foretold." He recovered well and stood from the couch. "You will remain here in my home, which is an honor I don't bestow upon members lightly. You will come to understand our ways and learn our teachings...if you wish to survive what's coming."

I heard him moving around the room and then he was back at my side. He grabbed my wrist hard and yanked me off the sofa. "Since you are unable to see, you will have someone with you at all times. For your protection. Can't have you wandering off and being eaten by an alligator," he said with a chuckle. Then he yanked my left arm closer to him, causing me to cry out in pain. My shoulder was better, but still tender.

"You *will* do my bidding, Cassidy Mackenzie. You will fall in line or you will be suffer the consequences. And so will the ones you love. I am a benevolent leader, as long as my wishes are fulfilled. You'd better get used to that. Now, let me show you to your room."

He led me to a door that didn't feel as though it was in the same direction we'd come from. When the door swung open, there was only blackness before me.

"I won't bother bringing you a light since you have no need for it. I will keep you close to me, and you will serve your purpose. If not, you will become expendable."

He pushed me forward, and I stumbled into the darkness.

"There's a compost toilet in the corner. Someone will bring you clothes. You'll get food and water when I feel you've earned it." He paused in the doorway and sighed loudly once more. "It didn't have to be this way, Cassidy. You could have ruled them by my side. You made the wrong choice. Pity."

The door closed and took with it all remaining light, leaving me in dark and silence.

Part of me was relieved. No secrets, no pretending to believe.

But no light. No way out.

Helpless.

If he was right, and no one was coming for me—which didn't seem possible—I didn't have much time left.

Because End of Days was code for disaster, and I worried I might not survive whatever he had planned.

CHAPTER 14
JUST A LITTLE PATIENCE

Jackson

Three days.

Cassidy's plane went down three days ago. Instead of barging in there and rescuing her, I'd listened to Ryder and our new pal from the FBI, Todd Barringer, but Jesus, Cassidy could have been rescued by a damn tortoise at this rate.

I sat on a chair in the men's room at Ryder's station. We'd fallen back to this spot with a Barringer and his partner to make a plan almost 24 hours ago. Too many cooks in the kitchen had me agitated. I just wanted to start the mission.

"Now, hold still," Ryder said as we completed the last step of preparation before I was dropped off in Everglades City at a spot where day laborers were picked up. Todd had an informant who said that folks from Maker's Plan showed up there regularly to get work. The plan was for me to go out on a job with community members and then ask if I could tag along back to the camp. My cover wasn't too far off; Army veteran, down on his luck, looking for a place to make a difference. If it weren't for Nigel and Havenhart Academy, that very well could have been my story.

Once I got to camp, I would try to locate Cassidy, get the lay of the land, and on the next workday, get any intel to Todd and Ryder, who would coordinate an official response. It was a sound plan. Sound enough. But I was restless. Impatient. Every minute Cassidy spent with the community was a minute she was in danger, or suffering, or miserable—

"I can't tell you how much pleasure this is going to give me," Ryder said. He wrapped a towel around my shoulders and gave a maniacal laugh as he clicked on the clippers.

"Man, I'm going to miss this mop."

Ryder chuckled. "She must be something if you're willing to cut off your mane."

My smile slipped a little. "Yeah. She is."

He nodded and made his first pass. I made him chop off the pony-tail first and promise to donate it to a charity for kids with cancer. I loved making him do nice things just to hear him bitch about it, especially when I knew he had an even bigger heart than me. After a few minutes of buzzing, the cool air-conditioned air hit my scalp and gave me a chill.

"I'm going to leave some and we'll dye this shit, otherwise it ain't gonna matter. Your pretty boy looks are likely to get you recognized, though, you know?"

"I can fix that," Geoff said. He slammed down a bag from the local drug store and whipped out his giant hunting knife, flipping it over in his hands.

"Uh, I was thinking contacts." Ryder raised his eyebrows at Geoff's knife. "You swamp people scare me."

"No, he's right," I said, coming up with a brilliant plan. "Contacts will be a pain in the ass and who knows what the accommodations are out there. A little plastic surgery would be good. I gestured to the knife. "Go heat that up."

"What the fuck, Howe? Cutting your hair is one thing, but permanent disfiguration?"

"It's not permanent. You ever seen what happens with a curling iron burn?"

Ryder frowned. "Do I look like I've spent much time around a curling iron?"

"No, but you have sisters, dumbass."

"I never paid attention."

Geoff whipped out a Zippo, held it under the blade for several long seconds, and then handed the hilt to me. I took it from him carefully.

"Darcy, the bartender in town, she burns herself with her curling iron on the regular. Leaves a nasty red mark that lasts for weeks but it doesn't scar, not really. I'll be out of there before it fades."

I took the curved blade and sucked in a breath before pressing it to my cheek, under my right eye, for a few long seconds.

"*Fuuuuuuuck* that smarts!"

I looked in the mirror and winced at the crescent-shaped red welt raised up on my flesh.

"Oh, man! I should get to burn you, too," Ryder said with a pout.

"Go for it," I said, handing the knife back to Geoff. "I'll let you take a turn. I owe you after that fucking kid shot you in Nasiriyah. That left a nasty mark."

Ryder pulled up his t-shirt sleeve and showed his deltoid, which had a rugged scar from where the bullet grazed him. He'd gotten an infection and they'd had to remove some of the skin and muscle. It finally healed, but he'd been pissed that it fucked up his tattoo.

Geoff heated the blade again and offered the handle to Ryder, who turned on me with a way-too-excited grin on his face. "Where you want it, pretty boy?"

"How about the eyebrow?"

"I can't believe you're going to let me do this."

"Yeah, right there—*ow!*—but not too close, fucker! Don't want me going in blind."

I looked in the mirror and was creeped out at my appearance. The buzz cut I recognized like an old friend from my service days, but the fresh burns, which I knew would scab over soon, were shocking.

"We'll dye your hair and then even *you* won't recognize yourself."

"That's the point," I said, shaking my head. "That means Cassidy won't recognize me, either."

Ryder grunted. "You'll have to rely on your charm and wit."

He and Geoff looked at each other.

"Damn. This op is fucked then."

There was a knock at the door and Todd poked his head in.

"Oh…wow, yeah, you look different. Look, we're a go, so Jackson, I'll take you with me tonight and we'll drop you off a few blocks from the day workers' pickup spot in the wee hours. You're going to need a good night's sleep."

"Not likely to get it," I muttered. Every time I closed my eyes, I found myself in Cassidy's shoes. I couldn't see much of anything, which led me to believe she'd had some injury to her eyes. I knew she was okay because I could hear her breathing and feel her pain, but I could also sense her thoughts. She wasn't terrified—she was determined. I could sense her taking steps to remain calm and focused on survival. Her inner strength gave me the drive to move forward with the operation. If she could be so brave, I wouldn't let her down. She believed someone was coming for her, and I was that person. I had to be.

Once my transformation was complete, I helped Ryder clean up the bathroom and said my goodbyes.

"We'll be out there. I'm stepping up my patrols around the perimeter, but not too close that I spook them. Geoff will be around more with his family, but they're stealthy. You won't know they're there. They hunt those grounds, so if they run into any of the Maker's Plan folks, they won't create a concern."

I shook hands with Ryder. "Thanks, man. I'll see you on the other side."

"A-ffirm. You watch your six."

We bro hugged, and then I left the visitor center with Agent Barrington.

The drive to the motel was short and he made small talk while I listened.

Like me, he was from Virginia originally, and he wasn't a huge fan of Florida but knew good agents were needed everywhere. He'd only been in the field a few years, but he'd done four years in the Navy and had an impressive amount of education under his belt; BAs in psychology and criminal justice, and he'd earned an MA in abnormal psychology.

at my temples. My jaw throbbed with the pressure I'd placed on it. I didn't want to speak, didn't want to make anything about this situation harder for her. I turned on the shower, grateful it was a big stall with a stone bench built into the wall in case she needed to sit down.

"Jackson? I think I need help."

I turned to find her standing in plain, shapeless white cotton briefs that were too big for her and struggling with her pullover top. Some floral shit with no buttons, just a v-neck.

"I'm sorry," I said, moving behind her, then thinking twice about it. I didn't want to see her in the mirror. I stood at her side and tried to lift the top over her head.

"I can't...I can't lift my left arm over my head," she said, her voice barely a whisper.

"Of course. Uh..." I spotted a pair of scissors on the counter. "You're not attached to this garment, are you?"

She barked out a laugh, turned and looked at me with wide eyes, then lost it in peals of hysterical laughter.

"God, Jackson. How could you ask me that? You think I dress like this all the time?"

I snorted. "Well, you never know. This shade of...what would you call this color? Chartreuse? It's very flattering against your, um, well, the cut is definitely flattering—"

"Cut it off, cut it off," she said, gasping for air. Her laughter was more than the situation called for, but she was visibly releasing the tension from her body with each round.

"You sure?" I asked, the scissors poised at the bottom of the shirt in back. "I can save the fabric and we can, I don't know, make a dish towel out of it. A toilet rag."

"Fuck that. I want to burn this shit."

"Fair enough," I said with a sigh as I snipped slowly. "Would you call this a blouse? I don't even know what to label it."

"I'd rather wear a burlap sack than this awful clothing."

I got toward the top and I moved her wet hair to the side, exposing her neck. When I got through the material, she tugged it off and threw it on the floor.

"At least they let me keep my bra, but I want to burn that too." She

My blood boiled thinking of what she'd been through. "I'd rather be shot by Rains' fuckups every day for the rest of my life than for you to have been through this, sweetheart."

The corner of her lips turned up and she squeezed my hand.

"You want me to…"

"I'm not modest, Jackson. It's okay. Trust me, it felt like everyone in that damn camp saw me naked in the beginning. At least I know it's you."

I clenched my jaw, wishing I could break something, break *someone*.

You just keep that trap shut, Howe. She doesn't need your shit right now.

I let go of her hand long enough to shut the bedroom door. "Let me grab you some clothes." I opened a couple of drawers and found a pair of flannel pajamas with hippos on them. "These okay?"

She smiled. Her first real smile since our escape. "I love hippos."

"Well, all right then. After you?"

Her smile slipped, and she turned for the bathroom. I followed her in and she went to the sink and looked in the mirror. I sat the pajamas on the far edge of the counter and then pulled a towel down from the cabinet and hung it over the shower door.

"I'm glad I don't have total clarity of vision. I don't think I want to know how bad I look."

I stood against the wall, trying to give her space. I stared a hole in her back. "You don't look bad at all. You look like you've been through hell and made it out the other side."

"Thanks," she said with a humorless laugh. "I definitely feel like hell. It hasn't settled in that I'm out, though."

"It might not for a while."

She nodded, less in agreement with my statement than to herself to accept that it was time for her to move. She slid the ghastly blue polyester pants they'd given her to wear down her legs and stepped out of them. I pressed my lips together to avoid cursing when I saw the yellowish bruises that told the story of her wounds. Her left leg from the hip down to her ankle bore most of the bruising. She'd clearly fallen onto her side, probably when she'd escaped the burning plane.

I needed to stop watching this parade of hurt.

"Let me get the shower going for you," I said, my heart pounding

"The FBI seemed like the best place to go if I wanted to do the most good."

"I don't blame you," I said, stifling a yawn. "After everything I saw overseas, I figured I'd come home and teach. Kids are awesome. They haven't had the chance to get fully fucked up yet."

Barringer laughed. "Or," he said, "it's not too late to turn it around if they *have* fucked up."

"Amen. You got kids?"

"No, sir. This is not the career for a family man," he replied. "I don't anticipate that in my near future."

The way he pursed his lips when he said it let me know that, a) he'd tried and failed at a relationship and was speaking from experience; and b) he very much wanted kids but was terrified. I didn't blame him one bit.

"I wanted to ask you more about Rains."

"I figured you might," I said. We'd been over the basics. He knew I worked at the academy, had no idea of the scope of our work, and he knew that Rains had a kid there. He also knew about our run-ins. But there were a lot of holes, and I'd assumed he would ask more questions when he got me alone.

"I remember when the Marshals picked him up in Florida. It was a big win for them. A friend of mine bragged about how they'd nabbed one of their most wanted and that he wished he'd been there to take the bastard back to Texas." Barringer looked around, changed lanes, and slowed as we drew up to an older single-story motel. "How does somebody like that just walk away from a Texas maximum-security facility?"

He pulled the car up to the curb and stopped.

"Agent Barringer," I began, "you ever stared real evil in the eye? You ever get up close and personal with someone who enjoys the suffering of others? A true narcissist who believes they've been put on this earth for a purpose and no one can stop them, not even the laws of physics or reality as we know it?"

Barringer flexed his fingers on the steering wheel. "I heard old timers talk about Bundy like that. I know I've hauled in some dangerous men who'd just as soon feed their families to the gators than go to prison."

I turned to him and shook my head, my cheek tight from the burn. It was a reminder that I was going to be playing a role, one that would hopefully get me close enough to Cassidy to save her.

"If you'd seen what this man did to his daughter. If you'd seen the depravity… He truly believes he is untouchable and acts as such. He's careful to a point, but he's gotten away with murder, escaped from the authorities and faked his own death. This is not a man we're dealing with, but a monster who believes he's above God and the laws of man. He's not going to give up without a show, and I'm convinced he's got a plan that's going to put a lot of lives in danger."

Barringer squeezed the steering wheel again. "No offense, Howe, because I'm sure you can handle yourself as well if not better than me or any other FBI agent, but I'm not fully comfortable with this plan. If we send in a team of agents—"

"He will kill every last one of his followers and anyone who comes near them. I truly believe that."

"Then how do you hope to waltz out of there with Miss Mackenzie?"

I grinned and tapped my temple with a finger. "I've got a secret weapon."

You know this poor man is going to be so confused unless you tell him everything.

Joanna. I breathed a sigh of relief.

I have a few things to report so get rid of the guy.

Joanna was having way too much fun playing secret agent.

"If that's all, I'd love to shower, get the remnants of my hair off me, and get some shut-eye."

"Fair enough. I'll have dinner delivered. Any requests?"

"Something that will fill me up and put me in a food coma, otherwise I won't be able to sleep even a little."

"Roger that."

He showed me to the room where I could crash and left to take care of a few things. As soon as he was gone, I showered and flopped on the bed in a towel.

Are you ready to strategize? Joanna nudged.

"Girl, give me a break," I said with a laugh.

My cell phone rang, and I answered it.

"It's easier to talk on the phone, and I have things to tell you before you leave."

Her sweet voice made me smile. She was so damn brave. "Hey, my little soldier. You got some intel for me?"

"Yes, Mr. Howe. Now listen carefully, this is important."

"Yes, ma'am"

I listened as she spoke so fast, I wondered if she was even breathing.

"He's blocking me, I can tell. There are things he specifically doesn't want me to know, and that's bad. Cassidy is close to him and she's in the dark. I don't know what that means."

"I think I have an idea," I said on an exhale. "She can't see well."

"No, it's more than that. And watch out for the pregnant one. She thinks he'll protect her, but the child is all he cares about."

"Oh God. There's a pregnant lady?" This bit of knowledge further convinced me it was better that I was going in alone. Barringer was giving me a week. If I didn't contact him before that time, he was going to send in the troops. I let Joanna know and asked her about weapons.

"There's a metal shed. The men spend time target shooting. There are tanks of something that have the flame sign on the side of them."

"Excellent. Thank you, sweetie. I'm so proud of you."

"I'm scared," she said. "Not like I was before. I knew Miss Frost was coming for me...but I can't tell what's going to happen this time. You have to come back here. And you have to find Miss Mackenzie. It's important."

"Yes, ma'am. You sure you ain't been to Ranger school yet? You'll be Spec Ops before long."

She giggled, and it made my heart sing. I wanted her to be a kid, I wanted her to have her innocence, but at every turn she blew me away with her strength.

"I'm going to talk to you as much as I can, but Miss Frost said I have to rest."

Alarm bells went off at that. "Of course you do. Is Miss Frost there?"

I heard her speak to someone else. "Here she is."

"Hello?" Delaney came on the line, and I smiled.

"Hey, you. What's the story?"

Delaney exhaled, and I heard rustling, like she was on the move. "I'll be right back, Joanna."

"You don't have to leave the room," Joanna said. "I know what you're going to say."

I burst out laughing, and it felt good, a bit of a stress release. I probably laughed harder than what was called for.

"You can't even be mad," I said. "She can't help it."

Delaney grumbled something I didn't pick up because I was yawning again.

"What I was going to say," she whispered into the phone. "Is that the last time she contacted you, she got a nose bleed, so I'm worried. I don't want her to have any setbacks."

Damn. "I get it, Del, I do, but it's all hands on deck right now. I need whatever I can get from her, but I don't want her hurt."

"I know." She paused for a minute. "So. Did you do it?"

I frowned. "Do what?"

She clucked her tongue at me. "You know. Your hair. Is it really gone?"

I chuckled. "Yeah, and it sucks. I worked hard to grow that shit."

She sighed. "It was really beautiful, Jackson. We'll have to have a proper memorial service for it when you return."

I knew she loved me. You didn't go through the kind of shit we'd been through in the fall and not develop a bond. But it was just that. A bond formed by trauma. I understood that now.

"I'm gonna bring her back. Cassidy. I promise."

"I know," she said, her voice breaking a little. "You have to. And you better not get hurt. Joanna needs you. We all need you."

"Yeah, yeah, yeah. You just want me around to keep an eye on your cousin."

"Jackson, that's not funny." She was getting too heavy for the moment.

There was a knock at the door.

"I'm sorry. Look, the agent in charge is outside with my dinner."

"Be careful, Jackson," she said. "Please."

"You got it, Counselor."

I hung up as Barringer knocked again. "Howe?"

"Yeah," I said. I got up and slid my jeans on. I didn't feel like entertaining in a towel.

"You fall asleep?" he asked as I opened the door.

I reached for my hair and cursed to find it gone. "Nah. Last-minute talk with Joanna. Wanted to see if she could give me any further intel, but Rains kept a lot from her."

Barringer set down two bags of fast food. "I'm sorry, this was all that was open."

"Don't care," I said, pulling a plain white tee over my head. "As long as it will put me to sleep."

We sat and dug in. I noticed he was eating a salad with grilled chicken, and he'd brought me a greasy burger, humongous fries and a giant milkshake.

"Eat up, you're going to need your strength. I'm guessing they're not going to have much food where you're going."

"You got more info?"

Barringer nodded and wiped his mouth. "I just got an email from the field office. The sheriff's deputies down in Everglades City have been monitoring three men who have been coming into town and buying up huge amounts of ammunition and pallets of food from the local Walmart. Then they load up a truck on the edge of town and take off into the Big Cypress. Deputies tried to follow them, but they lost them on some back roads. They've got enough ammo and food to do... I don't even know. They get paid under the table for day labor, and there's no regularity to their shopping. Sometimes they go three days in a row, sometimes they go two weeks in between shopping trips."

I dipped a fry into my shake and Barringer gave me a look.

"What? Salty and sweet. It's good." I took a drink of water and got serious. "This is exactly why you can't just rally the troops and go storming the stronghold. If the intel I've got is good, there are innocent people there. Kids, even. You don't want to have a Jonestown or even a Ruby Ridge on your hands."

"You're right. I just have a bad feeling about this."

"Tell me about it."

I savored the last few bites of my burger and my gut let me know it was sufficiently full.

"I just wish I had more info about the camp. The only records I could find listed a handful of dwellings, but if they've been there a while, who knows? And drones are out. They'd spot them."

"I hear you. It'll be fine. I've got the names of at least two members who aren't fully loyal to Rains. I'll find them."

Barringer sat back in his seat and frowned. "You got all of this from a little girl who's never been to this place? I know you told me to trust you, but this is... How can she know?"

You can trust him. He wants to believe.

I tapped my temple. "Let's just say she's got ways of communicating with me that don't require technology."

Barringer leaned forward with his elbows on the table. "Telepathy?"

"Sort of."

I waited for him to whip out the cuffs and take me in or call the whole thing off. It was a big chance, telling him this. Nigel wouldn't like me giving out sensitive information about the kids, but this mission had to be a success, and I needed this agent to have my back.

"I've seen it happen before, but not like this. Is she talking to you now?"

I nodded.

"Tell her I would very much like to meet her someday."

I heard Joanna giggle in my head and it warmed my heart. I'd love to see her open up and start to smile more. I wanted her to have fun and get to be a kid.

When you get Miss Mackenzie back, you can take me to Disney World.

I barked out a laugh. "Already bargaining. Alright, you got it."

Barringer gave me a look.

Tell him I'd like to meet him too.

"She says she'd like to meet you, too."

The agent smiled. "Sounds like a plan."

"And if you can throw in tickets to Disney World, that'd be great."

He laughed, and Joanna poked me.

I didn't say that.

"I know, but why not make him work for it?"

Barringer narrowed his eyes but his smile eased my concern. "I'll see what I can do. You need to get some shut-eye, Captain Howe. Or should I say, Retired Captain Luke Stephens."

I saluted him. "At your service."

We went over the details of my cover one more time, he gave me all of the documentation I'd need, including dog tags, passport, driver's license, and cash with serial numbers he'd recorded. Any information he could get on these folks would ultimately help take them down. I gave him my weapons and my correct identification for safekeeping. I hated being naked, but it was necessary for my cover. I'd have my knife and my training. That would have to be enough.

He left to get some shut-eye of his own around eleven with plans to be back by five a.m. We'd grab some breakfast sandwiches and then he'd drop me off to begin my journey that would hopefully lead me to Cassidy.

Sleep did not come easy, but that was mostly due to Cassidy. When I climbed in bed, I opened the Connection. She was awake, wherever she was being held, and she was feeling around the room, checking the wall boards for weaknesses. There were some big cracks between boards that let moonlight in, and I watched as she pushed her fingers through and pulled, seeing if she could get one loose. I wished I could communicate with her and let her know I was coming.

Hang tight, sweetheart.

She gasped and turned to look behind her—as if she'd heard me.

CHAPTER 15
FELLOWSHIP

CHAPTER FIFTEEN - FELLOWSHIP
Cassidy

Rains had kept his word that he would keep me close. I'd barely been allowed to leave my room, which would have been fine, but I was restless. It had been four days since the crash and I still felt it in every bone, joint, and muscle, but I was stronger every day. Denise brought me breakfast, and then in the middle of the day, she brought me out to help her with the laundry. She was friendly and spoke to me about the community, sharing with me a little about what they'd accomplished, but careful not to give away any details I could really use.

Like how to get the fuck out of there.

"I told His Right Hand that I think we should bring you to our dinner and prayer service today. If all goes well, it might be good for you. You can meet the others, and by sharing in fellowship, you'll learn to love it here as much as we do."

"Thank you," I said to her, careful not to speak too much. I couldn't exactly say to her that there was no way in hell I would ever believe the bullshit her man was spewing, but I was raised right, and I could

Rains patted him on the shoulder. "You've always been such a good lieutenant. I swear to you that you shall be rewarded for your loyalty."

"Yes, sir." He bowed to Rains and the two men climbed into the boat. "We need to get you to safety. It might be good to get to our California clan, or perhaps the Oregon community? Wherever you feel can shelter you best."

"Oregon would be good," Rains said as they climbed aboard the boat. "John has amassed a large cache of weapons and they're holding on to a lot of cash at the moment. It'll be good to see him and my grandchildren."

The motor started—and I couldn't breathe.

More groups? More children? *Grandchildren?*

Oh, we'd so underestimated this man.

Cassidy moaned against me, and I slid over as far as I could on the bench, letting her body slide down. She rested her head on my thigh and slept while my thoughts spiraled with the information I'd just heard. I really needed to get that intel to Nigel and Damien, maybe even to Agent Barringer. Maker's Plan was a much more organized adversary than we'd originally thought. If Rains had two or more other groups prepared for war, his reach was much more dangerous than we'd assumed.

Why couldn't I See it? Joanna's voice was less confident than usual, it sounded more like the voice of a young girl whose entire reality had just been blown.

"You have other siblings." I kept my voice down to avoid waking Cassidy. "Abel, more in California and Oregon, it seems. And somewhere, hopefully safe, you have a new baby brother."

And I never knew. Why did he keep me with him? What of their mothers? Did he hurt them like he hurt mine?

"Hey, shhh," I said, hoping to keep her mind on our current status rather than on what she had no control over. There would be time later for her to fall apart. I hated to do it, but I needed her help. "Joanna, can you get to Mr. Preston or Mr. Hart? I need you to tell them I have Cassidy and we're out of the camp, but not out of the woods, if you get my meaning?"

I'll tell them. What else can I do? Are you safe?

"Not quite, honey, but don't you worry. I'll be back there soon to hassle you in person."

Good. I'm going to tell Miss Marcia that I need Mr. Preston.

"Thank you, Joanna."

I brushed Cassidy's wet hair back from her face and sighed. The rain poured down around us, the air grew colder, and Cassidy slept. As the sky grew dark, I mentally prepared myself that we'd likely be stuck out here all night. Water pooled around our feet in the blind and I willed myself to be calm. I'd been in worse situations and survived.

But I hadn't been in close proximity with a powerful yet fragile woman who I'd been dreaming of for months. A woman I'd Connected with. A woman who, no matter what happened, would always be a part of my consciousness.

After everything she'd been through, I feared how she would react to the fact that I'd found her because I'd been watching her. Could she forgive the intrusion? Or would she be so disgusted by the mental violations she'd experienced at the hands of Rains that she'd be done with those of us who were different? She knew about Delaney, or so I thought, but what would she say about me?

"I'm sorry. I was just outside the hunting blind keeping an eye out. I'm sorry if I scared you."

My teeth were chattering so hard I could barely get any words out. I'd thought of Jackson so often since I'd met him, wondered about him, and then throughout this disaster, I'd thought I'd never see him again. The fact that he'd rescued me, that he was here in the flesh—all that flesh—was overwhelming. I felt as if I should be more thrilled to be this close to him, and yet, I wasn't eased.

"Thought I'd dreamed you."

"Nah, sweetheart, we're in this nightmare together." He held me tighter.

"You have to be freezing."

"I'm okay. As long as I move around a bit, it keeps the circulation flowing." He gazed down at me with concern. "I wish I had something to keep you warm, or that I could build a fire, but we're exposed here and if any of those security guys are still looking for us..." He trailed off as he looked out of the hole we were in, as if he'd heard something.

"I swear," I said, sitting up a little more and pushing my damp hair back from my face. "If I never come to Florida again, it'll be too soon."

"Aw, you can't blame the whole state for one evil man and his posse of doom. What would Mickey Mouse say? And alligators are just damn cute, you have to admit."

I knew he was trying to cut through the tension, but I wasn't there yet.

"At any minute, we could become gator food or end up back in the clutches of that evil man."

"Hey," Jackson said, tipping my chin so I was forced to look at his face. I could make out his features this close, but there was still a halo of blur around his head. "I won't let that happen, Cassidy."

I reached up and touched his scalp. "What happened to your hair?"

"Disguise," he said with a laugh. "You like my makeover? My pal Ryder, who's out here somewhere looking for us, he had way too much fun cutting my hair off and dyeing it black." He made a face, and I ran a finger over his cheekbone.

"Who did this to you?"

"Oh, these?" he asked, pointing to two circular red marks on his

CHAPTER 23
ESCAPE

CHAPTER TWENTY-THREE – Escape
Cassidy

Cold.

Wet.

Dark.

Alone. I woke up alone, and in the darkness. I began to worry that the escape had just been a dream, that I was still in my cell. In the dark.

I pushed myself up and felt metal underneath my hands. Metal?

"Jackson?" I called out, but kept my voice low. "Jackson?"

"Shhh, hey, hey, it's me."

Jackson climbed through an opening in the darkness, his big body crowding me in the small space. I reached for him, allowing him to take me in his arms and hold me close. He'd pulled off his white t-shirt somewhere outside of the camp and he was still shirtless, his skin warmer than mine but still wet from the rain that continued to pour down upon us. I sighed in relief that I was no longer in that cell, that we'd gotten away from the camp, but I still felt uncertain, and it was more than the fear of recapture that had my stomach in knots.

I sensed her confusion as I stood motionless with the bottles in my hand.

"Jackson? Are you okay?"

Her voice filled my head as if it were my own. The hot water poured down my skin as though I were the one under the spray. My left shoulder throbbed as if I were the one injured.

In my exhausted state, I'd let down my guard and allowed the channel to open. As happened previously, it was so much stronger with Cassidy. Sometimes it was more like being an observer, like I was watching a live camera feed focused on their movements. With my father, I felt his pain. But as Cassidy's movements became my own, I was aware of my *own* sensations as well as hers. I experienced our nervousness and joy together. I'd never seen myself in someone else's perspective, touched my own body as someone else. I felt her appreciation...and desire. For me.

Trying not to panic, I bent and placed the bottles on the bench, nearly dropping them as my depth perception was off. I fumbled, trying to get them to stand up because I was seeing myself set them down from opposite me. You ever try to fix your hair or, hell, put a bandage on your own arm using a mirror? That's what it was like, seeing myself through Cassidy's eyes.

"Guess I'm a little tired myself," I said, hoping I could get through this hair washing without making a total fool out of myself. Or worse, hurting her.

I stood by her side and reached for her hair, running my hands through it, though I couldn't feel it. Instead, I felt the gentle pressure against my own head, the sharp pull when one of my fingers got caught in a tangle.

"I'm sorry," I said. "I don't want to hurt you."

"You didn't," she said. "It feels nice." She had her eyes closed, so I had to feel around, using my memory of where things were to get the shampoo into my hand and onto her hair. It worked, but damn I felt clumsy, and worse, I was disappointed I wasn't getting the full experience of washing her hair since it would probably be the last time she ever let me.

reached behind her back to unhook it, but couldn't get her left arm to work. "Would you?"

"Am I giving this the same treatment?"

"Yes! Please." She continued to giggle, but as soon as I lay a hand on her shoulder to keep her still, she grew quiet. I cut the back of the strap and she held the cups in place against her with her hands for a brief moment before letting the bra fall with the discarded rags. It was as if she realized she'd have no place to hide from me. She only paused for a short second before yanking the panties off and standing up straight. Her gaze landed on her reflection in the mirror, and she let out a disgusted sound.

"I can't even stand straight. My shoulder won't work. I can't fucking see. Jesus." She shook her head and then turned for the shower. I held the door open for her and she stepped inside, her battered body stiff, her movements hesitant, as though she didn't trust her footing. Once she was inside, she tested the water with a hand before moving under the spray and letting out a moan so strong, her whole body sagged. "God, that feels amazing."

I had to turn away. I had to force myself to look elsewhere, but the brief glimpse I'd caught of the water pouring over the top of her head and down her throat to her chest and between her breasts...I was a dirty fucking disgrace for looking. I stared at the floor, at her feet, ready to leap to her rescue if she started to fall.

"Hey, Jackson? I'm sorry, but if there's some shampoo, can you please wash my hair? I can't—"

"Yeah, sure."

I opened the cabinet beneath the sink and found some coconut-scented shampoo and conditioner. I set the bottles on the counter and bent over to remove my trashed boots and peeled the soggy socks off my feet. Leaving my cargo pants on, I grabbed the bottles and stepped into the shower with her.

And that's when things went sideways.

My brain went a little fuzzy, and instead of seeing Cassidy, I got a load of *me*.

The Connection.

smile and fake it with the best of them. "I *would* like to meet the other residents here."

Denise squeezed my arm. "We'll turn you into a Maker's Disciple yet!" She clapped her hands together then paused to place a hand on her lower back and one on her swollen belly. "Whew, this baby," she said. I could see her fairly well since she was right next to me, and she seemed to sway a bit.

"Why don't you sit down and let me finish this work?"

"Thank you, Cassidy. I appreciate it."

She lowered herself onto the couch and blew out a breath.

"Are you in pain?"

She continued to breathe harder than I thought she should.

"I'm thirty-four weeks along, but I was hoping to make it to at least thirty-six weeks."

"I don't know a lot about pregnancy, but some amount of discomfort is normal, right?"

"It is. This is a little more than discomfort," she said from between clenched teeth.

"Should I get your mom?"

She didn't speak for a moment…and then she nodded. "Please."

"Okay. I'll get help, just hang in there for a few minutes, okay?"

The washing machines were just off the kitchen, and I recalled it was a straight shot to the front door. I had no idea where His Right Hand was. He hadn't been in his office when Denise brought me through.

I made it to the front door and opened it. I recalled there were six steps down to the ground, so I held onto the railing and let my heel brush the back of each step until it touched the next. It was slow going, but better than falling.

When I stepped onto the soggy ground, I froze. This was the first time I'd been unaccompanied. If I could see better, this would be my chance to make a break for it, but then if something were to happen to Denise's baby, I'd feel terrible.

The sun was bright overhead, making it tough to make out shapes as my eyes adjusted. I didn't hear any voices, only birds chirping in the trees around the camp. I could slip into the tree line and vanish. I could get away.

I couldn't fucking see.

And this was the Florida fucking Everglades.

"Hello?" I called out.

No one responded. I began to walk slowly away from the house, counting my steps. I recalled there were about two hundred steps between the house and the infirmary. About every twenty steps, I called out, but no one answered.

Until I heard voices. Children's voices. They were singing. I headed in that direction, figuring they had to be supervised by an adult.

The sound of their voices gave me hope, however vague. No place with children who sang so innocently could be truly evil, could it?

"Oh, hello…Cassidy?"

A woman's voice, and not one I recognized.

The children's voices ceased their joyous hymn and fell silent.

"It's alright, children," she said in a soothing voice. "This is Miss Cassidy. Remember the lady who fell from the sky?"

The children began to chatter as someone grabbed my left arm, turning me roughly.

"What are you doing here?"

Esai. *Shit.* Of all the people to run into.

"I came for help. It's Denise."

"The baby?" asked the woman. "Oh, Esai, please go fetch Irene!"

He grunted and squeezed my arm painfully. "You stay here and do what they say," he said menacingly. "If I hear otherwise, you'll be sorry."

"I will."

I heard his footfalls leaving the area, and a gentler hand touched my shoulder.

"Please, sit with us. I'm Carol. Maybe you would let the children ask you some questions?"

I didn't know if that was a good idea or not, but since I didn't have a choice, I figured I would stick to safe topics. She led me over to the group and I could make out at least a dozen little faces looking up at me.

"Miss Cassidy can tell us what it's like to be saved by the Maker. Right, Miss Cassidy?"

Well, I can certainly lie.

My bullshit meter sent off alarms through my gut. There was no truth allowed with these kids. "How many of you have ever been on an airplane?"

The once-gentle hand on my arm tightened enough to grab my attention and remind me to watch what I said.

"I count six hands," Carol said. "That's very good. Some of you traveled by airplane to come with your parents to our community."

One of the children close to me stood up to speak. "Were you scared on your airplane?"

"Airplanes are usually a very safe way to travel," I answered, waiting for the squeeze that would let me know if I'd strayed from their beliefs. "I've been flying airplanes for almost twenty years. And I would get in another plane right now if I needed to go somewhere—"

"But she's joined us now, so she doesn't need another plane."

The squeeze was there again, reminding me to be careful.

"Girls can fly planes?"

I chuckled. "Yes, girls can do whatever they want to—"

"As long as it's part of the Maker's Plan," the teacher corrected.

"Right. Does anyone else have any questions?"

"Did your plane break? Is that why you crashed?"

"I don't know," I answered truthfully. "The women who were on my plane wanted to come here, but the only place we could land was a runway that was too short for my plane. I did the best I could, but we ran out of ground."

There were murmurs from the children, and a quick squeeze from the teacher.

"Our Maker wanted Cassidy to be here. It was His plan, and that is why He saved her when her plane crashed. She was chosen to join us."

A long squeeze let me know that's where I should end the conversation.

"I want to be a pilot when I grow up."

"Me too!"

The children began to chat over each other, and the woman next to me cleared her throat. "You will be exactly what the Maker has chosen for you to be. Praise Him."

A chorus of "praise him" could be heard…and then a hush fell over the students.

"Boys and girls, how do we greet The Second?"

"Bless us, for we follow the Maker's Plan."

The children recited the words as if they were saying the Pledge of Allegiance. A chill went down my spine.

"Praise Him," The Second said. His tone was that of a man who was used to people making him the center of attention, yet he didn't want to intrude. In any other place, he would sound nice and warm and kind.

The Second didn't give me creepy vibes, but I didn't trust anyone here besides Irene.

"You children have been blessed this day to spend time with Miss Cassidy. She's our miracle, and her arrival marks the prophecy.

Awesome. He was as nuts as his father, and just as dangerous.

"Miss Cassidy was just telling us that girls can fly planes," one of the children said.

I watched The Second crouch down in front of her, and the children hushed again.

"Chelsea, a woman may rise as high as a bird in the sky, that's the truth, as long as she lifts others up above her. Someday, you'll find the man The Maker has pledged you to, and it'll be your job to lift him up, and sometimes carry him like the air carries an airplane. That's a big responsibility, now, isn't it?"

"Yes, sir." Her voice sounded less bold and excited than it had before he'd spoken. The bastard. Oh, the loathing I carried for men like him, who made women feel less than from the time they're old enough to dream. *I'd like to take him up in my plane and drop him.*

Shit. I recalled what Irene said about watching my thoughts. I didn't believe it was true, but I needed to be more careful.

"Wonderful. Now, I have to take Miss Cassidy back to her room so she can rest. We all have to have our strength for what's to come, don't we?"

"Yes, sir," the children answered like robots.

"But before we go, I bet Miss Cassidy would love to hear 'Sinners Turn.' Miss Lottie, can you lead our children in that beautiful hymn?"

"Come on, children. You heard The Second. Everybody...one, two, three—"

The Second pulled me to my feet and turned me gently in the direction of the house. As we walked away, I heard the first lines of the hymn.

"Why will you die? Will you let him die in vain? Sinners, will you follow the Maker's Plan?"

The indoctrination at such an early age was frightening. Would any of these children survive unscathed?

"That was brave of you to come seeking help for Denise. I knew you were meant to be here. I just knew it was true."

I clenched my fists to avoid lashing out. The audacity...

"Is she all right?"

The Second walked slowly, allowing me to take careful steps. Being back on my feet reminded me of the fact I had a long way to go until my body was fully healed. I hoped next time I had an opportunity to escape that I'd be strong enough.

"She's staying in the infirmary for a while so the nurse can tend to her, but it doesn't appear that she's in any danger of going into labor. It was a blessing that you were there to help her. You, Miss Cassidy," he said, tucking my hand into the crook of his elbow, which brought me flush against his side, "are truly a blessing." He placed his other hand over mine and patted it. His touch shocked me and I waited for the sickness to come, indicating whether his intentions were good or...

"Glad I could help."

"And it's fortunate for us that you can take over some of her duties while she rests. My father relies on her."

"I'll do what I can, but I still can't see well."

"And fortunately for you, I'm here to teach you our ways and how Our Maker is to be served."

"Lucky me."

He stopped walking. "It's not luck, Cassidy. It's divinity. Things do not happen without being preordained by Our Maker. He places us upon a path to righteousness, and if we follow His plan, our lives will be worthy of ascension."

"So that means free will isn't a thing?"

"Oh no. It's very real. But free will leads us down the path of temptation and destruction. That is why the work we do is so important." He paused for a moment. "We are saving lives here. Just as we saved yours. Without Maker's Plan, I fear you would not have survived the terrible tragedy that occurred."

"You mean being hijacked and forced to crash land." We were away from others, and I was tired of keeping up the charade.

"That is the view a sinner would take, Cassidy. We both know you're better than that."

He lifted a strand of hair from my face where it had stuck in the ointment I was still using for my cuts. I flinched, but he made no move to hurt me and my stomach didn't clench.

"Hey," he said, his voice dropping to a soothing octave. "I would never hurt you. Please don't be afraid of me."

He was so close now, I felt his breath on my face. He smelled of something clean. Pure.

"You startled me."

"I apologize," he said, then placed his hands lightly on my shoulders. "But I hope you'll come to trust me. I know it wasn't necessarily your choice to come, but sometimes Our Maker takes the choice from us when we need Him to most. You've been feeling restless for some time, haven't you, Cassidy? Knowing you were on the wrong path? Knowing you were meant for something more?"

A wave of warmth flowed through my chest, and I gasped. How did he know?

"Is it too extraordinary to believe that your coming here was meant to be? That this detour is maybe the answer to your needs?"

I must have been feeling weak, as my whole body began to tremble. He spoke a truth...of sorts. It was as if he'd heard my inner thoughts over the past few months.

I shook my head to clear it and concentrated on my truth seeker. This had to be bullshit.

Instead of the sense of disappointment I usually felt, I was shocked.

He was like a bright light, a ray of sunshine striking a newly bloomed flower in a garden tended with love and care.

He was telling the truth, or at least the truth as he'd accepted it to be. He was one hundred percent committed to his beliefs and there was no sign of dishonesty anywhere.

Could he really be the son of that evil man?

We began walking again, and he hummed the tune of the hymn the children sang. Instead of creeping me out, it soothed me.

"Here we are," he said as he stopped. "There are six steps, are you ready?"

"You're really good at this," I said. "Thank you."

"My mother was blind. I used to take her around whenever we left the house."

Was, as in no longer with us? "She's lucky to have you," I said as we climbed the steps together. He was patient, letting me set the pace. When we reached the top, he opened the door for me.

"That's kind of you to say. Please, step inside."

"Thank you."

He didn't lead me in, only stepped aside to let me pass.

I must have shown my confusion.

"Men are not allowed in the house when His Right Hand is not present. My father is away on an errand, but he will return for tonight's service."

"Oh." *Weird.* Was he going to leave me alone?

"I'll be here on the porch until it's time for supper. I'd be happy to escort you and break bread with you, if you'd care to join me."

"Thank you."

I stood hovering in the doorway, unsure what to do.

"Why don't you drink some water and then nap? You've had a big day and you need your rest."

As soon as he'd spoken the words, my eyelids felt heavy, and I leaned against the doorjamb to keep from falling over.

"I think I will rest. Thank you..."

"You may call me Abel. In fact, I'd very much like it if you'd call me Abel."

"Thank you, Abel. I'll rest now."

"I'll be here if you need me."

I turned to enter the house and my room seemed miles away. I staggered a couple of steps and reached for the back of the sofa to steady myself.

It wouldn't matter if I just lay here, would it? Denise wasn't coming back, and I'd hear whoever entered the house...

A moment later, the soft cushion met my cheek and I slipped into unconsciousness. The last thing I remembered was Abel humming the hymn just outside the door.

CHAPTER 16
INFILTRATION

Chapter Sixteen - Infiltration
Jackson

The first part of the mission went swimmingly. Barringer dropped me off with a coffee and McDonald's sandwich before daylight and I waited at the day work pickup spot. Not too long after, a huge swamp truck pulled up and four men climbed out. They had water bottles and one of them carried a small cooler. Their clothes were worn and didn't appear to fit them well, and two of them had on tennis shoes with holes in them, while the others boasted worn work boots.

I'd spotted the one Joanna called Lance right away. He was a tall Black man, reserved, didn't really fit in with the three muscular white men.

They were all ex-military. It was obvious by the way they surveyed the assembled group and watched each other's backs. They were also armed, which wasn't unusual in Florida.

Besides the four of them and myself, there were six men speaking Spanish in another group and two solo Black men who didn't speak to anyone.

A van pulled up and the driver spoke in Spanish, asking for land-

scape help, and one of the Black men and the whole group of Latinos moved to get into the van before he'd even finished his request.

Another van pulled up and waved the other Black man into the car. Perhaps they had something prearranged?

I pulled out a stick of gum, missing my old tobacco habit right about now. There were only the four men and myself left, so I held out the pack.

"Anyone?"

Lance accepted the offer with a nod. The others watched me with interest. One of them cocked his chin at me.

"Where'd you serve?"

"Rangers 75th."

They looked at each other. "First Marine Expeditionary Force. Camp Pendleton."

I stuck out my hand, figuring I'd make the first move. "Luke Stephens," I said, the name sounding weird in my mouth.

"Nice to meet you," the leader said, his grip firm and appraising. He held my hand a beat longer than usual, and I noticed his eyelids flicker before he let go with a smile. It was subtle, but it was there, almost like he'd been trying to read me. "I'm Matt Jonas. This here is Earl Davis and Tony Hill. That gentleman is Lance Cooper."

"Pleased to meet you," I said, shoving my hand back in my pocket.

"You just passing through?" Matt asked.

"Yeah. Been working in Louisiana. My girlfriend kicked me out," I said, blushing a little. "Thought I'd see the sights before I settled down in a luxury apartment somewhere." My smirk let on that I'd definitely seen better days. "Florida's warm this time of year." I shrugged.

The men looked me up and down and exchanged looks.

"We got a regular gig with a guy that'll be here shortly. We could use someone with construction or painting skills. You interested?"

Another van pulled up, and the men picked up their things and started for it.

I pushed off the wall where I'd been leaning. "Don't mind if I do."

The worksite was a new home development, and I spent the day doing everything from hanging drywall to laying laminate flooring. I

worked closely with Lance, and while he was a quiet man, he was an easy guy to partner with.

The others invited me to eat with them and shared some of their fruit, as I'd only brought beef jerky and water for lunch. I had to play the part of a homeless veteran, and that seemed to be the best option.

The men prayed together before they ate, assuring me I'd found the right guys. Over lunch, they told me a little about their "church," and asked me about my service and what I planned to do now that I'd been discharged.

"I want to make a difference," I said. "So much of the work we did in the Rangers was about protecting people. I'd always thought I'd serve a short time and then join law enforcement, but I stayed until... well, until I got hurt. Can't pass the physical for the police department, so I'm just trying to find a place I can do some good work, you know? Help people."

The men exchanged looks yet again, and I hoped that meant I'd passed their test.

"Amen, brother. Sometimes it seems like all we can do is survive, but as long as we serve Our Maker, we're headed in the right direction."

I held up my water bottle. "Amen, indeed."

When the day was over, the foreman handed us each seventy-five bucks and we headed back to the van as a group. I knew I'd be sore the next day. Teaching art was tough, but nowhere near the backbreaking work construction could be.

"Here," I said, handing twenty bucks to Matt. "For your church. Thank you for sharing your lunch and your work with me." I thought the gesture might help my cause.

"Thank you, brother. You got a place to sleep tonight?" Matt asked me as we climbed out of the van.

"Heading to the shelter. I heard they got space."

Matt looked at the other men and back at me. "You're a good worker. I might have a more permanent option for you if you show up here tomorrow. How does that sound?"

I tried to keep my enthusiasm at bay. "Yeah, maybe. Thank you."

He nodded at me. "See you in the morning." They waved as they drove away, and I walked off in the direction of the homeless shelter Agent Barringer located for me. He'd made sure I'd have a spot, at my insistence. He'd offered to put me up at the motel again, but I didn't want to take a chance.

Checking in went well, but then I tangled with a guy who didn't appreciate me taking his regular bunk and, before I could diffuse the situation, he decked me in the eye. I didn't lift a hand to defend myself. I didn't want to hurt the guy. I ate the beef stew they served, and then I went out front to stretch my legs and wait for Barringer to show up.

About ten minutes later, he strolled by in a coat and beanie, looking right at home with my fellow shelter pals.

"Matt Jonas, Earl Davis, Tony Hill and Lance Cooper. Jonas is the leader."

"Okay," he said, his hand in his pocket. I assumed he had a recorder on. "I'll run the names. What the fuck happened to your face now?"

"Picked the wrong bunk."

"Shit."

"It's fine. The men didn't seem to talk to other folks at the worksite, but were friendly enough with me. Asked where I was staying and told me they might have a more permanent place for me if I was interested."

He nodded and glanced down at my boot. "Your tracker will give us your location, but I wish you had some way to communicate."

"Nope. Too conspicuous. Didn't see any of them with phones."

"Got it. You sure you don't want to come with me?"

I shook my head. "This is actually a nice reminder."

He frowned.

"What could have been, you know?"

He sighed. "I'm glad it wasn't. Too many veterans in this place as it is. Alright. Hopefully they'll take you with them to the site again tomorrow, and I'll be watching from a safe distance. I'll see what info I can dig up."

I nodded to him and then turned to go back inside. The guard at

the door looked me over, then looked toward Barringer, walking away.

"My sponsor," I said, and he smiled.

"Right on. Have a good night."

Once inside, I stretched out on the bunk I'd been given, knowing I wouldn't sleep well at all. It was so much like awaiting deployment on base, knowing that this time the next day, you might be in a different country in who knew what kind of conditions. It was a challenge to keep the adrenaline under wraps. Tempers could be high, but it was also a time for goofing around to get the ya-yas out.

The man you spoke to today is asking someone if they can bring you back to the camp. I can't See my father anymore, though, and I can't tell what's happening, only flashes.

"Why do you think that is?"

I hadn't realized I'd spoken out loud until the man in the cot next to me cleared his throat. Oh well, I didn't have a gift like Joanna, so out loud it was going to have to be.

He's blocking me. My father.

"It's okay. Talk to me about something else. Tell me what you've been working on. How's school?"

I swear I heard her groan in my mind.

Well, I almost have my research paper finished for Miss Frost's Sociology class. And I painted something special for you, but you have to wait till you get back to see it.

"I can't wait, sweetheart."

"Hey, man, it's lights out."

"Sorry," I called out. I lowered my voice to a whisper. "I have to be quiet now. My bunkmates are getting pissed."

Why are you with all of those people? It's a...sad place. Be careful. And when you hear them shout, duck.

"Right." *What the hell is that supposed to mean?*

"Man, will you shut up?"

"Sorry."

I was going to end up with more than a black eye if I didn't become a little less conspicuous. I stretched out on the cot that was of course too short for me. My backpack would be the best option for a pillow, and when I went to move my hair out of the way for the hundredth time that day, I thought simultaneously that it was now less hassle, but also that I missed my rebel hair. Immensely.

It'll grow back. Good night, Mr. Howe.

I shut my eyes, willing my body to relax. The sounds of the others shifting, grumbling, and snoring gave me comfort. Living alone these past two years, I'd forgotten how the night sounds of your comrades could be soothing. I actually slept hard, considering.

The next morning, I woke up with only twenty minutes to be at the work spot. I grabbed a quick bagel and fruit, then jogged down to the convenience store next to the pickup spot. I grabbed some water, more beef jerky, and a few protein bars to stash in my backpack. Hopefully I wouldn't die of scurvy before this was all over.

Once outside, I stood against the wall about ten feet from the group of Latino men who'd been there the day before. I asked them in Spanish if I'd missed any trucks and they said no. They asked whether I'd received any work the day before, and I let them know I'd gone to the construction site. One of the men shook his head.

"Cuidado, amigo. Los hombres son peligrosos."

"Gracias," I said, knowing full well that the men were dangerous and I needed to take care. I wished I had time to ask them more, but the same swamp truck pulled up and the same four men got out—this time with a fifth. A much younger guy. They flanked him and walked straight toward me. The truck didn't pull away.

"Morning, Mr. Stephens," the new arrival said, approaching with his hand out. Matt stood at his side.

"Luke, this is—"

"Call me Abel," the young man said. "My brothers told me that you might be looking for…community. A place to stay and be a part of something important."

"Yes, sir. Been on the road for some time now. Would be nice to have a place to belong, you know?"

"Looks like you've had a rough time of it," Abel said, studying my black eye. He patted me on the shoulder, then let his hand rest there. He, too, closed his eyes for a moment longer than a normal blink—and then he smiled.

These guys were reading me. I knew that's what it had to be. I'd seen Nigel do it before. I said a quick thanks to Morgan for teaching me how to keep myself guarded from psychic interference. I was strong enough that it was second nature, I didn't have to even think about it. My Connections, on the other hand, I didn't have as much control over.

"Picked the wrong bunk at the shelter last night. No biggie."

Abel laughed and squeezed my shoulder before letting me go. "I think we've got just the place for you. How about you come back with us after your shift? We'd love to have you for dinner and fellowship."

This was it. The invitation I'd been hoping for.

"I'd like that."

"Praise be! Well, alright! Bring your appetite and we'll see you at six."

He patted me hard on the shoulder and gave me a wide smile. He climbed back into the swamp truck and took off toward town.

The van from yesterday pulled up and Matt called me over.

"You joining us?"

"Don't mind if I do." Anything that would get me closer to Cassidy...

We went to a different worksite this time.

"Need you men to paint today. That going to work?"

"Yes, sir," Matt said. "We can handle whatever you've got."

I sat in the back row of the van next to Lance, who seemed nervous for some reason. He was studying the passing scenery as if looking for a way out.

When we got to the site, which was a church, we climbed out and I stretched my legs. I hung back to tie my boots, and Lance waited for me.

"You good?" I asked him when I stood. Matt and the others had gone a few yards ahead to talk to a man at the front doors of the main stuccoed building. It wasn't a massive complex, but depending on what we were painting, this was likely going to take more than a day.

"Just want you to know," Lance said as we walked together. "This offer he's giving you? Comes with strings. You think long and hard before you accept. There ain't no going back."

He wandered away toward a water fountain and filled up his bottle as I joined the others.

I knew exactly what he meant.

I spent the next few hours painting the sanctuary walls with Earl, who asked a helluva lot of questions. I gave as little information away as possible.

"So you go to church, Luke?"

"Haven't been in a while," I said honestly. "But I pray regularly. I know there's someone looking out for me, given what I've been through." I didn't think these men would appreciate the Pagan nature of my actual spiritual life.

"What denomination you belong to?"

"My mama raised me Baptist," I said, letting the drawl out like I'd had as a younger man.

"You been baptized? You know your scripture?"

"It's in here somewhere," I said, tapping my head. "Comes back, don't it?"

Earl laughed. "Reckon it does."

"Mind telling me why you asked?"

Earl set down his sprayer and wiped his forehead with his sleeve. "If you decide to come with us, you'll put that knowledge to the test. The Sec—Abel, he's a good teacher. Me and the other guys, we were like you. Needing direction in our lives."

"So you go to his church? He a pastor?"

"Something like that," Earl said. He turned to me and grinned. "We seen miracles out there."

My gut clenched. "Miracles?"

He nodded slowly. "Abel and his father...they're special. You'll see for yourself."

I bent and took a swig from my water bottle. "Looking forward to it."

The rest of the day went fairly smooth and then we were back in the van. I actually dozed on the ride back to the pickup site. When we arrived, Earl poked my shoulder.

"Didn't get much rest last night, huh?"

I stretched and smiled. "Nope. Been a while since I slept well." That was an understatement. My, uh, condition made sleep a rare occasion.

"You'll sleep well at the compound," Matt said, patting me on the back. "It's peaceful out there."

"Thank you," I said. "But…I can't pay my way."

Earl came up on my other side and put a hand on my shoulder. "You give what you can, that's all anyone asks."

I nodded and accepted an apple from Tony, grateful for the food. I needed a helluva lot more calories than I'd had the past two days if I was going to be at full capacity.

Before we'd left the worksite, the pastor of the church had given Matt a wad of cash. I didn't ask about my cut, figuring I'd wait to see what happened.

The swamp truck pulled up and the men piled into the bed.

"Ride on up here with me," Abel said, and I noticed the faint shake of Lance's head before he climbed into the bed.

I pulled myself up into the cab and sat next to Abel. I hadn't noticed the driver earlier. He gave me the damn creeps.

"Luke, meet Esai."

Esai nodded before putting the truck in gear and pulling away from the pickup site. He turned onto the highway and soon we were deep in the Big Cypress National Park.

I sure hoped my tracker was working.

"It's about a forty-five minute drive and then we'll take a boat to our compound. We'll get you some dinner and then you can join us for prayer service."

Abel was young, maybe early to mid-twenties, and he was eager. He was nearly vibrating with excitement over finding a potential new recruit.

"That sounds great. Tell me a little more about your church. Earl said you preach a unique take on the New Testament."

Abel's eyes flared and he smiled. "It's better if you hear it from our leader." He flicked on the truck's radio and slid in a CD. "This is a recording of one of his sermons."

The voice that filled the cab of the truck made the hair stand up on the back of my neck.

That's my father's voice.

I closed my eyes and focused on Joanna's voice inside my head.

This was one of his earlier sermons, when he focused on the need to repent before the End of Days. Repentance comes through pledging oneself to Our Maker. Whether through gifts or deeds, he would say it was important to be right with Our Maker before the signs begin, for then it will be too late to dine at His table.

I watched Abel out of the corner of my eye. He closed his eyes and smiled and listened to the sermon coming from the speakers.

I can't see you, Mr. Howe. Why can't I see you?

I couldn't respond to her, if I did, I'd call too much attention to the fact I had a little voice inside my head. I didn't think these folks would look kindly upon that.

If you can't talk, just listen. My father will try to persuade you, and he might succeed if you're unable to fight his Influence. I need you to hear my voice. Remember why you are there.

Her voice grew fainter the deeper we drove into the swamp. I was lulled into a state of relaxation by the swaying of the truck and the cadence of Rains' speech. When the truck came to a stop at the water's edge, I was in a pleasant state of mind. Relaxed. I recognized otherness at work, but despite my training, it affected me. I just hoped I was strong enough to fight it when I needed to be.

We'd stopped at a spot where there were four aluminum fishing boats tied up to a small dock.

"We don't take the truck in this time of year. We've had some flooding, so it's easier to get there by boat." Abel went around back to help unload supplies from the bed of the truck. I followed to give him a hand.

There were groceries, propane tanks, and medical supplies. I took several loads over to the boats and within a few minutes, the truck bed was empty. Abel climbed into a boat with Esai, and Matt told me to climb on in with him. The other three men took the two remaining boats and we set off into the swamp.

Abel began to sing, and his voice echoed along the tree corridor. My relaxed feeling lingered, amplified by the lull of the boat and his soulful voice. From a skeptical perspective, I knew that there was a purpose for all of their actions. One of the topics Agent Barringer and I spoke about the night before I went in were the behaviors and actions to look for when being recruited by a cult.

"They will offer praise and point out things about you that make you special. They'll introduce you to others who will share their stories. They'll share only the beliefs that will inspire, saving the sacrifices that need to be made for later. They'll use music and other methods to invoke emotion and share passionate monologues about how their lives have improved. The level of commitment will increase slowly until the new recruit feels trapped and has become so isolated from their families, they feel they have no one to reach out to.

"The process is very similar to how an abuser gets their partner to fall in love. They don't typically smack you around on the first date. It's an incremental build until your life is no longer yours to control. No one is going to ask you to drink the Kool-Aid at the first meeting. What they *will* ask is, 'Are you ready to take that next step in the name of your beliefs?'"

I kept his words at the front of my mind. I'd seen firsthand how mind control worked serving overseas. The "insurgents" we captured and questioned had been indoctrinated from an early age into the kind of thinking that made them willing and able to run headlong into a temple and blow it and its worshippers to bits, killing dozens in the process. The religion they'd been taught had beauty and love and peace as part of its central message, but fanatical leaders had twisted it to serve their purposes.

Given all of this knowledge and experience, though, I couldn't help myself.

"Great set of pipes, there, Abel."

"Thank you, Luke."

Matt shot me a worried look. I got the sense this guy was important, and I wasn't supposed to talk to him like a normal person. But then Matt smiled. "He does have a beautiful voice. Truly a gift from the Maker."

"Praise be," Earl called out from his boat next to ours.

The afternoon light was fading, and though I should have been paying attention to where I was going, I was way fucking lost. We took so many turns and there were multiple tributaries at each one...

Please let the damn tracker work.

Ryder had assured me he'd be close by. He and Geoff would be looking out for any signs of trouble.

I hoped they were right.

"Y'all make this trek every day?"

"Yes, sir. Six days a week," Matt answered. "We're on rotation. Some of us work at the compound and those of us that are skilled laborers, we go into town. The four of us trade off each week with another group of men. If you decide to stay, you can join our crew or the other one. Whatever we make at the job sites goes to benefit the community."

He let that sink in, and I nodded.

"Sounds like a great system. Small price to pay for community and fellowship."

Matt patted my knee and smiled. "Praise be."

A few moments later, just as the sun had dipped well beyond the horizon, we pulled up to a dock hidden by a thick copse of cypress trees. It appeared the woods were much thicker here.

"'Fraid you're going to get those boots wet," Matt said. "We'll hook you up with a pair of tall boots back at camp and dry them by the fire tonight."

I fought the panic that threatened to overtake me. I could handle this. I might have been out of practice, but once a Ranger, always a Ranger.

My tracker was sewn into my boot behind the circular label on the ankle. I had no clue if submerging it in water would short it out. There was no time to worry about it. I hopped out into calf-deep muck and began helping them unload the boats into another swamp truck that was parked by the dock. Once the boats were unloaded, we all piled into the back of the truck and Esai drove us along a tree-lined path. We only traveled about a half a mile before I heard a bell ringing. The other men began to stand up and the truck came to a halt.

"Home, sweet home," Tony said, and he hopped down. The ground was soggy but there wasn't the standing water like there'd been by the dock. I followed him down and ignored the squish.

"Bet you've served in some swampy places before."

"Sure, but as a soldier, I'd much preferred the desert to deployments in the wetter regions. I definitely did not enjoy training in the muck, but you do what you gotta do."

"Hoorah," Earl said. Tony and Matt gave him a warning look, and he dropped his head.

Peculiar. I'd have to keep my eye on their reactions to military discussions. They'd been fairly open during our lunches, but they'd mostly stuck to where they'd served, who they knew, etc. There wasn't the loose banter about being "in the shit." In fact, I hadn't heard these men swear at all.

I followed the men into camp, which reminded me of a Boy Scout camp I'd attended as a kid. I counted ten wood cabins, a pavilion with a pointed roof that was screened in, probably for for meetings and meals, a fire pit... In fact this very well may have been a church camp at one point. There was a little school building next to the pavilion, where a group of children who appeared to be of various ages under ten years old sat in a circle singing songs with their teachers.

"How many folks live out here?" I asked Matt.

"Full time? About forty or fifty, not including the children. We have a few folks that live in town who come out for services."

I nodded as I took stock of the camp. I didn't see a lot of folks milling about like I imagined I would if there were fifty people living here.

"We'll take you to our dormitory so you can stash your belongings and then we'll wash for supper," Matt said, guiding me forward. We walked through a denser bit of greenery, and on the other side was a large log-cabin style home that was much nicer than any of the other dwellings.

"His Right Hand, our leader, stays here." He leaned closer. "We refer to Abel as The Second. He's the son of our pastor. We don't use titles when we're among civilians because they don't want the attention. Esai, myself, and another man named Gabriel are their lieutenants. We take the safety of our members seriously," he said, and he gazed knowingly at me. Was he trying to warn me? Was he talking to me like a recruit?

"You have concerns out here? I'd think your biggest worry would be gators and snakes."

I figured I'd try the lighthearted approach, but Matt was obviously taking my measure.

"Natural safety issues we can deal with. It's the potential for human intruders we're more concerned about."

"Have you had trouble?"

His gaze darted about as we walked around the back of the fancy house. "Put it this way. There are locals who don't take kindly to having us here. We had a few run-ins with drunk hunters in the beginning, but now outsiders steer clear of us."

"I can see why that would be a problem."

"We've got kids here, you know? We're selective about who we let in."

"I understand. You never know who could be wandering around out here," I said.

We moved through another thicket and over a small footbridge. There on the other side, we came upon three long greenhouses.

"We grow as much as we can here."

I noticed lots of people moving around inside the plastic, letting me know where some of the folks were, anyhow.

Matt led me to the right and just past the greenhouses, there was another large structure.

"We have lookouts on duty 24-7 posted around the camp. If you stay, that would be one of your responsibilities...that is, if you're still comfortable with weapons."

"I am."

He patted me on the shoulder and led me up the steps of the large structure. "This is the men's dormitory. The women and families live in the cabins we passed earlier. We have about thirty single men. Many of us served. We have clothes and personal items in these cupboards here, so if you don't have something, you can take what you need. We have a team that takes most of the laundry into town once a week."

"Yeah, I'd imagine the logistics are tough way out here."

"We've got generators, but we don't want to pollute the water any more than it already is. The community tries to keep our carbon footprint down. There are compost toilets in each of the living spaces. We collect rainwater for showers and the greenhouses. We're doing our best. Life isn't easy out here, but we're happy making a go of it with others who believe as we do. Who want to be prepared for The Coming."

I wasn't ready to go deeper into the belief system of the cult, so I let that go.

"Thanks. For everything." I shook his hand.

Matt smiled genuinely, as though he was pleased. "Happy to have you with us, Luke. Now why don't you take this bunk right here next to Lance. Bathroom is at the end down there, just like the barracks."

I laughed because it was true. It was obvious that some of these guys had served because they were certainly keeping their space regulation.

I set my backpack on the floor next to the bunk and decided to change clothes before getting the bunk filthy. I grabbed a change of clothes from my backpack—I had brought three days' worth—and went to the bathroom to change and clean up. I was pleased to find soap and clean towels, a basket with new toothbrushes. There were shelves along one wall where the men had obviously claimed baskets, so I found an empty one. If I wasn't here under such sinister circumstances, I would be pretty keen on my new living situation.

I glanced up from the sink—and jumped, thinking I wasn't alone. Then I laughed.

It wasn't a stranger in the bathroom. It was me. I'd forgotten over the course of the past two days about my new look.

"Damn," I said, finally getting a look at my eye. It's a good thing I hadn't had this the first day these guys met me. They'd probably think I'd been in a bar brawl. The red mark from the hot knife was starting to scab over and looked like a nasty scar. Perfect.

I finished up, changed my clothes, and shoved my things in my backpack. There was nothing suspect in there, nothing of value, so if someone took it or went through it, they wouldn't find much, just a bottle of cheap lotion, a package of sunflower seeds, more beef jerky, Chapstick, and a battered copy of *Of Mice and Men*.

I put my things under my bed and went outside. There were about ten men hanging around outside, chatting and laughing, including my new workmates. When he saw me, Matt waved me over to join them. He introduced me, and I quickly figured out which of the new faces were also ex-military. They were all warm and welcoming, and as we walked together to the pavilion for our meal, they bantered with each other and traded jabs that didn't seem out of the ordinary at all.

Once inside, though, that all changed.

The men fell silent as they accepted their meals. Each plates held a scoop of spaghetti, a slice of bread, and canned green beans. We were given a small glass of milk or water to drink, and there was a bowl with apples or oranges available. I followed them to a table where they put their plates down, and then knelt on the wood floor of the pavilion. I followed their lead, and we waited there until everyone filed in with their plates.

My bad knee was screaming at me, but I remained still, glancing around as much as I could with my head bowed. Finally I noticed Abel —The Second—take his place at a table up front.

"My brave community, we take in this sustenance to fuel our bodies and mind for The Coming. We give our hearts and souls over to The Maker and prepare to be His soldiers. We are grateful for His gifts and bind ourselves to Him as his loyal servants in love and worship. In The Maker's name we pray. Amen."

The group said "amen" together, and then stood and took their seats.

I noticed the men didn't start eating until Abel took his first bite, and then they dug in with gusto. Well, as much gusto as you could with as much food as an elementary school student would receive for a school lunch. I ate slowly, savoring each bite of the surprisingly good food. I made eye contact with Matt.

"Thanks, man. So much. This food is… This place is…"

He nodded with a proud smile. "Had a feeling you'd appreciate it."

And I did. I might have been playing a role, but the hunger inside me, and that part of me that was constantly restless, really did appreciate the apparent peace here.

"After we eat, we wash and then we set up the chairs for evening service. I understand His Right Hand will be speaking tonight. You're in for a special treat."

"He doesn't speak all the time?"

Matt shook his head. "He still travels, spreading The Maker's word, finding the congregations that are worthy, recruiting true believers to join the cause. His missionary work is the backbone to Maker's Plan."

Just as we thought. Rains survived and he's continuing his manipulation.

I needed to find out as much as I could about the plan.

Esai came over and spoke quietly to Matt.

"Excuse me, gentlemen." They left together, and Earl picked up Matt's empty plate.

"They've got to escort His Right Hand," he said, explaining. "He doesn't go anywhere unaccompanied. His life is to be protected at all costs."

I noticed Tony elbowed him and gave Earl a warning look, as though he'd said too much. They were being awfully open about how the organization worked, so either I was being tested or they bought my story. Either way, I was on alert, although it would be easy to just accept this...especially for a guy like Luke Stephens, with nothing going for him.

I followed the men to clean up after dinner, which involved washing our dishes and then our own hands in a separate station. Then we filed back into the pavilion and set up rows of chairs. We took our seats and a man played guitar while we sat in silent communion.

A hush fell over the room, and I heard footfalls on the wood floor. Slow. Reminded me of my former drill sergeant, who would walk the aisles slowly during written exams trying to make us nervous. He'd lean over us just enough to raise our blood pressure.

This man's footfalls, however, made the hair stand up on the back of my neck.

He's there. My father is there.

I didn't like the fear I was sensing from Joanna. I wished I could cut her off so she didn't have to experience this. Her voice was faint, weaker than it had been before I took the boat here. Something was blocking her, but damn that strong little girl kept trying for me.

I can't see you there. I don't know why I can't see you.

The footfalls stopped right beside me and I fought the urge to look, since the rest of the group had their heads bowed as they waited for him to approach. I hated having someone at my back. Leftover occupational hazard.

The man paused, shifting his weight enough to make the boards creak, and then he moved past. He was a slight man, probably under 5'10", with short, thinning, nondescript brownish hair, and he moved as though he was in pain. I'd wondered how much damage Delaney had done to him back in Shreveport. We knew he'd been near death when the ambulance had taken him away. Damien recalled hearing the paramedics state his temperature was over 105 degrees, much too hot for the human body to sustain for long.

How had he survived? Did he have a Damien here? Someone who could heal with the touch of their hands?

Who else had he collected?

So far, I knew Lance and Matt and Abel all had some sort of psychic extra something going on. How many others did here?

Rains moved to the front of the assembled group and stood with his back to us for several long moments before he spoke.

"'Then I heard what sounded like a great multitude, like the roar of rushing waters and like loud peals of thunder, shouting: 'Hallelujah! For Our Maker, the Almighty, reigns.'"

"Praise be," the people said back to him.

"Here in our community, we are well aware of the rushing waters and loud peals of thunder, but we are confident in our work because we know we do The Maker's bidding. He has a plan for us, for we are His chosen soldiers."

"Praise be."

"And we have recently experienced one of the signs that let us know the plan is in motion. 'A great and wondrous sign appeared in Heaven: a woman clothed with the sun, with the moon under her feet and a crown of twelve stars on her head. Revelation 12:1.'"

His voice raised goose bumps on my limbs. My heart beat faster, and I realized I was hanging on his every word. I knew what was happening, but what about the rest of those gathered? Joanna was right. This man's power was ominous.

There were murmurs all around and Rains turned to face the group, his arms out to the side. "When our lovely guest came from the sky, I knew. Our time is getting closer. Soon, the Maker's plan will be fully realized, and your faith has made all of this possible." He stretched his hand toward the back of the room.

"Praise be."

The people turned to look, but I knew what I'd see, and I was terrified.

My gaze landed on Cassidy—and my stomach dropped.

Her poor face.

"Miss Cassidy's arrival was a miracle. Her clothes, burned by the heat of the sun and the fire. The moon tattooed on her foot. And the symbol on her jet...twelve stars. All of these point to her arrival as the sign we've been waiting for, and her miraculous recovery is further evidence that The Maker believes in us as we believe in Him."

Esai walked with Cassidy, guiding her by her elbow, and her steps were reluctant. Halting. He led her to stand behind Rains.

Her eyes were open, but they didn't appear to be looking at anyone in particular. She kept her face devoid of expression. She was so brave.

I had no idea if she would recognize me. I thought I'd feel relief at seeing her in the flesh. Instead, I fought to hold in the anger. The cruelty of not taking her to a hospital. What if there were injuries that wouldn't heal right? Her face had cuts all over, maybe from when the plane's windshield broke? She moved as if she were in agony. It didn't seem like she could see, which explained a lot. The previous few times I'd opened the Connection with her, everything had been black. I'd sensed her frustration and how hard she was working to stay calm. But I couldn't see through her eyes like I normally do when the Connection is open.

I knew it was dangerous to open it now, but I wanted to reassure her. The uncertainty of her movements broke my heart.

Help is here, Cassidy.

CHAPTER 17
PROPHECY

CHAPTER SEVENTEEN – Prophecy
Cassidy

I felt everyone's gazes on me even though I couldn't see. I hated that he brought me out in front of the congregation, talking about me as if I were a damned miracle. I hated being used for his nefarious purposes.

Help is there, Cassidy.

I nearly jumped out of my skin at the voice in my head. It sounded like a young girl's voice. I'd heard it before, when I was recovering from the crash in the initial days. The voice wasn't familiar to me, and yet I knew it was real and good, though how I don't know.

Someone is there. Someone...different. Someone who's there to help.

I tried to look around and internally cursed my stupid eyes. Would I ever be able to see again?

"Good evening, Cassidy."

Abel. Since our first meeting yesterday, he'd been very sweet. It was obvious he'd taken a liking to me, and I felt sorry for him. He'd been raised to believe this shit his father was teaching, and he was so dedicated. It was sad. I couldn't be angry with him, not when he'd also been a victim. Rains had stashed him away from the world with the three women who now ran the school here at the community. I'd wondered if I could get through to Abel during one of his visits to the house. I'd almost brought it up just today, my concerns about his father's teachings, but then I got so sleepy...I crashed on the couch again. And then I knew.

He'd been using some sort of influence on me. His voice was hypnotic, the way he dropped to a lower register and you felt it over your skin like a low vibration, and all of your muscles just...let go.

I felt him pat my arm and make a sound, almost like he'd read my thoughts.

One day, he would realize how evil his father truly was, and then he'd have to make some decisions about his life. I didn't envy him that day.

Rains continued speaking about prophecies and miracles and I shut it out, trying to listen for that familiar voice again.

I'd been shutting out the fire and brimstone speech my entire life.

I mean, why did these nutjobs get so fired up about Revelations? Why did they have to make faith about violent endings and terrifying events? I believed there was a higher power, but I *refused* to believe the crazy talk of a man who'd led his followers into a swamp to wait for The Coming of God. Not Jesus, but God. And from listening to his sermons and private conversations in his office, I'd learned some very disturbing facts about Maker's Plan.

Gerald Rains was a thief.

He was plotting to kidnap his daughter from Delaney's school.

He had a child on the way—with poor Irene's daughter—and he was sure this child would possess gifts stronger than even his own.

And he was going to use the birth of that child to kick off his terror campaign.

I'd heard enough to be horrified, and the feeling that I was stuck, that there was nothing I could do to help or put a stop to his plans, did not sit well with me.

"We're grateful for the gifts we've been given, and we're ready to return the good works. Let us show The Maker through song how much we appreciate Him, how willing we are to carry out His plan and ultimately bring about the salvation of our deserving brethren.

Our prayers will be heard on high. We will show that we will not swerve, we will not diverge from our path, and that through righteous works, we too will see the glory of the Kingdom of Heaven."

"Praise be," they all called out.

Fools.

This man was going to lead them to their deaths, I could feel it.

"The Second will now lead us in song."

Abel stepped away from me and I watched as his shadow stood beside his father. The room was silent for several beats and then he began to sing. The young man had a truly beautiful voice, and the few times I'd heard him sing I could completely understand how people had come under his influence. He could almost make me believe in this nonsense.

Abel's tenor was breathtaking, his range was wide and his voice climbed to the highest notes, echoing through the pavilion. It gave me chills. I knew it had a major effect on the community. Irene had told me it brought people to tears. She'd said hundreds of people would come up to him at the end of a song whenever he performed, giving him huge wads of cash, big checks, etc. All of that money made this community possible, so apparently Rains took him around from time to time to "collect alms," aka, rip people off.

"Bow your heads with me." I could make out the blurry form of Rains as he stood next to Abel and placed a hand on his shoulder.

"Our Maker, from whom all glory shines. We bow before you, most holy one, and bind ourselves to you to do your work, to be your sacred vessels of change. Your plan is nearing fruition, and we serve you without hesitation, without reservation. We will continue to bring the worthy into your dominion and when the end of days arrives, we shall walk hand in hand down golden paths of light, bathed in your love. We are your humble servants, your brave soldiers, your willing warriors. We give our thanks, our loyalty, our love to you. Our Maker."

Rains paused briefly and someone began playing a guitar in the back of the pavilion.

"If there are any of you who are weary, who feel your resolve slipping, who need the strength of our community, please...come forward. There is no judgement here, only love. Take from us what you need."

There was some movement as a few people came forward, I couldn't tell how many. Women sobbed, men pleaded, and Rains spoke in hushed tones, praying over each of them while the guitar music grew louder and more intense.

I shivered.

"Are you cold, Miss Cassidy?"

Esai. His presence washed over me like a cold sweat, making me nauseous.

"No."

I didn't want him touching me ever again.

He's there, Cassidy.

That voice again. Someone was here? Who could it be?

"Maker, these humble servants ask for your blessing. In your name we pray, amen."

"Amen."

I sucked in a breath when they finished. Listening to his words made my skin crawl.

"Tonight, we have a bit of a surprise. The Second was able to procure a special treat for you. You've all been working so hard to make our mission a success, and I want to reward you."

There was applause and excited cheers from the children who were present. Sometimes they were kept away from the adult service, but apparently they were present tonight.

"Would you like some ice cream, Miss Cassidy?"

Abel sounded so charming, as though he was asking a woman he was courting...and that's actually what it was. A courtship. My stomach lurched at the thought of being Connected to this group of fanatics.

"No, thank you," I said, looking anywhere but at his face, which I couldn't see clearly. Because these incredibly dangerous people kidnapped me and there's no way to pretend that anything about this was normal.

"Oh. Alright then. Would you like me to walk you back—"

"I'll take her. Sir."

Great. Another walk with Esai. I wasn't sure I could keep the contents of my stomach down. I put on a brave show, but he scared me almost as much as the leader of this awful place.

"Well, goodnight then, Miss Cassidy."

He sounded hurt, like a wounded puppy. In another place and time, I might have been flattered that a man like him paid attention to me, despite the age difference. Irene told me he was in his early twenties and quite handsome.

Esai squeezed my elbow, letting me know it was time to go. He practically yanked me to my feet. He always walked too fast for me to carefully keep up, and I tripped twice on the way to the door. The slam of the wooden screen made me jump. I stumbled several times on the way back to Rains' house.

God, not that room. Please.

"You'd be smart to be nice to him. He might be your only chance of a normal life here. If you refuse him, Rains won't ever let you out of that room."

I didn't say anything, just let him drag me along.

"The Second needs to choose a wife."

"He's a child," I whispered. He was at least fifteen years younger than me. He deserved to get away from this evil place and have a real life with someone his own age.

"He is The Second," Esai said, pulling me to a stop.

I cried out as he squeezed my arm so tight, I was sure I'd be bruised, if not worse.

"When the end of days occurs, he will have a very important role. You would do well to remember that your fate is undecided in the coming battle. Marrying him would ensure your survival."

"This is so wrong," I whispered. "All of this. What about you? Are you going to sit by and watch innocent people die?"

He yanked me so hard, I slammed into his body and my shoulder popped. Tears burned my eyes but I wouldn't give him the satisfaction.

"No one is innocent—"

"Excuse me? It's Esai, right?"

Every cell in my body was on alert.

I knew that voice.

"What are you doing here? You should have an escort—"

"I'm sorry, forgive me. I was with Earl, and we got separated as everyone was leaving the pavilion. I was just looking for the way back to the dormitory."

That drawl. Where had I heard it before?

Jackson.

Oh God! He'd found me. Just like the voice said. Help truly was here. But—no! He shouldn't be here. He was in danger.

"Luke, there you are," another man said as he came closer.

"Sorry, man," Jackson said to him. "Bent down to tie my boots and you were gone. Sure is dark out here."

"No problem." I heard something that sounded like a pat on the shoulder. "Come on, we should get some shut-eye. Oh-five-hundred comes awful early."

"Heard that. Thank you. Y'all have a good night now."

My heart pounded in my chest and my shoulder throbbed in time with the beats as they walked away.

"Let's get you inside." Esai stomped up the steps and I tripped over my feet. I would have faceplanted if he hadn't had such a tight grip on my arm.

I wanted to scream, wanted to run to Jackson, but I knew I couldn't. It would likely get us both killed.

Esai opened the door to Rains' house and dragged me inside.

"Come on, quit fighting me," he said.

"You're hurting me! I can't see where—"

"Shut up."

The light came on inside Rains' office and he opened the door to my prison cell.

"This would all be easier if you'd just quit fighting." He pulled me in close and ran a hand over my hair.

My whole body tensed. I knew he warred with himself. His darker nature wanted to have his way with me. The part that Rains controlled knew that there would be serious repercussions. From what I could tell, at least sex wasn't a part of Rains' diabolical plan. He had Denise, and though she was very pregnant, I heard them going at it every night he was in the house. Things might be different, though, once she was no longer carrying his child or able to be of service.

"Get some rest, Miss Cassidy. Hopefully you'll see things differently in the morning."

The polite part of me almost said thank you for seeing me to my room, but I wouldn't allow myself. I wanted him to go forward knowing he was taking part in immorality. There would be no clean conscience for him, whatever he hoped came out of this.

The door shut, taking the light with it, and I heard the padlock snap. I let the tears fall once I heard Esai shut the office door and leave.

Only Esai, Denise, and Rains had keys, apparently. The Second never came into the house without his father. Denise brought me food and came to get me to help her with the chores, but that was it. The rest of the time, I was kept in this shack.

There were big cracks in the outside walls, and I was terrified of what might climb or slither in here with me. In a way, not being able to see was a blessing.

But Jackson. Could it be true? Was he really here?

He'd made quite an impression on me when I met him, and to be honest, he'd been the subject of many dreams since then. Delaney had told me he was a Ranger, so hopefully he knew what he'd gotten himself into.

Let him be safe. I couldn't bear it if something happened to him too.

Moments later, I heard faint singing outside. It was so quiet, I could barely make out the words...

"If I go crazy then would you still call me Superman?" Then humming.

Superman?

"My superhuman might."

I went to the far wall and found the crack that was large enough for me to see out of...if I could actually see fully. I didn't know who it was, or who might be around, but I had to let him know that I heard him. Could it be *him*?

I cleared my throat.

The singing stopped.

I heard some other men passing by. I knew there was a men's

dormitory somewhere back there. And a shooting range. I'd sat in my room early one morning, hiding under my bed because I'd heard so many gunshots, until I figured out that they were doing some sort of target practice.

"I'm coming." One of the men spoke close enough to the wall of my prison.

I coughed a little louder this time. That was it. I couldn't afford to take any more chances. I had no idea who knew I was back here.

He started humming the song again.

"Kryptonite" by 3 Doors Down.

Superman…

Jackson.

I'd called him Superman when he'd showed me his gunshot wound. I hadn't believed him.

It seemed so far-fetched. If only I could see…I'd recognize him anywhere. His face had been emblazoned on my memory, his smile and that thick blond hair. I'd thought of him so often, even so far as to wonder if he'd felt the bizarre connection as much as I had. It had been different from an instant realization that a person was attractive. I couldn't explain it or describe it other than the feeling that you knew someone, even though you were seeing them for the first time.

But then there'd been the divorce to finalize, the liquidation of our joint assets, the condo to sell…I hadn't been able to do anything but have-to things. I thought there'd be time to start over, to actually live my life. And now I was locked in a room and trotted out in front of a bunch of lunatics once a day as a reminder that they should continue worshiping a false idol who was going to get them all killed. How was this my life?

And could I actually hope that someone was here to rescue me?

I curled up on my cot and tried not to totally lose faith. I had to believe someone would find me. Maybe he had. He was going to need a whole lot of luck to get us out of here alive.

CHAPTER 18
PATIENCE

Jackson

After three long days of hard manual labor around the camp, and evening worship services where Rains and his people elaborated on their theories about The Coming, I lay in my bunk and struggled to quiet my body and my mind. I tried not to toss and turn, didn't want to call attention to myself, but I was agitated. I was still no closer to getting Cassidy the hell out of here, but I was learning so much more about the bullshit Rains was teaching and the kind of people who had chosen to follow him. It was enough to give me permanent indigestion, high blood pressure, and a fucking aneurysm.

With Lance on one side and a guy named Wilhelm on the other, I lay there trying to get some rest, but not fall asleep too deeply. It took all of my former training but I managed to get a couple of hours of... rest. I wouldn't call it sleep.

And I dreamed of her.

She lay in the dark crying. Her vision was blurry in all of the Connections I'd made with her since the accident. Blurry or just black. Like that night. Darkness surrounded her. I sensed her losing hope, and I wished I could just break through the wall and carry her out of here. Who cared that there were thirty-something armed men between us and freedom? Or that some of them had supernatural talents on their side?

Patience, Mr. Howe. Miss Frost says patience.

I woke up with Joanna in my head.

"I got it, I got it."

"Oh good, you're awake."

Great. Matt caught me talking to myself.

"Morning person," I said, pushing myself up on my cot. I'd slept in my boxers and my last clean t-shirt. I stepped into my jeans and grabbed for my socks and boots, shaking them out in case any critters were nesting inside. "What's the morning routine?"

Matt looked around at the other men and stepped a little closer.

"You and I are going to hang back today. I'll show you around the camp, get you set up with your regular chores, and then I've got a special project I'd like you to work with me on."

There was something off about his instructions. I sensed he was going to test me. I needed to be ready for whatever he sprang on me.

"Whatever is best for the community. I'm at your disposal. I don't mind the worksites if it helps out, or if you need me to work around the camp, I'm fine with that. Appreciate y'all bringing me in. These dinners have been the best I've had in a while."

His countenance changed at my words. Instead of guarded, I could sense him softening toward me. "Just wait till you see what's for breakfast. It's Saturday. French toast and sausage patties. My favorite day of the week."

My stomach growled. "'Bout to be mine as well."

"Go get yourself cleaned up and you can help us with the water."

"Copy that."

I used the bathroom and joined the other men in going to the well to bring buckets of water up to the pavilion. We took the dirty water from the night before and ran it through a filtration system they had that Matt explained was a mini treatment plant.

"Gotta take care of the land," he said.

I was impressed with the systems they'd put together out here. I recognized a lot of hacks we'd used when deployed in remote areas without creature comforts. When we finished our chores, we went back to the pavilion and went through the same procedures as the night before, only this time there was free conversation amongst the people. I was introduced to some of the other men, but the women didn't mingle with the single men. They stayed with their spouses or together, and the single men ate together. I didn't want to ask too many questions, so I tried to learn as much as I could from observation. Too many questions could raise suspicions.

"Morning." The driver from yesterday sat beside me, and the other men greeted him warily. He was also the asshole who had been manhandling Cassidy the night before.

"Luke, you remember Esai? Esai, this is Retired Captain Luke Stephens. Ranger with the 75th."

"Fort Benning, huh?"

"Yes, sir," I said. I didn't get the sense this guy had served, but he'd definitely done time. I'd noticed the faded blue ink on the webbing of his thumb and index finger.

"Matt says you've got some experience with explosives."

I glanced at Matt, who nodded as if to say this man was safe to discuss my training with. Sure he was.

"Yes, sir." I didn't care to elaborate.

"Good. Matt's going to bring you out to the range a little later. I've got some questions about detonators."

"What's your purpose?"

The men looked around as if to dissuade me from discussing the topic here.

"Right. Later. Sure."

Esai nodded at me, his gaze holding mine for a moment longer than was comfortable. I went back to eating my food and he did the same. Matt and Earl carried on a discussion and Lance remained quiet, an outsider to most of the conversations. I needed to figure out how to get him alone. I needed to feel him out and see if he truly would be an ally like Joanna had said.

It was hard to focus with Cassidy so close but unreachable. I waited for her to come eat, but she never came in. After breakfast, we cleaned up and I helped Matt with some other chores around the camp while the men we'd been working with took off in the van for town and possible work. Matt was chatty. He talked about his past and how he'd lost his family in a divorce while he was overseas.

"I heard The Second speak at a church in San Diego after my discharge. I was still trying to figure out what to do with my life next, and it was as if I was meant to be there that day...meant to hear his message. The Second was a guest of the local congregation for about a month, and I went to every one of his services and meetings. My wife had moved with the kids back to Arizona, so there was nothing keeping me in California. When The Second introduced me to His Right Hand and they asked me to join the community, I jumped at the chance."

I nodded. "Feels good to be needed, included. When you leave the service there's that period of time when you're kinda lost and feel...directionless."

Matt grunted. "Amen to that."

We worked until lunch and, as we were walking back to the pavilion to eat, we walked around the back of the big house—and I felt a jolt run through my body. Immediately, I was pulled from my perspective, and I could see myself walking. Though it was blurry, I knew it was myself I was looking at.

Cassidy.

She could see me.

She was somewhere close.

I bent to tie my bootlaces and tried to control my breathing so as to not let on something was up.

"You okay there?"

I heard Matt's voice as an echo, the sound in my ears, as well as hers.

"Yeah, sorry. I'm forever feeling my laces untie. Nearly got me shot once in a firefight. No matter how many times I knot them, they always come undone."

Breathe. Breathe.

Cassidy.

I felt her gasp. I glanced up and through the bushes I caught movement. The back of the big house had a poorly constructed addition. It was built from scrap wood planks that were not well fitted together, leaving cracks in the walls that were nearly an inch to two inches wide. It had a slanted roof with a few shingles missing. The cracks were wide enough that I saw movement behind them.

Then I saw fingers at the same time I saw myself through Cassidy's injured eyes.

She was right in front of me, and I couldn't do a damn thing about it.

"All set?" Matt asked.

"Sure, yeah, sorry. Spaced out for a minute. Low blood sugar. Happens sometimes."

Matt patted me on the shoulder. "Let's remedy that, shall we?"

It was subtle, but it was obvious that Matt was trying to lead me away from the area. In the pavilion, he explained we needed to grab our sandwiches and head to the range out back of the dorm. Esai would be meeting us and they wanted to discuss tactical strategies with me. I noticed he took me the long way around, avoiding the back of the main house, as we headed past the dorm to the range they'd constructed.

Matt unlocked a large metal shed and held the door closed for a brief pause. "Luke, I need you to understand something." He turned to face me, his eyes hard.

"Sure. Yeah."

Matt glanced around and made eye contact with someone, lifting his chin in greeting.

I turned to see Esai stalking toward us. I moved to the side, not wanting this man at my back. He definitely gave off dangerous vibes.

"Joining our community means accepting our mission fully. Before we go any further, I want you to understand a bit more about the prophecy."

Esai gave Matt a warning look, but Matt held up his hand.

"He needs to know exactly what we're up against, Esai. It's better this way. Luke deals in absolutes, am I right?"

They both glared at me, challenging me to take them seriously.

They had no idea how serious I was about my mission.

"Absolutes. I don't like to be bullshitted, if that's what you mean. Be straight with me, that's all I ask."

Matt nodded at Esai, who stepped back and crossed his arms over his chest.

"Being part of this community," Matt continued, "means accepting the teachings of His Right Hand and our role in the coming end of days."

I swallowed hard. They were about to spring their evil plans on me, and I needed to pull on all of my acting ability.

"You mean like Revelations."

Matt and Esai traded looks. "In a manner of speaking. Luke, the end of days doesn't necessarily mean the apocalypse like most people would have you believe. His Right Hand explains that the end of days means an end to the persecution of true believers. It means the time has come for our community to ascend. There will be bloodshed as those who stand in our way are cut down, and we have been preparing for that. For too long, true believers in this country have been silenced by the laws of man rather than ruled by the word of God. Enough's enough."

They waited for my response.

"Understood. What would you have me do?"

They exchanged looks again, and I knew I'd answered correctly. If I'd have argued, they would have kept the shed shut and found a way to remove me from the community. If I went running, they'd kill me. If I was too enthusiastic in my response, they'd bide their time before they killed me.

Matt pushed open the doors of the shed and I was greeted with a stockpile of weapons and ammunition that would put any armory to shame. AR-15s, explosives, handguns, you name it. It all looked fairly new and well maintained, meaning someone here knew how to properly store munitions.

Esai put a hand on my shoulder and guided me inside.

"We've got C-4 but we need remote detonators set up. Earl can run you through the plans and what we need, but they have to be easily transported via train and bus to metropolitan areas.

Oh shit.

They were planning to take this show on the road.

"How many? What's the desired blast range?"

I continued to ask them matter-of-fact questions as though my heart wasn't threatening to break free of my rib cage and run screaming from this place. I hoped Joanna was hearing this. I hoped my locator chip was working. I had to get word to Barringer. I had to get Cassidy and the children the fuck out of this place before these zealots blew themselves to kingdom come.

Matt and Esai were delighted to tell me their full plan. They were talking multiple metropolitan areas.

Law enforcement targets.

State legislatures.

Educational institutions.

And there was more—this community wasn't the only group preparing for this day of reckoning.

Apparently Joanna had been kept in the dark about a lot of her father's dealings. And time was running out.

"So when do you need these ready?" I asked, as though I wasn't talking about committing domestic terrorism on a wide scale.

"Soon. We're waiting for the final signs. They should be happening very soon."

"Signs?"

Matt's eyes flared. "Signs. It started with the birth of The Second twenty-two years ago, and each one has brought His Right Hand closer to the Maker's Plan. Like the kidnapping of his daughter, and the most recent attempted martyrdom of His Right Hand. Like the woman falling from the sky. Twelve signs in all, and there have been ten, so two more are coming."

Esai cleared his throat as though to remind Matt that he still needed to proceed with caution.

"We want you to take inventory of what we have and begin to construct the devices. We're going to need you to instruct those who'll be going out into the field on how to properly transport them, set them..."

I set my hands on my hips and glanced around the room, nodding. "And you're sure about this? This is what must be?"

"We do not question orders here, Luke," Esai said. "Joining this community means swearing our allegiance to His Right Hand, and we are prepared to make whatever sacrifice is asked of us. That is our way." He stepped closer. "Are you prepared?"

"Yes, sir." It was the only answer I could give if I was going to save Cassidy and prevent this disaster from occurring.

This rescue mission just got a lot more dire.

That evening, after hours of discussions with Matt and Esai as we went through possible scenarios, we joined the rest of the community for dinner. I couldn't believe the men were able to talk and laugh with each other, join in fellowship, knowing they were sitting on an arsenal that could wipe out the entire camp. I engaged in the conversation as best I could, trying to reassure them I was onboard with their plans and their mission, while thoughts percolated as to how the hell I could possibly put a stop to this madness.

The service that night was much lighter in tone. It was led by The Second—Abel—and the guy was jubilant, full of light and love. It was difficult to accept that he was the son of Rains, unless I thought about Joanna. She, too, was thoroughly good. Whatever was broken in Rains, whatever evil lay within his tainted soul, had not been passed on genetically to his kids. I had no idea how Abel was raised, who his mother was, but he was utterly devoted to His Maker. He showed deference to his father, but he didn't appear to worship him, and that gave me hope. Perhaps the younger Rains could be reached. Maybe it wasn't too late for him.

Cassidy was brought to the pavilion for the evening service, but she hadn't been there to eat. I prayed they were feeding her. She was going to need her strength. I had to fight to focus on not looking her direction when all I wanted to do was take her into my arms and away from this nightmare.

As Abel spoke, I found myself slipping into a more peaceful state. The cadence of his speech, the breathy quality of his voice relaxing my nerves. I could almost forget the men had asked me to build explosive devices that would ultimately slaughter hundreds, even thousands of people. He ended his sermon by singing an achingly beautiful hymn that had tears pricking my eyes.

I could have been lost to the emotional pull if Cassidy wasn't sitting in my line of sight. One glance at her was a reminder of the malevolence here at this camp. That she'd been hijacked, forced to crash her plane, and kidnapped, which meant denying her proper medical care. I opened our Connection enough to feel the physical pain she was experiencing from her injuries as well as the underlying anger and frustration she felt at being trapped. She was afraid, but those other emotions were stronger.

Good. *Keep fighting, Cassidy.*

When Abel finished, Rains stood from his spot between the very pregnant Denise and Cassidy and approached his son. They embraced and he whispered praise in Abel's ear before turning to address his congregation.

"Tomorrow is the Sabbath, and we will spend the day in silent meditation and prayer. We will each take stock of our devotion and dedication and loyalty to our mission here. The signs have led us to this moment, and we must be prepared at any time for the end of days." He glanced around at his congregation, a pleased expression on his face.

And then his gaze landed on me.

"We have been given so many gifts here. We have so many reasons to be grateful. Each of you is a gift to our community, and Our Maker has plans for each and every one of you. Let us give our thanks together."

He led the group in a dramatic prayer that felt more like performance than worship. At one point, Cassidy lifted her head and glanced around. I wondered if her vision was improving. I wondered if she knew I was here. Had she recognized the tune I sang? Did she know it was me? I'd racked my brain trying to come up with a signal that wouldn't cause any alarm. I tried to think of how I could get close to her room without being noticed. They hadn't left me alone at all since I'd arrived, and they weren't likely to anytime soon. I needed a plan and I needed it fast.

The service stopped abruptly, and there was a flurry of activity as

Esai stood with Denise. Rains hurried to her other side. He walked her slowly out of the pavilion, leaving Esai to drag Cassidy behind them.

Abel stood and closed out the service, letting folks know there would not be a service in the morning, but instead the pavilion would be open if folks wanted to have silent prayer together.

"Let's go," Matt said, directing me toward the door Rains had exited from. Abel and Earl guided folks to the other set of doors, keeping the flow of traffic away from whatever was happening.

We got outside and found Rains supporting Denise's weight as she panted, her face twisted in pain.

"We need to take her to the infirmary, sir."

"No, I'm fine, I just need to lie—"

She collapsed, and I rushed forward to catch her when she slipped from Rains' grip. I scooped her up into my arms and waited for instructions.

Rains' eyes were wide. "Thank you. Please," he said, gesturing toward the infirmary. "Matt, go on ahead and make sure Irene is ready for us."

"No, please," Denise mumbled. "I just need to rest."

Rains brushed her hair back from her face and he smiled. For a moment it appeared he might actually sympathize with the poor woman's pain.

"I'm not taking a chance with my son. You'll be examined and then you can rest."

Esai grabbed Cassidy hard by the biceps and jerked her closer to his side. I ground my teeth together when she cried out.

"Sir, shall I take Miss Cassidy to her room?"

"No, bring her with us. I want her near."

Esai led the way with Cassidy clutched to his side. Rains walked beside me, speaking softly to Denise. Her body continued to tense and then release as though she were having contractions.

"When are you due?" I asked her.

"In another month," she said between clenched teeth."

"Oh boy, that's soon," I said, trying to stay lighthearted. "If I remember correctly, you're definitely within the time period that the baby should be safe, the lungs are fully formed—"

"Captain Stephens, what is your experience with pregnant women?" Rains sounded perturbed by my chatter.

"Oh, uh, my aunt was a midwife," I said. "And my mother was a medic and occasionally had to deliver babies. They taught me all the specifics of pregnancy as a deterrent when I hit puberty." I chuckled, but then thought maybe I'd gone too far.

When we approached the steps, Rains stopped me as the others went inside.

"This child is special, Captain Stephens. Everything must be perfect for this child's birth, do you understand? I will not take any chances with his health."

What went unspoken was that Denise's health was less important. I wondered how she felt about that.

"Yes, sir," I said, bowing my head a little.

He held out his hand for me to carry Denise inside. She moaned as we climbed the steps.

"Almost there," I said to reassure her. I had to duck to get inside. The infirmary wasn't much more than a shack sitting on the outskirts of the camp. I lay her on a table and stepped back as Rains took his place at her side, holding her hand for...comfort? Maybe.

Irene hurried to take Denise's vitals and then prepared to do a pelvic exam. I made sure I was out of their line of sight, so I stood next to the door. Next to Cassidy. Esai was focused on what was happening on the table, so I took a chance.

CHAPTER 19
SIGNS

CHAPTER NINETEEN – Signs
Cassidy

It was total chaos the moment Rains abruptly ended his prayer tonight. Denise had nearly fallen out of her chair as what seemed to be contractions hit her like a ton of bricks. She'd gripped my arm and whispered through clenched teeth.

"Lord, forgive me."

Rains took swift action to get her away from the community and outside, where he could assess the situation. I'd learned quickly that Rains only tolerated theatrics when he was responsible, and he certainly did not intend for there to be anything but health and holiness surrounding his child's birth.

The Third. The Closed Circle. The Eleventh Sign. I'd heard so many names attributed to this baby, and none of them boded well for the child, or for Denise.

And now as Denise panted and cried with the pain of her contractions, I concentrated on the latest bruises forming on my arm. Damn Esai. He was always so rough, as if that would make me fall in line. Fear of him. Well, I was sick of his manhandling, sick of this whole scenario. If only I had a weapon, I'd almost consider taking them out one at a time, using the techniques my cop brother taught me, and fighting until I could get away—

Oh yeah, except for the whole not being able to see business.

My vision was better. Things were still blurry, but I could definitely make out shapes and movement a little better. And I was getting good at knowing when people were around me and how many. Like now. As I stood against the wall of the infirmary, I knew Denise was on the bed, Irene was between her legs attempting to do a pelvic examination, while Esai's big body kept getting in the way. At least he'd let me go momentarily so he could fetch things for her.

The man who'd carried her had that familiar voice, and he stood between me and the door. He was huge. Taller than the doorway, bigger than Esai. I had no hope of overpowering him to escape. Unless...no, was I imagining that he was Jackson?

Rains was across Denise's body from where I stood. I knew because I felt his gaze on me as he continued to pray. Well, or just talk to himself. I knew he was trying to calm Denise down, but there was nothing loving or encouraging about his voice. All he cared about was that child, about the power this child was supposed to have, and about the child's destiny. This child's birth was supposed to be the second-to-the-last step before the end of days. I'd picked up that much from his conversations in his office.

He'd kept the details of the twelfth sign under wraps, however. It seemed he wanted to be able to play his hand when he thought it most opportune.

There was one other man in the room. Matt, I think was his name. He was a security guy, but I hadn't had much contact with him.

"Matt, I need you to go stand outside. I want this building secure," Rains said.

"Yes, sir." He moved. "Luke—"

"He stays here."

There was a pause. "Yes, sir." He hurried out the door and down the steps, and I heard him speaking to someone outside. The man next to me—Luke, I guessed—moved a little closer and exhaled, releasing some of his tension, but he was still wound tight, ready to spring into action.

A flurry of activity, muffled voices, and cries from Denise filled the room.

"Denise, honey, I need you to tell me your pain level," Irene said.

"Um, it's ohhhhh… Mom, it's a seven I think. Or an eight. I—"

"Okay, you need to remember that if you can, because it will be important later." Irene cleared her throat. "Do you want me to clear the room?"

"Everyone stays," Rains said calmly. "Irene, please continue."

Oh, damn. As much as Denise bothered me, I wouldn't wish a pelvic exam in front of random men on even my worst enemy.

"Do it, Mom," Denise said, her voice shaky as though she were crying. "I need to know if the baby is okay."

I saw Esai move to stand a little closer behind Irene, and it turned my stomach. Pervert. I had no doubt that if he were given any opportunity, he would take from a woman whether she agreed or not.

The man standing next to me moved closer still, I assumed to avoid blocking the door.

"Is there anything I can do to help, ma'am?" he asked, his warm drawl reverberated through me as he pressed against my arm subtly.

Was I crazy? Could this Luke really be Jackson?

I tried to make more room between us…but he followed.

"Mr. Rains? Can you please hand me that gel? Behind you on the shelf?"

Rains moved around to hand it to her and then remained in front of me, his back to us. I heard him murmuring to Denise and her teary voice in return, but I was too focused on the man next to me.

He took the pinky finger of my left hand between his fingers and squeezed, then he slowly turned my hand so my palm was facing him. He moved so slow, likely hoping to avoid notice. No one in the room reacted, so I assumed they couldn't see any motion. His hand disappeared for a second, and then he pressed something cool and hard into my palm, sliding it slowly until I was holding it. He closed my fingers around it before crossing his arms over his chest.

What had he slipped me? I so wanted to believe it was Jackson, but

I just couldn't be sure. What if it was a trick? What if they were testing me?

I slipped the heavy-ish object into my pants, hoping the tight elastic waistband would keep it from falling through to the floor. There were no pockets in these pants they'd given me to wear. I held my arm against it until I could transfer it to my bra. It was metal, cool, and had ridges and curves on one side. A pocketknife maybe? I could hope.

Please let it be Jackson. Please.

"Denise, you're dilated to two centimeters, but your water hasn't broken, and you haven't lost your mucus plug, right?"

"No, I don't think so."

"Good, okay. I think this could be Braxton-Hicks contractions. Just to be safe, you should stay here tonight, and I can give you an IV—"

"She goes to the house with me," Rains said. "You can come and set up an IV there. You can stay with her. Stephens, can you carry her to the house?"

The man next to me stepped forward. "Yes, sir."

"Good. Esai, carry the supplies for Irene. Close up the infirmary and let's go."

I stood still, hoping to be forgotten, but then I felt Rains' hand on my arm, and I cringed. It was bad enough being touched, but I always felt like I needed a shower after being around him. Evil seeped from his skin like grease through a cardboard container, staining whatever it came into contact. I knew no matter what happened, even if I managed to get away from this place, away from him, I'd always carry that stain.

I followed behind Rains as he struggled to keep up with the man carrying Denise. Whatever had been done to him before he came here, he moved like a much older man. It was quite a ways from the infirmary to the house, at least a football field and a half? But this Luke guy was keeping his pace like it was nothing.

"You doin' all right, Miss Denise? Need me to set you down for a minute to catch your breath?"

She laughed and then groaned. "I should ask you the same thing."

"Nah, I'm fine. I've carried much heavier weights, much longer distances."

"Were you in the military—"

"That's enough talking, Denise," Rains said, clenching my arm a little tighter. "You need to save your strength." He yanked me forward and I stumbled, causing him to grunt impatiently.

"Please do keep up," he growled.

This was new. There were definite cracks in his controlled exterior anytime there seemed to be an issue with the baby. After Denise dropped a plate in the kitchen of the house, he'd shouted at her and berated her for her incompetence, told her she needed to do better if she was going to be around to mother his child. I'd heard it all from my cell, even her apology in a low voice. Most of the time she acted as though everything was peachy, but I sensed she grew more afraid of him the closer she got to her due date. It didn't keep her from doing his bidding, but it was there. She couldn't bullshit me.

When we got back to the house, he stopped at the foot of the steps. The man they called Stephens started to climb the steps, but Rains darted in front of him.

"That's far enough. Denise, you can walk inside on your own."

"It's no trouble—"

"Men are not allowed in the house," Esai said quietly to Stephens. "Stay with her," he said, gesturing to me.

Stephens set Denise down and she panted, but she was strong enough to stand. Esai and Rains took her hands and helped her up the steps and into the house. When the door closed, the Stephens guy turned to me.

"We don't have much time. Matt's coming. It's me, Cassidy. Jackson Howe. Delaney—"

"Oh, God, Jackson! You shouldn't have come here!"

"There was no way I wouldn't," he murmured. His voice was thick with emotion, but then he exhaled and his words became clipped as though we were talking about the damn weather. "I have so much to say to you, but for now, keep that knife close, you hear me? Find a way to cut at those boards at the back of your room. I'm still working on a plan, but we don't have much time. They've got enough weapons to blow this place sky high."

"The birth of the child is the next sign. He hasn't said what the final

one will be, but he's mentioned seeing an interloper. God, Jackson...
what if he means you?"

"Here comes Matt. I swear, I'll get you out of here, Cassidy."

"Jackson, thank you—"

"It's Luke Stephens. Remember that. I'm so damn happy to see
you. God, I could kiss you right now." He barked out a laugh, maybe
to cover what he'd just said, but then I heard footsteps approaching. It
was dark, and I could barely make out movement.

"All good, Matt?"

"Yeah, but what are you doing with her? Miss Cassidy, you need to
be inside—"

"Cassidy, come now."

Rains had come back for me. I wished I could stop time and have
just a few more minutes with Jackson. I couldn't believe he was really
here. His voice was like a dream. And for the first time since I'd woken
up and realized what the hell was going on, I actually had a sliver of
hope in my chest that I might get away from this. Somehow.

I fought the urge to smile at Jackson and climbed the steps with a
blank expression. I was doing great until I misjudged the top step and
tripped, falling hard on my knees at Rains' feet.

"Come on," he said, dragging me up. "I don't have time to deal
with you right now," he snarled in my ear.

"Do you need anything else, sir?" Jackson called out then, and God
bless him, he was going to get us both killed if he wasn't careful.

"No. Thank you, Stephens. You can go about your duties."

"Goodnight, sir."

I heard Jackson and Matt leave as the door closed behind me.

"Get to your room," Rains said. "I'll deal with you later. Right
now—"

"Hello?" Irene was at the door, her arrival temporarily earning me
a reprieve.

"Come in," Rains said. "She's in her room. You are to stay with her
tonight, and if anything is not right with her, you need to wake me."

"Sir, maybe we should take her to the hospital?"

"No. She doesn't leave the camp. The child is to be born here."

"But sir, I have limited experience with childbirth. I don't want to take a chance—"

"Everything will be fine. The Maker will ensure the child is safe."

"But Denise? Sir? My daughter's blood pressure is a little high. She could be experiencing—"

"All will be well. She has you to care for her. See to her now."

He gestured for her to go upstairs and my heart hurt for Irene. Her worst fears had all come to fruition since she'd followed Denise here. Losing her daughter would break her. I'd have to be sure that if—God, hopefully *when*—Jackson got us out of here, I could convince him to take Irene too.

"Now, Cassidy. To your room."

I pushed past him and walked toward the back of the house. I knew my way.

"Esai, lock her in."

My stomach lurched. I concentrated on the feel of the slick metal against the skin of my waist. If Esai chose this moment to put his hands on me, it would be so tempting to cut his fucking balls off.

I heard his footfalls behind me as I stepped into my cell. I turned to face him, my chin up defiantly.

He stood hovering in the doorway. I knew he wanted to take what was in front of him, but his fear of Rains overrode his libido. Thankfully.

"Good night, Miss Cassidy."

The door closed and I heard the lock click. I pulled the knife out of my waistband and stood near the cracks in the wall, trying to find light. I ran my fingers over it, unable to see clearly how it worked. I found a ridge and slid my fingernail under it, gasping when I felt the blade move. I pulled it out and in the dim light, it appeared to be a three-inch-long blade. It locked into place, and I decided to leave it like that so it was easily accessible.

Rains and Esai were now in his office ,and I crept close to the door to try to hear what they were saying.

"How did he respond?" Rains asked. "When you showed him the shed, what was his reaction?"

"He didn't have much of a reaction. He asked questions, didn't seem surprised by our responses. He was solid."

The moment it took Rains to respond had me terrified. *Oh no.* What if they'd figured out he was here for me?

"And he agreed to the plan? Any reason not to trust him?"

"No, sir. He seems like a reliable guy, happy to be here and be a part of things. Abel and Matt both read him and neither picked up anything of concern. He's just another homeless veteran."

"Very well," Rains said. "I haven't seen anything to give me pause, but I've got one more test for him. Tell Matt to give him outpost duty with Lance, and to have Lance watch him. See what he does when he's alone. If he doesn't make any moves, then we'll proceed with the plan."

"Yes, sir. Anything else, sir?"

"You've been wonderful, Esai. Thank you for your loyalty. Once the child is born, the girl is yours to do with as you will."

"Very good, sir. Thank you, sir."

"Have a good night."

The door to the office closed, and I heard Rains' chair scrape on the floor. He stood outside the door to my cell, breathing heavily.

"It's really a shame you are immune to my Influence, Cassidy. When you first arrived, I had planned to take you as my bride for the ascension."

Did I answer him? He'd done this before, talking to me through the door, and I'd ignored him. Tonight I wanted to yell and scream. But I knew it would do no good.

"And now?"

The floor creaked under his weight.

"Now I think your value is for bartering."

"Bartering?"

"Mm. Yes. I plan to trade you for my daughter. Joanna. She's at that school, and despite my attempts to retrieve her, both legally and force-fully, I've been unsuccessful. Her place is here, for the ascension."

"I don't know what—"

"Don't play dumb. I saw you there. You and that counselor. Delaney Frost. Why do you think I had you brought here? I did a little digging and discovered that she's your best friend. She took something valuable from me, so I took something valuable from her. And if her and that headmaster aren't willing to return my daughter to me..." He paused and laughed in a way that turned my stomach. "Well, I'll send you back to them. In pieces." He patted the door as I shrank back into the shadows. "It's a shame I shall never lie with you. Our child would be quite strong. Not as strong as The Third will be, but strong. Pity. Goodnight, Cassidy. Get some rest. The coming days will be taxing for you, I'm afraid."

He walked away from the door slowly, switched out the light, and shut the door to his office.

And I promptly vomited in the toilet.

My hands shook so hard, I dropped the knife Jackson had given me. I patted the floor, terrified I'd lost it in a crack, and then my foot kicked it, knocking it under my cot. I found it and crawled into bed, clutching it to my chest.

That son of a bitch was going to get a big surprise if he tried to cut me into pieces. If I killed him, maybe I could end this nightmare. For everyone. Would it all fall apart without him? Or would Abel take up the mantle? Or Esai?

The next day, no one came for me. It was dead silent in the house. I had no idea if Denise was okay, if Irene was still here, or where Rains was. I used the time to feel around the room for the cracks that had some give, to try and find a weak board, something, anything.

The southeast corner of the room, behind my cot, had what seemed like big bushes in front of it, as all I could see was green and then the blue sky way high up. There was a spot where the floor and the wall didn't meet. I used the tip of the knife to dig out a few nail heads and worked at them until I could loosen the boards. It was exhausting, though, and I didn't think I'd made much progress. I managed to loosen two of the one-by-four boards that were weakened by the dampness.

If the opportunity presented itself, I could move my cot, lift the boards and perhaps get out from under the shack. That corner seemed as if it were higher than the ground outside. I'd work on it again later tonight

Breakfast, lunch, dinner...they all came and went, and no one brought food. The sky grew dark, and still nothing. It was as if the entire camp had disappeared. I was afraid to do any more to the room for fear of making too much noise in all the quiet, or in case Rains showed up. But no one came.

When the sun went down, and I still hadn't heard or seen anyone, I was terrified. The waiting had fried my nerves. I paced. I tried to focus on my breathing so I didn't hyperventilate, but the what ifs took over. What if they'd poisoned the entire camp like Jonestown? What if he'd killed everyone and disappeared, leaving me here?

Where was Jackson?

Sometime in the evening, hours after what should have been dinner, I lay on my cot and must have slept. I woke to a crackling noise outside my room, followed by a sound that sent icy spikes of fear into my chest. What the hell—

"Cassidy."

I gasped. "Oh God, is it...you?"

He hummed the Superman song.

"Jackson?" I whispered.

"I brought you some protein bars. I know Rains left. Esai and him went to town, I don't know why, and they haven't come back. The truck's still gone. I'm on lookout duty tonight, I snuck out the bathroom window to come here before my shift. Are you okay?"

"I thought everyone was gone. Or dead. It's been so quiet."

I couldn't hold back the tears.

"Shhh, shhh Cassidy, come here."

I followed his voice to the corner behind the bush. I felt the wall until I touched something crinkly. The protein bar. His fingers.

"Jackson," I said, touching his fingers, their warmth giving me courage. "Under the floor, I can lift the boards. I think I can get out if I can get a little more—"

"Good girl," he said.

I moved my cot a little and lifted a board. He was able to reach under and hand me the bars.

"Stay put for now. I can't get you out just yet. I'm being watched."

I choked back a sob. I tried to be strong, but being alone all day had affected me more than anything yet.

Jackson cursed. "It's going to be okay, Cassidy, I swear. I'm going to get you out of here. Listen. They're going to have me working with the explosives. They're building bombs, Cass, they're planning some crazy shit."

"I've heard Rains. People are going to die."

"I know," he said, stroking my fingers with his. "But we're going to get out of here. I'm going to see what I can see from the lookout tower. It's above the tree line, the one they're going to have me in tonight, and I'm going to find a way out of here. Then, when I have an opening, I'm going to blow the shit out of that shed. So when you hear the explosion, you be ready, okay? That means I'm coming for you. Do what you can to loosen enough boards to fit through, can you do that?"

"Yes, I will. But please be careful, Jackson." I choked out a laugh. "You know, I wanted to see you again after I left Havenhart. I had a plan. I was wrapping up my personal business and then I was coming back to stay with Delaney. And I wanted to see you." I wanted him to know. If this all went south, I wanted him to know. "I've thought about you..."

"God, sweetheart, I wanted to see you too. We have a lot to talk about."

I heard something. Someone was in the kitchen. I shushed Jackson and listened. The water ran, I heard ice cubes in a glass. Denise? Or Irene?

"I don't want to leave you, but I have to get to my post. I promise I'm getting you out of here and back to Delaney."

"Wait! Jackson. You have to be careful. The lookout position is a test for you. They talked about it last night."

"I figured. Did they say anything else?"

I squeezed my eyes shut to keep the tears in. "He said he was going to trade me for his daughter. That if they wouldn't let her go...he would send them...pieces."

Jackson cursed. "I'm getting you the fuck out of here, Cassidy. And no way in hell is he getting his hands on Joanna again. He needs to be put down."

We heard voices. Someone walking by.

"I gotta go. Be strong, sweetheart. I'm coming for you."

"Thank you, Jackson. Be careful."

One more stroke of his fingertips and he was gone. I didn't hear a sound. I couldn't see him through the cracks, there was no motion, nothing. It was like he'd disappeared.

I scarfed down one of the protein bars and then put the wrapper under the thin mattress on my cot. I made sure the knife was under my pillow in case I needed it, then I tried to relax enough to maybe get some rest.

Please hurry, Jackson.

CHAPTER 20
SIGNALS

CHAPTER TWENTY – Signals
Jackson

My heart pounded as I climbed back through the window into the bathroom. I'd been gone less than five minutes, but I worried. I'd waited until the rest of the men were in their bunks before heading into the empty bathroom. Now, I made it back inside and into a stall, so I could try to calm down.

God, the hell Cassidy had been through. I didn't put it past Rains to carry out his threats to harm her. I'd seen what he did to Joanna with my own eyes. His own daughter.

And the poor girl carrying his child. She was nothing to him. All he wanted was the baby and then she'd be discarded, I could just tell. He'd been so cold to her as her mother examined her.

I wanted to save them all, and that wasn't likely to happen.

I flushed the toilet, went to the sink to wash up, and then I headed back out. Matt said he'd meet me in front of the dorm. I prayed he hadn't been out there when I'd scurried through the bushes to get to Cassidy. There was good cover on both sides of the narrow canal that separated the men's dorm from the rest of the camp. I'd made the leap back and forth over the water without too much noise. I was running out of time, and that meant I was going to have to take chances.

Matt was at the bottom of the steps smoking a cigarette. That was a surprise.

"I know. Bad habit. I've cut back to one a night." He laughed and shrugged. "His Right Hand knows. He lectures me about sacrifice." He took one last drag on the cigarette and put it out on the bottom of his boot. "I've sacrificed plenty."

I patted him on the shoulder. "So where to tonight?"

Matt turned and looked away from the compound, pointing up above the tree line.

"Going to show you the ropes up in the birdhouse. We've got two tall towers at each end of the compound," he said, which wasn't news to me. I'd spotted them first thing. "We have armed guards up there twenty-four-seven. There are rifles, night-vision goggles, and all the sunflower seeds you can eat, from our very own community garden."

"Sounds like a party," I said. "Lead on."

We walked through the dense brush in the darkness, only his flashlight to guide us, until we got to the ladder.

"I'll just knock and Howard will come on down, then we'll go up together, I'll show you the routine, then Hyram will be here in six hours to relieve you." Matt chuckled. "So if you need to take a leak, now's the time."

"I'm good," I said. "I went before we left."

A heavy-set guy came down the ladder and landed with a grunt.

"Matt," he said with a nod. "All clear. I did spot some hunters out earlier this evening but they were carrying a good-sized buck with them, so I figured they were legit."

"Very good. We'll keep an eye out for anything suspicious."

"Copy that," Howard said. "Night, fellas." He took a step back and marched off through the greenery toward camp.

"After you," I said, wanting him ahead of me. He climbed up the ladder with sure grip and footing. I waited until he was through the bottom and on the platform, which looked big enough for a person and a half, maybe, but not two full-sized men like us. It seemed sturdy enough, but still. Thankfully I had no issues with heights. I could imagine a job like this might terrify someone else.

I started up the ladder and when I got about halfway, I saw a flash in the bushes. It looked like light reflecting off metal, but I wasn't sure. It happened so fast, I could have imagined it. I made it the rest of the way up and climbed through the hole in the bottom of the platform. Matt had a pair of binoculars out and was surveying the compound.

The second tower on this end was about fifty yards away, and the other end of the camp was about two-hundred-fifty yards away. I could see those towers as well, though the tree line was taller on that end.

"Lance is up in the tower across from you. Earl and Tony are in the far towers. There's a radio here. Channel one is for all of the compound, channel two is for the south towers—that's you and Lance tonight. Channel three is for ground patrol. There's a box here you can sit on, and inside there's plenty of ammo and night-vision goggles in case it's too dark. Moon will be full in a couple of days so you've got a lot of light up here."

"Yes, sir." I kept my back to the southern side of the platform, hoping Matt wasn't planning on staying too long. When we moved, the tower swayed some, reinforcing my belief that this tower wasn't big enough for the both of us.

"All right then," he said with a smile, clapping his hands together. "I'll leave you to it." He patted me on the shoulder and then lowered himself to the floor, dangling his feet out the bottom. "I'm going to get some shut-eye, but if you need anything, Esai always monitors channel one. I'm sure glad you're here, Luke. His Right Hand has some big plans. It's taking all of our manpower to keep the compound moving and to take jobs and bring in money to keep everyone fed. Folks are tired, and things are going to pick up here soon. It's good to have a man I can trust."

"Whatever I can do to help," I answered when everything in me was screaming *I will end you and anyone who gets in my way.* "For now, I got this. Go get some sleep."

"Thanks. When you're done, grab some breakfast and then get a couple hours' sleep. I'll meet you at the shed at thirteen hundred hours to get you started with the devices."

"Roger that," I said with a relaxed smile. No need to let him know there was no way in hell I'd build even a light switch for these mother-fuckers.

"Night, Luke."

Matt descended the tower and I took a deep breath finally. I broke out in a cold sweat, my hands shaking while I tried to keep my freak-out to a minimum.

Holy shit, this was bad.

Not just the explosives and the plans, but the fact they were keeping Cassidy locked up and threatening her with dismemberment? I'd kept it cool in front of her while she'd matter-of-factly told me what she'd heard. This was the first time I'd been alone since coming to camp, and I took in some extra oxygen from the clear night to settle myself.

The swamp was peaceful except for the occasional moan of a gator or the snuffling sounds of some other creature. Probably a hog. I'd seen tracks earlier in the day and thought that yeah, there had to be a lot of wildlife just outside the compound.

I thought of Lance up in the other tower and figured now might be a good time to see if Joanna was right about him. Lance was alone too, but how could I be sure no one else monitored channel two?

Time is running out, Mr. Howe.

I sighed in relief.

"Joanna," I whispered. "So good to hear your voice. How are you doing?"

You don't have much time. The final sign is imminent and if you don't escape before it happens, I'm afraid... I can't see what happens to you and Miss Cassidy...

I let that sink in.

"I know, honey. Is there anything you can tell me? Anything I can use? How about Lance, anything I can ask him to find out if there's a chance he'll help me? Without blowing my cover?"

Tell him you know about Chattanooga and that the girl says thank you.

"Do I want to know?" I could only imagine the awful things Joanna must have been through.

He tended to me after the first time my father took a belt to me. He said I'd done nothing wrong. He said someday my father would have his reckoning.

"You're damn right he's going to have a reckoning."

I turned the channel on the radio to two. "Lance, this is Luke Stephens, you copy?"

"Affirm," came the reply. "Good evening."

"See anything worth noting?" I asked.

"Negative. All's clear."

It was now or never.

"Is this line secure?" I asked him.

He hesitated. "You'll hear a beep if someone joins in."

"Good. Hey Lance? I appreciated your words, you know, before I came here." I had no idea how to be subtle so I just spit it out. "And I'm supposed to tell you from a friend, 'thank you for Chattanooga.'"

The other line was quiet. Then, "Your friend is a smart girl. She's okay?"

"Yeah," I said, smiling. "She's doing great."

I heard him sigh. "Thank you for letting me know. You watch your back, Stephens. You can't trust any of them."

"Why do you stay?"

"Protect those who can't protect themselves. My wife brought us here. When she died, I had nowhere else to go and he started talking about plans. I got nervous for them kids and the women. When it all goes down, I'll help the innocents." He cleared his throat. "You here to get that woman out?"

"That what you think?"

"I figured."

"You heard talk?"

The moment it took him to answer nearly killed me.

"Nah. They're too focused on their plans."

"Good man. I'm going to move soon. You'll know my signal. Thanks, Lance."

"Over and out."

I exhaled harshly. Damn, thank God for Joanna. I'd been terrified that I wouldn't be able to get to him without others around.

He's such a nice man.

"You heard that?"

I did. I hope you all can get out okay.

"Thanks, honey. Get some sleep."

Mr. Howe?

"Yeah?"

Her voice in my head had been such a balm for my nerves, but tonight she sounded truly fearful for the first time.

Please come back. I couldn't stand it if something happened to you.

"You're a good girl, Joanna. Get some sleep."

Look behind you, Mr. Howe.

I frowned and turned around.

A flash once again.

I waited.

Another flash.

I put on the night-vision goggles and gazed in the direction the flash had come from.

Fucking Ryder!

My good buddy was in so much camo it was hard to make him out, but he flipped me off sideways, which was our thing.

I grabbed a flashlight and was about to flash back. But then I looked around the perimeter carefully. Before I did any further communication, I wanted to make sure we didn't have any company. When it appeared the coast was clear, I crouched in the corner and flashed Morse code to Ryder through the slats in the wood.

Fuck you sideways, motherfucker.

I waited for the flashes to come my way and slowly deciphered his message.

Ready to storm the place when you give the signal.

Fuck. That was the worst thing they could do.

No. Huge cache of weapons. Explosives. Have a plan.

I sort of had a plan. It wasn't a great plan, but it was a plan.

We'll wait for your signal.

Shit.

I'm going to try tomorrow afternoon.

The radio crackled. "Stephens?"

Lance.

"Stephens," I answered.

"We're about to have company."

"Copy that."

That was that. I couldn't take a chance to continue communicating with Ryder.

A minute later, I heard faint footsteps through the bushes down below. Two men I didn't recognize were making their way around the perimeter of the compound, checking things out. I hoped Ryder and his backup were out of sight.

There was a sound farther out, and I froze.

So did the men down below.

A moment later the radio crackled.

"Lookout. What's going on at your two o'clock?"

I looked in that direction and picked up the rifle. "I saw some feral hogs darting around in the brush out there. Maybe that's what you heard?"

The patrol guys went about another twenty yards outside the perimeter, and I had to force myself to breathe.

Shit.

It was too quiet.

"Son of a bitch!"

Sure enough, a group of hogs came hauling out of the bushes and chased the patrol guys my way. They scrambled up my ladder, making the tower sway.

"I fucking hate those devils!" the man shouted.

I tried to keep my chuckles quiet.

"Y'all okay? They're pretty nasty, them hogs."

The men continued to curse, but the hogs continued out of sight.

"We're solid," the man said. "We'll be out of your hair now."

"No problem," I said. "Be careful out there."

They climbed down and headed back out on patrol, headed in Lance's direction, leaving me to my thoughts.

Tomorrow. I would be in the shed tomorrow. I could survey the supplies and come up with a good enough distraction that would have the whole camp in an uproar, but not actually hurt anyone.

The rest of my shift went by without any excitement. I glanced out toward Ryder's position a few times and I saw some movement, but had no idea how many men were in the area.

At six, there was a knock on the bottom of the ladder and I climbed down the twenty or so feet to the ground.

"All's good?" the man asked. I recognized him from meals, but hadn't met him yet.

"Yes, sir. Luke Stephens," I said, holding out my hand.

"Hyram Brown," he said, giving my hand a firm shake. "Matt said for you to come by the pavilion and grab some breakfast."

"Will do," I said. Hyram climbed up as I trudged off toward the pavilion.

I whistled the Superman song as I passed Cassidy's room.

Soon, sweetheart. Soon.

CHAPTER 21
IT'S TIME

Cassidy

Thank goodness for Jackson's protein bars because no one brought me breakfast. I worried about Denise even as my stomach growled. I also had an ominous feeling of foreboding. I'd lost track of the days, but I knew I'd been here at least...a week? Maybe more? My cuts had all healed to pink lines, the scabs gone. But it was a blur.

I hadn't heard or seen Rains. And that terrified me.

Peering through the slats of my cell, the sky appeared gray. Perhaps it was going to storm today? The temperatures had been steady the entire time I was here, but there was a slight chill in the air and a feeling of heaviness, the kind that made it difficult to breathe easily. I'd been through some Florida storms before and knew that they could be fierce. It wasn't hurricane season, however, so that was good news.

A shout sliced through the air, followed by a sob. It sounded close by. It sounded like Denise.

I heard footsteps pounding down the steps and toward my cell. I grabbed for the knife Jackson had given me because, well, I was going to be ready no matter what.

Someone entered Rains' office and I heard a feminine voice swear.

Whoever it was tried the lock, and when they couldn't get it open, they ran away and then came back.

"Stand back!"

Oh God. "Irene?"

There were several loud bangs and then a thud on the ground. The door swung open and a harried Irene stood in the doorway.

"I need your help! She's going into labor, Rains is gone, and I don't want anyone else coming in this house."

"Whatever you need me to do."

Irene led me through the house. "How's your eyesight?"

"A little better every day."

"Good." She turned back around and locked the front door. "Help me with this." She had me help her push a large cabinet in front of the door. "This will hopefully slow whoever it is down. Come on."

We ran up the steps and into a bedroom at the top of the stairs.

Denise was in the bed panting and whimpering. "Mom?"

"It's okay, honey. We're going to deliver this baby. The three of us. And then we're getting out of here."

I could make out their facial features well enough to see the strain they were both under. Denise's eyes were wide and her skin covered with a sheen of sweat. "I'm so sorry, Mommy."

She was obviously terrified. Maybe she'd finally gotten the hint that she was expendable.

"I know, honey. Okay, let me do one last check and see if you're ready to push." Irene had gathered necessary items and they were at the foot of the bed. She had Denise turn so her bottom was at the side of the mattress, and Irene sat on a low stool between her knees.

"Cassidy, listen to me carefully. We don't have a lot of time. I'm going to deliver this baby, and then I need you to help me get Denise ready to go as soon as she's able. Rains went into town to bring back a midwife. I told him that I didn't think I could handle this on my own, which is bullshit because I was a goddamned ER nurse for years. I've delivered babies before, that evil bastard."

"Okay. But there are armed guards everywhere, watching from the towers—"

Irene grabbed my arm. "He told Esai that when the baby is born, he's to dispose of my daughter. In front of us! There's no way I'm letting either of them touch her ever again!"

I glanced at Denise, who lay there panting with tears streaming down her face. "I'm so sorry. I should have listened to you. It's my fault."

"You stop that right now," Irene said as she slid on gloves and squirted gel onto her fingers. "Save your strength. You're going to be in pain, honey, but we've gotta get out of here, and this baby…" She drifted off while she gave Denise a pelvic exam. "Okay, Denise. You're dilated to nine centimeters. Let's get up and walk around again and see if we can't speed this up."

"It hurts! Oh God," Denise said as Irene helped her up from the bed. I hurried to her other side and let her lean on me.

"I know, and you're so brave. Let's just make one more lap here."

We helped her walk around the room slowly with frequent stops as the contractions hit her hard. She started to scream at one point, and Irene placed a hand over her mouth. "You have to keep quiet or those guards are going to come over."

A few minutes later, a particularly hard contraction had Denise nearly doubled over in pain, but she handled it like a champ.

"I think we might be ready after that," Irene said as we led Denise to the bed and propped her up against the headboard. She sobbed while we got her in position and then I listened carefully as Irene told me what she needed me to do.

"All right, Denise. When that next contraction hits, I want you to push like your life depends on it."

Denise nodded, sucked in a few breaths and said, "Okay."

I'd never thought I would witness a birth. I couldn't be there when my nephews were born, and neither myself nor my closest friend, Delaney, had children, so I'd never experienced this miracle. I found it ironic that with all of Rains' boastful beliefs about himself, the true miracle was happening here without him.

Denise was so brave, and Irene so steadfast. After just thirty minutes of pushing, Denise gave it one last effort—and Irene held her grandson in her hands. Despite her fear, Irene gazed down at the miracle in her arms and smiled.

"He's beautiful," she murmured, letting her fierce mama bear I slide briefly. She cleaned off the boy and wrapped him in a towel before handing him to Denise.

"Oh, Mom." She smiled and held the little bundle close.

"You did great, honey. Now take a couple of minutes to get to know your son."

Irene hopped into action and I followed her, taking orders as we went.

"We need to make a sling to carry him. We need water and food. One of the men told me which way to go if I ever decided to make a break for it. I'm going to follow his directions and, well...pray."

"There's a man here who's planning to break me out. He said he would be making a distraction soon."

Irene raised an eyebrow at me. "We can't wait, Cassidy. You can come with us now, or stay and wait for him. Either way, escape isn't likely. I know Rains will be back at any moment. I'm surprised he actually left, but I convinced him his precious child needed the care..."

I squeezed her arm. "You're amazing. I'll do whatever I can to help the two of you."

We rushed around and gathered what we needed, including a handgun Irene knew Rains kept in his desk drawer that was miraculously still there. We were just getting Denise out of bed and cleaned up when we heard a knock at the door.

"We're out of time."

There was another knock.

"Denise? Open up, hon. We brought you some food."

Mother and daughter gazed at each other, and the gravity of the moment settled in. They could very well die trying to get to freedom. Irene tied a makeshift sling around Denise that held the baby against her chest, and then Irene slid on a backpack. She had camo rain ponchos for both of them, and I helped her get one on Denise.

"I'll take care of it," I said. "I'll distract them. You two go out the back."

Irene paused, then she hugged me. "If we get away, we'll send help."

"Take care, you two."

Denise moved quickly for a woman who'd just given birth. Youth was resilient. I followed them down the steps and Irene helped me move the cabinet before they slipped out the back.

"Who is it?" I called out.

"It's Carol, is everything all right?"

I peeked through the window on the door and saw two people on the porch. "Just a moment," I said, giving Denise and Irene time to get out the back door. I waited as long as I could. I pulled it open and smiled as though I absolutely had not just helped deliver a baby and aided in an escape. In no way should I have been opening the door, and just the sight of me would alarm anyone on the other side.

"Miss Cassidy," said the surprised teacher. She was accompanied by Lance, one of the men who did security. "Are you...is everything okay?" she asked.

"Oh, yes, I was just helping Irene get Denise cleaned up and doing some laundry," I lied, trying to come up with an excuse for being out of my cell. Not that these people likely knew I was living in a locked room, but for sure this woman would question why I was walking about freely in Rains' house.

"We didn't see her or her mother at supper, nor for breakfast, so I wanted to bring some food by," she said, holding a tray with covered dishes on it. "I know His Right Hand is away on business overnight. If you'll let me in, I can take it up to them."

"Thank you," I said, reaching for the tray. "They'll appreciate it. It was a long night. Denise has been having contractions for a few hours. She'll likely be in labor before nightfall," I said, glancing in Lance's direction.

Carol didn't let go of the tray. "Nonsense. I know you're still recovering and have trouble seeing. It's not safe for you to be using the stairs." She smiled, but her lips were pressed together and her nostrils flared as though she was very uncomfortable with this situation.

"It's okay. I'm feeling much better and can see well enough to put one foot in front of the other." I gave a gentle tug on the tray and she let go. "I'll be sure they get something to eat."

The teacher looked at Lance and then back at me in confusion.

"Very well. I'll be sending The Second over to check on them in His Right Hand's absence. Good day, Miss Cassidy."

Lance gave me a long look as the teacher descended the steps. He didn't say a word, but he raised his eyebrows. I gave him a slight nod and closed the door with my hip. I set down the tray and then locked the door behind me.

I carried the tray to the kitchen and, like a barbarian, I ate as much of the food as I could, shoveling in pancakes and sausages with my fingers, hoping that my nerves would allow me to keep the food down. I didn't want to be weak now. I needed strength no matter what my escape plan would be.

I could either wait for someone else to come in—with my luck, Rains and Esai would come back at any minute—or I could make a break for it myself. The back door was just a few feet away. I had no idea what would greet me outside, but honestly, getting shot by some guy on patrol would be better than waiting here to face Rains' wrath.

I wanted to wait for Jackson's signal, but I knew I was out of time. It was late morning and after the strange encounter with Carol, it was likely someone else would drop by to see why I'd been the one to answer the door. With the camp on high alert, there was no doubt they'd come back.

At that moment, the sky opened up and buckets of rain poured down on the metal roof of the house, so loud it drowned out the pounding of my heart. I needed to act, so I hunted around the kitchen for a flashlight and a water bottle, wishing I had a compass or a map. Anything. I was usually pretty good with finding my way through situations, but not nearly blind, not on foot, and certainly not in the middle of the swamp. I found another poncho hanging in the mudroom in back and there was a pair of men's rubber boots. I took those too. With my knife in hand and the other items stashed in the front pocket of the poncho, I placed my hand on the doorknob and exhaled.

It was now or nev—

A massive blast knocked me on my back and glass from the door rained down on me.

Over the thunderous rain, I heard children screaming and men shouting, and I figured if Jackson was going to offer a signal, that very well could have been it.

I scrambled to my feet, grateful the poncho had protected me from more cuts, and I opened the door a crack.

A series of smaller explosions went off and a fireball flew into the sky. My vision was still blurry, but I could see large shapes, and I could see a row of shrubs between the house and the fire.

"Stephens! Oh my God!" I heard a man shout. "Anyone see him come out?"

"No one could have survived that."

Stephens...

Jackson.

He had to have gotten out. *He had to.*

I made my way to the shrubs and looked through them to the shell of a metal building that was on fire, despite the pouring rain, although it would likely be put out in a short time. There were no buildings close enough to it to catch fire, so the men stood and watched from several yards away.

"What is this?"

That voice.

Dread filled my stomach and I feared it was too late for me.

Through the bushes, I saw Rains and Esai join the group of men watching the fire burn. They had a woman with them who was wearing scrubs, and by the way Esai had a grip on her arm, I didn't think she'd come willingly.

I heard a branch snap, and I peered around the corner of the house.

"Jackson!" I whispered.

He'd come for me. He crouched at the corner of my cell and was about to pry the board away when I snapped my fingers, figuring it wouldn't be heard over the sound of the rain and the continued popping sounds from the fire.

His head swung my way and even from twenty feet, I sensed the relief coming from him. He made his way toward me and pulled me into his arms.

"I've never been so happy to see another human being in my entire life," he said, pressing a kiss to my drenched hair. "But we've gotta move. *Now*."

He took my hand and led me in the opposite direction of where he'd come. He pulled me into a crush of bushes and we crouched down.

"We have to get through the creek and then head that way," he said, gesturing to the fire line beyond the shed. "We're going to pass close, but we should be safe if we hurry." He looked down at my mud boots and smiled. "Good girl. Stay close to me, all right? You got that knife?"

I nodded, too terrified to speak.

"If anyone approaches, you keep that at the ready. If anything so much as slithers close to you, you fucking keep that handy, you got me?"

I nodded, my teeth chattering. I wasn't cold but I was going to be in shock if we didn't move now.

Jackson crouched low and we crawled through the thick brush. The boots were too big and they got sucked into the mud a few times. I almost lost one, but Jackson was patient as I yanked my foot free with the boot intact. We reached an embankment and the creek roared below, fed by the current downpour. I could barely see through the blur as it was, but the rain was so heavy it pooled in my eyes.

"It's moving fast, but it's only about a foot and a half deep. You think you can handle it, or do you want to climb on my back?"

"Give me a break," I said. "I might be in distress, but I'm no damsel."

"Damn," he said with a laugh. "All right, sweetheart. Don't let go of my hand, you hear me?"

"I won't let go."

There was a bend between us and the fire, so I doubted the men in camp had a clear view of this spot, but we had to move fast. We'd have plenty of cover on the other side once we made it across and up the embankment. I poured as much energy into my limbs as I could and followed Jackson into the rushing water.

CHAPTER 22
EVASIVE MANEUVERS

Chapter Twenty-Two – Evasive Maneuvers
Jackson

My heart was filled with hope the moment I saw Cassidy's face, but that hope was short-lived. I hadn't realized we'd have a torrential downpour the moment I'd hit the detonator. I'd also planned to do it later, when we would have less daylight to contend with, although the filtered light coming in through the canopy of the trees surrounding the camp played tricks on the eyes. That could be to our advantage.

I knew I was out of time when Matt let me know that Rains and Esai had gone to town to bring back a midwife, that Denise was about to have her baby at any moment. I knew that Rains considered the birth a sign, and the next one was supposed to be the start of the uprising. Well, I'd just gone and blown up his ammunition and C-4, so hopefully I'd put a damper on that plan, but I didn't trust that to be true. As much thought and effort as had been put into this plan, he had to have other resources I didn't know about.

Thankfully, I'd discovered a loose piece of metal at the back of the shed that I was able to push free enough to slip out. I'd need a tetanus shot when we got out of this mess, but otherwise, I escaped unscathed.

I wired that fucking place to go up like a truck crashing into a gas station but I'd used a remote detonator instead of the damn suicide bomb shit they'd wanted me to use for their twisted plans.

Somehow, Cassidy had gotten free, but she was still moving tentatively, probably still sore, definitely still visually impaired. And the fucking creek was rushing so hard that it about knocked me over when I stepped in. I should have just carried her but instead, I half dragged her across the water. She got soaked in the process, even going under the water that was by now close to three feet deep, but when she popped up, she blew out a breath and showed me she still had the knife.

"That's my girl," I said, wrapping an arm around her shoulder as I led her toward the embankment. I turned to look over my shoulder and realized we were really fucking visible right here. I whipped off my bright white t-shirt, hoping my tanned skin would stand out less against the mud. Cassidy had on a camo poncho with the hood up and her dark blue pants were soaked underneath.

"Sorry to get fresh, but I need to give you a boost up this hill." I put her in front of me and shoved her ass up the hill with one hand while I pulled myself up with the other hand, grabbing onto vines and branches, whatever I could use, just to get us out of the water and out of view.

When we reached the top of the embankment, we heard the shouts.

"Oh no," she said, looking back toward the house.

We saw Rains and Esai go into the front door—then Rains roared. Esai came running back out and whistled, using the signal for security. Matt had given me the basics on how they ran security, but to see this ragtag bunch come together, I knew he'd downplayed the level of sophistication this group had going on.

I pushed Cassidy into the darkness of the trees. "What happened in there? How did you get free?"

"Irene delivered Denise's baby this morning and I helped them leave," she said through chattering teeth. "He's going to be livid."

"He's going to come unglued." I looked down at her. "Do you know where they went?"

She shook her head and wrapped her arms around herself. "Irene said one of the men told her which way to go if they could ever get out."

"Probably Lance. He's a good man." I needed to get her to shelter and out of her wet clothes. The temperature had dropped, and while it wasn't necessarily cold, Cassidy was soaked and the adrenaline was bleeding out. She was bound to go into shock. Damn, she was so brave. So strong. If I wasn't already half in love with her...

I pulled her against me and willed some of my body heat into her.

"Are you ready to move? There are people out here waiting for us—"

Gunshots rang out, and I tackled Cassidy to the ground. I couldn't tell where they were coming from.

There were more shouts, but they sounded far away. Could it have been more of the ammo from the shed?

"Stay here," I said to Cassidy. She was completely covered in the bushes. I searched for a tree that would give me cover. I scrambled up a massive cypress that let me see over the top of Rains' house. There were ten men meeting in front of the porch, taking weapons from Esai. He directed them to split up—and he sent three in our direction.

I climbed down as quickly as I could and grabbed Cassidy. "We've gotta move. We may have reinforcements but they're a ways off. I'm not sure if they'll approach—"

"Luke!"

My head whipped around to see Matt running toward the creek. I witnessed the moment he went from grateful I was alive...to realizing I'd set this all in motion.

I didn't want to hurt him. I knew he was doing what he thought was right, staying in this community, following this megalomaniac, but there was no way I was going to let him be a part of hurting Cassidy. I reached for the gun in my waistband as he raised his weapon.

More gunfire erupted, distracting him.

This time, I recognized gunshots from the camp and answering shots from the woods beyond the fire. Ryder's or Barringer's men must have moved in.

The shooting was concentrated in the area around the men's dormitory, so I prayed the women and children had been led to safety away from the compound.

"Luke," he said again, leveling his gun in our direction.

I pushed Cassidy behind me. "If he fires, you run like hell."

"Jackson, no!"

A flurry of pops rang out and a line of crimson appeared on Matt's neck just as he sank to his knees, his eyes wide in disbelief.

I couldn't tell if he'd been shot intentionally or if it had been bullets exploding from the shed. I needed to get Cassidy out of there. I had no choice. I had to lead her away from the invading men. We couldn't get pinned down in the middle of the firefight and that shed wasn't finished spitting out deadly metal. I'd snatched a Sig Sauer and four clips before leaving the shed, shoving them all in the cargo pants I'd taken from the closet this morning, but that wouldn't last long.

"We've gotta make a run for it. Trust me?"

"I do, but he's not going to stop looking, Jackson. Even if we get out of here."

I pulled her close and rubbed her arms. It was no use, she needed to get into some dry clothes and I had no clue when that was going to be possible. The rain wasn't letting up. "He's like a bad rash."

She gave a humorless laugh. "If I never see him again it will be too soon. I'm not a bad person, or at least, I never thought I was… Is it wrong that I want him dead?"

I shook my head. "I know the feeling. Come on."

I took her by the hand and we moved at a fast walk through the trees, which weren't as thick the farther we got from the creek, a blessing and a danger, considering we were likely being pursued. I stopped every so often to see if anyone had caught up to us, but so far the only sounds I detected were our loud breaths, the snapping of twigs and sloshing of mud under our feet, distant gunfire, and shouts.

A voice rose above the din through a bullhorn.

"This is the FBI. Lower your weapons. We have you surrounded."

The children screamed, a terrified chorus of cries that brought me to a halt.

"Oh God," Cassidy said. "The kids!"

I ground my teeth together and planted my feet to keep from running in that direction.

Cassidy pulled on my arm. "They won't hurt the kids. They can't—"

"The agents won't hurt them. They won't fire if they know the kids are in danger."

Sure enough, the gunfire stopped.

I scanned the area and saw no movement, but I wasn't about to get complacent. Not with Cassidy. "Come on. A little more, let's get as far away as we can."

"Okay."

We continued on until I felt like I'd yank her arm out of the socket if I dragged her any farther. "Let's take a break," I said, leading her to a pile of collapsed trees. She sank down as though her bones had gone liquid.

"I'm so sorry to push you," I said. "I know you've been through hell."

"And I'd still be there if it weren't for you, so don't apologize." Her eyes lingered on me a moment longer. "It's just been a while since I've done cardio."

I stood with my hands on my hips, not feeling winded in the slightest, but fully aware her body had been battered in a plane crash about a week before. I recalled from looking at maps with Agent Barringer before I left that there was a waterway not too far from the camp in the direction we'd been going. I wasn't sure we could get across. We might have to follow the tree line as far as possible.

I had to rely on the knowledge that Ryder knew we were out here, otherwise...I didn't want to think about reviving my survival tactics to keep us safe. It was wet as fuck out here, not a good sign for getting a fire started. I hadn't had a backpack to use to bring food or anything. All I had was a bottle of water, some protein bars, a lighter I'd snagged from the shed, and the gun.

"I'm going to see if I can get up this tree and check out our location."

She nodded and sighed. "I just need another minute and then we can go."

"Be right back, sweetheart."

I climbed up the tallest tree, taking care with some of the weaker limbs up high. I couldn't get high enough to look out over the entire area, but I did see that fifty yards ahead was indeed a clearing and a significant waterway. We were definitely going to have to change direction. If we made our way south, maybe we'd be far enough outside the line of fire that we could safely connect with Ryder's men.

Things were still quiet in the direction we'd come from, and my chest tightened.

This had been too easy.

We weren't out of the woods by a long shot.

Just then, I heard the whir of an engine, faint...but headed our direction.

Shit. The fucking swamp boat.

I climbed down and jumped the last five or six feet, running over to Cassidy.

"We need to move. We need to find cover."

She heard it too.

We ran south about two hundred yards until we came to another clearing. If we tried to make it across and they came this way with the boat, they'd see us for sure. I pulled Cassidy back against me, her body trembling and her breath coming in hard pants. She wasn't going to be able to go much farther.

Ahead, there were the ruins of a dock and a collapsed structure that must have been a hunting cabin at one point. A hunting cabin could mean there was a blind nearby.

"Come on," I said, leading her in that direction. The structure itself wasn't safe, although in this rain, it might provide some shelter, but I had another idea.

Twenty yards past the structure was a large area of sawgrass and the perfect place to hide. "This way."

The boat's motor grew louder and in moments, whoever was on that boat would be within sight. We reached the clumps of sawgrass and I held the leaves aside so Cassidy could climb inside, where someone had cleverly hidden a blind. There was a slanted wood roof covered with dried sawgrass and a metal bench inside. The backside was protected with another piece of wood, and though the floor was soggy, it would get her out of the rain. From the outside, you couldn't see the blind unless you were looking for it, and it obviously hadn't been used in a while as there were no breaks in the growth for a hunter to see prey. I prayed it was hidden enough from the waterway that a passerby wouldn't see us.

I also hoped there were no snakes. We didn't need any close encounters right now.

I squeezed in beside her and pulled the large fronds of grass around us. I smacked at a mosquito, one of the dozens that had bitten me since we'd made a run for it, and I tried to calm my breathing and my heart rate.

The boat came into view and slowed as the people onboard saw the ruined cabin.

Shit.

It was Esai. And Rains.

Esai pulled the boat up to the ruined dock and hopped out. Rains stood and looked around, his hands on his hips.

"I don't see any fresh tracks," Esai said. "But with this rain, it'll be tough."

Cassidy pressed closer to me, holding my arm like a life preserver.

Rains stepped onto the dock and took a deep breath, letting it out before raising his hands at his sides. His lips were moving. I couldn't make out the words, but I stiffened when I realized what he was doing.

Cassidy's body jerked and she tried to stand up.

"No," I whispered, wrapping my arms around her.

Rains was using his Influence. Cassidy was too exhausted to fight it off.

"Come out, come out, wherever you are," Rains said in a louder voice. "Come to me."

Cassidy gasped and pulled at my arms, trying to get free.

"No, sweetheart. Here." I pressed her head to my chest. "Listen to my heartbeat. Focus on that, not on him. Don't let him in."

"I can't...I have to—"

"Shhhh."

I cursed. I didn't have the kind of gift that allowed me to have any sort of Influence over others. My ability was strictly an information-gathering and monitoring kind of thing. God, I needed Joanna.

And on cue, a voice filled my head.

Singing.

"Joanna," I whispered.

Cassidy gazed at me in wonder. She heard it too. Joanna sang a beautiful incantation, somewhere between folk song and hymn. The words didn't matter as much as the feeling that her voice evoked.

My head felt fuzzy, like just after a deep sleep, and my body felt as though it were tucked into a warm comforter on a billowy bed drenched in morning sunshine. All of the comforts I'd need to never want to move again.

Cassidy slumped against me, her eyes closed, her breathing steady.

Thank God.

Rains continued for another minute or so, and then his shoulders dropped as though he'd given up in frustration. He stomped a foot and looked around, his gaze skimming over the top of the tule we were hiding in, but he made no move to leave the dock.

Esai walked up to him, his eyes downcast.

"There's no sign of anyone. I'm sorry, sir, but we've got to get out of here. The FBI will be looking for you."

Rains growled. "Without the woman, I have no chance of getting my daughter back. Without the baby, our plans cannot move forward. Without Abel… I can't believe the fool turned himself in! He *knew* to avoid capture. I need my children with me! The Maker's Plan requires they be with me! And now, without the weapons…"

"Then we start over, sir. I swear to you, I can build our arsenal once more. We will take back Joanna, and we'll find the child. I've already contacted our lawyer. He'll get Abel out of jail. Abel knew nothing of the plans, so they'll have no reason to keep him."

Rains shook his head. "And we lost Matt and that Stephens fellow. Pity. They were good soldiers. They would have been helpful."

"Yes, sir. But there are more where they came from. More soldiers who are disillusioned with current leadership. We'll find what we need."

face. "My version of plastic surgery. They'll go away. The shiner was compliments of a fellow guest at the St. Francis Rescue Mission. I stayed there a night before I connected with the guys from the camp. I picked the wrong bunk."

I sat up and pulled my hand away from his face with a jerk. "You did all of this...for *me*?"

His mouth turned down at the corners but his eyes were full of mischief. "Well, I heard they had great food and knew how to party. It wasn't that much of a sacrifice." He winked at me, and I shook my head.

"You are every bit the charmer Delaney warned me about. Although, I didn't see it last time I met you."

He peeked outside again. "There was a lot going on then, and I, uh...well, I was kinda dumbstruck meeting you."

"Dumbstruck? Why?"

Jackson gazed at me, and I sensed he had something of importance to say. His switch to a serious demeanor was jarring, but not unexpected. We'd just been through a traumatic experience. Of course he'd have to be off-balance too.

"Let's just say when I met you, you were more than just the friend of a co-worker to me. I was...affected by you."

"Oh," I said, rather lamely. "Um, same here."

Way to go, Mackenzie. Way to play it cool.

He smiled, and relief was evident in the gesture.

"I'm so glad I found you," he said. "As soon as I knew you were missing, there was no keeping me away." Abruptly, he sat up straight and his eyes flared. "You probably should eat. Here," he said, pulling a protein bar out of a pocket in his cargo pants. "You'll need your strength. You already conked out on me once."

I took the bar and tried to tear into it in a civilized manner, so he might not guess how starving I was. I broke off half of it and tried to hand it to him.

"No, thank you. I had a big lunch before we took off. Don't you worry about me."

"Thank you. I had a few bites of food before I left, but I can't remember when I ate before that. The last twenty-four hours are a blur.

The last thing I remember before I crashed in here was singing. Who was that singing?"

"Ah," he said, turning away from me enough to lean back against the wall of the blind. "That was Joanna."

"Joanna?"

"Mmhmm," he said, resting his head back and closing his eyes. "Rains' daughter. She's, uh, gifted. Like him, but not. She's something else, that girl."

"What do you mean, gifted?"

He frowned, keeping his eyes closed. "She Sees things. She's also able to communicate mentally. Like a telepath."

"If I hadn't experienced that evil man's power, I wouldn't believe that was possible."

"It is indeed. If it weren't for her, I might not have found you."

There was a fondness in his voice when he talked about her, but something bothered me about his explanation. "So, she's like him? And she's at your school? That's gotta be dangerous."

"No," he said, opening his eyes and turning to face me. "She's not *like* him. She'd never hurt anyone."

"It's wrong. Messing with people like that."

"Cassidy, sweetheart. Not everyone who is gifted is evil." There was an edge to his voice, as though my words had struck a wrong chord.

I gazed up at him and inched away. "You mean there are more?"

He started to speak, but after a moment, he clamped his jaw shut. The expression on his face said he'd just experienced the worst disappointment. Then he tried again. "Yeah. There's more. Look, Gerald Rains is powerful. He uses his Influence to hurt people. I get it—"

"You don't know. I've been around his brand of religious bullshit before. My parents...their church had them believing some insane dogma. It affected my whole life. Ask Delaney."

"Cassidy—"

"I'm sorry. I don't know that I can *accept* that some girl was talking to me in my head, someone related to that man. I'm...kind of freaked out by all this. It's not normal."

The protein bar threatened to come back up, and I had to fight to keep calm, keep the food down. "I knew Rains was evil from the moment I met him. He made my skin crawl. He tried to...he tried to get *inside* me, Jackson. I felt it. He was going to make me his wife. He tried to—" God, when I thought of those icy tendrils trying to slither into me, that cold dread, I felt panic creeping in. "He was going to have Denise killed after she gave birth and take me as his wife for this so-called ascension." My whole body shook as it tried to create some sort of heat, some sort of protection where there was none.

"I know, sweetheart. I'm so sorry. Did he..."

"God, no. Thankfully. Honestly, I think I was more in danger of *that* happening from that Esai creep. He... I can't, Jackson. I don't even want to think about what could have happened."

"I'm so sorry," he said. He reached for me, but hesitated. Maybe he worried I wouldn't feel safe with him. I wondered if anyone would ever make me feel safe again...but if I did, Jackson would be the one. All of this talk, this facing the reality of what could have happened...it opened me up, left me raw. I was afraid that if I let go of any more control, I'd fall apart and there'd be no putting me back together again.

"If only I'd have caught him back in the fall, when he came for Delaney, this wouldn't have happened to you."

I fell silent. Anger boiled up inside me. Anger at this evil man and the people he'd convinced to do his evil will. All of this was because of my relationship with Delaney? These people had gone through all of this trouble to kidnap me because we were friends? I was furious, and resentment threatened to settle into my heart, but I knew it wasn't fair. Delaney was at that school to help kids.

But then, she knew about all of this? People with strange gifts? And she never said anything?

"You couldn't have known what he'd do." I mostly meant it.

"Not this, no. We thought he was dead. But I guess I knew deep down he wasn't."

"He faked his own death?"

Jackson nodded, his solemn expression doing more to unnerve me. "He used his Influence to convince the hospital folks up in Shreveport."

"If he did that, can he ever be stopped? I mean really?"

Jackson sighed. "I won't rest until I see his dead body myself."

I wanted to believe him, but there was something…off about his words, and it occurred to me that he hadn't given me the whole truth.

"How *did* you find me, Jackson? You said Joanna was part of it, but how?"

The pain in his blue eyes nearly took my breath away, as if he knew I would hate whatever he told me, and yet he also knew he *had* to tell me. He started to speak—

Then he held a finger up to his lips and climbed slowly from the blind we were in.

I listened, but it was hard to hear anything over my heart pounding in my ears and my teeth chattering. Alone once more and unable to hear or see anything, I quickly began to panic. I didn't even realize my breathing was growing shallow until what was left of my vision began to go spotty.

I tried to call for Jackson, but the pain in my chest took all of my breath away. I reached for him, gasping.

"I think we're safe, sweet— Oh, God! Cassidy!"

I lost my balance and tumbled off the bench, landing in the puddle on the floor of our hideout, where it was cold, wet, dark…

CHAPTER 24
ABHORRENT

Jackson

"Jesus Christ, Howe. What the hell are you doing all the way out here?"

"Thank God, Ryder!" Relieved, I leaned back into the blind to let Cassidy know we were safe.

"Cassidy!"

In the single minute since I'd popped outside because I heard someone approaching, Cassidy had passed out face first in the water on the floor of the blind.

I reached in and yanked her up, wincing when I thought about her injuries, but there was no time to be gentle. I got her under the armpits and dragged her out of the blind onto the soggy ground. The rain hadn't let up and her skin was ice cold. She coughed twice and moaned, letting me know at least she was breathing, but she wouldn't be for long. She needed proper shelter immediately, or she wasn't going to make it.

"Let's get her to the boat," Ryder said, grabbing her feet. "Geoff will get us to shelter so we can get her into some dry clothes and warm her up."

"Thanks, man."

We carried Cassidy to Geoff's waiting swamp boat and I took her in my arms, sheltering her with my body as much as I could. Ryder wrapped the two of us in a mylar blanket and Geoff took off at a slower pace than he had the first time I'd ridden with him. He had giant spotlights to guide the way. I was grateful...so grateful they'd found us. All I cared about was the woman in my arms and getting her to safety.

Cassidy had a sturdy build and was fairly tall, but right now, she felt as fragile as fresh-picked flowers in my hands. I'd been so relieved to get her away from the camp in one piece, but after the conversation we'd had in the blind...now I was terrified.

It was obvious she was going to need time to heal from the trauma she'd experienced, and I knew I'd have to give her that time. Though, any hope of a future with Cassidy had been dashed by her expression when we talked about gifts.

Even without this horrific experience, she carried around a lot of baggage that meant she would likely never see my fucking curse as anything but evil. Wrong. Abhorrent. I wouldn't blame her. She'd never trust me. And I couldn't keep it from her. She'd find out, and then she'd hate me, and I couldn't live with that. Better to have her fear me or keep her distance than to have her hate.

"Closest place to take her is my house," Ryder shouted over the motor. "Otherwise we can drive y'all into Everglades City, but that's going to be at least another hour."

I wanted to ask Cassidy her preference, but she was out of it.

"Your place will be fine, thank you."

He nodded and then shouted back to Geoff.

"Jackson," Cassidy moaned. She started to pull away, but I held her tight.

"I'm sorry, sweetheart. We're with friends. We'll be off this boat and to safety real soon, and then we'll get you dried off."

Her eyes widened and her body shook much harder than just from the boat.

Hold on, sweetheart. Hold on.

It seemed like we were on the water for hours when we finally pulled up to a dock. I recognized the area as where we'd met Geoff the first time.

"My truck's just up in the lot. Can you walk, ma'am?"

I passed her to Ryder. "Here, hang on to her for a second and then pass her to me."

I felt Cassidy stiffen as I let her go. I jumped out onto the dock and then reached for her as Ryder lifted her off her feet. I scooped her up and followed Ryder at a quick clip to his truck. I eased her into the cab and onto the bench seat, the rain whipping at our faces now, and then climbed in behind her.

Geoff waved from outside and I mouthed "thank you" to him. I'd be sure he was compensated for his help. Handsomely. Ryder too.

Ryder flopped into the truck and slammed the door, making Cassidy jump and scoot closer to me.

"Cassidy, sweetheart, this is Ryder Simms. He and I served together."

"Good to meet you, ma'am," Ryder said as he turned on the truck. "I'm so glad we found you in one piece."

She melted into my side a bit, shivering violently. I looked down at her, but she only stared out the window, the blank look worrying me more than the shivers. She was shocking out on me. I didn't get her this far only to lose her.

"Ryder," I said, looking at him over her head, and I gave him a look that I hope conveyed the seriousness of the situation. She needed a warm, dry bed STAT.

"I'm on it."

Ryder drove as fast as was safe, and thankfully the rain began to subside. Finally.

"Any word from Barringer?" I asked him as he turned off the main road and onto a gravel one.

"I texted him when we found you, but he hasn't answered. I'll let him know we've arrived and I'm sure he'll get here ASAP. Dude about lost his shit when you blew up that shed. Nice work, by the way."

I snorted. "Thanks. Think I singed my eyebrows a little. Caught my thigh on some rusty metal on my way out, so that's awesome. I'm sure I've got tetanus in my future."

"Oh, dude, I've got shots. Let me give you one."

"How the hell do you have tetanus shots?"

"I'm the fucking EMT for these parts, friend. When I ain't patrolling the park, I'm on the volunteer fire brigade. They paid for me to go to EMT school last year. Figured I'd be a triple threat."

"Yeah, cuz your ass ain't singing and dancing despite your decent acting chops."

We continued to bust each other's balls until we ran out of driveway in front of a sprawling ranch-style house.

"Holy shit, Simms. This is your place?"

"Indeed. My brothers and I built it over the years and when I retired, I bought their asses out. None of them want to live out here anyway, so they took the money and bought an apartment complex in Miami. Mom and Dad are about a mile away, my grandparents are in a prefab on the other side of the property. One big happy family."

Cassidy dozed against my chest and as miserable as we both were, all soggy and cold, I didn't want to let her go. I knew this was likely the last time she'd let me close to her like this.

"I'll come around and help you," Ryder said, and I was grateful for the moment alone with her.

"Jackson?"

"Yeah, sweetheart. I'm here. We're at my friend Ryder's house. We're safe. I'm going to get you warm and dry. I promise."

"Jackson?" she repeated.

I had no idea if anything I'd said registered with her. "It's me, Cassidy."

She opened her eyes and though they seemed glazed over, I knew she was lucid.

"Please don't leave me alone. Not yet. Please."

"Whatever you need," I said, cradling her face. "Let's get you dry, fed, and rested, and then we can make a plan."

She blinked a couple of times and then nodded.

Ryder opened my door and stepped back.

"Barringer hit us back. They're still processing all of the people at the camp, all the kids. They had to haul the whole lot of them into

Everglades City. The whole fucking FBI field office is out there, along with state police. He's got Rains' kid in custody."

"Abel. Rains was pissed he turned himself in."

"Well apparently he's talking, but Barringer's not sure how much he actually knows."

I needed to know everything, but Cassidy had to come first.

"Let's get you inside," I said.

She nodded, pulling the mylar blanket around her.

I climbed down first, not losing contact with her, and then I turned and held out my hands. She came haltingly into my arms, sliding down my body and onto her feet.

"Want me to carry you?"

She shook her head. "I'm okay. Just, stay with me?"

"You got it."

I kept an arm around her waist and she leaned into me. We followed Ryder up the steps and he unlocked the door. He had us wait while he disarmed what appeared to be a sophisticated alarm system.

"Shut the door, would you? And hang on one second. You're about to be attacked in 3...2..."

I heard the scrabble of claws on tile just before two slobbery bloodhounds came sliding around the corner and into the foyer.

Cassidy gasped, and I stepped in front of her...but then she laughed.

"They're gorgeous! What are their names?" she asked.

"Simon and Garfunkel," Ryder said, and I burst out laughing.

"That's perfect," I said, bending down to let the dogs check me out. I got a face full of slobber before they moved around me to press against Cassidy's legs as she laughed again. It was the first time I'd heard her laugh since meeting her last fall, and the sound gave me hope.

"I know, I know, I'll get you treats, you beasts. Hang on a minute." Ryder bent over and allowed the dogs to check out his scent. "My parents come over and feed them in the mornings and evenings if they know I'm working. I told them I didn't know when I'd be home, so they were over earlier. But these two will pretend like they haven't been fed in a year, just you watch."

"I don't blame them," Cassidy said. "They're gorgeous dogs." She smiled, leaning against me.

Ryder grinned and then wiped his gooey hand off on his pants. "Gross, but gorgeous. That's my boys."

I pulled Cassidy close, grateful she was still next to me. She hadn't left my side since we got out of the truck. I worried after that conversation in the blind that she'd be leery of me. I supposed there was still time for that to happen, so I was going to take whatever contact I could until that time. Until I told her everything.

"You two, go lay down," Ryder said to the dogs, then he gestured for us to follow him. "Let me show you guys where you can get cleaned up."

Ryder led us down a hallway to the right.

"I've got two rooms and an adjoining bathroom on this side," he said, pointing to the right as he ushered us into one of the rooms, "and my office and bedroom are on the other side here. Back that way," he said, pointing toward the foyer, "is the kitchen, living room, game room, etc. Cassidy, my sister-in-law left some of her clothes here in the dresser, and you're welcome to whatever you find. Howe, you're outta luck for anything other than shorts and t-shirts, I'm afraid."

"S'all right," I said with a shrug. "You can't help your short-man DNA."

"Yeah, well, we didn't call you Jolly Green Giant for nothin'. I'll go grab you some gear."

"Thanks, Frodo."

Ryder shoved me in the chest playfully and then left the room. Leaving us in all kinds of awkward.

"I'm guessing you want a shower," I said, raising my eyebrows.

"A shower sounds amazing."

I stood there, hands on my hips, dripping on Ryder's floor, stalled out. Which was not what she needed. "I don't want to crowd you, sweetheart, but you seem a little shaky—"

"Please." She lowered her head and swayed on her feet. I reached for her and she took my hand. "I don't want to be alone. They locked me in that room, and for two days no one came and I thought... I don't think I can be alone again and not lose it."

I started to hum to keep my mind on my task instead of on this bizarre situation.

"That was brilliant," Cassidy said. "You humming that song."

"'Kryptonite?' Well, I needed some way to let you know it was me, and you called me Superman."

She laughed, and I wished I was able to focus enough to break the Connection so I could see her smile.

She opened her eyes and turned to look at me, and I immediately saw the concentration on my own face. I looked like a huge dork. My tongue was sticking out the side of my mouth and curved up. I quickly pulled it back in. *Idiot.*

"You *are* Superman." Her gaze traveled over my wide shoulders and down my torso. I sensed her appreciation for what she saw, felt a shift in her mood from hesitant to...engaged. Oh, God, this was awkward. I'd forgotten I didn't have a damn shirt on. She tilted her head and looked at the spot where I'd been shot.

"It's barely there. Your scar." She reached out to my stomach and the moment she made contact, the Connection dropped, and suddenly I was staring down into her lovely face, which was now so close... mere inches. She swayed forward and her breast brushed against my arm.

We both gasped, and she gazed up at me, her lips parting, her chin lifted.

"Here, let me rinse this."

She turned away, her lips tilted up in amusement and she let her head fall back under the spray.

I shuddered at the feel of my fingers in her hair this time, taking the utmost care with her. When the water ran clear, I reached for the conditioner.

"Do you miss your hair?" she asked.

I gave an exaggerated sigh. "Yeah. So thanks for letting me wash yours. By the time it grows back out again, I'll probably forget how. I don't even know if I have the patience for the in-between stage."

"That's the worst," she said, her eyes closed again as I massaged her scalp. "Mmm, you can borrow mine anytime, that feels so good."

"At your service, sweetheart." It helped to talk. It kept my mind off of our proximity, off the hunger I'd felt from her as she stared at my bare chest. I knew I wasn't unattractive. There was a reason people gave me shit and called me pretty boy, but it was an entirely different matter to *feel* the way someone felt when they looked at me. To feel the way Cassidy felt.

It was time to rinse her hair again so I guided her back under the spray, taking care to keep the conditioner from running in her eyes. The cuts on her face had mostly healed to bright red marks, the deeper ones still holding the remnants of scabs. I thought perhaps Damien would be able to work his magic on her wounds and heal her, I just didn't know if it had been too long for him to be able to correct the more serious issue—her vision.

If her eyes were beyond repair, well, that would be the worst thing Rains had taken from her. Her ability to fly. From what I knew of her, being a pilot was interwoven with her identity. She wouldn't recover easily from that loss.

"You want to get out of those pants and have your turn?" she asked.

And there was the dilemma. If I took off my pants, barriers would be removed. She'd see all of me, including my response to being this close to her naked, although there was enough weight on this moment that I didn't think I'd embarrass myself by being fully erect. She'd also see the remnants of my wounds, the injuries that nearly cost me my life and forced me to retire from the service.

Maybe it would…I don't know, make her feel better? Or worse. I'd hate for her to pity me. I hadn't been naked in front of another person who wasn't a medical professional since I'd been injured.

That realization hit me hard and added a layer to this situation I hadn't considered. Was I ready to be exposed like that?

"Uh—"

"Oh, come on, Jackson. You've proven yourself to be the perfect gentleman, and like I said, I'm not modest."

"Maybe I am," I said with a laugh that I hoped covered my hesitation.

She gave me a fake-shocked expression…and it slowly melted into disbelief.

"I'm sorry," she said genuinely. "I don't want to make you uncom-fortable."

I smiled at her and reached for my belt. I unfastened it, undid my fly, and shoved the pants down, wincing a bit when I remembered the rusty metal shed.

CHAPTER 25
SAFETY

Cassidy

"What's wrong?"

I hadn't meant to bully Jackson into getting undressed. He'd been shirtless around me all day, and though I'd noticed the scars on his back, he hadn't seemed to be self-conscious or anything. I couldn't tell if he was actually uncomfortable, but then I'd seen it in his eyes. Worry. And then he'd grunted when he pulled his pants down.

"Oh, close encounter with some metal." He turned and tried to inspect the back of his thigh, but he couldn't get a good look. He yanked the pants the rest of the way off, along with a pair of boxers, and turned his back to me. "How bad is it?"

I gasped.

How bad was it? The poor man! If I'd thought the scars on his back were bad, that was nothing compared to what was below his waist.

The backs of his legs had deep, ropey scars that slashed through both calves and one thigh. And there was dried blood. A crusty wound about four inches long ran from the side of his left thigh under his glute. The skin around it was red and angry and seeping blood. I couldn't tell how deep it was, but I knew it needed to be cleaned immediately, although it might've been too late to avoid complications.

"Jesus, Jackson," I breathed, bending down to look closer. "How were you able… This looks painful!"

I glanced up and swallowed when I realized I had my hand on his perfect ass. I pulled it back and stood, trying to play it off like I hadn't just accosted him. He'd been so good about not touching me inappropriately and here I had a handful of his tan skin.

"I don't have a lot of feeling back there," he said with a shrug. "I felt it happen when I was getting out of the shed, but I didn't have time for any skin care routine, you feel me? I only wanted them to *think* I'd been blown to bits."

"Well, here," I said, moving him under the spray. "Do you need me to—"

"I think I've got it," he said with a wink. He reached for the bar of soap and under any other circumstances, I would have drooled over his male beauty.

His body was muscular, his arms powerful, his chest thick and broad, his shoulders wide and strong. From the front, his thighs were toned, but from the back they appeared misshapen, as though someone had taken an eraser and removed whole pieces of what should have been there. The deep grooves pulled the skin taut and the scars themselves were keloid in appearance. He must have been in agony when it happened.

"What…happened?"

Jackson glanced behind him. "What? Oh that? A little shrapnel. No biggie. Here, let me wash the blood off and then maybe you can tell me if you see bone or anything."

"Jackson!"

He laughed. "What? I don't think it needs stitches, and I really hope not, because letting Ryder go at my ass with a needle does not sound like a good time." He lathered up his hands and then reached back and ran his hand over the wound, his face scrunched up in obvious pain. It was enough to keep me from staring too long at his rippling obliques, his V, or…lower.

God, I was a horrible person.

"Thaaaat does not feel good. Wow. Okay, let me get the soap out." He pulled the nozzle down and hissed as he sprayed the wound directly.

"Be careful," I said, reaching out a hand. Like, what the hell was *I* going to do?

He hung the nozzle back up and blew out a breath. "Okay, how bad is it?"

I crept closer, hesitant to look, and crouched.

"Oh God." I was pretty sure I shouldn't be able to see fat cells. The cut welled with blood and it ran down the back of his leg. I pressed my lips together and looked away as I stood up.

"That doesn't sound good."

"You said Ryder's an EMT?"

"Yeah? Why?"

"I, uh, better go get him."

I reached for the towel he'd hung up for me and stepped out of the shower. I did a quick job drying off and wrapped the towel around me.

"Cassidy, wait."

I turned to say…something cheeky or encouraging, but I was rendered speechless by the view of him there under the spray, the worried expression on his face.

"No, you stay there. I'll be okay. I'll…be right back."

I hurried from the bathroom, ignoring the chill in the room and the pain in my shoulder as I pushed the door open to the hall.

"Ryder?" I called out, and then headed toward the kitchen, calling again.

I heard the scrabble of claws on the tile and was greeted by his gorgeous dogs.

"You two are so precious. Where's your daddy?"

"What's up?"

Ryder came out of the kitchen, and his eyes popped out at my current state of undress. Then he frowned, all businesslike.

"Um, Jackson needs you," I said. "He has a bad cut."

"Hm. He mentioned he might. Here, let me go get my first-aid kit."

I hurried back to the bedroom, the dogs hot on my heels. I went into the bathroom and Jackson had turned off the water. He cupped himself with his large hands. *God, he's incredible.*

"Ryder's coming," I said.

"Can you hand me a towel?" he asked, pointing at the far cabinet.

I held my towel closed with one hand and grabbed him one with the other. I turned to hand it to him and chuckled.

Simon and Garfunkel were sitting in the doorway. They were in the exact pose, their faces identical.

"I don't need more of an audience," Jackson said to them.

They gave him an uninterested glance and then focused on me.

"Here, let me grab these pajamas and I'll get out of the way," I said.

"Hey," he called.

I paused in the doorway.

"I'm...sorry, Cassidy."

"For what?"

He wrinkled his nose. "I'm sorry you had to see all this. I swear, I—"

"You'll always be my Superman," I said, giving him a brave smile, one I hadn't been sure I'd ever have again.

He shook his head and looked down at his feet. I heard him chuckling as I entered the bedroom.

"He in there?"

I turned to find Ryder trying not to look at me in a towel. Thank God I'd been fortunate enough to wind up with two gentlemen. It was such a relief after Esai and the other creepy men I'd been with at the compound.

Ugh. I hated even thinking about them.

"Yeah, he's waiting for you."

"Thanks. Move, beasts."

He stepped through the dogs' shoulders and they didn't budge, not until he pulled the door mostly closed. Then they came to me and plopped down on their hindquarters as if waiting for instructions.

"Well, hello there," I said, smiling at them. "Aren't you two the most handsome boys?"

One of them gave a little woof and his tail thumped on the ground.

I removed the towel and made quick work of pulling on the hippo pajamas, mindful of my shoulders. They were a little big, and a little short, but they were soft against my hypersensitive skin. Now that I was out of the shower, I shivered a bit. I glanced longingly at the bed, but I wanted to see if Jackson needed anything.

"Hey, do you need—"

I pushed the door open and froze.

Jackson stood, leaning on the counter with one hand and holding the towel in front of his groin with the other. Ryder was on his knees behind him.

"This might sting a little," Ryder said, before jabbing Jackson in his gorgeous ass with a needle, a wicked smile on his face.

"Motherfucking scum-sucking bastard that hurts!"

"Yeah, well, I'm not done. That's for the tetanus. I'm going to have to give you a local and stitch this shit up, although…you should probably see a doctor, dude. I don't like the color of this."

"I'm not going anywhere," Jackson said. "Just clean it up and slap a bandage on it or something so I don't bleed all over your damn house."

"Ooo, you're so cute when you hate me," Ryder said, and Jackson cursed some more under his breath. "I better stitch it. I think I've got some penicillin. I'll stick you with that too."

"Goddammit, I hate you," Jackson growled as Ryder dug around in his kit.

I let a giggle slip, and they both turned toward me.

Jackson's scowl was so comical, I couldn't help but laugh harder.

"I'm sorry, I just wanted to see if you two needed anything."

"Yeah, I need for him to not stick me with any more needles, the son of a bitch."

"Oh, you love me and you know it," Ryder said.

"Better shave it and get to it then."

"My pleasure, good buddy."

Ryder shaved the area carefully and gave Jackson a local, which brought forth an elaborate curse from Jackson, something about catching a parasite in the swamp in a prized body part that sounded terrifying. I watched him carefully stitch Jackson's thigh, doing the best he could with the jagged cut. He winced every time Jackson growled at him. It was obvious that despite the teasing, he hated hurting his friend and was worried about him.

After he'd finished close to twenty stitches, he placed a large gauze pad over the wound and then reached for the tape. "Cassidy? You mind being my extra set of hands?"

"Sure." I knelt beside him, sucking in a breath as my left knee touched the ground.

"Cassidy," Jackson warned.

"I'm fine."

He grumbled some more, and Ryder chuckled heartily.

"Here, can you cut me some tape? Four pieces."

I pulled the tape and cut, handing him the pieces as I went.

"All done. I'll send you a bill," he said as he pressed the last piece in place. Then he slapped Jackson's opposite ass cheek.

"Grrrr, I'm going to get you back, just you wait," Jackson said as Ryder climbed to his feet.

"Aw, quit your bitching. Now we're even for the shoulder," he said, his smile fading as he studied the back of Jackson's legs. "Although, if I'd known about the roadmaps you've got going on—"

"That'll be all, Captain Simms," Jackson said, giving him a look that said *we'll talk about this later*.

"I've about had my fill of your ass in my face anyway. You two want something to eat? I don't have a whole lot, but I can whip up some comfort food if you're hungry."

Jackson looked at me, his eyebrows raised. "What do you want, Cassidy? You want to eat or get some sleep?"

"I could eat," I said, suddenly really hungry. I'd forgotten about food until now, and once my stomach got the message that food was near, it would not be placated.

Jackson gestured for us to exit the bathroom. "What the lady needs, the lady shall have. Now if you two will give me one tiny ounce of dignity, I'll meet you in the kitchen."

He made eye contact with me to make sure I would be okay without him for a minute, and I nodded.

Such a gentleman.

The dogs were at my side the moment we stepped out of the bath-room and they followed us to the kitchen.

"I think I've got some bachelor food, some cans of soup, some Kraft Mac and Cheese—"

"That sounds like heaven."

He grinned. "Coming right up."

He started pulling out the necessary tools to make the creamy food of the gods a reality, and I watched closely, trying to keep my stomach growls to a minimum.

"Sure glad we got you out of there okay," he said as he filled a pot with water, covered it, and then set it on a gas burner to boil. "Those sons of bitches were no joke. Me and my boys been out in the woods watching since Jackson got himself recruited, and I didn't have a good feeling about the outcome. We had a hard time keeping the damn FBI guys from barging in there, but once I got intel on that weapons shed, I knew we had to wait or…"

He trailed off, as if he realized he was headed in a dark direction with that train of thought.

"I'm so grateful, I can't even tell you."

"I'm just so damn sorry it took so long. When Howe showed up and told me what happened, and then we found your plane? I didn't have high hopes, I'll tell you that. I don't know how you survived that crash."

I sighed and hugged myself with my arms. "Me either. The nurse at the compound, Irene, she was real good to me. If it weren't for her, I'm not sure I would have made it." I sat up a little straighter. "Do you know what happened to her? She and her daughter Denise escaped just before I connected with Jackson. Denise had just given birth. She had a newborn with her."

Ryder rubbed at the stubble on his chin. "I'm not sure, but I bet Barringer, the FBI agent, would know. He's the lead on this situation. He's the one who got Jackson into the camp. Young guy, but he knows his shit, especially about the cult stuff."

I shuddered. "Well, then I'll have to thank him too."

Ryder checked the water and then ripped the box open. "I think we can get him to come out here tomorrow to interview you two. I hate for you to have to go anywhere. You're gonna eat this delicious and nutritious meal and then I bet you crash for about eighteen hours."

I laughed. "I feel like I could sleep for a week, you're right about that."

Ryder stirred the macaroni and smiled. "I thought he'd lost it when he showed up. Jackson? I hadn't seen him since we was discharged around the same time. He got out of Walter Reed and went off to work at that fancy school, and I came home."

"How long ago was that?"

Ryder frowned for a minute. "About two years ago? Maybe longer? I lose track of time down here. Usually just dealing with injured hunters and drunk morons traipsing around in the swamp. Then Jackson shows up, talking about your plane going down, and how he was having visions. Thought he was fucked up or something, hallucinating."

"What do you mean, visions? Did he tell you how he knew where to find me?"

The timer went off, and Ryder turned off the fire. He carried the pot over to the sink and used the lid to drain the water.

"I told him that Joanna had Seen you."

Jackson stood next to the counter beside me. Ryder turned around and the two of them exchanged a look that left me feeling nauseated.

What the hell is he keeping from me?

"Yeah, and he was a mess. Hadn't slept, hadn't eaten. Hey, just like right now." Ryder laughed it off and stirred in the milk, butter, and cheese powder.

Jackson bumped me with his elbow. "You need anything for your pain, sweetheart? Some Advil?"

I shook my head, fully aware he was trying to distract me. "I'm fine."

He gave me a small smile and then asked Ryder where the bowls and silverware were. I watched the two of them work together and had the faintest thought that they'd probably been really close at one time. They moved around each other like a well-oiled machine. Maybe tomorrow, after I'd had some rest, I could get them talking about the younger versions of themselves. I wanted to know more about Jackson, and Ryder sure seemed willing to share embarrassing stories. As long as they were safe, I guessed.

There was definitely something Jackson wasn't telling me about all of this, and as much as his presence was a soothing balm for my battered self, I couldn't totally relax.

What if there was something more to him being in the right place? At the right time?

What if he'd actually been working with Rains…?

No, that was ridiculous. And Delaney had told me many times that she trusted him completely.

Then what was this uneasiness about?

Jackson handed me a bowl of cheesy goodness and smiled.

"I'm sure I would have made it better, but you know what they say about beggars." He winked at me as Ryder cursed.

"Whatever, Howe. You really want to start with the stories? Cuz you know I've got a bounty of them."

"And I want to hear them all," I said, slipping a spoonful of deliciousness into my mouth. I moaned at the taste, then had to rein myself in before I began shoveling the stuff in my face.

Jackson and Ryder traded a few more jabs as I leaned over my bowl and let the scent wash over me, taking me back to days spent at Delaney's as kids, her mom fixing us Mac and Cheese for lunch. I could never resist, even though I knew when I got home I'd be in big trouble for accepting food from her family. I'd stay as late as possible before running all the way home, terrified I'd miss my curfew and be told I couldn't play with Delaney anymore. Her house was my safe place, my comfort zone. I always wished I never had to leave.

"Hey, there. Easy."

Jackson slid his arms around me and lifted me up.

"Hmmm? What?"

"You fell asleep over your Mac. I'm just going to take you to bed, all right?"

I let my head loll against his shoulder and yawned. "That's the best Mac and Cheese I've ever had in my life."

Jackson chuckled and then slowed to ease through the doorway. He set me down gently on the bed, and I felt two jerks to the mattress.

"Oh, where do you two think you're going?"

I opened one eye and smiled. Simon and Garfunkel had decided to join me.

"You two, come on out of there," Ryder said from the doorway.

The dogs looked at him with their long expressions as though he'd lost his damn mind.

"It's okay," I said. "They can stay."

Ryder grumbled about loyalty and obedience, and Jackson walked out into the hall with him.

"Jackson?"

"Yeah, sweetheart?"

I loved that he called me that. It felt like more than just a generic term of endearment when he said it. Or maybe I was fooling myself.

"Are you coming back?"

He stood in the doorway, the hall light illuminating his big body that took up most of the frame. He'd thrown on a t-shirt and a pair of loose sweatpants that were too short, so he'd bunched them up below his knees.

"Is that what you want?"

I looked around the dark room. It was nothing like the room at the compound. The dogs' panting shook the bed, their rhythmic movements soothing.

"I can grab some extra blankets and crash on the floor—"

"No, please. You need rest, too."

He rested his hands on his hips and shifted his weight. "I don't want to crowd you, Cassidy."

"You're not. I'm asking."

He blew out a breath through his nose and nodded. "Yeah, all right. Let me just go check in with Ryder. I'll be right there."

I should have cared. I should have been embarrassed that I'd basically begged him to go to bed with me. I should have had some fucking pride, but I was beyond all of that.

I turned to lay down on the queen-size bed and stretched out my legs. I had just enough space to slide my feet between the two dogs. The sheets were soft, the bed was comfortable, the room smelled like...well, a house. Not rotting vegetation, brackish water, and whatever the hell other dank odors came from the damn swamp.

I groaned. I just wanted to forget about that place. Forget about that horrible man. Forget about that awful room and the terror I'd felt at being in the dark and thinking I would die alone. I'd never had issues being on my own until this. I'd lived alone for years before marrying Robert. I could handle it.

"Yeah, she's right here, hang on."

Jackson came trotting back into the room. He had his hand over a phone.

"I'm so busted. I forgot to call Delaney the second you were safe and now she won't believe me that you're okay. You feel up to talking to her for a few minutes."

"Sure," I said, pushing myself up to a sitting position once more. My whole body ached, and Jackson must have seen it on my face.

"I'm bringing you some Advil, okay?"

I smiled at him and mouthed "thank you" as he handed me the phone.

"Hey," I said, bracing myself for the onslaught.

Instead, I heard sobs.

"Oh, Cassidy, I'm so sorry! I feel awful that you were affected by any of this! Are you okay? I'm going to get a flight down there—"

"Hey, shhh. It's okay. I'm okay…or at least I will be."

"Jackson said you're hurt. I'm so sorry! I want you to come stay with me. Will you do that? And I'll take care of you?"

My breath caught. I didn't really have a lot of alternatives. I definitely didn't want to stay with my parents. At some point I would have to contact them and let them know I was safe, but I didn't want to see them. My parents still practiced a version of Christianity that believed in a lot of the same shit Rains taught his people, and if I never heard another Bible reference, it would be too soon.

My brother? No, he had no room in his life for drama. He'd expect me to suck it up and move on. And if Rains was to be believed, my crash pad was no longer available. Not that it was any sort of home. I'd been planning to move out of LA, still considering my options…

The truth was, Delaney was the most important person in my life, and I wanted to be close to her, even though right now I had a lot of tough questions to ask. The answers to those questions would determine whether she *continued* to be the most important person in my life.

"Cassidy?"

"Sorry. I'm here. I do want to see you, but don't come here. Let me talk to Jackson after we get some sleep. I know we have to talk to the FBI. Let me...can I call you tomorrow? After I know more?"

"Sure, of course. I'm sorry. I'm so glad Jackson is there with you. He's behaving, right?" She huffed a laugh. "I know he can be intense."

Jackson was currently standing next to the bed with his arms crossed, a frown marring his forehead.

I grinned. "Yeah, he's intense, but he's been a perfect gentleman. I'm in good hands."

He ran one of those hands over his mouth and looked away, smiling. He went into the bathroom and shut the door.

"I'm glad. He's such a good man. And Cassidy...he was beside himself when you went missing. He took off immediately to come find you, but it sounds like he hit some red tape when he got down there."

"But he doesn't even know me," I said, still confused. "Why would he come all this way for someone he's only just met? Risk his life? I still don't get it."

"Has he, um, talked to you? About...about how we knew what happened?"

And speaking of tough questions.

"Very little. Delaney, I'm going to need to know. I have so many questions."

"I know you do, and I'm sorry. There's a lot I haven't been at liberty to tell you, and I *hate* that I couldn't tell you, but you understand how important confidentiality is to my work."

"Of course I do, but Del, this is different."

"You're right," she said. "It's very different. And I'll tell you everything, but I want you to see it for yourself. I want you to come here, to Havenhart."

I exhaled and slid down in the bed, unable to hold my head up any longer. "Yeah, okay. I'll think about it. As soon as we're cleared to go,

I'll let you know." I barked out a very unattractive laugh. "It's not really like I have anywhere else to go."

"I'm so sorry, Cass. I hate that this past year has tossed you around like a lost sock in the dryer, but I promise—come here. I'll take care of you until you're ready to make some permanent decisions. You can stay with me, or we can get you set up in the bungalow next door. Remember the one you stayed in? It's still vacant. The headmaster wants you to know his offer of employment still stands."

My throat felt thick and my nose burned. "Thank you. I've gotta go, Delaney. I'll call you tomorrow." I was about to lose it if this conversation continued.

"Hey, I love you, girl. I'll see you soon, okay? And if you change your mind, I can be down there in a few hours."

"Love you, too."

I hung up the phone before she could say anything else. Jackson came out of the bathroom, where he'd clearly been trying to give me privacy to talk to Delaney.

"Here's your phone," I said, holding the thing out like it was on fire. I hadn't been ready for that conversation, and the shakes were back.

"Hey," he said, sitting on the edge of the bed next to me. He took my hand in his. "What happened?"

"I'm just not…ready. She wanted to come down here, she asked me questions…Jackson, I'm… I want time to stop for a little while. I know it can't forever…"

"I get it," he said, brushing my hair back from my face. "I get it. Real life will be here soon enough. Sweetheart, let me hold it off for you. Call me your reality bodyguard, all right? Let me shield you from all I can."

"Why do you always make me feel better?" I asked him, scooting over and patting the mattress next to me. "You know what I need before I do."

He looked down at the spot I'd just vacated and his warm expression faded to one of wariness. "Are you sure? I can take the floor—"

"Jackson, are you with someone? Like…do you have a girlfriend?"

"No! Why would you think that?"

"Because I get the sense that I'm asking you to do something that goes against your morals or something."

He exhaled, swore under his breath and then pulled off his t-shirt. "Well, when you put it that way." He slid into bed next to me, taking the spot I'd made for him and upsetting Simon. Or Garfunkel. Whichever it was, they walked over my legs and curled up behind me, pressed against my back. I was grateful for the warmth.

"Jackson, I'm—"

"Shhh. Come here," he said, sliding his arm under my head and pulling me against his body.

I can't even begin to describe the relief, the peace, the comfort I found in his arms. I'd felt safe with him from the moment we escaped together. Actually, before that. From the moment he'd hummed that Superman song and I realized it was him. Or even further back, from the time he'd held me after Delaney was shot.

I'd barely known him then, I barely knew him now, but he was the embodiment of safety and warmth. I knew instinctively that I could trust him, although I also knew I was pushing my worries about him to the back of my mind.

He was still keeping something from me. And tonight, I wanted him to continue keeping it away.

"I'm not going to attack you, I swear."

"I know you won't attack me," he sighed. "You fell asleep in your Mac and Cheese. I think my virtue is pretty safe."

I snorted and snuggled closer, my forehead pressed against his neck. "Fine. Call it a temporary reprieve. I'm a known virtue-taker."

He gave a deep belly laugh, and I loved the sound of it. I ran my hand over his chest to his other shoulder, and he sighed.

"In any other situation, my virtue would be yours for the taking."

"Wait...we're not talking about real virtue, are we?" I asked him. I knew he had a sense of humor, but I didn't want to be an ass and assume. I knew nothing about his past. For all I knew he might not even find me attractive. Not that I have a huge ego or anything, but I was pretty sure he felt the chemistry between us.

"Well, if you mean the virtue of a forty-something guy who hasn't had sex in at least, oh...what decade is it?"

"That long, huh?"

"Well, I haven't been with anyone since a fucking bomb ripped me to shreds, so at least three years? Wow. Yeah. I got blown up three years ago. After rehab and retirement, I went to Havenhart, which requires me to act virtuous at all times."

"Damn. Yeah, you're definitely virtuous. Well, if it makes you feel any better, I can measure my virtue in almost a year as well."

He held up a fist and I bumped it with mine.

"Here's to virtue."

I laughed. "To virtue."

He rubbed my back and we both fell quiet. I almost thought he'd fallen asleep until he rolled onto his side and pulled me against his chest.

"I'm here for you as long as you need, however need. I'll keep you safe…even from myself. Okay? We're on your schedule here."

I sighed and snuggled closer, slipping my knee between his thighs. "See? Superman."

"Goodnight, sweetheart."

The last thing I remembered was him humming the tune and running his fingers lightly up and down my spine.

CHAPTER 26
CRUSHED

Jackson

I didn't think I'd sleep at all, holding Cassidy all night, but at some point I stopped warring with myself over the propriety of my actions and accepted that whatever she needed from me, I'd give her…and I'd deal with the heartache when she was ready to move on.

Because I wasn't fooling myself that, despite finding my one, even though this felt like everything good and right in the world, and even though she was everything I'd ever thought I could possibly want in a woman…she was already lost to me.

I hadn't missed her comments. I knew she saw me as a temporary hiding place, something to keep the real world from encroaching until she was ready. And her real world didn't involve anything like communicating through telepathy, healing through energy exchanges, or the ability to form a psychic link with someone through a simple handshake.

Jesus. She was never going to accept this. It would be better for me to hold her at arm's length, be there for her however she needed, and then let her go when she was ready to spread her wings. I'd survived Delaney finding Damien, I could survive Cassidy—

Yeah, fuck that.

Delaney had been a schoolboy crush. Cassidy would crush me.

And no amount of bourbon at Shenanigans would be enough.

Unlike the others in my life who I'd had the same experience with, she touched a part of me I never shared with anyone and drew me further into her existence.

Eventually, though, my body was tired of fighting, at least for this night. I crashed hard, but then I dreamed of some crazy shit. Running. I dreamed of running like my life depended on it, but I didn't know if I was running from something or to something, or someone. I was tired, my lungs burned, and I felt like it was too late, that *I* was too late. And it didn't make any difference. I couldn't stop it. Or get away from it. Or get to it.

I woke up covered with sweat and panting, feeling trapped.

And then I smiled.

Cassidy was still wrapped around me, her legs tangled with mine. Simon or Garfunkel was laying behind my bent legs on top of the blanket so I was well and truly trapped. And wasn't that fitting.

I heard kissing noises from the hallway and the dogs got up and stretched. They stood on the bed, wagging their tails, not wanting to leave their charge.

"I know how you feel, boys, but nature calls."

Ryder kissed at them once more, and they groaned before hopping down from the bed and woofed as they passed him in the doorway.

"Sorry to wake you," he whispered. "You need anything?"

I pushed myself up and rubbed at my face. "Yeah, I need to pee like a damn racehorse."

I stood and stretched, wincing when the bandage on the back of my thigh pulled at the hairs on my leg.

"Yeah, probably should have shaved that area. We can get you fixed up after breakfast."

"Shit. You're enjoying this."

Ryder grinned. "I missed you, Howe. I forgot how much you hate needles."

He took off with the dogs and I stretched out my back. Cassidy stirred in her sleep, and I tucked the blankets around her. I thought I'd make her a plate, bring her breakfast in bed. Then started fantasizing that maybe we could make our way to one of them fancy resorts in Miami and I could get her all pampered, treat her to some luxury and shit. I'd do anything for her.

And wasn't that a bitch.

"Jackson?"

God, I loved the way she said my name. "Yeah, sweetheart?" I needed to pee, but I needed to care for her even more. I sat down on the bed next to her and she started to stretch, then winced and grabbed her left arm.

"I need to remember not to do that."

"I think it would be good to get you some medical attention today. What do you think?"

She pulled the blanket over her head. "Uh-uh."

"Uh-uh?" Damn, she was cute.

"Uh-uh. I don't wanna." She pulled the blanket down with a huff. "I know, I know, I can't hide forever."

"You can hide as long as you want. I'm not going to make you do anything you don't want to do," I said. "Well, except eat some breakfast, but I'll bring it to you so you can keep hiding."

Her smile lit off that hopeful feeling in my chest and, warning bells be damned, I let myself feel hope.

She reached for my arm and gave it a squeeze. "Thank you. I know I have to face the music, though. Delaney wants me to come back to the school with you."

Another hopeful beat of my heart. "What do you think about that?"

She blew out a breath. "I don't know. I have a feeling there's a whole lot about that school that's not going to sit right with me."

And the hope melted into a puddle and ran down a storm drain.

"Look, I'm not going to tell you that it's all unicorns and rainbows there. Or maybe it is. Unicorns and rainbows are things that aren't supposed to be real, right? But we love them, we think of them as being peaceful. Beautiful. But life is ugly. And the people at Havenhart? They've seen a lot of ugly. They deserve unicorns and rainbows, and that's why I work there. I don't know if I'm making any sense."

She watched me closely, her frown severe. "I don't want to go from one place where they were trying to manipulate me to another one. It's going to be a long time before I trust anyone again."

Hope. Gone. *Poof.*

I held up a finger and walked into the bathroom. I needed to relieve myself and think for a minute. I didn't want to fuck this up, and I felt like I had one chance to come clean with her, or else she'd slip through my fingers. It wasn't about me, though; it was about her having someone to trust. How fucked up would it be if she leaned on me and I pulled the rug out from under her?

I was washing my hands when I heard a scream.

I nearly tore the door of the hinges to get to her.

"Gimme it back!"

I slumped against the doorframe in relief. "Apparently, those two aren't going to let you hide anymore."

Simon and Garfunkel had ahold of the blanket and Cassidy was trying to pull it back from them—and losing.

"Don't hurt your shoulder," I said, whistling for the dogs to let go, which they did, and then they went outside the room and sat on their haunches in the hallway.

Ryder came running. "Aw, hell. I'm sorry, Cassidy. I taught them some bad manners. They do that to get me out of bed on my days off."

Cassidy was hanging off the bed, cracking up. "It's fine," she said, gasping for breath. "They're the best. I loved sleeping with them last night. Do they sleep with you?"

"Hell no. I don't let them on my bed." But Ryder's smirk let us know he was full of shit. "Breakfast is getting cold."

"Thanks, man."

He took the dogs and left us alone.

Cassidy smiled up at me, but then it slowly faded. "Why do you look like you're about to tell me there's no Santa Claus?"

"I wouldn't dream of telling you such falsehoods," I said, but I shook my head. "About before...I know you don't trust easily, and I'm not going to push you to. And I have things to tell you, but I'd like to get you fed. Why don't we eat and then talk? Then I can give you some space to decide what you want to do next. I'm going to reach out to Barringer, the FBI agent, but if you're not ready to talk to him, you don't have to. I promised you last night I'd keep everything away from you as long as I could."

She pushed herself off the bed and walked over to me. "Jackson, you can't hold back the whole world. Even Superman...well, yeah, *he* can. But I don't expect that. I appreciate you. I...yeah. I just want you to know, no matter what, I will always be grateful for you." She placed her hands on my shoulders and stood on her toes to kiss my cheek. "Thank you."

She went into the bathroom and closed the door.

And I remembered to breathe.

The peace lasted long enough for her to have seconds of bacon and biscuits.

Barringer didn't wait for us to make contact. Ryder let him in, and he went straight to Cassidy.

"Boy, am I glad to see you." He stuck out a hand. "Special Agent Todd Barringer."

"Thanks for helping Jackson get to me," she said, shaking his hand.

I moved to her side, ready to shield her from Barringer if he pressed her before she was strong enough to talk. She leaned into me, just enough to reassure herself, and she crossed her arms over her chest.

"Good to see you, Jackson. I brought your stuff," he said, setting a manila envelope on Ryder's counter, along with my guns and my hunting knife. "I won't take too much time, at least not today, because I know you need rest, but I wanted to see if you need anything else?"

"I do want to know... Did you find two women and a baby?"

Barringer looked at me and then back at Cassidy. "Yes, ma'am. They're in protective custody. We took mother and child to the hospital to be checked out and they're under observation." He smiled. "They asked if you were safe."

"Thank God," Cassidy said, bringing her hands up to her face. "I couldn't believe she gave birth and then took off running."

"Sounds like you were instrumental in helping them escape. But how are you? Irene was concerned about your injuries."

Cassidy smiled, but I saw her lower lip quiver when she spoke. "I'm okay. The worst is probably my shoulder. Well, and my eyes. Between the crash and the fall, I got pretty banged up, but Irene saved my life. Helping her deliver her grandson was the least I could do."

I wrapped my arms around her and she grabbed my forearms, almost to shield herself.

Barringer seemed curious about us. I told him we'd met before briefly, but stressful situations change dynamics. That's what he could continue to think.

"So, I won't keep you long, but I do need to get statements from both of you. Can we do that? Do you feel up to it, Miss Mackenzie?"

She sighed, and I squeezed her to let her know it was up to her.

"Yeah, okay," she said, her shoulders shrinking in.

He looked between us. "He can stay with you, if that helps. Howe, I can debrief you after her. I have some questions."

"Oh, I bet you do. I hope none of your men were hurt?"

He shook his head and barked out a laugh. "Only my informant, one Retired Captain Luke Stephens, who died in the blast. May he rest in peace."

I grinned. "Helluva blast, huh?"

Barringer shook his head. "Jesus, Howe. You're one lucky sucker."

"Not totally lucky," Ryder chimed in. "You should see his ass."

Barringer's eyes shot to mine. "You injured?"

"I'll live. I might be gangrenous, but at least I won't get tetanus, thanks to that asshole."

"You need to see a doctor. Why don't I take you in?"

I shook my head. "And let Ryder miss out on the fun of sticking me with his needles? I think he's got some more drugs he wants to stab me with."

Ryder rubbed his hands together. "Yes! *Please* let me do the penicillin. It'll hurt like a bitch."

I rolled my eyes. "Fine. And then you can finish shaving this mess off my head. This black shit looks like shoe polish."

Cassidy covered her mouth to hide the giggles.

"What? You want to get in on this?"

"Yeah, it's not really your color. I like the blond much better."

I held out my hands. "The lady has spoken."

The next few hours were filled with a lot of talking. I learned a few new things that nearly sent me on a homicidal rampage: some of the men had tried to use the kids as shields to escape the compound; two women admitted that they'd been sexually assaulted by Esai; and speaking of Esai, he and Rains were nowhere to be found.

"Don't worry," Barringer said when he got a load of my anger. I knew my face and neck were red. "The info we got from Irene and Denise, and that guy Lance who was with them, will help us. That, and what you two heard. I'm already in contact with agents in Oregon and California. We're putting together a task force to bring down the rest of this organization. And," he said, raising an eyebrow, "we've got Abel Rains in custody. And he says he will tell us whatever we want to know."

"Yeah, lotta good that's going to do," I said, pushing away from the counter.

"Jackson." Cassidy had been sitting on a stool the whole time, and she looked ready to fall over.

"Hey, why don't we take a break and I'll take you back to bed. You could use a nap."

"No, I'm okay, but I wanted to say…Abel is different. I could tell."

I frowned. "What do you mean?"

She took a deep breath. "He's…innocent. Yeah, he believes all the crazy dogma, but he *really* believes. He's naïve. I think he's ignorant of the shady shit Rains is into. He was never allowed into the house, and that's where Rains held all of his meetings with Esai and people on the phone. He kept Abel away from it all."

Barringer and I exchanged a look.

"I'm serious, I can tell when people are bullshitting me. I don't think he knew about the plans. I never heard him speak about anything other than the scriptures and, like, their beliefs."

"That's kind of what I get from him, too," Barringer said. "He could be telling the truth."

"Or he could be as big a manipulator as his father," I said, clenching my jaw. "If you'd seen what Rains did to his daughter…" But then, Joanna was also an innocent. It could very well be that Rains kept his own children out of the plans and only used them for their gifts.

"That brings me to what I wanted to ask you," Barringer said. "I'd like to talk to Joanna."

I stiffened. "No."

The three of them raised their eyebrows at me.

"Excuse me? No?" Barringer was not pleased. It seemed his nice-guy understanding bit only went so far when it came to his investigation.

"No. Joanna is finally moving on with her life. She doesn't need to get pulled back into this mess."

Mr. Howe.

Oh, God. Not now.

"No."

But Mr. Howe! I want to help.

"I said *no*."

"And we heard you," Ryder said, moving closer to me, a frown on his face.

"It's bad enough Cassidy has to go through this—"

"Jackson—"

Mr. Howe, I want to know. I want to know about the plans and...about my brother.

"I said *no*, Joanna!"

Fuck.

"She's talking to you," Cassidy said. "Like in the woods. I wasn't imagining that. She...she talks to you. How?"

"Howe, I'm not going to put her in danger—"

"Bullshit. She's in danger just by you knowing where she is!"

Mr. Howe—

I turned away and smacked the wall on my way out of the kitchen. I needed to breathe. I needed to think.

I had to keep them safe, not bring them further into this.

I went out the front door and down the steps to the gravel driveway. I forgot I was barefoot until I tried kicking some of the gravel.

"Son of a bitch!"

"Jackson?"

Cassidy stood on the porch, her arms still wrapped around herself.

"I'm sorry. But I don't want to put her through any more. She's just a *kid*. She didn't deserve to be put through the shit he put her through. None of you. Her, Delaney, you—"

"Jackson, how did you find me?"

My stomach turned to lead.

"Somehow, this girl talks to you in your head. But there's something else."

I really wanted to kick something, throw something, scream…

I sighed. "Yeah, there's something else." I planted my hands on my hips and sucked in a breath through my nose, trying to find my calm center or whatever Morgan called it.

Fuck. I couldn't lose it. Not in front of Cassidy.

"Tell me. Please."

"Sweetheart, if I tell you…let's just say I know you're not going to be okay with it, and I know you need to trust someone right now. If I tell you…I doubt it's going to be me any longer."

She stared at me as if to say she wouldn't ask me again.

Morgan's breathing shit wasn't going to help me now.

"Do you remember when we first met?"

She smiled. "I do. You shocked me when I shook your hand."

"You felt it too?"

She nodded.

"What if I told you…that was no static electricity? That the current you felt was something real, something way more powerful?"

She frowned. "Are we talking physics or psychic phenomena?"

"A little of both? I don't know why, I don't know how, but Cassidy…I'm different."

"Right. Superman," she said with a laugh. I could tell it was a show of bravery, that she was just as worried as I was about what I was going to say next.

"It's not a superpower, and it's not really the gift that the headmaster considers it to be. And sometimes it just plain sucks to be like this. Like me. But what happened between us? When we met? It's the reason I was able to find you."

"What are you saying?"

It was my turn to try laughter to break the tension. It didn't work. "Sweetheart, when I say we Connected, I'm not trying to be all corny like a romcom. It's not me trying to be romantic, although it felt that way for me. *Feels* that way for me. Cassidy..." I took a deep breath and stepped off the cliff.

"When I say Connected, I mean we were linked. I make Connections with people. It's different each time, how much I'm affected, and with you it was instant, it was powerful...and it scared the hell out of me."

"Connections?"

"Yeah. When I Connect with people, I can see them. I can see their past, their thoughts, what they're doing, what they're feeling. It's like surveillance cameras, monitors in a hospital room, a wireless mic. And usually I can control it. I can flip a mental switch and tune in or out. But with you? It hit me like...well...like a goddamn plane crash."

Cassidy placed her hands on the railing and gripped so hard, her knuckles turned white. "I don't... How?"

"I have no idea, Cassidy, and honestly, it's haunted me ever since I saw my father put a fucking gun to his head and pull the trigger, miles away from where I was. I can't control who I Connect with. I can usually turn it off...but not with you."

"Jackson."

If I kept talking, I feared I'd turn into the raving lunatic I'm sure she thought I was, but I couldn't stop the words from tumbling out of my mouth.

"I tasted the smoke. I felt the glass cut my face. I sensed your panic when you thought you couldn't get out." I swallowed hard. "I saw you look back at that evil wench in the skirt impaled by the fucking tree, and I knew you thought about trying to save her before you realized it was too late."

My chest was on fire, my throat was raw, and any minute now she was going to run.

"I was *with* you when that plane crashed, Cassidy. I was with you while you agonized over whether to take any more phone calls from your ex-husband. I felt your terror at seeing Delaney nearly die. And I panicked with you, surrounded by strangers you couldn't see, in a place you couldn't escape—and I *had* to find you. I've always hated my gift. But goddamn, I am so glad I Connected with you. So glad I was able to find you."

Cassidy's expression was blank. After long, agonizingly silent seconds, she stepped back from the railing, toward the door.

"Cassidy?"

She turned and walked into the house without a word.

I sank down on the gravel, ignoring the cut to my fucked-up legs.

I'd done the right thing. I'd told her my truth...and she'd walked away.

I had to let her. She'd hate me, think I was a freak, and probably beg Barringer to take her away. It was probably a good thing he was here. She could trust him in title at least, as a sworn officer of the law. Ryder, too, for that matter.

But she'd never trust me. Not now.

For a moment, I was tempted to open the Connection...see what she was thinking and feeling, but that would be the worst betrayal of all.

Instead, I locked it up tight, closing all of the mental barriers against her that I could still access in my exhausted state.

I'm sorry, Mr. Howe. I'm so sorry.

Tears stung my eyes at the pain in Joanna's voice.

But I closed her out, too.

I was alone in my consciousness.

And wasn't that damned fitting?

CHAPTER 27
PIECES

Cassidy

The FBI agent met me just inside the front door.

"Is everything—"

"No, it's not, but let's get this over with. Please."

"Is Jackson coming back?"

I walked into the kitchen and sat back down on the barstool at the counter. My gaze darted to Ryder, and he seemed to understand that he should check on Jackson. He moved swiftly toward the front door.

"What do you need me to tell you?"

Barringer sat down across from me. "I'm sorry, Cassidy. I know this is awful timing, but I really need to know what you know. If you have any information that could help us find them…"

"All I know is what Jackson and I heard just before Ryder found us. He mentioned someone named John, and he talked about a clan in California and a community in Oregon. Before that, when I was locked in the room next to his office, he and Esai spoke in soft voices, so it was hard to hear everything, but the plan was that when the child was born, Denise's baby, it would be the second-to-last sign before an interloper would come in and divide the camp, which would kick off his stupid holy war. He had a list of cities, I'm not sure if I can remember them all, but they were going to attack them with bombs. But Jackson said he blew up all of their weapons, so maybe that last part won't happen?"

Barringer stopped writing on his little notepad and his pencil dangled in the air above the paper. "But if they have other locations, California and Oregon, chances are they have more weapons. The question is, will he go ahead and play his twisted game if not all of his chess pieces are on the board?"

"That's a good question. He often seemed very cold and calculating, but as Denise got closer to having the baby, he started to get violent. Angry. His control was slipping. I swear..." My throat went dry and I grabbed for my orange juice and swallowed half the glass.

"It's okay, Cassidy. Take a minute."

I set the cup down harder than I meant to because my hand was shaking.

"I swear he was going to kill Denise after she delivered the baby. And I'm pretty sure I would have been right behind her, since I had no intention of letting him cut me into pieces to send to that school where they have his daughter."

Barringer's jaw twitched, and he cracked the knuckles on his right hand. "Thank God Howe was able to get to you first."

The massive breakfast I'd shoveled into my face now felt like dead weight in my gut. Like it was wrong, like it shouldn't be there, and I worried I was going to vomit it up.

"Do you believe that psychic powers are real?"

Now I sounded disturbed.

"You mean the girl? Joanna? If I didn't believe him about her before, I do now that he found you, and things were exactly as he predicted they would be. I've read Rains' file, too. Guy is unbelievably slippery. How he managed to escape from maximum security in Texas, of all places, and then fake his death in Louisiana...seems to me he's capable of just about anything."

I thought back to the first time I'd been brought to him. "He does this thing...I don't know, maybe I was still fucked up from the crash."

"Tell me."

"Rains made me leave the infirmary after a couple days, had me brought to him. I'm not sure if I realized it then or later that he was the one who'd orchestrated the whole thing—that he'd sent the women to abduct me. But that first time I met him alone, he sat me on a couch in his office, I couldn't see much. My vision was worse then; now I can see shapes and some detail, but things are blurry and I have some dark spots.

"Anyway, he started asking me questions, and I just felt…wrong. I wasn't sure at first how much of that feeling was my natural dislike of organized religion or just him, but as he was talking in that way of his…you know, people who like, try to hypnotize you with their voice? I felt, like, cold fingers snaking around my neck and something was trying to get *into* me. I know it sounds insane, and again, I'd just been in a plane crash, Agent Barringer, so believe me, I know how wild this sounds."

Agent Barringer put his hand on top of mine on the counter, and I knew instinctively that he wasn't about to commit me or be condescending in any way.

"Rains has years of manipulating people under his belt. Psychic powers or not, he knows how to get under people's skin. He's done it for a long time to a lot of parishioners. He's bilked thousands of people of their life savings. He's swayed whole congregations to join in his teachings. He always moves on before the authorities can catch up to him, but the FBI has records that go back at least twenty years, Cassidy. We've had him in custody a few times, but somehow he gets away, either escapes or talks his way out of punishment. If I can convince him, I'm going to get Jackson to let me speak with Joanna, and then I've got permission from the higher ups to dedicate a task force to bringing him down."

He pulled his hand back and ran it through his hair, and I could see the strain on him. I imagined it was hard for someone like him, who leads a life of chasing bad guys and protecting good folks, to imagine a person like Rains gaining so much power.

"I don't believe in the whole psychic *woo woo* stuff," I said. "I guess that's the hardest thing for me. Accepting that what happened out there was anything other than a good con man and a bunch of gullible, ignorant people who followed him and did his bidding."

"Cassidy, I've studied cults and groups who use manipulation tactics for years. I did my master's thesis for my criminal justice degree on Scientology. I'm telling you, there are other forces at work sometimes. We do blame the victims in our society, but I think education is the best way to prevent it from happening. Children should receive training in how to question what's being taught to them, they should understand programming like what Rains and his teachings are all about. Young people are susceptible. Former military folks are ripe for it as well; they spent years of their lives programmed to think and act a certain way, and here you have someone telling them their skills can be used for a greater good, and they want that redemption."

"I get what you're saying," I said with a sigh. My energy was flagging. I needed to lay down. I wanted Jackson—

Jackson. Oh, God. He'd opened his heart to me, he'd told me his truth…and I'd walked away from him. But there was no way what he was saying was true.

"Cassidy?"

"I'm sorry. Did Jackson tell you anything about his so-called gift?"

Barringer shook his head. "No, but when he mentioned his conversations with Joanna, I figured there was something more there. Why? What did he say?"

Could I talk to the agent about it? Without betraying Jackson? Didn't I owe him more than that after he saved my life?

"I'm sorry, Agent Barringer. I really need to lie down. Can we…"

"Of course," he said, standing from his stool. "You rest. I'm going to have to get back to the field office but…wait, are you sure you don't want to see a doctor? I can try to bring someone out—"

"Not yet. Thank you. There's nothing acute going on, so whatever I need fixed is likely too late anyway. Not without more than a simple office visit. I'm going to rest. If you could, please leave your phone number."

"Jackson and Ryder both have it, if there's anything I can do. When you're ready to leave, let me know, I can arrange for transportation. If you need a place to stay…"

He was really very kind and genuine, and that made this easier.

"Thank you, and I'm sorry I'm not more help. I will talk more, but for now—"

"Yes, you go relax. I'll probably be back later today or tonight." He held out his hand, and I shook it. "Thanks for speaking with me."

"Thank you for helping those people. I hope Irene and Denise are okay. And the baby. Please tell them I'm thinking of them, you know, if you're in touch."

"I absolutely will. Thank you, Cassidy. For what it's worth? I think you're one of the bravest people I've ever met."

My cheeks flushed at his words. "I don't feel that brave, especially not in hippo pajamas."

He laughed. "Especially in hippo pajamas." I followed him out of the kitchen and into the foyer. "Alright, get some rest." He was almost to the door when he turned around. "Cassidy? I know it's not my business, but I feel like I need to share something."

I crossed my arms over my chest, wishing I'd at least had a bra on for our conversation. "Okay?"

"I just...when I met Jackson at your crash site, I've never... Well, I've seen people who are very driven but with him, it was different. As law enforcement, we accept the fact that we're not always going to catch the bad guy and save the day. For Jackson? Failure was not an option. He was going into that compound to get you, no matter what we said, how hard we fought with him to let us go in as a team. He would have marched straight in there. But he had a plan and he convinced me his entry could be a little less conspicuous than some long-haired, jacked-looking guy marching into camp looking for his woman."

I snorted. "I'm sorry. Yeah, that wouldn't have gone over well. Thank you."

Barringer nodded. "You mean a lot to him. He knew he was risking his life for you, and now that I've met you and seen you together, I can see why. So go easy on him, would ya? Us men are pretty thick-headed sometimes, but his heart is in the right place."

And I knew that, and that's why I was so torn.

"Thank you. I appreciate it."

He smiled once more and then went outside. As he opened the door, I saw that Ryder and Jackson were sitting on the front porch, shoulder to shoulder. Jackson had his head in his hands. I could tell by the slump of his shoulders that he was exhausted, and I felt terrible for how I'd responded to his admission.

Instead of going to him and reassuring him, I turned on my heel and went into the bedroom, crawling into the bed we'd shared the night before and pulling the covers over my head.

Brave. Yeah, right. I chose to hide rather than care for the man who'd risked his fucking life for me, all because he believed some wild scenario where a little girl hundreds of miles away told him how to find me and he'd had a little empath thing going during my crash.

It was all too much. I sucked in a breath and tears stung my eyes before I squeezed them shut.

Two heavy weights landed on the bed, and Simon and Garfunkel curled up on either side of me. I had never had a dog, but I'd always loved them. It was obvious these two knew somehow that I needed their comfort.

How was that different than Jackson knowing that I needed help?

Not that he was a dog. But was it so weird to believe that some people had a little extra something, like animals did, that could sense when people were in danger or hurt? I mean, they have dogs that know when your blood sugar is too high or too low to help diabetic people.

What if Jackson *had* seen my plane crash?

Oh, God. Survival had been at the forefront of my mind until we got here, and I'd had things to occupy it since, but alone with my thoughts was not a good place for me to be.

I ran through the plane crash over and over in my mind and bile rose in my throat when I thought of how close to death I'd really been. That feeling of dread when I knew the plane would come up short, that the runway wasn't long enough for my Challenger 300. When we'd hit those first trees and I lost control of steering, it was the first time since becoming a pilot that I'd truly thought I would die doing the thing I loved most in the world.

Which led me to my current panic: who would I be if I wasn't

Captain Cassidy Mackenzie? If my eye injuries were permanent, or my shoulder was beyond repair, and I couldn't fly again? Or, what if I lost my nerve? What if the thing that made up my identity was gone? Who would I be? What would I do?

My heart pounded so hard in my chest, I thought I might pass out. My peripheral vision, what was left of it, turned fuzzy, and I felt as if I'd been holding my breath, the strain too much.

One of the dogs crawled closer and nosed his way under the blanket and licked my face. I felt the other one at my back press closer to me and then he whined, followed by a soulful howl.

"Cassidy? Sweetheart?"

All I could do was sob.

That was all he needed to hear.

Jackson coaxed the dog at my back to move and he crawled in behind me, wrapping his arms around me. I focused on his fingers in my hair, smoothing it over and over, and the warm pressure of his body against mine. The panic subsided to angry tears, which led to a hard sleep that I desperately needed, body and soul.

Apparently, Jackson needed it, too. When I opened my eyes next, the room was dark. I felt the dogs jump down from the bed, but there was still that warm, comforting presence at my back. I turned over to find Jackson sleeping fitfully. His face twitched and a crease formed between his brows. I watched him for several minutes, until he twitched all over and moaned, the crease getting deeper.

I pressed my index finger into the muscle there and rubbed gently. "Shhhh," I whispered, wishing I could ease him, but I was afraid to wake him. I rubbed at his crease, then his temple, then I gently massaged his earlobe, his jaw, and I was running my thumb along his cheekbone when his eyes popped open.

"Hi."

He pulled back and let go of me, but I held on to his shoulder.

"Are you okay? Were you having a bad dream?" I couldn't make out much about his features, but that crease was still there.

"Are you all right, sweetheart?"

"I am now," I said, snuggling closer to him.

He pulled me against his chest and let out a long breath. "I was so scared when I came in. You weren't breathing."

"Yeah," I said. "I think I was having a good old-fashioned panic attack. The dogs helped, then Superman saved the day." I smiled, and for the first time today it felt genuine, not something I was doing to try to make myself feel better.

"Cassidy, I'm so sorry—"

I put a finger to his lips. "Please, don't. You have nothing to be sorry for. I can't believe I was such a jackass, to walk away from you earlier. You were telling me something very important, and I was too chickenshit to hear you out. I'm the one who's sorry."

He tucked his chin on top of my hair, rubbing it gently. "I told myself I could handle it if you hated me, if you never wanted to speak to me again—"

"No, Jackson," I said, pulling back and placing my palm on his cheek. "I could never hate you. Never. You saved my life, and you continue to save me from myself. I can't believe you came in here and held me after I was so awful to you."

He splayed his hands on my back, and I loved that there was so much of him that I couldn't see over his broad shoulders, that the only place for my leg to go was in between his. Being this close to him felt right, like the only place I'd ever feel whole again.

Woo woo stuff or not, Jackson was a good man, and I needed that right now.

"Trust me, if I hadn't lived and breathed my stupid curse for over twenty-five years, I wouldn't believe it either. Like I said, it helped me save your life, so I can't regret having it. But I regret that it put a wedge between us when you sure feel like someone I want to be close to."

I looked down between us and stepped off the ledge.

"The only thing I see between us are clothes."

I felt him smile, his stubbly cheek lifting under my hand.

"Well, yeah. Clothes."

"Let's do something about that."

And his smile was gone. He tightened his grip on my back. "Cassidy—"

"Jackson, I want to be close to you. I need to feel something good, something safe, something to make me feel alive. I need to feel *you*." I slid my hand up under his shirt, and we both moaned at the contact.

"Sweetheart, I don't...we don't...this doesn't..."

"Are you attracted to me? Do you feel the way I feel for you?"

He swallowed audibly as my hand moved from his back to his abs and then his pecs, his muscles twitching as I used my nails to lightly score his skin.

"If you mean totally gone, all the way, one hundred percent into you..."

"Yes," I gasped as he let his hand drift down to my hip and pulled me flush against his pelvis. "Like that. I feel that. Want to feel you."

Words were a lost concept at that point. I tugged at his t-shirt until he yanked it off, while I worked at the buttons on the front of the hippo pajamas. I pulled my right arm out but that damn left arm didn't want to cooperate.

"Here, let me help you," he said, sitting up. He turned and glanced at the hallway and then stood to close the door. He took my good hand and pulled me up to a sitting position and then slid the top off of me.

I lay back and pulled the pajama pants down, lifting my legs to pull them the rest of the way off. When I stretched out naked before him, I was happy we were mostly in the dark. If I would have seen my own body covered with ugly bruises, I might have lost my courage.

Jackson was frozen next to the bed. When he didn't move to come back, a chill ran across my skin.

"Am I too forward for you?" I asked him. "Because I realize I'm throwing myself at you, and I don't know if your hesitation is because you don't want this or if you're trying to be chivalrous."

He barked out a laugh. "Chivalry has its place, but darlin', I don't want to hurt you. And as wound up as I am right now, I don't trust myself."

"I won't break. You won't hurt me. And I'm in full control of my faculties, in case you were worried about that."

He chuckled again and slid back onto the mattress next to me, his hand finding its way to my hip once more. "I haven't even kissed you yet. Maybe you'll hate it and kick me out of bed."

"I won't," I laughed, his hesitancy driving me crazy.

"Right. You say that now. Maybe I just won't take that chance."

I started to ask what he meant when he went on the offensive.

Oh, he kissed me all right...but not on the mouth. He started at my neck, his kisses hungry, desperate. He knew just how to take me out of my head and out of the physical pain I'd been in. He focused on places I loved to be touched, as if they had flashing neon signs on them to guide him. He rolled me onto my side, facing away from him, and moaned as he ran his fingers and then his lips down my spine. I tried to look over my shoulder but I was too blissed out. I allowed myself to enjoy not being able to see after nearly two weeks straining to make out the basics around me.

"Only what you want. Only what you need," he murmured against my ear as his fingers traced the curve of my ass and brushed my core.

"Yes," I moaned, pressing my hips back into him, letting him know that was exactly what I wanted, exactly what I needed. "More. Please." I lifted my leg and tucked it back over his, opening myself to his tentative touch, hoping he'd take things much further.

Jackson grazed my core, a little more insistently this time, and with a little more pressure, and he gasped as he found my slick entrance, desperate for him. Aching for him to take me away.

"More?" His voice was higher now, and as he panted, puffs of warm air caressed my shoulder. He slid one finger inside me. "More, sweetheart?"

"*Yes.*" I pushed back again, taking his finger deeper, and he groaned.

"God, sweetheart. I want to give you everything."

He slid a second finger inside, and I rode his hand until my body seized...and the release was epic, so strong, so right, so *good*.

"More?" he asked as I came down. He licked and sucked at my neck as I shivered in the best possible way.

Jackson proceeded to give me the sweetest gift, reminding me that my body was still able to experience exquisite pleasure despite the torture it had been through. And while his kisses were delicious and he hit all of my spots, he stoked a fire in me that would soon spread uncontrollably if he didn't...let...me...touch...him.

"More."

CHAPTER 28
HUMBLED

Jackson

Never in my wildest dreams did I imagine that I would be given such a precious gift as Cassidy's body, and despite her encouragement, I was terrified.

Let me count the ways.

One, it had been years since I'd been intimate with a woman. Like 365 days times at least three. Damn, maybe even four. Between my deployment, my injury and then isolation in Arkansas...yeah. It wasn't like I was going to sneak chicks into my apartment in the boys' dormitory, where I was actually supposed to be a role model.

Two, I was afraid I would hurt her, and that was a raging boner killer. Her injured shoulder, her sore back...she was so strong and brave, would she even tell me if I caused her pain?

Three, I knew she was hiding, that she wanted to escape, and normally I'd approve of such behaviors, but I felt like a shit even considering what she was offering. But then was that being condescending? To think I knew better what she needed? I tried my damnedest to never be that guy.

Four, I didn't want to be her regret.

"Jackson?"

God, the way she said my name sent a flood of heat through my body.

"Yeah, sweetheart?"

"Jackson, you have incredible hands. And talented lips. And I want more. Are you going to give me more?"

I lay beside her and exhaled harshly. "Cassidy, honey, I'm...I don't know what the right move is here. Believe me when I tell you that I dream about getting between your thighs and...well, now I'm blushing over here just thinking about what I want to do."

She sat up and slowly, gingerly, hoisted her leg up and over me until she was straddling my hips.

"Oh, God. Cassidy."

It was so dark I could barely see her, but there was enough glow from under the drapes to bathe her curves in soft light, for me to see that she was smiling.

"You're going to feel really guilty if I have to do all the work," she said, running her fingertips over my stomach. I gripped her hips and held her in place.

"Oh, you think because you're up there, I'm going to let you do the work? Maybe I'm just enjoying the view."

I ran my hands up her sides and stroked her breasts with my thumbs. She sighed and her head tilted to the side.

"Has anyone ever told you how incredible you are? How utterly beautiful?"

She fidgeted a little and shrugged. "I'm okay."

I sat up and pulled her against my chest, brushing her hair out of her face.

"Sweetheart, there is nothing *okay* about you. Apparently I haven't worshipped you enough. You need convincing." I took her hand and placed it on her chest. "You have such a strong heart, and when I feel it beating against your chest, it's like I'm stronger just being closer to you." I slid her hand over to her left breast and ran our joined hands over her tight nipple, loving the way it felt brushing our entwined fingers. "Your breasts are perfect, but that's a given."

"A given?" She laughed and squirmed.

"Mmm." I moved her hand to her hipbone. "This spot where your pelvis and leg meet, that little depression there that's so sensitive, and so close to where I want to be, where I want to taste."

Her eyes flared and she smiled, and that mischievous side I knew was lurking under the surface... Oh yeah, here it comes.

"Come on up here, sweetheart."

I lifted her hips and slid down the bed. With her knees on either side of my head, oh Lord, I was in heaven.

She was incredible, the way she took from me what she wanted, the way she let me in, opened herself to the pleasure. I thought about opening the Connection to discover how she was feeling, whether she was enjoying—

"*Ohhhhhhhhhh, Jackson!*"

Her whole body quaked with the force of the second orgasm I gave her, but I was far from done. She said she wouldn't break, and damn if I was going to quit before I'd had my fill of the sounds coming from her, the taste on my tongue.

She tapped out after the third time.

"God, the view from down here is humbling, darling. You make such a pretty picture when you come."

I brought her down to my lap and sat up with my back against the headboard. She lay against my chest trying to catch her breath.

"I'm beginning to think maybe you *are* Superman."

I chuckled. "Nah, I've just been saving it up, woman. You are the recipient of a lot of pent-up sexual energy."

She laughed hard. "I'm lucky. But tell me, do you have any left? Because I want to see what other tricks you've got up your sleeve."

"None," I said with a smirk. When she clicked her tongue at me, I said, "I'm not wearing any sleeves."

She huffed out a breath and scooted down so she could work on my fly.

Oh, God. This is really going to happen.

"Get these pants off, Captain Howe. Ha! We're both captains."

"I'm retired, though, so you outrank me," I said, my voice gone gravelly. I tried to control my breathing, but watching her hands unfasten the shorts I'd borrowed from Ryder and try to slide the material down… My erection sprang free at the same time she sucked in a breath.

"Oh, Jackson," she said, running her fingers over one of the deeper scars that wrapped around my thigh and onto the top of my pelvic bone.

"I know, right?" It was easier to laugh about it now.

"I mean, that's impressive too," she said, gesturing to my dick with one hand. "But this…I can't believe—"

"You can thank Ryder. He carried my fat ass out of harm's way and held off the bad guys until medics could arrive. He saved my life, which is why I let him stick needles in me now. It's the little things that keep a relationship alive."

She shook her head and bent down to kiss the wounds that tried to end my life. Good thing I was stubborn. I'd have been pissed to know that dying in the fucking Afghan desert meant I'd never experience the touch of this woman.

"I'll be sure to thank him. Now," she said, running her fingers lightly up my shaft, which didn't need any help standing at attention. I'd forgotten how much more intense everything felt with a partner. It was one thing to experience an erection while flying solo, but it was so much *more* with the anticipation of anything other than the heat of your own hand.

"You want to help a wounded gal out here?"

"Yes, ma'am." I tugged my shorts off and I held out my arms to her. "You more comfortable laying down, or—"

She straddled my hips, licked her hand and stroked my dick from base to tip, running her fingers lovingly around the ridge, the visual almost my undoing. She was so goddamn sexy I was going to be done before we even started.

"We okay with this? I've got an IUD."

"We're definitely okay with this," I said, getting two handfuls of her incredible ass. I groaned as soon as I felt the heat from her slick core, and when she had me in position, we moaned together as she took me inside her. She smiled and started to move, then winced.

I held her in place and shook my head. "Let me do the work, sweetheart," I said, looking down to where we were joined. "Just tell me, fast or slow? Easy or hard?"

"Slow and hard, Captain. That's an order."

"Fuck yes," I said, pulling her down hard until we both groaned together. "Like that?"

"Yes! More. Fuck me, Jackson."

I punctuated each word of my answer with an upward thrust. "Yes. Ma'am." I was rewarded with gasps from her, followed by the most delicious string of curses. When I figured she wouldn't kick me out of bed, I couldn't wait another minute to taste her mouth.

"Kiss me, Cassidy."

She threw her arms around my neck and kissed me hard, as hard as I thrust into her. I loved the feel of her firm nipples brushing against my chest, the way she bit my lower lip, the way she pulled back to watch me pumping into her.

It was a good thing she'd given me the go-ahead, because true to my word, I lost control. Then *she* lost control.

"God, Jackson, I'm coming!"

"That's beautiful, sweetheart. You're beautiful. Take what you need."

She moaned for several long moments as her whole body tensed and then she turned to putty in my hands, her head falling back on her shoulders as she laughed.

"So good. That was so good. Do it again."

"I'd love to." I turned her carefully onto her back, and we managed to get her there again. This time when she came, she said my name over and over.

She tightened around my dick so hard, I groaned and knew my release was close. I drove into her, slower this time, as my whole body shook and I felt every brush of her velvet heat. I sucked at her neck and her earlobe until another string of colorful language came from her.

"Cassidy, sweetheart...you feel so good."

My body tensed so hard my vision went spotty. My breath caught and a screamer of an orgasm was ripped from my goddamn soul. I lost my rhythm—well, pretty much all control of my large muscle groups

—and wave after wave of pleasure hit me as if I were caught in the most wonderful of all riptides.

I held myself up on shaky arms so as not to crush Cassidy, who lay gasping underneath me.

"Please tell me you're okay," I said, terrified I'd hurt her despite her protests that I wouldn't.

"Definitely not okay," she said, letting her legs fall open. She smiled up at me and ran her hands up and down my sides.

"No? How about better or worse than okay?"

"Better. Definitely better."

"Dare I hope for good?"

She tapped a finger against her lip. "Hmmm. Good is a start."

My arms gave out and I caught myself before I landed on her, rolling to the side.

"I'm not sure my heart has found a sinus rhythm yet, and I'm pretty sure I nearly had an aneurysm or embolism. One of those isms that are bad."

She laughed, rolling onto her right side to face me. "Nonsense. Superman doesn't have isms."

"Right," I said, still gasping and wiping sweat out of my eyes. "How silly of me." I cleared my throat. "Before I get up and take care of you—"

"I can take care of myself. You just lay there and bask in the quality performance you just put in. I'll take care of *you*."

I watched her get up from the bed and was relieved to see that she moved loose limbed to the bathroom, gone was the tension in her body that I'd been so worried about. If nothing else, I'd given her some freedom of movement and hopefully distracted her from darker thoughts. She turned the light on in the bathroom and the sight of her naked form silhouetted in the doorway, well, she was a goddamned work of art, and I appreciated the hell out of her.

Job well done, Howe, was my last coherent thought.

Until I felt something wet on my face.

"Hmmm, sweetheart. Give me a second, I'll be ready to go again."

Cassidy's laugh came from across the room.

I opened one eye to see the floppy jowls of Simon or Garfunkel, still wasn't sure which was which.

"Oh, I love you too, buddy," I said, scratching him behind the ears.

I spotted Cassidy at the door to the bedroom. Dressed.

"I'm sorry, they beat me in here, I was trying to let you rest. But Agent Barringer is here and he wants to talk to you."

"Come here," I said. "I just need to see something, come here."

She approached me with a satisfied smile. "What do you need to see?"

I grabbed her around the back of the thigh and ran my hand over her ass and up her back. I hoped she saw the gravity in my gaze.

"If you're really okay. With what...with this."

She bent over and pressed the sweetest lingering kiss on my lips.

"I'm really good, Jackson. Thank you, and I'll want to do that again, so I hope you've got some of your super-strength left."

"I'll find it. Anything for you. Hey, one more of those." I pulled her down for one more kiss before I faced reality.

"I'll meet you out there. He brought food, by the way, and if you don't hurry, I might eat it all. I feel like I could eat a whole cow right now."

"I'd bring you one. I'd do anything for you, Cassidy."

She paused at the doorway and her smile was teary. "You already have."

Then she was gone.

And I had to quiet all of the alarm bells going off in my head.

You're in deep, Howe. There's no walking away unscathed from this woman.

I cleaned up in the bathroom and tried to shake off my fear. Maybe I wouldn't have to walk away. Maybe this was really happening.

Maybe I was dreaming.

"Hey, Howe? It's Nurse Simms," Ryder called out in a falsetto that cracked me the hell up.

"In here."

He came to the doorway with gloves on and a syringe in his hand. "Time for your penicillin." I groaned, and it was his turn to crack up. "Kidding. But let's see it."

He didn't like the redness around the wound on the back of my thigh, so I let him stick me with his big-ass needle.

"Motherfuckingwhorebastard, I hate you!"

"You love me, you know it."

I really did. I'd missed him a lot, and though I'd never choose to have this be the reason we saw each other again, I knew after I left I wouldn't wait three more years to visit.

"I do, man. Thank you. For everything. I'm in your debt."

"Yeah, well, I'm sure we'll be back here again, and you'll do me a solid."

"You know it. You need me, you call."

He patted me on the back, and then slapped my ass cheek as he shuffled out the bathroom door.

"Asshole." I turned to wash my face and looked at my fucking hair. "Wait. Get back here. Come shave my head."

"Demanding little shit," he said as he came back in. "Thought after all that noise you two just made, you'd be in a better mood."

"I'm in a great mood."

Ryder whipped out a pair of trimmers from under the sink. "Yeah, I think I miss the blond on you. Let me be the brunet in this relationship."

It didn't take long for him to have my hair buzzed down to stubble on the scalp, and by that time, I had better control over the emotions that ricocheted around my head.

Fear

Worry

Anger

Longing

Bliss

Love

Terror

"There you go, Howe. Much better. Now rinse off and let me rebandage that ass."

"You're having way too much fun with this."

He rubbed his hands while I hopped in the shower and rinsed all of the itchy hairs off. Then I let Ryder shave the spot on my thigh around the wound and rebandage it.

"Was it as good for you as it was for me?" He walked out of the room cracking up at his joke.

He really was an asshole, and I loved him to pieces.

I found Cassidy sitting in an overstuffed leather chair with one of the dogs next to her and the other one on the ottoman. She was petting them both and laughing at something Barringer said. She'd changed into a t-shirt and sweatpants, and she looked so much more relaxed, almost where she'd been when I'd first met her.

She looked up as I came in the room and squinted.

"Jackson? Come closer, I can't see you. What's different?"

I ran my hand over my head. "The shoe polish look is gone. I figured my career as an Elvis impersonator could wait a bit. Someday I'll make it to Vegas, but until then, I'm a blond. Now I just gotta grow my curls back." I shook hands with Barringer, who shook his head at my newest new look.

"I like your curls, but this is hot too," Cassidy said as I took a seat next to the beast on the ottoman, getting a lick from him. Cassidy ran her fingernails over my scalp, and I held in the moan of pleasure. I gazed at her for a long minute, wishing we were still alone.

Barringer cleared his throat. "Afraid I've got some news for you both."

Time to focus. I tore my gaze away from Cassidy and linked my hands between my knees. "Hit me."

CHAPTER 29
THE GOOD, THE BAD, AND THE UGLY

Cassidy

"I've got the good, the bad, and the ugly. Which do you want first? Actually, I'm going to start with the good because we could all use a little hope."

I was so happy to have Simon in my arms right now because I knew that whichever category of news the agent gave me first, it was all going to take away from the relaxed vibe I'd been in after an evening in Jackson's arms.

The man was… Fuck Superman, he was a *god*. He'd managed to fly me so high my problems, my pains, my preoccupations were all tiny specks on the ground from about 35,000 feet in the air. It was a crime to have to play civilized and deal with reality when I knew what heaven awaited with his body wrapped around mine. I prayed for a repeat soon.

"So the good news," Barringer said, interrupting my musings. "Is that Lance was able to give us a name in Southern California and a possible location of a group there. They're less involved in the religious aspect and more about carrying out the plans Rains masterminded for an uprising. But it's a start.

"The bad news? Still no sign of Rains or Esai Ramirez. We've got airports, buses, harbors all on alert, but nothing. We think they may have connected with five other men from the community who weren't present at the time of the raid. They'd been in town on a worksite and hadn't come back yet."

"Earl and Tony were two of them, right?" Jackson asked. "Shit. I forgot they'd been on rotation. They're just as skilled as Matt was. All ex-Marines. They likely still have connections in So Cal from their Camp Pendleton days."

"Yes. Lance was able to give us lists of all of the people in the compound and he gave us descriptions on them, as well as a place in Escondido where Earl's name is still on the lease."

"Good, so it's a place to start."

Barringer didn't answer.

"And now the ugly…and this part is going to be hard for you to hear, Cassidy."

I tucked my legs under me and held onto Simon a little tighter. He shifted but didn't move. *Good boy.* I didn't know how I was going to leave these boys behind when I left… Eventually. Which I didn't want to think about. I had fantasies of staying here in this house for an indefinite amount of time cuddling with the dogs, making love to Jackson, forgetting about life…

"What is it?"

Barringer pulled out a file from his briefcase and sat it on the counter next to him.

"We found another link between Maker's Plan and your abduction and the hijacking."

The ringing started up in my left ear again. It had lessened over the past few days, but stress seemed to aggravate it.

"Robert Crane."

I flinched at hearing his name.

Jackson frowned at Barringer and then turned to face me.

"What the hell does my ex-husband have to do with this?"

Barringer cleared his throat. I wiped at my face as Jackson moved closer to me and reached for my hand. I took his and held on for dear life.

"We identified the two women on the plane, Rachael Smith and Sophie Jones, AKA Rachael Dunbar and Sophie Herman. We traced their movements prior to the flight and it turns out that theirs are the names on record for one Maker's Plan Foundation, a 501(3)(c) out of Coral Gables, Florida. The organization's records are pretty much on the up and up, but they'd paid for the flight hours with a credit card, and through that piece of intel, we were able to get phone and financial records. In those phone records, we found calls to Robert Crane." He cleared his throat again and leaned his arm on the counter. "I spoke to him this afternoon. Cassidy, you knew that he'd been trying to build a private charter company, right?"

"Tried and failed. He lost all of our money."

Barringer sighed. "Which went into the hands of Maker's Plan. They told him they'd invest in the company as long as you were the pilot they'd be working with. They'd been trying to get to you for months."

A wave of nausea washed over me.

"Oh my God. That explains the phone call from him a few days before the flight. He tried one last time to get me to go into business with him. He said he had clients and he needed me to fly them. I told him no, and he said they were going to kill him. I just thought he was being dramatic."

Barringer nodded once. "And lastly, I'm sorry to say, we have reason to believe he'd been having an affair with Sophie Herman. For years. They served together in the Air Force. Cassidy, when Robert couldn't get them a plane...he told them exactly how to get to you."

Simon turned and nudged me with his nose, giving me a slimy lick on my cheek. I buried my face in his muscular shoulder and tried to slow my breathing.

Jackson squeezed my hand and then stood from the ottoman. He began pacing the living room.

"Honestly, none of this surprises me," I said, wiping my tears. Any residual guilt I had about divorcing Robert was gone.

"We've taken him into custody. He's going to be charged as an accessory."

"Good." If it meant I'd be free of him, all the better.

"So where does this leave us?" Jackson asked. "Those two are dead, but Rains and Esai are on the run with possibly Earl and Tony. They wanted Cassidy so bad, they went through all of this to get her and a plane…"

"I think their plan was not for Cassidy to crash," Barringer said. "But for her to bring them a plane they could use to transport weapons and people for their attempted uprising. And if she didn't cooperate, they'd have her to trade for Joanna."

"He was so mad when he couldn't manipulate me," I said, thinking back to that first visit with Rains. "He talked to me as if I would just accept everything about his beliefs and…he thought he could turn me and that I would help him. When I didn't, he was furious. And he used me as one of his signs. He had his people believing that I was part of some ridiculous sign from the scriptures."

"Abel talked about that in our interview," Barringer said. "He explained the teachings about the twelve signs, including the lady who came from the sky, and how his father preached that the last sign would be the interlopers' invasion that would lead to the armed uprising."

I turned and stared at Jackson. "And we gave them what they wanted."

He had his hands on his hips, his eyes darting between me and Barringer.

"The invasion. The interlopers. And now that we know some of the people escaped…and there are others out there—"

"Which is why I'm here." Barringer set down his file, turned to face me and laced his fingers between his knees. "I'm going to be heading up a task force with three goals. First, locate and apprehend Rains. Second, eliminate the threat from Maker's Plan. Last? Untangle the financials for the organization, in which case we may be able to get you restitution for not only your losses but your time spent with the group."

"That matters less to me than making sure this guy doesn't do it again. And you gotta make sure he doesn't hurt anyone else, especially his kids."

"Yeah," Jackson said. "Joanna? The baby? And what about Abel? If he finds out Abel talked at all, he could be in serious danger."

"I'm already on it. He's in protective custody and will remain there until we capture Rains, and Denise and the baby are also in protective custody. He won't get to them—"

"Barringer, I hate to doubt your plans, but I explained before what this guy is capable of, yeah? Escaped? Faked his death? He can get to anyone, anywhere."

Barringer nodded. "Which is why I think it's a good idea to get you two to a safe place. I hate to rush you in making any decisions, Cassidy, but it might be best to get you out of Florida."

"My place is secure, Agent Barringer," Ryder said. "Wired it myself. I'll get a text if anyone passes the halfway mark on my driveway and the doors and windows are all alarmed. We'll know if anyone gets close."

"I understand that, but with just the two of you to protect her against potentially four or more men—"

Suddenly, both Simon and Garfunkel sat up straight and stared in the direction of the entry hall.

Ryder pulled out his phone and frowned at the screen. Simon growled low in his chest and Garfunkel went to Ryder's side with his hackles raised.

Jackson pulled me out of the chair and shielded me with his body.

"We've got company. Barringer, if anyone was looking for her, they could have followed you out here," Ryder said as he pulled out a handgun from an ankle holster.

Barringer pulled his weapon out of his holster and stood behind me.

"Simms," Jackson said, and Ryder nodded.

"Safe is in my bedroom, you know my combo. Here," he said, handing Jackson his pistol. "Shotgun in the pantry. Safest place is your bathroom."

"Copy that. Sweetheart, let's get you safe."

I let him take me by the hand and into the bedroom, Simon on my heels the whole time. Jackson made me crouch-walk to the bathroom and sit on the floor. There were no windows, which was a blessing, but I hated feeling so vulnerable.

"We're going to check the perimeter. You stay here, please."

"Jackson, I can handle myself with gun. I've been to the range with my brother and I'm certified. I've got a Sig P365 at home."

He smiled and kissed me. "That's my girl. Take this," he said, quickly showing me where the safety was on the 9MM. "You want this or my .22?"

"I've used one of these before."

"Good. I'll be right back." He winked at me, but he wasn't smiling. I watched him walk low past the window and out into the hall. The bathroom had a pocket door and wasn't much protection, plus I wanted to see what was coming at me.

My heart pounded out of control the moment he was out of my limited sight. The lights outside the bedroom shut off, and I reached up to turn off the bathroom light and then crouched against the wall away from the door, where I could see anyone coming.

I clutched the gun to my chest and tried to get my breathing under control. Simon pressed against me and whimpered.

"I know, buddy," I whispered. "I hate it, too."

The house was way too quiet for way too long.

Then the window in the bedroom shattered, and I heard a thud like feet landing on the floor before the alarm started its piercing siren. There was another thud, then there were two men in the room outside the bathroom.

Simon growled ferociously—and all hell broke loose.

Jackson sprang into the room from the hallway and caught someone with a rifle, who he quickly disarmed, tossing the rifle into the hall behind him. Grunts and shouts filled the room as shots rang out in another part of the house.

Garfunkel had come charging in with Jackson and lunged at a second dark figure heading toward the bathroom. A gun went sliding across the floor. Simon was up on all fours, his growling now a menacing echo bouncing off the bathroom walls.

In the moonlight, I saw two figures grappling before one of the men fell to his knees. Then Jackson's face was illuminated, he was still on his feet with his teeth bared. He moved with deadly grace. A huge knife flashed in his hand and he swung it in an upward motion, driving it into the other man's torso before the body collapsed to the floor.

The other intruder struggled with Garfunkel latched onto his arm, and Jackson went into motion again, the knife held out in front of him and a macabre smile on his face, welcoming what was no longer a surprise attack.

I heard a scream and a snap as Jackson broke the arm of the guy and shoved his face into the ground. He pressed a knee into his back.

"Where's Rains, Earl?"

"I'm not telling you shit, interloper! You're supposed to be dead!"

"Surprise, motherfucker. Now tell me where Rains is before I break off your other arm and feed it to you."

He bent the man's arm up at an unnatural angle, and the guy screamed again.

"Howe, hold up."

Ryder took over subduing the man and wrapped his hands behind his back with zip-ties while Jackson got his feet. He stared down at Earl, his chest heaving, the white shirt he'd been wearing now covered in blood. I prayed none of it was his.

As if he felt my relief, his gaze found mine in the corner where I hid, and he moved forward. Simon's growls grew more intense and he barked in warning, so Jackson stopped.

"It's okay, boy. Cassidy," Jackson held out a hand for me. I pushed to my feet and placed a hand on Simon's back.

"Shhh, buddy, he's okay. You're okay."

Simon looked up at me and whimpered again before pressing against my leg.

"Are you okay?" I asked Jackson, who had turned to say something to Ryder.

"Yeah, but we gotta go, sweetheart. There are more men out there."

And though I'd just seen him kill one man and maim another, I didn't fear him. I took his hand and we ran through the house.

CHAPTER 30
TRUST

Jackson

I hated that Cassidy had seen any of that, but I didn't have time to dwell on it. Besides the four in the house, we apparently had more guests outside. We had no alternative but to make a run for it, and Ryder, bless him, was willing to part with his vehicle and provide cover so we could get past them before they had a chance to breach the house again.

We got to the garage and Ryder called the dogs into the Hummer and shut them in.

"You want us to take the dogs?" I asked him. "Actually, that's probably a good idea. Here, Cassidy, let's get you situated."

Ryder stood blocking the passenger door, staring silently at something in the dark corner of the garage. The dogs went nuts in the vehicle, clawing at the window and snarling.

"Thanks man." I held out my hand to Ryder for the keys—and I'll never forget the change in his expression. The moment when he went from my decades-long friend to my enemy.

Instead of the keys, he gave me however many thousand volts his taser was packing. I only had a split second to turn toward Cassidy before my entire body froze and pain rendered me unconscious.

Cassidy's horrified expression was the last thing I remembered seeing before I hit the ground.

I came to and my entire body ached like the time I'd gotten too close to an IED blast in Nasiriyah. My ears were ringing and my brain was sluggish, but I knew it was imperative that I get moving.

And then I felt the zip-ties that held me to Ryder's dining room chair, biting into my wrists and ankles.

I was still in Ryder's garage, but Cassidy was gone, Barringer was bloody and crumpled on the floor next to me, and Ryder stood a few feet away—now with a gun pointed at me.

An eerie voice filled the echoey space from behind me.

"If he manages to get out of that chair, shoot him. And shut those dogs up."

Ryder adjusted the grip on the gun, and turned to give hand signals to the dogs, quieting their barks to whines. When he turned back, his expression was blank. He stared into my face, but he wasn't looking at me.

Damn. Not Ryder.

It took a few tries to get actual words out of my mouth.

"Well, if it isn't the boogieman."

"Captain Jackson Howe, U.S. Army Ranger. Retired. Not Luke Stephens. Art instructor at Havenhart Academy, Eureka Springs, Arkansas. Munitions expert. Counterintelligence agent. Gifted artist. Psychic." The last was said with disgust, the hard "c" ringing out through the space.

"All that and we've never dated? I'm impressed."

"Smart mouth as well. Tell me, Jackson. How does it feel to be responsible for countless deaths? To be a kidnapper? Do you sleep well at night?"

I swallowed and put on my most winning smile. "I sleep just fine, Gerald Rains. Charlatan. Manipulator. Thief. Child abuser. Murderer."

"And currently the only person standing between life and death for you, Captain Howe. Tell me, did you really think you would come into my community, *my house*, and take what belongs to me? And live to speak of it?"

"'Fraid you've got me confused with someone who believes in your bullshit, Gerry."

"You of all people should know how belief equals power, and I've gained the belief of so many. The community was just an experiment, a small-scale replica of what will be when the totality of my plans come to fruition."

Rains stepped in front of me and he looked...unhinged. His combover was sticking up in a few spots, his plain-joe face was ruddy with anger, his eyes bloodshot. Seemed we'd put up more of a fight than he'd expected us to, and he appeared to be having a tough time keeping his shit together.

As if he read my thoughts, he smoothed down his hair and took a deep, cleansing breath.

"I'll never forget the first congregation I turned. The rush of power I got from the adoring faces of men, women, and children desperate for salvation. They'd seen the signs. Society as we know it can no longer sustain itself. The secular leadership in this country has created a violent and corrupt world that so many people are seeking respite from. I see it in their eyes, feel it in their emotions. I can give them peace. I can deliver them from their suffering."

"So you *do* actually believe your own lies," I said, shaking my head. "I think I would have had more respect for you if this whole thing was a ruse to get you to the Promised Land. The fact you actually believe in shit like women falling from the sky as signs that God is coming like a sex addict on payday is really sad, Ger."

His eyes flared and he stepped closer to me. "You have no idea what I'm capable of, Howe. You have no way of comprehending the amount of money they handed to me, the properties...I have access to some of the most powerful politicians and some truly desperate folks who will do *anything* for me, their faith is so strong. There are only a few people like yourself who have any chance of resisting me. It's so easy. I can go wherever I want, with whomever I want..."

I took that as a reminder to lock my mind up tight as a drum. No way I was letting this piece of shit get ahold of my gray matter.

"Interesting," he said, pulling up a chair. He looked over my head and smiled. "Earl, would you please tell Esai to move Cassidy to the car. We'll be leaving soon. Thank you." Then his snake-like eyes turned back to mine, and I felt his icy feelers trying to worm their way into my psyche.

What the fuck had he done to Cassidy? If I let myself get distracted by thoughts of her, this would be all over. All would be lost.

Instead, I grinned at him. *Thank you, Morgan.* I really needed to be much more gracious to her when I returned. She'd prepared me well for this, even after getting tased, which now that I thought about it, I must have had an adverse reaction. My heart felt a little racy and my head hurt as if I'd maybe smacked it on the ground.

Yes, you do need to be gracious to her, and you need to concentrate. Be careful.

Shit. Joanna shouldn't be here right now. I tried to shut her out, but I had to concentrate on keeping my mind closed to Rains. I didn't want her to see any of this. Joanna's voice was crystal clear, as if she was on the other end of a cell phone with all bars of service.

I mentally pictured cutting phone wires with a pair of snips, and then she was gone. She would be safe from all this.

"You are quite extraordinary, Captain Howe. You managed to get past not only *my* notice, but even my two strongest readers didn't discover your deception. And even now..." He trailed off and I felt a fresh assault on my mind. What started as eye strain soon turned into a massive migraine as I fought to keep him out of my head.

"So disappointing. I could have used your strength, and Cassidy wouldn't have your death on her hands. She, too, is strong. She would have made a perfect partner for my ascension if she'd just cooperated, but alas, I may still have use for her. She's older than I'd prefer, but still fertile. With her uncanny strength, she'll produce a miraculous child."

And that was my undoing.

"There is no fucking way—"

"Oh, but there is. It's only a matter of time until she's ovulating."

I bared my teeth and fought my restraints, even though I knew better than to react. He was doing this on purpose. He knew Cassidy was my weakness, probably had been watching the house long enough to know just how close we were. God, I could not let her fall into his hands again, but I hadn't thought of everything. Poor Ryder stood there dumbstruck with a fucking gun pointed at me, and at any moment Rains could direct him to take me out.

I couldn't let that happen. I should have prepared him. I should have done a better job.

"You're sadly going to have more deaths on your hands, I'm afraid. And once again, you have failed Cassidy. Shame, really." He stood and strolled over to stand near Barringer, clicking his tongue against his teeth.

"Now, it won't be long before your friend Agent Barringer awakens, and I plan to be long gone before that happens. I wanted to give you one last opportunity to let me in. Come on, Jackson. Join me and you can be close to Cassidy, you can use your valuable skills, and once you help me get my daughter away from that school, we can be a real family."

The pain was back with a vengeance. Rains was giving his all, trying to pry into my brain, but my walls held firm, thank the gods.

A trickle of blood ran from Rains' nose and the corner of his eye. Seemed he'd reached his capacity and it wasn't enough.

For a moment, I considered playing along for Cassidy's sake, but I couldn't...there had to be another way. If only I had the gift of Influence and could get through to Ryder, or a gift more like Delaney's and I could burn the fucker, boil his insides...

"And help you murder innocent people? Give you access to your daughter? Never. You'll never get your hands on Joanna again."

His eyes glowed red for just a moment, and he struck me so hard in the jaw I saw stars. The force knocked the chair over and my temple bashed against the concrete floor.

In those mere seconds, however, the situation changed—and though I was the one tied to a chair and on the floor bleeding, I now had the upper hand.

All it took was that one point of contact to completely turn the tables. It was clear that Rains had no clue what he'd just done, and whereas in the past I would be deep in the throes of regret and cursing the defective part of me that had tormented my life since I was seventeen years old, this time, I reveled in it. If I weren't in so much pain, I would have squealed with delight at this development.

"And you will have to live with your failure," Rains was saying, but it didn't matter anymore. "Despite what you think, I am not a murderer. Mr. Simms? If you would be so kind as to incapacitate Mr. Howe once more."

Ryder stepped closer and pulled out the taser. Before I could say a word, he shot me again, but this time I managed to stay aware... enough to know I was having a seizure. Ryder stared down at me as Rains continued to spout more of his bullshit as he left the room but I was beyond being able to hear what he said.

"Hey...HEY!" Ryder snapped out of the Influence as Rains left the room. He pulled his gun and fired after Rains but he was already through the door into the house, shouting orders as he ran.

"Howe, what the... Oh fuck, what have I done?"

He started to undo my ties, but I growled at him.

"Stop them! Get Cassidy. Go!"

As Ryder flew into the house, every muscle in my body pulled taut and I fought to stay conscious. It hurt so, *so* fucking bad, but I couldn't let go.

Mr. Howe, I got through to your friend, but I'm so sorry you got hurt again! Hold on. Hold on.

I heard more gunshots, then groaning from Barringer's direction.

My muscles were mostly done fighting me and had settled into a series of twitches. I had enough control now for me to use my shoulder to scoot myself around so I could see Barringer's battered body. "Barringer, you okay?"

He groaned again and lifted his head. His handsome, clean-cut, fresh and innocent-looking face was a bloody mess. I had a fleeting thought that this might have been his first beating, unlike the countless ones I'd had in my lifetime. I remember being livid when I got to my feet after that first one. I'd been spurred forward by a superhuman strength fueled by a lust for blood I didn't quite understand. I wondered how Barringer would emerge from his beating.

"These people better pray to whoever they believe in for deliverance," he said in a cool voice. "When I get ahold of them, they're not likely to receive any mercy."

I barked out a pained laugh. "Hallelujah. Are you restrained? Can you move?"

Barringer pushed himself slowly to a sitting position, and I cursed when I saw his hands were indeed zip-tied, but thankfully his feet were not.

"Give me a second." He was a bit woozy, his body listing to one side. "When I only see one of you, I'll try to move."

"Copy that," I said. I glanced around at Ryder's meticulously organized garage. "There's gotta be something we can use to cut these ties off."

"I got it, I got it. *Fuck!*" Ryder ran back into the garage and pulled out his knife. He knelt beside me and I pulled away as much as I could with a big-ass chair tied to me.

"Are you Good Ryder or Bad Ryder?" Joking only made it slightly less awful that one of my best friends had nearly killed me.

"Fuck, I'm so sorry, Howe. What the fuck happened?"

"Gerald Rains happened. Welcome to the world of the unseen terror from within. Tell me what you know."

Ryder cut my ties and I rolled over onto my back, every muscle in my body shrieking and laughing at me for foolishly thinking I was ready to get to my feet.

"That Earl guy, Rains, and that fucker Esai took Cassidy. They're driving a gray Blazer. I've got partial plates," he pulled out his phone and then cursed. "They must have used a jammer. No service. Let me get to my office and see if I can use the radio." He held out his knife, and when I flinched from him, his face crumpled. "I'll get a BOLO out and then you can kick my ass."

He ran back into the house, and I focused on making my arms and legs cooperate enough to crawl over to Barringer.

"You had quite a seizure," Barringer said. "I was faking unconsciousness, foolishly hoping that bastard would stop wailing on me. He's a big guy," he said, rubbing his bruised jaw.

"Yeah, seizure is a new experience for me."

"That's because I have my tasers reconfigured to pack a wallop in case I run into one of these fools on bath salts," Ryder said, returning yet again. "It's not really allowed, but I'd rather have to ask for forgiveness than permission. In this case, I'm damn sorry, Howe. I fucked up."

"Yeah, yeah, let's cry about it later. For now, we need to find Cassidy."

Barringer and I got ourselves cleaned up while Ryder was able to use his CB to get in touch with the local sheriff. An alert was sent out to law enforcement, but I didn't think that was how we were going to find them. I needed Morgan and I needed Joanna, and I needed my two associates to suspend disbelief a little.

Ryder was able to get the Wi-Fi working and eventually the cell service came back on, meaning they probably had their jammer with them and were out of range. As we sat at the counter in his kitchen, I tried to work out the best way to explain how my curse worked—or rather, my gift—which I was finally ready to accept as the blessing it truly was.

"It's about to get weird in here," I finally said as I pulled up Morgan's number. "I've never done this in front of anyone other than the people I work with, and I'm not even sure it will work remotely like this, but I need you two to not...I don't know... Give me shit about it."

Todd and Ryder looked at each other and then back at me.

"Does it involve nudity?" Ryder asked. "Because if it does, I probably should sit this one out. I wouldn't want to distract you or anything."

"Leave it to you, Simms, to make it weird."

He held up his hands in surrender and I rolled my eyes.

"What about you, Agent Barringer? Do I have your agreement to keep this out of official channels? Or should I expect a visit from some G-men and a vacation in a government-run facility complete with those scratchy robes that let your ass hang out?"

Barringer laughed and then winced. "That really hurts. Remind me not to laugh, and no, Howe, I will not share anything about your psychic powers with management. That would likely get me a vacation in a padded cell as well."

"Roomies!" I held up my hand for a high-five, but he just groaned and repositioned his ice pack.

"Okay then, let me tell you what's going to happen. Normally, I try not to use my little internal spy cam. Morgan—she's what you'd call a Mystic—anyway, she taught me how to be intentional about it, taught me how to use what I See to help people. It's how I found Cassidy before, and hopefully it will help me find her again. I'm going to call Morgan. She…helps me focus. I don't know…well…you'll see."

I hit the call button and waited. After a few beats, my screen was filled with fiery red hair and Morgan's scowl.

"You sure you want to do this with an audience?"

"What? No hi? Hello? No 'I missed you'?"

Her scowl turned epic. I couldn't see her stance, but somehow I knew she was crossing her arms on her end and probably tapping her feet.

"Fine. Yes, I want them to be here."

"Very well. Do you have access to a candle? Something to help you focus?"

I looked to Ryder, and he blinked twice before darting off to the pantry. He returned with a large white glitter-covered pillar candle.

"Sparkles? Really?"

"Fuck off, Howe. It was a gift."

He handed it to me along with his lighter.

I propped the phone up against a basket full of napkins and set the candle right in front of me. "Should I light it?"

"Take a few cleansing breaths first. The more centered you can be before you start, the better."

"It's a little hard to center on anything right now. I feel like I've got my finger in a light socket—"

"Dammit, Howe, I said I was sorry."

I chuckled and then closed my eyes. It took four or five deep, slow breaths before my body felt calm enough to not distract me from my purpose. I lit the candle and then rested my hands on either side of it. I realized that usually I had to pull my hair back before I got started and that made me miss my hair. Before I could get all resentful and angry again, I focused on what was important.

Cassidy.

Cassidy.

I chanted her name in my mind and closed my eyes. I mentally turned the dial of what I called my rack system. I pictured my gift as a sort of sound system with a receiver, speakers, all set up on a shelving unit. Underneath the hardware were shelves packed with vinyl. It looked very much like my dad's setup back in Virginia. I guess since he was the start of all this, it was my way of honoring him. He had a massive record collection, and we often sat together and listened. When I finally picked up guitar, we'd pick out tunes and play them by ear. Mom forced the piano lessons, but dad was all about organic music. I missed them both.

I heard Morgan's steady voice as I moved toward the rack. Cassidy's "album" was already on the turntable as I'd been tapping into the Connection I had with her a lot. I visualized myself placing the needle on the record and then I stepped back and listened for the crackling sound that signaled contact.

I gasped as I was thrown into her point of view.

The backseat of a car. A hand gripping my arm so tight, fingers felt like shards of glass slicing into my muscle tissue. Darkness outside as we bounce on ragged seats. Windshield is dirty and wipers can't keep up with the rain.

"It's raining," I said aloud, thinking Ryder would be able to, I don't know, take notes? Use a weather tracker? "Four people in the car including me. Cassidy."

I shut out all sound except for what was in the car. Rains' voice rose above the drone of the car's engine and the tire noise.

"Call Dawson and let him know we'll be arriving in a few hours. We can stay there until I arrange the exchange."

Earl spoke from the passenger seat. "Yes, sir." Earl called someone and I tried to make out any details, which I spoke out loud when I picked them up. I tried to figure out approximately how long it had been since they'd left and how far they could get in any direction by the rendezvous time.

"I need to use the bathroom," I heard Cassidy say.

"You'll go when we stop. We're nearly there."

"It's your backseat," she muttered.

Rains leaned close to Cassidy, and I felt his breath on her cheek.

"I hope you know better than to think you can manipulate me. If we stop and you try anything, you will pay, is that understood?"

"Yes, sir," she said so viciously, the venom in her tone felt good coming out of her mouth.

Rains signaled to Esai to pull over, and the latter yanked Cassidy out.

Her skin immediately went clammy, and I had to fight not to vomit.

He *wanted* Cassidy. He probably prayed harder for a moment alone with her than for all the things Rains asked of his followers to pray for.

"You can go behind that bush," Esai said. "And know that I will have my gun trained on your location. If you try to run, you won't succeed in getting away."

Cassidy stiffened her back as she walked away and, rather than trembling, she clenched and unclenched her fists, her nails biting into the flesh of her palms with each step. She stomped to the bush he'd pointed out and turned around to face him, unwilling to have him at her back. She wanted to see him coming.

And oh, the ire. She was imagining all the ways she wanted to castrate him, so vividly I covered myself as a reflex.

That's my girl.

I stepped back from the image of the sound system and lifted the needle off Cassidy's record, giving her privacy and moving onto the next selection.

I pulled out another album ,and this one repulsed me. The cover felt wrong as it made contact with my skin, and my hand shook as I lifted the needle.

"Concentrate, Jackson. You can do this." Morgan's voice grounded me, reminded me of my purpose.

I set the needle on the record, closed my eyes, and when I opened them, there was a phone in his hand. He hit a pre-programmed number and lifted the phone to his ear.

He was physically strong, stronger than he looked, and I felt that power in his small movements. It wasn't that he was muscular or fit, it was like he was running on some sort of generator. He was somehow siphoning physical power from the big men surrounding him.

Fascinating.

He smoothed down his hair and his calloused, scarred hands felt like rubbing a snake the wrong way. Scaly, rough. Revolting.

Everything about him was just repulsive, down to a cellular level, and being Connected to him filled me with so much dread I wanted to run, slit my own throat rather than bear his touch, hear his voice.

Did he feel this way about himself?

"Put me through to the school."

"Yes, sir."

He was using some sort of third party to place the call for him. The phone rang three times before the connection went through.

"Nigel Hart."

CHAPTER 31
EMPOWERED

Cassidy

I wasn't above squatting on the side of the road to pee, but with that disgusting Esai watching me, I'd almost rather die than pull my pants down and take the chance of exposing myself to him. I walked around the lone bush near the spot where they'd pulled over the car and tried to tell my bladder to do its job and be quick about it, keeping my eyes on my captor the whole time.

Rains was pacing, talking in a low voice to someone on a cell phone and gesturing angrily. It filled me with glee to know that things weren't going well for him, especially after the nightmare at Ryder's.

Yeah, I was once again in his clutches, but things were different this time

We weren't in the middle of the swamp.

I could see better, still not like before, but my vision improved every day.

I knew for a fact that people would come looking for me.

I had to keep those things at the front of my mind, otherwise I'd throw myself at Esai and his gun and beg for him to kill me.

Watching Jackson get tased and have a seizure was awful, but the fact that he'd been alive when I'd been yanked out of the room gave me hope. Plus, I don't know, maybe we really did have a Connection... because I knew he was with me. I felt something, extra? Something inside of me that gave me more confidence than I had before.

"Hurry up," Esai shouted, and I gave him a nasty smile before flipping him off. Fuck it, they weren't fooling anyone with their holier-than-thou cause. They were killers, manipulators, liars, and in Esai's case, rapists.

When he'd pulled me out of the garage and into Ryder's kitchen, he'd made it clear that once I'd served my purpose, Rains had told him I was his for the taking, and he planned on taking a lot. It should have terrified me, but I knew better.

I'd kill him with my bare hands before that happened. Somehow, some way. I'd listened to my copilots talk about their adventures in the military, heard their stories, and I knew there were ways. And once this nightmare was over, I was going to learn more. I'd get Jackson to teach me, or maybe Delaney's cousin James, but I would learn how to kill. I would never be a prisoner again.

I took a moment to stretch out my legs and hips since we'd likely be in the car for several more hours. At least they hadn't thought to blindfold me. I'd seen a couple of signs that let me know we were headed toward Arkansas. I tried to look at everything I could so maybe Jackson would pick up something when he was able to Connect with me again.

"Bring her here," Rains growled to Esai.

Esai approached and I made sure my pants were fastened before he grabbed me with his brutal hands. He dragged me back to the side of the car and shoved me at Rains. There were no more pretenses of civility. They wanted me to know they didn't give a shit about me except for barter value.

"They want proof of life," Rains sneered. "Let them know you are unharmed, Cassidy dear."

"But that would be lying, Gerald dearest," I sneered right back. I was so sick of this man and I knew talking back was reckless, but I couldn't help myself.

His backhand to my right cheekbone knocked me on my ass and

rung my bell, but I didn't utter a sound other than a small grunt when I hit the ground. I wouldn't give him the satisfaction.

I scrambled to my feet and smiled coldly. He couldn't break me, not after everything I'd been through. I refused to be afraid of him now.

"Give me the phone." I held out my hand, a little unsteady on my feet but upright. I held the phone to my left ear since the right was ringing loudly again.

"Miss Mackenzie, this is Nigel Hart, Headmaster of Havenhart. Are you alright, dear?"

"I'm fine," I said, shooting a glare at Esai. "Thank you for asking."

"Listen carefully. Captain Howe is well and assures me the situation is under control. He is aware of your circumstances."

My acting skills deserved a golden statue. Warmth flooded my body, but I merely nodded. Jackson was with me, watching probably at this very moment, in that way only he could.

"Please make sure no harm comes to Mr. Simms." That had been my biggest concern, that Jackson would hurt his old friend for acting not of his own volition. I knew he wouldn't be able to live with himself if yet another person was hurt because of Rains and his evil ways.

"Mr. Simms is perfectly fine, thank you. Whatever happens next, please have faith. Do all in your power to return to us safely, Miss Mackenzie. We *want* you returned to us."

Us. That sentiment was almost my undoing. My eyes burned but I refused to show any other emotion than dissatisfaction with my current situation.

"Thank you—"

Rains ripped the phone out of my hand and shoved me against the car.

"We'll make the exchange tomorrow evening. You will receive instructions when it's time. You will bring Joanna to me if you want Cassidy Mackenzie to live. There will be no law enforcement, none of your security staff. Only you and Joanna. If you don't follow my instructions, you'll find Cassidy's mutilated corpse. I'm tired of playing games with you, Hart."

My stomach turned at that part, but I had faith Jackson would once again find me.

Please find me.

Rains hung up the phone, called another number, and walked away while he spoke to them. Meanwhile, Esai grabbed me and shoved me into the backseat of the car, which was actually a great thing, as my energy was flagging. My head was killing me and I'd started seeing lightning flashes in my peripheral vision. If my retinas hadn't been detached before, that blow probably did the trick.

I rested my head against the seat back and closed my eyes. Moments later, Rains slid into the seat next to me. I didn't have to open my eyes to know it was him. He had a peculiar scent about him, it was almost metallic. Maybe he was ill. Maybe all this psychic battling had taken a toll on him.

Good. I hoped he suffered.

"You really disappoint me," Rains said as Esai climbed in and started the car. The tires spun in the gravel and kicked it up, rocks pinged under the car as he pulled away, fishtailing a bit before he straightened out on the highway. My head jerked back-and-forth from the movement, sloshing my damaged brain around in my head like a sponge in a bucket, and it was starting to be too much.

"Perhaps you should sleep." While his tone was warm and kind, the icy tendrils stroking at the back of my neck were a clear warning.

I stiffened, but they became more insistent. They pulled at the sensitive spots where each hair emerged from follicle until my scalp burned and stung. My face heated and I squeezed my eyes shut, attempting to push them out, to remain in charge of myself, to maintain, to—

"Shhhh there, there. It's so much easier if you just...let...go."

I gasped as a heavy load of ice was poured over me, or at least that was the best way to describe the sensation, weighing me down, pushing me into the seat, the sharp corners of individual cubes cutting into my skin, stinging me. I gasped and sucked in shallow breaths, trying one last time to keep him out.

I jerked forward, my hands shooting out to grasp at anything to keep myself from drowning. My eyes flew open and I made one last ditch effort. I grabbed ahold of Esai's seat belt and yanked hard, figuring if I was going down, I was going to take them with me.

The car swerved and I was thrown against the door. My left temple made contact and sparks shot through my vision. I hoped we crashed. I hoped it killed them both.

Esai tried to pull the belt from my grasp while keeping the car on the road. Rains was being tossed around beside me, his head slamming into the seat in front of him at one point as he wasn't wearing a seat belt. I hoped his self-preservation had kicked in and he'd leave me alone.

But then he grabbed my wrists and clamped down, the pain overcoming any ability I had left to fight him. His gaze locked on mine and his voice was unbearably loud in my ears, booming against the insides of my skull, rattling my teeth against each other.

"Let…me…in…Cassidy."

I was seconds from passing out, the pain and lack of oxygen too much for me to fight.

"Go…to…hell," I bit out, and my last act of rebellion was to kick my feet against the seat in front of me as hard as I could, breaking the seatback and launching Esai's face forward into the steering wheel.

The car lurched and went careening across the road.

"Then you'll join me," Rains snarled. My bones creaked under the force of his grip, and I screamed into the blackness as the cold permeated me, filling me with the devastating knowledge that he'd won before I was sucked into the oblivion. The last conscious thought I had was that I heard singing…a lovely young girl's voice that I'd heard before.

Sleep, Miss Mackenzie. Sleep and save your strength. We're coming for you.

I felt the car go airborne and I let go, hoping that if Jackson was watching, he'd seen that I'd fought my hardest and hopefully be proud of me.

I woke up to a massive headache and a hard wooden surface beneath my cheek. I ran my tongue over my teeth and tasted blood, and once again, my stupid eyes wouldn't work. But my ears were filled with an ethereal sound, one people often used to describe Heaven. Multiple children's voices rang out in an echoey space, singing hymns with angelic grace. As much as religious music made my skin crawl, there was no denying this music was beautiful, pure. Holy.

Welp. I'm dead. At least I went down fighting.

But it seemed the fight wasn't quite over.

CHAPTER 32
RECKONING

Jackson

I had no desire to be the Lone Ranger for this mission. I'd never been so grateful to have people at my back that I trusted as we surveilled the site Rains had chosen for the exchange. Being Connected to him may have felt like bathing in excrement, but it did have its advantages. I knew what he planned to do, and we were ready.

With Simms, Barringer, and Delaney's cousin James by my side, I could almost hold it together, although my control was tested when I saw that bastard Esai carry an unconscious and bleeding Cassidy from the car into the secluded church outside of Fayetteville. The force that held me back was not the grip of my good friends and trusted allies. No, it was seeing Rains and Esai with bloodied faces and knowing that Cassidy got her licks in, and feeling her through our Connection, alive.

But also weak and in pain, a condition that I'd promised her and myself she'd never be in again.

I was also held back by the fact that I didn't want Joanna to see me kill her father. As much as she feared him, and as much as she wanted him out of her life, seeing the man she trusted do the deed would scar her forever and potentially ruin our bond.

No. I wouldn't put her through that unless it was absolutely necessary.

James had scouted the location as soon as I learned of it, and we met him there. It was an historic site, a two-room clapboard building with a modest cross on top that had been built in the late 1800s and used alternately as a schoolhouse and a house of worship ever since.

Nigel had done a little digging and discovered that Rains had been using this church as a base of sorts during the time we'd thought him dead. At least twice a month, he'd given a sermon as a special guest, and the current pastor was completely enamored with him. They'd been raising funds to go to Rains' community in Florida, and Nigel confirmed that the church's leaders hadn't been informed about the community's demise.

We'd managed to evade notice by the six men from the congregation guarding the church, and we were able to monitor each of the three entrances to the building. The plan was for Nigel to arrive and attempt to bargain with Rains. We would incapacitate the sentries, and then we would move in and rescue Cassidy.

Joanna would remain in the car with her security detail. Period. I didn't even want her there, but Nigel was confident we could keep her safe.

My confidence in this entire mission was enhanced by the fact that I now knew exactly what Rains had in his head.

The Connection had been a surprise. The moment he'd touched me, backhanding me in Ryder's garage, the reel-to-reel of his memories had whirred to life. The images weren't far off from the life I'd imagined someone like Gerald Rains would have experienced.

A pre-pubescent Gerry in a white short-sleeved, button-down shirt and gray pants that were too tight and too short, watching with admiration as his father won over a congregation by giving a passionate speech about the will of Our Maker. Gerry being bullied, beaten to a pulp behind the school gym with his own Bible, which he carried with him constantly. His first sermon before the congregation at the age of sixteen, which gave some members elation and others envy. The home invasion a year later that claimed the lives of his parents and his older brother while he hid in a pantry—which was the moment his "gift" was born.

The invaders were no mere robbers. The group was made up of church members, some of whom were in law enforcement, who were pissed at the elder Rains for not only messing around with their wives, but also the church's finances. He'd left a paper trail, a mistake Gerry wouldn't repeat.

Little Gerry learned from his father's foibles, and as he became a man, he was determined to amass power slowly, undetected by those around him. No one was to know they'd been manipulated. He was careful, calculating. He spent a year with his grandparents in Indiana before heading off to college, convincing his local congregation to cover his tuition to the church's college, where the plan was that he would earn his degree and then return to lead them to the Promised Land. He knew who to manipulate and how far to take it instinctively. And he was good at what he did.

On the drive to Fayetteville, I opened up the Connection further so I could take as much of his evil into me as possible. Any miniscule fact I could use to defeat him, I would do it and face the consequences later. There were moments in the "film" playing in my head where I found myself believing him, accepting what he was saying, hell, even finding him compelling when he spoke, eager to please when he asked for obedience...it was almost easy to forget these were images from the past, they were so vivid.

My Connection was strong with Cassidy, but this one—with a man I loathed more than any other—affected me in a way I hadn't anticipated. I had empathy for the younger Gerry. But knowing what he'd become, what he planned to do—yes, that all became clear as well—there was no room for any other emotion than the desire to put an end to his terror.

He must have been tired because he made no attempt to hide this part of himself. He must have assumed no one around him was powerful enough to read him. Maybe he didn't know anyone with my particular skillset. It gave me the advantage.

Ryder and I waited in the brush surrounding the driveway to the church, James was at the rear, and Barringer was covering the side exit. Nigel drove his Bentley into the small asphalt parking lot and parked it in the spot next to the handicap space in front of the building.

Are you there? I can't see you.

"That's good," I whispered. "You shouldn't be able to see me."

Ryder frowned at me, and I gestured to the car. Ryder made a quiet whisper through his teeth and shook his head.

It was approaching dusk and the sky was filled with pink and purple hues that filtered through the canopy of hickory and oak trees, deepening as the clock pushed further into the night. By the time this exchange was supposed to take place, there would be no light in the sky, very little light surrounding the church, as there was only one light in the parking lot and one above the back door.

Nigel made no move to exit the car. He remained seated in the front, chatting amiably with a young woman who sat on the passenger side rear seat. My stomach dropped.

"No. You can't be here!"

It's not me. But it looks like me, doesn't it?

I pulled out my binoculars and, sure enough, I stared at Joanna, but slowly her features morphed and—

"Charisse?"

Joanna's security detail hadn't looked anything like Joanna when I'd met her before. Now? They could be twins.

Nigel was using his own power of suggestion, and damn he was good. Even her psychic signature felt similar to Joanna's.

I loved having him on our side.

The front doors of the church swung wide open and my attention honed in on the mission.

Esai surveyed the space, looking for any telltale signs that Rains' directions hadn't been followed. There were none that he could see from the front of the church. We'd hoofed it in from a mile away and had the congregation members who were waiting to ambush Nigel subdued behind a shed out back of the church, where James could keep an eye on them.

Esai gestured for Nigel and Joanna to enter the church. Nigel opened the door and grabbed his cane, which was mostly for show, and he stood to his full height with a polite smile for Esai as he closed the car door firmly.

"Bring the girl."

Nigel straightened his overcoat. "She stays where she is."

He climbed the steps, and Esai made a move to stop him but he was frozen in place. Nigel merely walked past, head held high as if he hadn't a care in the world, into the church. As if he were untouchable.

Esai watched him with a scowl and as soon as Nigel was inside, he was able to move. He hurried toward the car.

Ryder trained his weapon on him but I held out a hand.

"Wait."

Sure enough, Esai reached for the handle of the rear door on the driver's side—then yanked his hand back with a shout. He shook it out while Joanna's doppelganger watched from inside the car.

"What the…" Ryder whispered.

"Nigel's a badass, I'm telling you."

Ryder returned his sights to Esai, who walked around the car and tried another door with the same effect. This time he jumped back after making contact and held his hand to his chest, curse words flying.

Headmaster has some neat tricks.

"Yes he does," I whispered, a grin on my face. "You okay?"

I'll be better when this is all over.

"Me too."

Ryder looked to me, his eyebrows raised.

Then all hell broke loose.

CHAPTER 33
BURNED

Cassidy

I struggled against the rope that tied me to a chair beside the altar of the antiquated church and wished for the madness to stop, to just be over. Every inch of my body hurt, I was tired, and with every new trauma, I wanted to give up and go to sleep...even if that meant forever. I'd won my battle of wills against this horrible man and that was enough.

I'm sorry, Jackson.

The sanctuary was stark white with dark wood pews and warm light emanating from flickering candles strewn about the place that cast shadows all around.

Delaney's boss, the headmaster of Havenhart, walked into the church with a jovial smile that was unexpected, but I was more surprised by Rains' reaction to him. The usually composed Rains, especially when he was in front of those he thought he could manipulate, was breaking under the strain. He didn't even try to charm the man.

"Where's my daughter?"

"Ah, Mr. Rains. I won't disrespect you with dishonesty by saying it's wonderful to make your acquaintance face-to-face. I'd rather hoped you would never return to Arkansas."

Rains turned to glare at me and then plastered an impatient smile on his face. "Nigel Hart, you wound me. What kind of a father would stand back and allow his daughter to be held against her will without taking action?"

"I might ask you what kind of father would abuse and neglect such a remarkable young woman, but then I know exactly the kind of father you are. Now, I have come to fetch Miss Mackenzie, the remarkable young woman *you*, in fact, are holding against her will. Are you willing to make the exchange voluntarily?"

The doors slammed shut behind Nigel without human aid.

Nigel didn't even flinch.

No wonder Delaney and Jackson held him in such high esteem.

I fidgeted on my chair, trying to make some slack with the ropes, but my energy flagged. I just couldn't anymore. I was so tired. I couldn't even keep my head up any longer.

"There will be no exchange," Rains snapped. "Give me Joanna and I might let you walk out of here."

"That's never going to happen."

Rains inhaled impatiently and rested his hands on his hips. "In here, in this place, *I* am in charge." He held his hands up and smiled. "My will shall be done."

I heard singing again. Live singing, not a recording and not in my head. I'd thought I was dreaming, but no. It was coming from above me. I looked up and groaned. *God, no.*

There was a choir singing in the loft above us. A *children's* choir.

"Enough with the theatrics, Rains. You are surrounded. You will not be given the opportunity to hurt another person." Nigel began to walk toward me and the candle flames grew bigger, brighter. Suddenly the temperature rose in the room, as though I were standing before a bonfire.

"Don't come any closer!" Rains growled.

Nigel stopped and pulled out his phone. "It's over, Rains." He touched the screen, and it lit up.

"Father?" a familiar voice asked. I couldn't make out the face, but I knew that voice.

"Abel." Rains' back stiffened. "You should have had more faith."

"Father, you need to stop this. You're a benevolent leader, you have a critical responsibility to your community, to your new child. You need to stop this madness!"

The sound of a baby fussing caught Rains' attention. "My son."

"*Both* of your sons. Please, Father. Stop hurting people. Give yourself up."

Rains clenched his fists at his sides and then he pulled a lighter out of his pocket, flicked it to life, and dropped it on the carpeted steps. A ring of flames spread around the perimeter of the sanctuary as though someone had poured an accelerant.

"You turned your back on me, on our community, the moment you turned yourself in."

Nigel glanced around at the flames, but he remained unflappable.

"You've reached the end of the line, Mr. Rains. It's time to surrender."

"When it comes to Our Maker, I will never surrender. As for you, Hart, I'm done talking to you. You were warned, and these deaths will be on your conscience."

The flames surrounded the sanctuary and began traveling up the stairs to the loft. The singing turned to screams.

"No, children," Rains said in his booming voice. "You must sing."

Their screams stopped and they carried on with their hymn, their innocent voices climbing over each other's, forming harmonies so lovely that the hairs rose on my arms. I renewed my fight against my bonds, determined to get free.

The front doors burst open at the same time as the side door, and three men entered while shouting, with guns trained on Rains.

"Nigel, go!"

Jackson.

He grabbed ahold of Nigel with the hand not supporting his rifle and shoved him toward the doors as he moved toward Rains.

I feared I'd never hear his voice again. His commanding tone gave me a burst of strength. I was able to yank one arm out of the rope, abrading skin as I went.

"Hold on," a man whispered next to my ear.

I whipped my head around to find James, Delaney's cousin, behind me with a huge knife.

"Here, take this," he said, shoving a gun toward my free hand.

He went to work trying to cut the ropes and Rains held his hands up.

"I see you survived your friend's amplified taser. How delightful. Now I can finish you off myself."

"Like you did Abel's mom? Joanna's mom? Like you planned to do with Denise? Tell me, Gerry, does your 'maker' approve of strangulation? Blunt force trauma to the head? Asphyxiation?"

Rains' whole body jerked with Jackson's accusations. "You bring lies into the Lord's house?" he seethed from between clenched teeth.

"Sorry, you're the liar, Rains. You do it all the time. Like the time you coerced this congregation's secretary to give you the combination to the safe and then you raped her."

The fires grew hotter and Rains vibrated with anger. "Shut up!"

"Or the time you told your father your Bible was stolen at school, but in reality those bullies used it to beat you to a pulp and then made you eat pages of it—"

"*Shut up!*" Rains raked his hands over his hair and took a deep breath, trying to get ahold of himself.

Sirens sounded outside, and Rains glanced around, looking for an escape route.

"Face it, Rains. You've always been weak, and you always will be, and you're not going to manipulate another person ever again!"

James cut my last rope and whispered in my ear, "I'm going up for the children."

"Be careful," I whispered.

Just then, a window shattered upstairs and the children began to scream again.

"Barringer," Jackson shouted, and Todd ran back outside, shutting the side door behind him.

Rains started to laugh maniacally. "So you've been doing a little digging. Fair enough. Since you destroyed my property in Florida by fire, I think it only fair that you die by immolation—you and this woman you seem so determined to save. I think it's perfect that the two of you will die here. Together. With the children, Howe. It'll be just like Nasiriyah. Yeah…Ryder told me all about the little boy you let die in the fire. Sadly, you'll add several more children to your death toll today."

Then Rains turned to me, saw that I was freed—and *I* saw his bravado had been demolished by Jackson's words. *Good.*

His eyes darted around and he made a move for the rear.

"Don't," I said, holding up the gun. No way was I letting him out of here. "You're not leaving."

He continued toward the door and I clicked off the safety.

"You aren't a killer, Cassidy. You don't have the stomach for it."

"Watch me," I said. "My time with you has changed a lot about me."

My arms trembled from the exertion. I was nearly out of gas.

"I'll take my chances."

He turned for the door—and I fired. But the smoke now rolling down the stairs was thick. I couldn't see if I'd hit him. But I heard him grunt, just before fresh flames exploded around the perimeter of the church.

"Cassidy!"

I ran forward, blinded completely now, and I stumbled, nothing but air beneath my feet—

"I got you, sweetheart."

Jackson hauled me against his side and took my weight. I coughed and he shoved fabric against my face. "Hold this here." He looked around, coughing as well. "James? You got 'em?"

"They're safe," James shouted back. "Get out now!"

But there was nowhere to go. We were surrounded by fire.

"I'm so sorry, Jackson!" There was no escape route. Jackson pulled me tighter against him and he coughed again, his whole body convulsing from the force.

"Hold on, Cassidy. Just—" He coughed yet again, and we sank to the floor together.

"Thank you. My Superman."

"Cassidy, hold on!"

I wondered if this was how Delaney felt all those years ago in the church's nursery, as fire licked up the walls and the children screamed. She'd somehow made it out unscathed...but I wouldn't. I thought about how sad she would be.

I hated that my new life was cut short. I hated that I'd survived the stupid plane crash and time in the swamp, only to die in another fire. And I hated that Jackson was here, and yet, I was grateful not to be alone.

The next time I woke up, everything was bright and soft and clean. Voices chattered around me as if they were trying to be quiet but were too excited to keep it down.

A man with a British accent raised his voice above the whispers.

"All I'm saying is that we need to give her the choice. Given what she's been through, I'll not act without her permission."

"Delaney?"

After what happened in the swamp, I'd hoped I'd never hear my voice sound all scratchy like that again. I'd healed from that. I had to believe I could heal again. I was beginning to have a great appreciation for the healing powers of the human body.

"Cass, oh my God! Are you awake?"

"If I'm not, this is an awful dream. I demand a refund."

"What—?"

"It's the drugs, darling," Damien said. "I gave her something for the pain to keep her comfortable."

"And bless you for that," I moaned. My thought process was slow and murky, sort of like the dreamy effect they used in movies as a person was walking toward you. Or like on the show *ER*, when people would blink their eyes and see the friendly face of George Clooney or Anthony Edwards leaning over the bed, only this time it was my best friend and her handsome doctor boyfriend.

"Doctor. That's right. You're a doctor. Hi doctor."

"Hello, Cassidy," he said, smiling at me with more wattage than George Clooney ever managed on that show. "How are you feeling?"

"How long you got? My pains have pains." Speaking of pain. "Oh God, Delaney—where's Jackson?!" I reached for her but got tangled up by a tube that must have been an IV.

She placed her hand over mine. "He's fine! He's with the FBI agent just down the hall. He wanted to be told as soon as you woke up, so let me go get him, okay? And, um," she looked at Damien and bit down on her lip, "Damien has something to discuss with you."

She started to let go of my hand but I reached for her. "What is it?"

"It's okay, everything is okay. Let me go get Jackson."

She turned and trotted from the room, and Damien laughed.

"You'd think she'd be better at that, seeing as she's the counselor," I said, rolling my eyes. My vision was no worse than...when? "What day is it? Where am I?"

"You're going to have a lot of questions," Damien said, patting my hand, "and I'm here to answer them. First, today is Saturday. It's been three and a half weeks since you were hijacked. You do recall what's happened?"

The creepy guys, the plane crash, the blindness, the community, Esai, Rains, Jackson. The escape. Ryder's house. Simon and Garfunkel. *Jackson.* Rains again. The church. The children.

"Oh God, the children—"

"They are all perfectly fine and back with their parents. It seems that Rains had arranged for there to be a choir practice during his little drama. James and Ryder were able to get them out through an upstairs window and the fire department's net. Now, we have some medical issues to discuss."

"But how were we not burned? How am I even here?"

"Nigel was able to protect you all from the flames. His gift is quite powerful." Damien's smile faded a bit. "So that's one less worry, but you sustained new injuries in the car crash before they brought you to the church."

My eyes blurred as they filled with tears. "I'm not sure I want to know." A sob broke loose, and he started to speak but I held up my hand. "After everything I've been through, I should be grateful just to be alive. I'm not sure I'm ready to hear the rest."

"Sweetheart?"

Jackson hurried into the room and toward the bed, but then he stopped short. He shoved his hands in his back pockets. "I'm…I'm glad you're awake."

What? What was this? After everything we'd been through, he was just going to stand there? "Excuse me? Get over here," I said, lifting my sore and heavy arm to reach for him.

"Thank God," he muttered as he bent down and held me close, kissing the side of my head. "Thank all the gods, thank everything. I'm so damned glad you're okay." He squeezed a little too tight, and I sucked in a breath, but when he tried to back away, I held him to me. He laughed and dropped to a knee. "Thank all the things you're awake."

"You saved me. Again."

Jackson shrugged. "I had help." He winked at me.

"Whatever. Thank you for coming for me."

"Always." And I knew he meant it.

His gaze dropped to my lips as he brushed my hair back. *Wow, he still wants to kiss me after all that, he must be a keeper.*

Damien cleared his throat.

"We were just going to discuss Cassidy's health concerns. Would you like Jackson to stay?"

"Please."

Jackson squeezed my hand and reached over to pull a chair close so he could stay on my level. Which was good, because when he stood, he was just outside my clear vision range.

"Very well. I'm not sure how much Delaney or Jackson have told you about my gift?"

"They told me that you do some kind of healing."

"I do, but today I've treated your abrasions and we've given you oxygen because of the smoke inhalation. I want to keep you here overnight and then perhaps we can discuss your shoulder and your eyesight after you've had some rest."

I could no longer see him through the tears, but the pressure on my hand from Jackson kept me grounded.

Grounded. No more flying. My whole life upended. I'd been too busy trying to survive since the hijacking to thing about exactly what all this damage to my body meant.

"Does that mean you can help her?" Jackson asked. He handed me a tissue, and I smiled at him as I wiped my eyes. Gently. Because everything hurt down to my eyelashes, though the drugs made it bearable.

"That is entirely up to Cassidy. I won't do anything without her consent."

"What would you do?" I asked. "Like, surgery?"

"Not in the way you think. It's a much less invasive process, and I would do my best to shut off your pain receptors." He tilted his head. "I've seen worse, actually. I believe I can make you whole again, Cassidy. That is, if you want me to try."

Damien's smile was so kind, so warm...if Delaney trusted him, I could. Right? I closed my eyes and reached down inside myself, repeating his words in my head.

There was no nausea, no hollow feeling...so he fully believed his words to be true, which I'd come to understand was the one flaw in my bullshit meter. Like with Abel. Abel was kind and innocent because he truly believed all he'd been taught. I wondered if he still did, after everything he'd seen at the camp.

The truth was, *I'd* been able to tell the difference, I just hadn't accepted it. I could separate the lie from the liar, and that was the skill I needed to hone, needed to trust. Needed to have faith in.

I'd seen proof of Damien's gift. With Delaney, with Jackson...there was no dishonesty.

I turned to gaze at Jackson. I trusted him implicitly, and he trusted Damien. I knew Damien had saved his life. Jackson had helped me escape from the camp, the swamp, and the church, but I'd also fought back and survived when it would have been easy to give up and accept my fate.

I'd never given up. And I wouldn't do it now. Even if Damien's healing didn't fix me, even if I could never fly again, I would survive. I had other things to offer. After everything I'd been through, I wanted to share my gift with others. The ability to know the truth, the ability to protect oneself. Survive.

I could do this. I could trust these people, and I could help.

"All right. Let's talk more tomorrow. I can barely put together words and stuff."

"Very well."

Jackson squeezed my hand and bent down to kiss my forehead. "You are so goddamned brave."

"Thanks, Superman."

His answering smile gave me the last bit of comfort I needed before I let myself drift off.

CHAPTER 34
HEALING

Jackson

I left Cassidy to get some rest and plopped down on the bench in the hallway next to Delaney. She stared at me for a long moment before she spoke.

"So."

I barked out a laugh. I knew Delaney had been itching to ask me a bazillion questions from the moment we were brought back to Havenhart Academy.

I'd never been so glad to see the gates out front than when we returned from the nightmare inside the church.

Cassidy had passed out from smoke inhalation in my arms, just as the fire department burst in and were able to suppress the fire enough for me to carry her out. We'd both been singed a little but, miraculously, we had no life-threatening injuries. Damien had been there to give me a little once-over before I gave my statement to the authorities. He gave me strict orders to get rest, as my lungs were unhappy and I was running a fever, and that was *before* I told him about the seizures. I told him I'd rest when I was damn good and ready, which wasn't at all as immature as it sounded.

"What do you want to know first?" I asked Delaney. She sat beside me on the same bench in the hallway where Cassidy had comforted me when *Delaney* was the one in the infirmary, last fall. Maybe I should carve my name in it, put a plaque on the wall or some shit.

"Everything! Wait, well, Cassidy…"

I sighed and leaned against her shoulder a little, absorbing that special energy she exuded that helped heal even the deepest emotional wounds.

"I don't need to tell you how amazing she is."

She laughed and rubbed my arm, giving my hand a squeeze. "She's the best. But are you two…is everything…"

"God, I hope so. She's…I…"

I turned to face Delaney and saw the happy tears in her eyes. "You *loooove* her!"

"Ugh, when you say it like that—"

"I'm sorry! I can't help it. I'm so happy. For everything; that you're both okay, that you found her, that she found *you*…" She poked me in the chest at the last bit.

"Ow! Hey, I'm injured over here."

She rolled her eyes and gave me that expectant look.

"She did, I just…God, I hope she can accept all of this, accept me. I don't know, Delaney."

"Give her time. She's been through an awful ordeal and it takes her time to warm up to things."

I understood what she was saying on a surface level, but my heart hurt just thinking about losing Cassidy again after all we'd been through. I was nervous having her out of my sight—even knowing Damien was with her and would protect her from anything—but I knew here she was safe. I just hoped she felt the same about me.

"Mr. Howe?"

I turned to find the person who had kept me sane the past few weeks, standing before me in the flesh.

"Oh, come here, girl!" I leaned forward and opened my arms to Joanna. She tackled me with more force than I'd thought she was capable of. She nearly bowled me over. *"Oof."*

"I'm sorry, I'm just so glad to see you!"

I held her tight to me and breathed a sigh of relief. "Me too, darlin'. You saved my damn life, you know that? And Miss Cassidy's."

I pulled back and wiped away Joanna's tears. I smiled at her security detail, Charisse, and thanked her for being there for the girl.

"My pleasure," she said, her Russian accent thick. She hung back while we talked to the very affectionate Joanna.

"Can I meet her? Miss Cassidy?" Joanna rubbed the top of my head and frowned. "And are you going to grow it back? It's not you like this."

I barked out a laugh. "It's good to be home. I might get a big head if I stay away too long."

Joanna giggled and rubbed my fuzz again, which was probably full of soot.

"You can meet Cassidy in a little while," Delaney said, smoothing down Joanna's hair. "She's healing right now."

Joanna nodded. She was fully aware of Damien's power to heal. He'd saved her life, too. Man, I may have taken a bullet for Damien and been the one to run into the jungle to rescue Cassidy, but Damien's power to heal had saved us all. Him and Delaney, working together, were so important to the academy, and all who found safe haven there.

"I was so afraid when the fire started," Joanna whispered, and I squeezed her tight.

"I know, darlin'. It was a close call, but everything's okay."

She pulled back. "Where's my father?"

And my smile fell.

"He and Esai got away. But don't worry. Agent Barringer and the entire FBI are on the lookout." I tapped my temple. "Plus, I've got inside information on his whereabouts."

Her eyes flared. "You do? Oh! You *do*!"

The Connection had been quiet. I was sure with Morgan's help I could tap into it once more, but after Damien had gone over my injuries, and I'd told him about the seizures in Florida, he said I shouldn't try to tap into my Connections with anyone until he could send me for tests. Apparently he was concerned that they may indicate there's something else going on in my brain. Figures. I survived bombs and gunshots, but a taser might take me out of the game for a bit.

"I do, but Mr. Preston said I need to rest." I lifted the corner of my lip and pouted, knowing it would make her laugh.

"And he's shut me out. I can't see him at all anymore."

I smoothed down her hair. "It's probably better that way, Joanna. You don't need to see what he's up to."

She kicked up her chin. "I can handle it," she said, and I knew she could, but she needed to be a kid, to have a life where she felt safe, not one where she was exposed to her father's evil plans.

Delaney joined our hug. "I can't thank you enough, Joanna, for helping bring my best friends home. You're my hero."

Joanna blushed from the praise and let us both snuggle her until we were a big giggly mess in the hallway.

"Are you ready for class tomorrow?" Delaney asked her. "I'm looking forward to hearing your presentation on the institution of religion." In addition to her counseling duties, Delaney also taught a Sociology class.

"Yes, ma'am. I'm nervous though."

"I'm sure you're going to be fine. How about you come by my office in the morning and we can take a look at your slides before class, okay?"

Joanna gave Delaney a relieved smile. "That would make me feel better, thank you."

I let go of Joanna and took her hands in mine, squeezing them gently. "Now, go on and get your dinner. Miss Cassidy is resting, and as soon as she's up for visitors, I'll introduce you, okay?"

She nodded. "Thank you, Mr. Howe. It's really good to see you smiling." She waved at us as she skipped off toward the commons, spotting at a group of girls on the way. She ran to catch up to them, and Charisse trotted behind her.

I exhaled a little more tension out of my body. It wouldn't all be gone until I had some time with Cassidy to talk, preferably when she was no longer medicated. I still wasn't sure how she would feel about me—or a potential future with me—after everything that had happened, especially after I let her get taken again, after she'd already been through so much...and I knew it would be some time until I could expect her to make any decisions. We all knew patience wasn't my best virtue.

"It's going to be fine, Jackson. I have a good feeling that Cassidy—and the two of you together—are going to be fine."

"I hope you're right."

We sat in silence waiting for Damien to come out, and the whole time I felt Delaney's healing energy working its way into me, through me. By the time he emerged, looking wrung out, he offered me a smile.

"She's resting. She's doing really well."

"How about you, though?" Delaney jumped to her feet and put her arms around his midsection.

Damien pushed his hair back from his face and sighed, leaning against her a little. When I'd first met him, he had one white streak that began at his temple. And now? It was hard to tell whether his hair was mostly black or white.

"I think, if she'll allow it, I'll have you be there when I heal her. I want her to rest and get her strength up before we do anything. I hate to wait, but she's got a lot going on."

Delaney frowned. "Let's get you home—"

"Actually, I'd like for you to stay with her and see what you can offer when she wakes up. Jackson, if you wouldn't mind taking a walk with me? Since you aren't going to go to bed yourself like I told you to?"

Delaney and I exchanged looks, and I nodded.

"Sure, man. Let's go."

The two of them shared a kiss and a moment of connection that at any other time would have made me roll my eyes. But now I knew. I knew, and I was so close to having it. Was it still possible?

Damien and I walked out through the boys' dorm and into the fading afternoon light. The air was chilly and I was grateful.

"If I never go back to the damn swamp, I'll be a happy man."

Damien chuckled, his voice a little hoarse. "You've been to hell and back, my friend."

"You can say that again, but Cassidy had it way worse."

He nodded solemnly and looked straight ahead. "Her poor body,

Jackson. Look, I can't disclose the extent of her injuries, but I swear to you I will do everything in my power to make her well."

I placed a hand on his shoulder and gave it a squeeze before letting go. "I know you will, man. But I don't like how much this is taking out of you."

In the past year since the troubles with Rains began, Damien had aged considerably. He even used to be taller than me, and now his shoulders seemed to have a permanent slouch to them.

"Delaney is worried as well," he said, his voice low. "I'm not sure how much longer I can continue—"

"You need to recharge is all," I said, hoping I was right. "As soon as we get Rains in custody, you and Delaney should take off for a few days. Go to the beach or something, maybe your place down in New Orleans."

Damien's lip quirked up. "That's not a terrible idea. I don't know. Let's see how Cassidy is doing, how Joanna is—"

"Preston, I'm telling you, I know I'm the last one who should be giving advice about this shit, but hear me out. We can manage without you both for a few days. We need you long-term, and not just for your gift, you feel me? Your leadership is crucial to this place. And your friendship, man…"

It was his turn to place a hand on my shoulder. "The feeling is mutual. We were so worried while you were gone. Delaney had nightmares. Even James sulked more than usual."

I bumped into him. "Aw, it's like you care."

He bumped me back and laughed. "You know I do, Jackson. Very much."

"I know you do." One thing Havenhart Academy had taught me was how to be open with people about my feelings. The people here would know anyway and would call me on my bullshit, so I'd learned to share like a good boy. Turns out I didn't hate it that much.

"And so does Cassidy, that's very clear."

My face heated and my chest was full. "She's so strong," I whispered.

"She really is. And she'll need us to be strong *for* her as she recovers. Which means you need rest too. We all do." Damien glanced at me.

"I want you to know I hear your concerns. I'm going to suggest to Nigel that he start looking for another healer. I'm not going anywhere, but I'm not too proud to admit that I could use assistance."

"Then you'll get it. If there's anyone out there with a skillset even remotely similar to yours, we'll find them. You need to rest, maybe get a full health workup yourself. I don't like how much the healing is taking out of you, and neither does Delaney."

He nodded. "You're quite right. Let's get through this latest calamity and then we can talk about how getting old really sucks."

"Speak for yourself. Only one of us is getting old around here and it ain't me," I said, raising my eyebrows at him.

"Right, that wasn't arthritis you came to me about several months ago when you had trouble putting on your pants, you old codger—"

"That's not fair. Those are war wounds, asshole."

"Keep telling yourself that, coffin dodger. You'll be an OAP before you know it."

"OAP?"

Damien smirked. "Old Age Pensioner."

Sometimes Damien's Britishisms tickled me, and this was one of them. By the time we got up to his apartment, and I made sure he was inside and hydrating, we were both in tears. It was one of those ridiculous laughter sessions when you're bent at the waist, gripping your sides in agony but continuing to say inappropriate and outrageous things. It eventually becomes a contest, as do most things when guys are being guys together, and you hope you're the last man standing.

"Enough, enough," Damien said, finally holding up his hand. "Give it a rest, mate. I think I've ruptured my spleen."

"Right. Can't have you pushing up the daisies just yet," I said in my lame attempt to sound like him.

"You either. Thanks, mate. Glad to have you back. Now get some rest. We've still got a school to run. I think your students are ready for something a bit more challenging than the paint-by-numbers I brought in, and ready to get back to art after Morgan had them doing research—"

"Research? Oh, man. Poor kids. Thank you guys for covering for me. I missed them."

Damien smiled. "They missed their teacher."

I sighed. "You know, there were moments out there, especially in the beginning, when I thought, 'man, I miss undercover work, I miss the adrenaline.' But no. That was a different time in my life, and while I'm grateful for having the experience, there's nothing like seeing one of my students have a breakthrough and figure out how to get the texture they want, or make the colors pop in a new way... They always seem to have a little more pep in their step when they leave, and I'm glad I can give that to them."

"I've told you before," Damien said. "You're worth far more to us than your skills as a Ranger. This academy needs you. We wouldn't be the same without you."

This time when I wiped at the tears, I couldn't blame the laughter.

"Thanks, man. I think I'm going to get back to Cassidy—"

"Jackson, go to bed. Let Delaney sit with her. And get yourself something to eat. Delaney has the cottage next to her own prepared for when Cassidy wakes up. Nigel has made it available for her permanently, if she decides to stay."

"Right. If she decides to stay."

Damien's words hit me like an ice bath. I'd put off thinking about a future without Cassidy because I needed to focus on getting her home safely.

But what now?

Rest. Yeah, I got that. Knowing me, it would be a whole lot of stewing and sulking.

CHAPTER 35
FACE THE MUSIC

Cassidy

I actually slept soundly after talking to Damien and I felt a little stronger, at least ready to face the music. The next morning, Delaney brought me breakfast, which I devoured. She also let me know that Jackson was running a fever and Damien had sent him to his apartment to rest.

"Is he going to be okay? I'm so worried…"

"He's been through a lot, but he's tough. And so are you."

That was all she needed to say for me to completely fall apart.

I cried and cried and cried on Delaney's shoulder, until there were no tears left. Then Grace checked my vitals and said I could go to Delaney's cottage and rest if I preferred. Apparently that was what I needed because once we arrived, I crashed and slept for nearly 24 hours.

I woke up the next time, tucked into Delaney's bed with Simon and Garfunkel staring at me, I felt like I'd turned a corner.

"Where did you two come from?"

Delaney peeked her head in. "Ryder brought them. He and Agent

Barringer have been staying with Nigel, and I guess the dogs have been going nuts without you."

I snuggled closer with my two new best friends and accepted all the love they had to give. Then I made a decision.

I was done feeling defeated. I was ready to reclaim my life.

Well. After breakfast.

"Feel up to going to the commons?" Delaney asked when I emerged from her room showered and dressed in more borrowed clothes. Thankfully, she had a sports bra that fit, so I was feeling much more comfortable.

"I think so. And then at some point, I need clothes and a cell phone."

"No problem. We can have some things brought over. The tailor in town is great. She's got a little boutique and does custom work. She's responsible for my makeover," Delaney said, turning in a circle. I admired her comfy-looking rayon pants and blouse outfit.

"As long as she's got underwear. There's just something empowering about knowing you're not facing the world flapping in the breeze."

Delaney laughed and pulled me in for a hug. "You seem much more yourself today."

"You have a way of doing that."

Delaney stepped back and winced. "And how do you feel about...me?"

Not once had my bullshit meter gone off in Delaney's presence. Occasionally in our friendship, I'd known she was keeping things from me, but I sensed an openness about her now, like she was ready to tell me anything I wanted to know and not hold back.

"You know I love you. This has all been...hard to swallow, but I'm getting there." *Could* I get there enough? A part of me was missing, somewhere else on campus with the man who'd risked his life to save me. I had to stand on my own before I was ready to deal with all of this...extra, but I knew for certain that I wanted him.

"Good. You'll get no pressure from me, okay? But I'm here for you, however you need."

"I know. And I love you for it. Now feed me. I'm starving."

Simon and Garfunkel were ready to go, too. They stood by the door and woofed happily.

"What shall we do with the boys?"

Delaney shrugged. "Bring them. George will have some goodies for them until we can get them proper dog food."

"Were Ramses and Clio okay with the dogs?"

Delaney wrinkled her nose. "They're over at Damien's place. Ryder wasn't sure this was the best time to introduce them to cats. They love Damien, though. I'm sure they terrorized him overnight, but they do it to him here, too, when he stays over."

I clipped the leashes on the boys and we went outside into a bright spring morning. The weather was perfect, even a little chilly, and not too humid. The boys both sniffed like crazy outside and did their business by a row of bushes at the edge of Delaney's small yard.

"How are things with Damien? Is it weird? Working together and being together?"

"Not at all. We've done well as a team from the start. I did worry about what the kids would think, but they're cute about it. I've never had a man around my students before, never dated anyone I worked with, so I had no idea, but it was pretty seamless."

"Seamless." Funny, I'd describe things with Jackson nearly the same way. I'd been so grateful when he rescued me, then I panicked, and now...I was justified in being cautious after all I'd been through, first with Robert and then the abduction. I knew Jackson understood that, too. I'd managed to space out as we walked and now we were entering the commons, which were bustling with a bunch of teenagers.

Maybe I hadn't thought this through. Was I really ready? To be in this place permanently? Around all these kids...who weren't like regular kids?

Delaney pushed the doors open and held them for me to bring the boys inside. They stuck close to me and ignored all of the stimuli. There were about fifty or so students eating at tables, and three tables held more adults. Damien waved us over to a table where he sat with Agent Barringer, and Delaney headed in that direction.

The men stood as we approached the table, and Damien pulled out a chair for Delaney.

"You look well," Barringer said as I took a seat.

"I feel so much better," I said. "I slept like a rock last night, thanks to Delaney."

I couldn't put it into words, but I knew she'd done whatever it was she does in her counseling with me. When the tears started, she held me to her and I felt a warmth surround me, like sinking into a soothing bath. I was able to say what I needed to say, finally put it into words how I felt about the abduction, the community, and all the shit my experience brought up from my past. It didn't hurt quite as bad when it was all out. Then another wave washed over me when she tucked me into bed, and I'd managed to stave off the nightmarish images that had been pinging around in my head since this all started.

"She's quite wonderful, isn't she?" Damien said, leaning over to kiss Delaney's cheek, causing her to blush a lovely shade of pink.

"Good morning, ladies." A man in his fifties with a jolly smile and disposition brought us each a plate of delicious-looking waffles and breakfast sausage.

"Cassidy, this is our treasured chef, George Walden."

"I remember you, from my visit in the fall. I hear you're brutal with a needle."

He tapped his nose and winked at me. "I'll be back with some bowls for your friends there," he said, smiling at the dogs. "So well-behaved."

"Thank you," I called out as he hurried back to the kitchen at a trot.

"Would you mind if I asked about your…gift?" Barringer asked Delaney as we dug into our breakfast. "Damien was kind enough to show me how he heals people yesterday." He shook his head. "I'm stunned. Honestly. I've read stories, you know? But I never imagined I'd ever see it in real life."

Damien took a sip of tea and leveled his gaze on Delaney. "Jackson had two wounds that were in need of attention. He had a significant fever. He really should have been seen by proper doctors."

"Is he all right?" I asked. "Will he be…okay?" My chin quivered, and I thought one move might shatter me. Simon nudged my hand and I stroked his ear to keep the tears at bay.

"Cassidy," Damien said. His deep, warm voice commanded attention and his British accent gave his words weight, but he was so...*kind*. That's the only word I could think of to describe his demeanor. "Our friend is quite stubborn when it comes to his health, and please believe me when I tell you that his wounds were not life-threatening. I was able to heal the thigh wound and the resulting infection, but that scrape from the metal will add a new landmark to his roadmap, I'm afraid. Systemically, he will recover after a few days' rest, which he's assured me he will take." He wiped his mouth with a napkin and when he brought it away, he had a smirk on his face. "I might have threatened to put a padlock on his door if he didn't agree to voluntary confinement."

Delaney laughed. "Oh, boy. Yeah, that sounds like Jackson." She reached for Damien's hand on the table and squeezed it. "Thank you for taking care of him."

"Yes," I managed to squeak out. "Thank you. I..."

They exchanged a glance, and then Delaney leaned toward me. "Take it from my experience, Jackson is hard-headed, but he'll be okay." Then she looked up suddenly and smiled at someone, waving them over. "There's someone who really wants to meet you."

I put my fork down and turned to see a slight girl with long black hair and wide, pale blue eyes standing several feet away, her hands clasped in front of her. She wore a floral sundress that matched the color of her eyes and a fearful expression on her face.

I smiled at her, and instantly her fear melted. Beside me, the boys popped up from where they'd been lying and their tails went wild.

"Joanna?" I said, and she nodded.

"I didn't want to intrude but I wanted to see you for myself."

I stood up to greet her, and as she approached, the boys began jumping and barking and pulling to get close to her. She held her hands out to them, and they licked her hands and arms, and then her face as their big bodies pushed against her.

"Well, Joanna, meet Simon and—"

"Garfunkel! You good boys." She petted them both and they kissed her once more before George arrived with their food. "You did a good job."

Her words made me flinch, and I tried to recover. "Sorry about the slobber," I said to her, and she just giggled.

"They're so cute. I'm glad they came with you," she said. "They're going to take great care of you."

"I...oh, yeah, they're great. I've never had a dog before."

"And now you have two." She smiled at me and my throat got tight.

"Joanna, I don't know how to say—"

"You're welcome," she interjected. "But I need to apologize, not only for intruding in your mind. I need to learn to get permission before I do that, and sometimes I get too enthusiastic and I forget. I'm just so sorry my father dragged you into this mess."

Gone was the innocent little girl. Her face darkened as she spoke, and I sensed the old soul inside of her.

"This is in no way your fault," I said. "And as for the intrusion, thank you for saying that. I'm not sure what to think of all this," I added, and she winced. I took a deep breath. "But I want to be... comfortable. With all of it."

She nodded. "I hope you can be. For Mr. Howe. He's—"

"Jo-an-na," Delaney interrupted with a gentle warning tone. "Remember, we talked about sharing your truth, but not that of others?"

She exhaled and glanced down for a second before she nodded and looked up at me. "Right. It's hard sometimes to know things, know what should be, and have no way of helping."

"I understand," I said to her. "And I am forever in your debt for helping Mr. Howe rescue me."

She shrugged. "I'm glad you're okay." She turned toward Barringer and frowned. "Mr. Howe says I'm not supposed to talk to you, but he didn't say I couldn't introduce myself." She stuck out her tiny hand and lifted her chin. "I'm Joanna Rains, and I really *do* want to talk to you, when Mr. Howe says it's okay."

Barringer smiled. "I'm very pleased to meet you," he said. "And for now, let's respect Mr. Howe's wishes." They shook hands and she winked at him.

"Okay. We'll talk later. Goodbye."

She smiled at the dogs, gave me one last look, then she hurried over to a table with other girls, all of whom were looking at us and whispering.

"Welcome to Havenhart Academy," Delaney said with a laugh.

"And how often do you have conversations like this?"

She looked at Damien, looked down at her watch, then back at me. "I don't know, twice—?"

"Twice an hour, perhaps," Damien said. "Speaking of which, Cassidy, when you're ready—*if* you are ready—I would like to discuss healing your injuries. Delaney can absolutely be present. Jackson, too, or whoever you'd feel comfortable with. I'm a board-certified medical doctor with an internal medicine specialty, in case you're concerned, and I can provide you copies of my credentials if you like."

"I...yes. I would like to try...the healing thing. I'm ready."

"I can evaluate what I'm able to correct in regards to your injuries. I'll only do what you are comfortable with." He tilted his head and his nostrils flared. "I can definitely provide you relief from that shoulder pain. Your eyes, well...we can talk. For now, I must meet with the headmaster." He stood and bent over to kiss Delaney's cheek. "Until later. Todd? The headmaster would like to speak with you, too."

Todd wiped his hands and picked up his tray, following Damien's lead. "I'll see you both later?"

I smiled at him, feeling the weight of everything pressing me down into the chair.

"Before you're completely overwhelmed, how about we do this: let's go see Diana, my assistant, and we'll have her set up the tailor to come by this afternoon. I have class this morning, which you can come watch or you can rest at my place, and then after lunch, maybe you'll feel up to seeing Damien?"

Time to be brave, Cassidy. You know Delaney is looking out for your best interests.

"Okay."

. . .

I'd never been able to watch Delaney teach before, and it was thoroughly entertaining, especially when her student Sergei from Russia got her talking about mesmerism and hypnotism.

"But isn't it true, Miss Frost, that the power of suggestion is strongest in those who do not have a clear sense of self-awareness?"

"That is true," Delaney said, hopping up to sit on her desk. "Your mind is open to suggestion in certain ways, but awareness is one of the best tools you can possess to combat negative suggestion. Like, for example, if you're watching a horror movie, once it's over, you'll likely still be jumpy and afraid, even though you know the likelihood is slim that some dude in a black cape and a white mask is going to slice you up with a knife."

"Or a hockey mask!"

She laughed and pointed at the kid. "Or a hockey mask. But, it can also make you think of ways you're vulnerable, like maybe you keep your drapes open at night, or you walk around with head-phones on too loud when you should be paying attention to your surroundings.

"If you find yourself in a situation where it's a high-pressure sales scenario, or a friend is trying to talk to you about this new opportunity they'd like to share with you—'would you like to have coffee and talk about it'—these are all situations when asking questions, and also questioning your own beliefs, is crucial. You possess vast knowledge within yourselves, and as you get older, you'll be faced with situations where you need to ask yourself: what does this person have to gain? What motivation might they have for being dishonest? And what might the consequences be if I say yes or no? You need to evaluate everything. Trust your gut."

She shot me a look, and I raised my eyebrow. Then it was time for class to end.

The kids all asked to pet the dogs and said goodbye to me. Once they were all out, Delaney smiled.

"That kid was a plant, wasn't he?"

She laughed out loud. "See? Question everything. No, darling. If he was a plant, I would have brought you into the conversation and had you talk about your inner bullshit meter."

I snorted and stood up. "I probably should. If the shit I've been through helps anyone *not* go through this hell, it would be worth it."

She smiled at me expectantly.

"Oh, no you don't, Delaney! You manipulative little—"

"What? Just pointing out that you have so much to offer."

I pressed my lips together and my eyes burned. "You mean if I can't fly."

"I'm sorry, babe, but you know that's what I do. I'm a problem solver. And I know it's bothering you, thinking about what you're going to do, although you don't have to worry about it. Not for a long while. You can stay here indefinitely, and your company said they'd give you leave…"

One of my tasks this morning after breakfast was calling my personal stakeholders. My parents were given very basic information: plane crash, stuck in the swamp, brought to stay with Delaney. My company, however, bent over backwards to tell me how sorry they were, and they promised they would be sending me an accident insurance payment to tide me over. Agent Barringer had explained everything to them, and they'd already been out to the crash site to investigate, but they weren't holding me responsible at all. Janet was fine, thank God. They were very generous, and said I could take as much time as I needed to heal and that they'd be in touch.

As for my personal belongings? Well, they didn't fare as well. My roommates at the crash pad took the call as fact, packed up my shit, and put it in the garage, which flooded when the water heater went out. Who knew if anything survived.

"You know, I read a book many years ago about survivors of accidents and how certain people have more of a sense of self-preservation than others. I thought about that book a lot when I was…" I cleared my throat. I didn't even want to think his name again. "When I was with the community. Before I knew Jackson had come, I was focused on getting to know my surroundings and paying attention to patterns so if I had any opportunity, I might escape. I wonder…"

"What is it?"

"I wonder if my, you know, my inner bullshit meter…I wonder if that's part of something bigger? Whatever I end up doing, I want to learn more about survival and how to protect myself. Who knows? Maybe it will help me get over the nightmares."

She gave me a gentle squeeze. "I think you're onto something. There are plenty of folks here who would be excellent resources as well."

We left her classroom and headed to lunch, and Delaney continued on the subject.

"You have the gift of time right now. Take it. Use it. Decide what you want to do. That's all I'm saying. And if whatever you decide involves staying here," she said with false innocence, "I'm certainly not going to complain."

"I can't stay with you forever, Delaney. You can't sleep on the couch."

"It's fine! I will until you feel like you can stay on your own, and then you can move next door, or…wherever you feel comfortable."

Truth was, I wanted to be with Jackson. I missed him terribly. I wanted his scent around me, his strong arms, his deep voice with the slight Virginia drawl telling me everything would be okay. And if I asked myself the questions Delaney posed to her class, this is what I came up with:

What does he have to gain by having this Connection, or whatever he called it? Well, what does any man want?

Sex. That was mutual in our case.

Money. From what I could tell, the dude was doing just fine. True, he lived in an apartment in the boys' dorm, but if he had a military pension and was getting paid as well as Delaney said *she* was being compensated, he didn't have need of my measly salary.

Love?

Oh God…I really *did* love him. I wanted to be with him right now, taking care of him, tending to his wounds, cooking for him, rubbing his feet…I loved how well we fit together, how well we got along, and how easy it was…

What motivation did he have to be dishonest?

A big one. He'd kept his "gift" from me because he knew I'd freak out. That could be considered dishonest, but guess what? He'd been right. I *had* freaked out at first, but I'd learned to trust my gut and accept that I needed to have a little faith in myself and the people around me, the ones who I knew I could trust.

If I accepted all that Jackson was, all I felt for him…could we navigate a relationship given all of the uncertainties in our worlds?

I'd never known love like he'd shown me. I'd never felt the way he made me feel; safe, cherished, loved.

The more questions I asked, the more the answers led me to a choice.

Give him a chance. Or break both of our hearts.

We entered the commons and Delaney held onto the boys' leashes while I grabbed food. George waved to me and said he'd bring out some food for the pups. I was so grateful for these people. I knew they cared for me because I was Delaney's best friend, but they were genuinely nice. Every person I'd come in contact with had gone above and beyond so far, or offered to.

Like Damien.

When I sat down with my food, I leaned close to Delaney. "Can we see Damien after lunch?"

She nodded and smiled, relieved. She patted my hand and we ate our burgers and fries, complete with moans of delight.

One thing was for sure, I'd eat like a queen here.

Damien and Barringer showed up and joined us.

"Are you free after lunch?" I asked him.

He gave the same relieved smile Delaney did. "Absolutely. And before you ask, he's eaten and he's resting. That's about all I can tell you."

I wanted to see for myself, but I wanted to see Damien first. Actually, I wanted crawl in bed with Jackson and not leave, but I wanted to test my new bravery and trust with Damien. I wanted to know more about the school and what they did here before I decided just how deep I wanted to get. I knew Delaney and I would always be friends, but I needed to know if I could really settle down in this place?

I turned to Agent Barringer. "After lunch, will you take the boys to see him?"

He nodded. "I think that would be a great idea."

Damien asked Delaney to go with him. It was obvious they weren't going to give Todd full access to the school, and I thought that wise. As much as I thought Todd was a good guy, he was still a federal agent and these kids were vulnerable.

"So you enjoyed watching our illustrious counselor teach this morning?" Damien asked, after we finished out meals. He looked at her with so much love. I was so damned happy for her. For them both. It was just kind of funny thinking of awkward pre-teen Delaney ending up with a posh British doctor. A picture of her with braces and the mouthpiece she had to wear afterward flashed in my mind, and I snorted a laugh. They all looked at me with concern.

"It was *that* good? Were there any videos?" Damien asked, and Delaney elbowed him.

"Stop it, you! There was no science video, and no, we don't need to go back over your surprise visit to my old school and my subsequent humiliation. Brat."

The rest of us chuckled, even Todd. "Was it one of those reproduction videos? I remember them splitting us up and showing the boys one video and the girls another, except in my class, the teacher put it on and left the room and it was the wrong one. We were all scarred by the visual reality of menstruation as sixth graders." He shook himself, and I cracked up. Damien tried not to laugh and failed. Delaney dropped her head in her hands.

"All right. Have we had enough fun? I think it's time for Cassidy's appointment." Delaney stood up first and carried her tray off while we laughed. It felt so good to laugh. It really was the best medicine.

But then it made me think of Jackson and how much fun we'd had before things went to shit at Ryder's.

I missed him.

"Hey," Todd said. "Let me take the boys outside for a walk and then over to Jackson. Delaney? Want to show me the best place for them to do their business?"

"Sure. Cassidy? You okay? I'll be there as soon as I can."

"I'm fine. Besides, I haven't had a chance to tell him embarrassing stories yet."

"You wouldn't dare," Delaney said with mock seriousness.

"You're right. I definitely wouldn't."

I gave her a finger wave and followed her man out of the commons.

He turned to me and placed a hand on my back. "Oh, please tell me you would."

"Would what?"

"Tell me embarrassing stories. I want to hear all about young Delaney. Was she just as adorable when she pouts? Was she boy crazy? Tell me everything."

"Wow, okay, Hugh Grant. Let's see if you're any good at this healing stuff and maybe I'll tell you *one* story."

He rubbed his hands together and opened the far doors of the commons. We entered a small hallway, then we turned right, and I immediately recognized the hallway. The bench. The vending machine.

"Welcome back to the infirmary," Damien said, gesturing for me to enter the room. He pressed a call button on the wall as he followed me inside. "We treat all manner of ailments here, from homesickness and the common cold, to broken bones and—"

"Gunshots?"

He exhaled. "Gunshots. Right. We've treated bullet wounds, and I pray to God there are no more. Now, go ahead and have a seat here."

He had me sit on the hospital-style bed before he went to the sink to wash his hands. The door opened and Grace entered.

"Grace Walden is our nurse extraordinaire and wife of our beloved cook."

"I remember. Thank you for taking care of me."

"Of course. We're so glad you're here."

"Now," Damien said, roping his stethoscope around his neck. "Let's walk through your injuries from the crash."

I frowned at the stethoscope. "Okay, um, first- and second-degree burns on my face, cuts on my face, my hands, dislocated left shoulder from when I fell from the cockpit to the ground. Uh, she monitored me for a concussion. The nurse was very nice. She took good care of me. Well, as best she could in a shack with limited resources."

"And your eyes?"

"She worried that maybe I had detached retinas from the fall. I didn't have glass in my eyes that she could see. It could have been the impact of the crash, or when that evil church lady backhanded me."

"One of your abductors?"

"Yeah." I shrugged. "I got a little lippy with her."

He chuckled. "Why does that not surprise me?"

"Guilt by association? It's not like Delaney has much of a filter."

"Precisely. All right. Let me do an exam and see what we can see... or not. I won't do any sort of manipulation without telling you. This is just a diagnostic pass."

I sucked in a breath for courage. "Okay."

He placed his hands on either side of my head and closed his eyes.

"Uh, Damien?"

He opened his eyes and removed his hands. "Yes?"

"Don't you need *your* eyes to, uh, check out *my* eyes? And like, tools or something?"

Grace chuckled from behind me, and Damien smiled, flicking his hair out of his eyes like a damn model.

"I don't require tools. My medicine is more hands-on. Is that all right?"

"Well, that's what I thought, but then..." I pointed at the stethoscope. "What about that?"

He looked down. "Oh this? Makes people feel better. Seems more doctory."

Oh, I liked him.

"You may proceed," I said in my best British accent.

He smiled and placed his hands on my head. This time when he closed his eyes, I felt a low-level current run through me. He breathed in slowly through his nose and out through his mouth.

"How about tinnitus?"

"Oh, my ears? Yeah. Ringing off and on, sometimes it gets like there's cotton in my ears."

He nodded, and then after a moment he stepped back and exhaled. "Let me check your shoulder."

"Okay."

He ran his hands over my shoulder and I felt the current again. The pressure from his hands was light, but there were a couple of spots that made me suck in a breath and grimace.

"Sorry," he said as he sat back. "Anyplace else?"

"Just aches and pains."

He nodded. "All right. Here's my full report. You've a torn rotator cuff and a hairline fracture of the clavicle. As for your ears, you have a ruptured left eardrum, which will likely heal on its own, or I can help things along. Your eyes, indeed, are a concern. There *is* evidence of injury to your retinas, but it's difficult to tell after the time that's passed. I can certainly heal your eyes, however your vision may not be fully restored and the potential for a repeat injury is high."

I exhaled a shaky breath. "So what do you suggest I do?"

"You have options. I can heal your shoulder and eardrum with no lasting issues. Your eyes, well, I'd like to send you to a specialist. If your livelihood didn't depend on your eyes, I would feel confident healing you, but I'd rather your vision be in the hands of someone with more experience than me. At least for a consultation. Then you may decide how you'd like to be treated."

"I appreciate that," I said, and I really did. I admired that he was aware of his limitations, or at least admitted that he had them. I still wasn't sure I believed he could heal my shoulder and eardrum. But now that I was here, I really wanted to take a chance. If it worked? Awesome.

If it didn't, though...how would I face Delaney and say, "Your man is a fraud"?

"You have reservations. Completely understandable."

"I'm not worried you'll hurt me or anything, but, like—"

"What if I'm a quack? A charlatan?" His serious expression made me giggle, and my cheeks flushed.

"Well, since you put it that way…"

He patted my knee. "Do you believe me that I won't cause you pain?"

"I do," I answered honestly. "Okay. Let's see what you can do, charlatan. But if you bring out the snake oil, I'm gone."

He smiled. "Deal."

CHAPTER 36
A GOOD PATIENT

Jackson

I'd never been a good patient, but after the hell I'd been through, I figured I'd earned some recovery time. If they were gonna bench me, put me on bed rest, then by God, I was going to be an overachiever.

But on day three, I'd had enough.

The only visitors I'd had were George and Damien with food, Barringer with the mutts, and Joanna with Marcia. It was tough to be cheery when I was feeling poorly. Damien was sure the fever was from an infection. Apparently Ryder's penicillin shot hadn't quite done the trick, or I'd picked up something else in the swamp. Damien took my blood—what was it about my friends liking to stick me with needles? —and said he'd run it over to the lab himself to see what was going on.

I was bone tired, a mere Jackson husk ready to blow away, only an echo of myself. I knew I'd survive this. I'd survived a lot.

I was tired of surviving.

But the visitor I had the evening of my third day in bed provided the kick in the ass I needed.

"Headmaster. Sir, I'm...sorry, please come in."

Nigel Hart had never stepped foot in my humble abode in the three years I'd been on staff here. Whatever the reason for his visit, I really wished I'd taken a shower. Brushed my teeth at the very least.

Tonight, he walked in with his walking stick, his portly belly straining at the buttons of his tweed vest, and his shoes shined so well they reflected off my dim lighting. Delaney followed him in and closed the door.

Thankfully I'd picked up my apartment earlier and it didn't smell too terrible, but I hadn't dusted, there was fresh dog hair from the boys...

"Jackson, my friend, I've come on a reconnaissance mission. I am forever grateful for your work in retrieving Miss Mackenzie, both in Florida and in the debacle at the church."

I swallowed hard and rubbed my sweaty hands on my sweatpants. "I'm glad to help, sir."

His gaze traveled up and down my severely underdressed self. "Your friend Mr. Simms and the FBI fellow have given me as much information as they have about Rains and his potential whereabouts... but I understand you may have a more useful bit to share."

"I...yes, sir. He, uh, well, he touched me and it opened a Connection. I have it locked down though, right now. I needed to recover."

Wading through the filth in Rains' consciousness on top of the nasty cut, the seizures, the smoke inhalation...I'd never been so wiped out in my life. Even when I was at Walter Reed recovering, I still had all of my mental faculties. But this time, I was exhausted. I hadn't wanted to take a chance that he could get to me through the link, even though that had never happened before with one of my Connections. You never knew *what* he was capable of, although we'd done an excellent job of stripping away his support base.

"You and I have much to discuss regarding your trip to Florida, but that can wait. I want you to see Damien for a follow-up on your medical issues, and then, when you're feeling up to it, I'd like you to resume your classes. I think the return to normalcy will be just as good for you as it will be for your students."

"Yes, sir. I'm looking forward to it. I also wanted to ask about Joanna."

Nigel raised a bushy eyebrow. "What is your inquiry?" He lowered himself onto my couch, and I remained standing. Delaney offered me a supportive smile and sat down next to Nigel.

"Well, it's about Agent Barringer, sir."

"At ease, Ranger," he said with a grin. "I spoke to Agent Barringer at length, and I've agreed to give him access to Joanna."

"But sir—"

"I am her guardian, Jackson. I believe the information she has will benefit the effort to put Rains behind bars permanently. Having him out of commission has to be our end game, and if the FBI wants to give it a shot, I want to support their endeavors. Joanna has asked that you be there, but I told her I needed to be sure you were fit for duty before I agreed."

"I am, sir. And as much as I trust Todd, I'm worried about the government not only learning about her and what she can do, but about the other kids here. I'm not sure that type of disclosure benefits the academy."

Nigel rested his cane across his knees and ran a knobby hand across the wood. "I've been very clear with Agent Barringer what sort of information he is at liberty to discuss with his colleagues, and I have ways of ensuring his cooperation."

That tidbit brought my concern level down considerably. I knew Nigel worked in mysterious ways, and I had no doubt he was capable of keeping Barringer in line.

"Okay. I would like to be there—as her legal guardian. If she'll have me." This was not a decision I'd come to lightly. I'd wanted to say something to Joanna when I returned, but it was probably best that I discussed it with Nigel first.

Nigel and Delaney gazed at me in surprise.

"That's a big step," he said, and I was glad he hadn't said no.

"I understand. She and I...she hasn't had a real family in so long, maybe ever. She's missed out on so much, and while I believe our community is the best place for her, I want her to have someone she can call her own. Maybe not a parent, but someone she knows will have her back no matter what. If it weren't for her, I doubt Cassidy and I would have made it out of the swamp alive. I owe her my life...and I'd like her to have it. Sir. If you think it's appropriate."

I hugged myself to keep the shakes under wraps. This was a huge step, and parenting of any sort was not something I'd ever wanted for myself, but ever since she'd used the word daughter when I was on the airplane, having the first of several freak-outs, I'd wondered what it might be like, to be that person for her.

"I'll take that under advisement, Jackson. It's an admirable suggestion, however unprecedented it may be."

"We haven't exactly had to deal with a situation like this before—"

He held up a hand. "I'll consider it." He effectively ended that discussion, and I knew better than to push with him. "On that note, I've asked Delaney to be here because it occurred to me that you may require more than physical healing after all you've been through."

I cleared my throat and planted my hands on my hips, then I crossed my arms over my chest, then I dropped my hands to my sides.

"To be honest, sir, I don't think I need—"

"Before I clear you to return to your duties, I want to be sure you are fit to do so. I also want to know where you stand before I invite Miss Mackenzie to remain here permanently. She and I had a conversation today, and she is considering my offer."

My heart thudded in my chest. "I… Is she okay? Is she okay with…us?"

"I'll let her discuss that with you when she's ready. For now, please let Delaney know how we can best support you."

I raised an eyebrow at Delaney. "Isn't that a conflict of interest?"

She rolled her eyes at me, and Nigel chuckled as he pushed himself to standing. The old man was moving a little slower these days, and I feared he might not be in the best shape to lead us for much longer. I knew he was in his late 70s, although his health remained that of a much younger man, but time catches up to us. Damien and I were feeling it as well.

"If you'd rather speak to Morgan—"

"Delaney's fine, thank you."

He chuckled again. "I know you and Miss Forrester have had your differences—"

"It's not that—"

"I happen to appreciate the fact that we have so many strong women in positions of leadership here at the academy."

"Yes, sir," I said, shaking my head, knowing there was no use protesting.

"Jackson, I want you to listen to me carefully. When I took you on as our art teacher, there were those who had reservations about your suitability for the position. Then when I put you in charge of the boys' dormitory, you once again exceeded my expectations. Time and time again, you've proved to everyone that I made the right decision. I believe you will continue to do good work for us, but I don't think *you* believe it, and frankly, I think it's time you…how do you young people put it these days? Marie Kondo your life a little?"

Delaney bit her lip and looked away to keep from laughing, and I frowned.

"Sir? Marie Kondo?"

"Yes, Jackson. You need to go through your emotional house and hold each item, decide what you need to keep, what gives you joy, and what you need to let go. Because you're carrying way too much emotional baggage for a man your age, and if you're going to continue in your current capacity, or serve in another, you need to, well…clean house. Especially if you're thinking of becoming the guardian to a child with special needs."

He looked around my cramped place and frowned. "I hadn't realized this apartment was so dreary. I think you could do with some new window dressings, to say the least. How an artist can live in a cave like this is beyond me."

Delaney chuckled and then pressed her lips together.

"I'll take it under advisement, sir."

He nodded, then smiled at Delaney.

"Very well. Delaney, dear, please check in with me after you're finished here, and then," he turned to face me, "we will determine whether you're ready to resume your duties, Jackson."

He held out a hand, and I shook it, but when I went to let go, he held on tighter than I'd imagined he could. "I'm grateful you are here, Jackson. Your bravery and wisdom are a tremendous asset. But I also want you to be happy and healthy. I hope you will allow us to help you find that state."

"Yes, sir."

He nodded, gave my hand a squeeze, and strolled out of my apartment with his head held high.

I flopped onto the couch dramatically with a groan, and Delaney laughed.

"That was heavy," I said, dropping my head back against the wall.

Delaney turned to face me. "Jackson—"

I cut her off like the asshole I was. "I really wish you weren't here right now."

She held my hand in hers and it immediately warmed. "I know. You hate being vulnerable, but let me help you. I'm not asking you to let me do therapy with you. Let me help you let go of some of this heavy stuff you're carrying. I swear, I want to cry just feeling this pain coming off you. You're my friend, Jackson. Let me be here for you."

I exhaled and let my eyes close. "Nothing for you to do, Delaney. You can't fix this. I just need to get over this belief that what I do is a curse. I know I can use it for good, and I have, but I also let people down in the past. Lives were lost because I was too busy trying to suppress it. After everything that's happened, though I'm almost ready to accept it is truly a gift, I swear."

"Right," she said. "Well, since you don't want my help, then I'm going to give you a news update."

I turned to look at her and nearly laughed as she pulled her legs underneath herself on the couch, a fierce look on her face. I thought better of it.

"While you've been recuperating, Cassidy has been getting her bearings and becoming acclimated to our little community. She's moved into the bungalow next door to mine. She's allowed Damien to heal her shoulder and her eardrum, and she's going to be doing physical therapy with Grace. Tomorrow, I'm taking her into Fayetteville to see an eye specialist Damien found for her. He wants a second opinion on how best to treat her eyes."

"That's…that's great. I'm happy. I know she's worried."

"Mmhmm. But don't you see what this all means?"

"That she's feeling better. I get it."

"No, Jackson. Come on. It means that she's giving our ways a chance, and she's going to stay...for a while at least."

Hope roared to life in my chest.

"Good. That's all good. All I want is for her to be okay."

Delaney raised that damned eyebrow. "That's all you want?"

I groaned. "Dammit, Delaney. What do you want me to say?"

"Nothing. I don't want you to say anything." She placed a hand on my cheek. "She misses you. We all miss you. And I miss your hair," she said, laughing again.

I smiled and leaned into her hand. "I miss it, too."

We looked at each for a moment, she let a tear slip out, and I gave up.

"Goddammit, Delaney. I hate crying!" But as the tears poured out and she hugged me, I broke. And at first it felt like water breaking through rusty pipes, but then she started with that damned feel-good-ness and it was like the sun came out from behind a cloud. Immediately I felt better, the tears dried up, and I could fucking breathe. She stroked my hair and another wave of warmth washed over me, and I sighed.

"Thanks a lot," I growled, and she cracked up, reluctantly pushing me away.

"Why do you have to be so difficult about this? If you just let me in without a fight—"

"Said the Big Bad Wolf. You'll huff and puff and blow my house down."

She shook her head. "Your house is made of Army bricks, Jackson. There's no way it's falling down. But it's big enough to let other people in, okay? Especially—"

"Cassidy is your friend, and I don't want you in the middle of this. If what you're saying is true, that she's accepting our ways, then let us work it out, okay?

"You're right. I'm sorry. I don't want to be meddlesome. I just want to see... You know what? Go take a shower, get cleaned up, and be in the commons in an hour. Got it?"

"Yes, ma'am." I rolled my eyes, but I really did feel better after she did her trick. I'd never admit it to her, mostly because she brought out this stubborn streak in me like no one else—and wasn't that my big problem? Not admitting when I needed help. Not asking for help.

Guess it was time for this old dog to learn some new tricks. I just hoped the reward would be a beautiful, stubborn, sexy, and brave woman to love me.

But for that to happen, I needed to get my shit together.

"Good. I want to see her. I've just been all up in my head. Worrying."

Delaney squeezed my arm and then stood up. "She's out with Ryder having her first training session. He's leaving the dogs with her. Nigel thought it might be great to have them here as added security."

"Good. They're pretty awesome, and they took to her right away. Ryder had mentioned that he was thinking about taking pick of the next litter from Simon and Garfunkel's parents so he could train another pair. I'm glad she'll have them. Plus, they're kind of cool."

"They are. It's nice having dogs around here." She stood up and held out a hand to me. "We were talking about going to Shenanigans tonight. Think you might want to join us?"

I took her hand and stood from the couch. "I don't know. I need to get out of *here* though. I think I want to see what shape my classroom is in."

"Well, text me if you want to come. We're not going until later. And by we, I mean Damien and James and Skye. I'm not sure if Cassidy is up for it yet."

I nodded. Maybe after a shower I could work up my courage and go see her.

Delaney gave me a hug. "I'm so glad you're back, and thank you so much for bringing my bestie to me."

"Anything for you," I said, kissing the top of her head. "Now let me go start conga-ing my life, or whatever you call it."

She burst out laughing and did a little dance move I recognized from the '80s. "Not conga. Marie Kondo. I'll bring you a copy of her book."

I waved as she shut the door behind her and then took a deep breath.

Shower. Shave. Clothes. Classroom. I could do this.

The kids were all in the auditorium watching a movie, which I'd learned from Joanna, who kept poking at my brain. I'd been keeping my mind locked up tight, but I let her in because, well, I missed her little voice.

We're watching The Goonies. Have you seen it?

"A bunch of times. It's a great movie."

Will you come watch with me?

My chest swelled with something sweet, and longing for something I never thought I'd have. Never really *had*. Family. I'd thought I was too old when I came here. By forty-six, I should be sending my children off to college or something, expecting grandkids, I don't know. Not thinking about providing a home for a fourteen-year-old.

"I'm going to do some chores that I've been putting off, but I do want to talk to you tomorrow. I've got some things to discuss with you."

You mean about the FBI?

"Yeah. If you want to do it, I'll be with you."

Good. That's good. Okay, you're missing popcorn and sodas.

I sighed so loud it sounded more like a groan, and she laughed.

"I promise. Tomorrow."

Good. I'm glad you're feeling better. And talking to me.

"Yeah, but you're not supposed to talk in the movies, so shhh."

She giggled in reply and then I shut things down. I needed some space. I needed some music. I entered my classroom…and blew out a breath.

I'd expected a mess, but everything was miraculously neat, even neater than I required. And there were drawings. Tons of them. Hung up on wire across the classroom, with notes on them.

We love you, Mr. Howe

We miss you, Mr. Howe

Hurry Back, Mr. Howe

Don't get blown up.

That one was Matteo's. Poor kid. I hoped someone was able to tell him that no, I did not in fact blow myself up. Hopefully…

"Knock knock."

"Come…here." I'd started to invite whoever it was in, but when I saw it was her, I wanted the distance between us gone. I held out a hand to her and held my breath.

Cassidy stood in the doorway, looking as if the last three weeks hadn't happened. She was dressed in black leggings, a long white t-shirt with a sage green cardigan over it, and Dr. Martens finished off the look. Her hair was down and brushed the tops of her shoulders.

She blushed so sweetly as she walked toward where I stood in the middle of the classroom. She paused before me, took my hand and smiled. "How are you feeling?"

I shrugged. "A little more alive every day." I tugged on the sweater sleeve. "Nice threads. I mean, it's not polyester, but it'll do."

She rolled her eyes. "Delaney's clothing chick had some stuff that actually fit me. I can't tell you how nice it is to be wearing actual panties!"

I bit back a crass joke, but I could tell she knew where my mind was.

"You know what I mean."

"I do." There was so much I wanted to say to her, but the words got all jammed up in my mouth. Instead of speaking, I gestured with my head to one of the stools in the room. "Will you take a seat?"

She frowned a little but her smile was still there. She was so confident, so strong. She'd overcome such an awful situation…and I couldn't even tell her how I felt.

So I did what I knew best.

I picked up my charcoals and sat on my own stool.

"Oh," she said, and she hopped up on the stool. "What do I need to do?"

I shook my head and smiled at the picture she made. The afternoon sun cut in through the windows high up on the walls, illuminating her face. I tried to pour all of my emotions, all of my admiration for her into the drawing. I wanted her to see it and know.

"Your students really missed you," she said, looking around at the artwork hanging everywhere. "They're so lucky to have you."

"It's the other way around. I'm the lucky one."

She tangled her fingers together in her lap and I focused on them for a few moments. I thought about how they'd felt when we first met, when I'd first formed a Connection with her, and then how I'd seen them curling around the edges of the wood panels in that infuriating cage Rains had kept her in.

When she'd taken my hand and we'd run, how cold she'd been in the blind and when she'd passed out and I thought I'd lost her. How she'd held my hand at Ryder's, trusted me, all the while knowing I was keeping something—my gift—from her.

How she'd touched me intimately. How she'd walked away but then came back, and we'd started the path toward acceptance. How she'd still trusted me after she'd watched me kill a man, taking my hand once more to flee danger. And then when she'd reached for me in the fire, and I'd thought it would be the last time I'd hold her.

We'd been granted a miracle. The fact that we were even here, living and breathing, seemed impossible after everything we'd been through. Was it impossible to think the miracle could continue? That she could stay, accept me and this place?

"Remember that movie *Speed*?" she asked, and I nodded. "Remember that scene at the end where they roll away from the bus on that dolly thing, and she says that part about relationships formed under stressful situations?"

"Yeah. It's bullshit."

She barked out a laugh. "You think so?"

I set my charcoal down and looked at what I'd drawn. "Some of my strongest friendships have been forged during insane experiences. Ryder and the guys in my unit, Delaney and Damien. I think people show who they really are in stressful situations, and if you make it out alive, you know that person will always have your back."

She stood from her stool and approached me, placing a hand on my shoulder. I couldn't look at her yet, I was barely keeping it together, worried about how she was going to react. I was tempted to open the

Connection, but I was too raw. I wasn't sure I could handle any form of rejection.

"Jackson? Jackson...look at me."

I sighed, took one last look at the drawing, and then prepared myself for the worst.

CHAPTER 37
SHOW DON'T TELL

Cassidy

Jackson lifted his gaze from his drawing and when his eyes met mine, I nearly staggered from the weight. And then I looked at what he'd been working on.

"Oh my God. Jackson."

On a surface level, it was clear he was ridiculously talented. But then I fell into the details, and they told me what I needed to know.

He'd given me a soft smile, which contrasted with the strong angles of my jaw and my clavicles, where they met in the middle. He'd added my freckles, even the ones on my chest, which made me love the drawing even more. They were a part of me that weren't considered traditionally beautiful, but they were me and I loved them. My hands he'd drawn in the position I tended to place them in when I was nervous. He'd seen that. I tended to rub at the base of each finger in a pattern with my thumb, it was just a quirk I'd picked up along the way, probably when I tried to stop cracking my knuckles so much.

My eyes were hazy, though, in the drawing, as if he saw the truth. I could see so much better than after the crash, but it was hard to visualize where my life was going since my vision was still a question. And my view of myself had changed through this whole ordeal. I'd always considered myself a capable pilot, an intelligent woman, and a strong person, but I'd lost my way through my marriage and divorce.

Strength meant something different to me now. It had a physical component, like the fact that I'd survived despite my injuries, that I'd learned to rely on my other senses, including the one that I'd hidden away for so long in order to endure the torture I'd experienced. But it was the strength inside me that mattered most. I hadn't given up or given in when that would have been easier, and I'd learned to trust myself. My vision wasn't as important as those parts of me, and Jackson saw that.

Jackson saw *me*. And I was pretty sure he loved me.

"Hmmm," I said, stepping away and holding my chin in a silly way, like an art critic. "It's good, but I think it's missing something. Let me try."

I was terrible at dealing with heavy stuff, and yeah, I needed to tread carefully with him as I knew he was much more vulnerable than he liked to let on. But I wanted to show him how I felt, since it seemed that showing was an easier way to communicate for him.

I ignored his confused expression and picked up a sketch pad from another easel. "May I?"

He nodded, his brows meeting in the middle.

I touched his hand, which had picked up the charcoal again, and took it from him. Then I stepped away and put a goofy concentration face on, making lots of noises. He stood from his stool and rolled his shoulders back. I noticed he was limping a bit as he walked toward the back of the room, and I hoped Damien had taken care of him like he'd done me.

Man. That guy was brilliant. I was a believer after just one session.

I had no more pain in my shoulder and I had full range of movement. I'd lost it when he was finished, totally bawled like a baby, and hugged him as he laughed quietly.

"I was afraid it was going to hurt forever, that I was going to be crippled by it. I can't believe—"

"Shoulders are probably the most flawed piece of engineering in the human body. If I could have a word with the designer, I'd love to discuss the problematic nature of its construction." He gave me some scientific explanation, but I was so busy moving my arm around and shimmying that it went right over my head.

"Let's see how that does," he'd finally said, "and then we can perhaps take care of some of these scars."

"Those I'm less worried about, since I can't even see myself clearly in the mirror yet."

Damien was sure he would be able to fix me all up, and though I was ready for him to tackle my eyes, he still wanted me to see a specialist.

"Fine," I'd said. "But the next time my arthritis acts up, I'm coming to see you."

He'd smiled, relieved that I was so happy. "I think you'll find that if you remain at Havenhart, you will not be troubled by arthritis. There's a certain magic about this place I can't quite explain, but ask Delaney. She doesn't even need her inhaler anymore."

I'd hugged him again—he was just going to have to get used to it. "You've made me a believer. I can't wait to see Jackson and—"

That was it. I wanted to share the news with Jackson that I was healed. I wanted to share everything with him. I'd woken up the past couple of mornings wishing I could roll over and talk to him about my dreams. I missed his presence like a plant needs the sun's rays to grow, to bloom. He'd made everything so much more bearable, and I knew with him by my side, everything would be just a little brighter, a little easier, a lot better.

While I'd been scribbling away, he'd turned on some music, and I bopped my head to Eve 6 and Disturbed, loving that we had the same taste in music. Delaney had told me he was a rocker like us. I wondered if there was anything *not* to like about this beautiful man.

"Almost finished," I said, now with my tongue hanging out.

I heard him chuckle as he moved around the room, arranging and rearranging paint brushes in their holders. He eventually made his way back to the stool and slumped onto it, a weariness I hated to see in him oozing from his pores.

"Just want to make sure I get the details right," I said, holding up my thumb and squinting. That got him to smile, so I took my thumb and forefinger and pretended to squish his head like a *Kids in the Hall* skit.

"You're quite the professional," he said, reaching one of his long arms toward me. "Let me see."

"Hold on," I said, adding one last item to make it complete as I moved toward him.

He took the pad from me in one hand and brought his other arm around my back, tentatively. I leaned into him and put arm around his shoulders.

"I mean, it's the best I could do under these conditions." I tossed my hair back for effect.

He barked out a laugh.

"Wow, Cassidy. I don't know what to say."

My drawing, unlike his highly skilled work of art, was us as stick figures, and his wore a cape. They stood side by side, holding hands with big smiles on their faces. Above my drawing, I wrote, "Will you go with me? Check this box."

"Here," he said, taking the charcoal from me. He placed it between his fingers and then adjusted it with way too much effort until he finally drew a perfect check mark in the box. Then he set my drawing on the easel and we admired our work side-by-side.

"Yours is definitely going on my wall," he said, wrapping both arms around me, pulling me into his body and between his powerful thighs.

"Will I be able to come see it? I'm quite proud of it."

"I don't know. They frown upon fraternization in the boys' dorm around here. Maybe we should put them both up at your place…that is, if you're going to stay?"

I linked my arms around his neck and pressed against him, loving the way his body sheltered me. He'd given me such gifts; my life, his love.

"I am. For now." He started to lower his head, but I lifted his chin with my finger. "I don't know what's going to happen, Jackson, but I know I *am* staying in this. With you. And since you checked the box, you're stuck now."

He smiled and licked his lips. "I didn't realize that it was a binding contract. Maybe I should have my lawyer look it over."

"You have a lawyer?"

He ran his broad hands up my spine and scored the back of my head with his fingers. "I do, around here somewhere. Isaac was a lawyer before he came here to teach. And Nigel is also a lawyer, among other things." He gazed deep into me with those green eyes. "I love you, Cassidy. I understand if you don't feel the same, but I need to be honest with you." He started to tremble and his chin quivered. "I know you have to figure things out, but I'm afraid of what that means."

"Jackson, you know how I feel, don't you? You can see things about me that even I don't know."

He shook his head and let out a shaky breath. "No, I shut it down. I won't do that to you."

"I want you to. See inside me, Jackson. See how I feel. I want you to."

I was just as frightened as him. I'd never laid myself bare like this for anyone, not Delaney, not my husband…no one had ever had the kind of access to me that I was giving Jackson. I hoped he knew what that meant.

He searched my gaze, his blue eyes—not sky or sea blue, but something darker, deeper—held me in place. He held me so close, I could even make out where the colors met and bled into each other. He took a deep breath, and there was a subtle shift as the gray took over the blue and his pupils widened, only for a split second, but it was a visual clue that he'd opened the Connection between us.

Then he gasped, and pulled me tighter against him.

"Cassidy." He placed his hands on the sides of my head and pressed our foreheads together. "God, sweetheart, thank you. I love you so much."

I wanted him to kiss me, and he did, and it was…everything. We clung to each other, our bodies communicating all the things we wanted to express. *I love you, I need you, I belong to you.*

When we'd been intimate before, the experience had been almost dreamlike. We'd been trying to escape our reality and our physical pain. But this time it was so much more intense. He kissed me like we were indeed binding ourselves to each other, making a vow to hold each other up despite the trials and travails in our path. He was saying he'd be there for me no matter what, and I was telling him he'd never be alone again.

We might not have the words to say all of these things now, but the kiss sealed our fate, bound us together in a way words couldn't muck up.

And just when I thought we'd shut out the world, the world let us know we weren't alone.

"Hey, Ranger, you in here— Oh...sorry, brother."

James had peeked his head in and was trying to leave when Jackson called out to him.

"Come on in." He turned me around and wrapped his arms around my waist. "Don't move, I'm not done...talking."

"I didn't mean to interrupt. Hey, Cassidy."

"Hi, James, you're not interrupting." Delaney's cousin looked scary on a good day. Today, he looked like he'd seen a ghost.

"Sorry. Howe, your buddy Ryder said you guys have some connections up in Oregon?"

"Yeah, I think so. Why? What's up?"

James ran a hand over his shaved head. "I got a weird phone call from a hospital up there. Some doctor saying she had some information about Tiffany."

Jackson sat up straighter. "Your daughter? What did she say?"

"That she had some questions was all, and the message cut off. I tried to call back, but the hospital said she's not on duty again for a couple more days. I'm thinking about heading up there to do a little recon, but Ryder said I should talk to you first. He's a good guy...for a Ranger."

Jackson smiled. "He's the best. Yeah, let's check in with him—"

"Tomorrow," he said, waving a hand in dismissal. "We're heading over to the bar for now. Besides, it's getting late. Cassidy, Ryder's out walking the boys and then he'll lock them up in your place, okay?"

"Thanks, James."

He grinned and tugged at his long goatee. "You two want to join us or...?"

Jackson looked at me with his eyebrows raised. I let him know in no uncertain terms that I needed to be alone with him and a bed as soon as possible, complete with mental visuals, and his cheeks turned red.

"No, man, but thanks. Let's make some calls in the morning, though, okay?"

James nodded. "It's probably nothing. Yeah, I'll see you in the morning." He waved at us as he left.

"It's like that, huh?" Jackson asked me as he buried his face in my neck, inhaling deeply before kissing the sensitive indent where it curved into my shoulder.

"It's totally like that. I would love to hang out and go to the bar, but if it's alright with you—"

Jackson stood from his stool and stepped away. "I heard you loud and clear. Let me just grab my phone." He reached over to pick up his phone from the dock next to a Bluetooth speaker when a familiar riff came on. He turned on me with wide eyes and a mischievous grin, snapping his fingers as he stuck it in his pocket, the tune continuing to play as he walked toward me.

"If I go crazy..." he sang to me, and I answered with "will you still call me Superman." He took my hand, and we sang the song together as we walked through the door and into our new life together.

EPILOGUE

Jackson

"Please can we do it one more time?"

Joanna hopped up and down on her toes as I groaned.

"How can you not be ready to hurl?" I asked her.

"Because it's so fun!"

Cassidy took pity on me. "Why don't you go sit over there with the other old people and I'll take her again."

I reached for her hand and held it up to place a kiss on my favorite special spot between her knuckles. She had a heart-shaped freckle there, which I determined I was the one to discover. "My queen."

She rolled her eyes, and the two most important people in my life trotted off together.

I parked my tired ass on a bench and watched them run into the gates of the Hollywood Tower Hotel at Disney's Hollywood Studios with the other crazy folks who enjoyed the wild ride. My stomach couldn't take another series of drops like that. The flashing lights weren't great either, with my newfound seizure disorder.

Yeah, I'd gained more than a couple of new parlor tricks from my time in the Everglades. I hadn't been that excited to come back to the Sunshine State, but Joanna desperately wanted to come to Disney World, and with Rains and his pals in the custody of folks who absolutely could not be swayed to let him go, Nigel felt confident that we could make the trip safely.

Barringer had been instrumental in his capture and while he hadn't been at liberty to share the details, it was clear he and Nigel had been working together to create the perfect place for Rains—and people like him—who chose to use their gifts for evil. Nigel made it clear that it was separate from Havenhart, and that he didn't want any of us involved. I had a lot of questions, and not many answers.

My phone buzzed in my pocket, and I pulled it out.

"Think of the devil and he shall appear. Agent Barringer, how's it going?" I pushed my hair out of my face and sat back. The in-between stage was killing me. I couldn't wait until it was long enough to pull back. I couldn't even count the times I'd gotten paint or glaze in it while working in the school's studio.

His laughter echoed through a lousy connection. "You enjoying the Magic Kingdom?"

"That's tomorrow," I said with a laugh. "She wanted to start with Hollywood Studios, and whatever she wants, she gets."

Barringer chuckled and I heard him speak to someone else for a moment before he was back. "Sorry. Taking care of some business. You've taken to parenting like a pro, Howe."

I shrugged, but I was curious what he was up to. "It's easy with her. She's such a great kid. Everything set up for tonight?"

"That's why I was calling. I'll collect you and the ladies from the hotel and we'll meet up with Abel's handler. We're going to meet at a safe house not too far from where Irene and Denise are staying with *their* handlers. They're going to be moved out of state soon, but we wanted to be sure the siblings got to meet before that happens. Once they're in witness protection, this won't be possible for a long while. I'm hoping after the trial there won't be a need for this level of security, but we just don't know how many of his people are still out there."

"No kidding. I appreciate the security. Charisse's colleague is here, too, but out of sight, so I feel okay with the meeting happening."

"Roger that. Does Joanna know or did you decide to surprise her?"

"Really? You think she wasn't going to find out? She's excited. Cassidy is understandably nervous to see Abel."

Barringer sighed into the phone. "I get it. She has every right to be, but I'm telling you, the guy has gone through quite a bit of personal growth these past few months. He's a total sponge, learning everything he can, cooperating with the task force. He wants to go to college, maybe even be an agent someday."

"Would he pass the background check?"

"I don't know," Barringer said. "But even if he can't be in law enforcement, he's going to do big things. I can tell. The kid is driven, Jackson. He wants to make amends for all of the awful things his father has done."

"Joanna is the same. That's too much of a load for these kids to bear. We have Joanna working with a therapist who specializes in PTSD. The nightmares were getting really bad."

"These poor kids. Okay, you enjoy your day at the park, and we'll see you guys after dinner."

"Thanks, man," I said. I disconnected just as my two women came running at me. "Ready to hurl yet?"

Cassidy rubbed her stomach but she laughed as she hugged Joanna to her side. "No, but this one is ready to eat again."

"Again?" I teased. "Are you sure you're not trying to grow a third leg or something?"

"Come on, Jack-son," she said, tugging my hand to pull me off the bench. "I want some more sugar!"

I let her pull and pull, knowing full well she couldn't make me budge. It had been a wild ride with her over the past year. From the moment Damien and Delaney had rescued her last August, to February and March when her father arranged Cassidy's hijacking and kidnapping, Joanna had been trying to acclimate to an unfamiliar world. She was more trusting with the adults on campus than she should have been, but thankfully we were all looking out for her best interest. She'd made a few friends, but there had been hiccups along the way.

After Cassidy and I returned to Havenhart, I'd known Joanna

deserved better than to just be a ward of the school, and so I'd discussed again the possibility of becoming her legal guardian with Nigel. Because of the circumstances, adoption wasn't possible at the moment, but becoming her guardian was my way of showing her that I'd always have her back, like she'd had mine and Cassidy's.

I thought I was being all chivalrous, taking her out to dinner in town to talk to her about it, but she'd already Seen it happening, and she was thrilled. Imagine that. Your life being so tumultuous that you'd be excited about having a wounded, retired mess of an Army Ranger—who hadn't done a great job of taking care of himself—as your legal guardian.

She hadn't cared though, and Nigel put the wheels into motion to make it so. This trip to Disney World was our celebration of being a family, and Joanna was happier than I'd ever seen her.

I hoped she'd still be that way after meeting her siblings tonight.

I finally let her pull me up from the bench, and I slung my arms around both of my women as we set out in search of more food for the Bottomless Pit. We found a Mexican-themed food court with an ice cream counter and she settled on a giant ice cream cone. Cassidy and I grabbed a table a few feet away from the line so we could see her.

Cassidy's vision had improved with Damien's help, and two surgeries to remove debris and repair her retina in one eye. She'd been cleared to fly a month ago, but she wanted to take her time. Once she'd decided that being a pilot didn't define her, she was able to be patient with her recovery.

"I've never had so much fun at an amusement park," Cassidy said, snuggling into my side.

"I'm glad you came with us." I kissed the top of her head and gave her a squeeze. "On this trip and on this journey."

Cassidy smiled up at me. "Of course. I wouldn't have it any other way."

We'd taken two weekend trips alone in the past couple of months, one to see Cassidy's parents and one to take the boys back to see Ryder. She'd decided if she was going to be their dog mom, she wanted to learn how to best utilize their training. Ryder had been thrilled to teach her how to do search and rescue. She planned to volunteer with the local authorities and was scheduled for a full course of classes in a month.

It was all part of Cassidy's healing process, and honestly it was good for me as well. We had a lot of trauma to work through, but our relationship continued to grow stronger every day. And she and Joanna were tight. They liked to gang up on me, which was perfectly fine. I'd take it if it meant they were both safe and in my life.

"So, I wanted to give you both a little update."

Joanna stared expectantly as she licked her ice cream cone. Cassidy handed her a napkin to catch the drips that were ready to roll over Joanna's hand. The sight of them working together had me rubbing at my chest.

My girls.

"I've given Nigel notice that I'd like to be relieved of my dorm duties for the next school year, and he was perfectly happy to do that, provided I accepted more responsibility in the running of the school."

Now both of my girls tilted their heads in concern.

"Is everything okay?" Cassidy asked, reaching for my hand. I linked our fingers together and smiled nervously. We'd been through so much and still, her touch gave me butterflies and grounded me at the same time.

"Yeah, it's fine, but this is confidential."

I gave Joanna a pointed glance and she made the symbol for locking up her lips in return.

"Nigel plans to promote Damien to Headmaster, and he wants me to take over Damien's responsibilities. I'm happy to do it. I owe my life to Damien and Nigel. We make a good team. And Nigel has some other business to attend to that's going to keep him away from campus, which I am not at liberty to discuss."

"It has to do with my father," Joanna said gravely. "I know he and Agent Barringer have been talking."

This was the part I needed to work on. It was hard to scold her. "Joanna, there's a reason they haven't kept you informed of your father's whereabouts."

She ducked her head and her shoulders hunched over. "I'm sorry."

I moved to her side, and Cassidy took the ice cream cone from her, placing it in a paper bowl.

"Honey, we know you can't always control what you See, but it's for your own safety. We want to keep him out of your head, and we're not sure how much it goes back and forth, you know?"

"I want to help, though."

I pulled her into a hug and kissed the top of her head, giving Cassidy a worried look. "You are, honey. You are so brave. But this is your time to be a kid. You won't get this time back, so let us grown-ups handle the icky stuff."

She groaned and rolled her eyes. "I'm almost fifteen. I'm not a little kid."

Don't I know it. "Which brings me to the other part of my news. Since I'm taking on additional responsibilities, I'll be moving out of the dorms and into Nigel's house. For some reason, he thinks I'll be a good caretaker of his big ol' mansion and all his fancy things."

I shrugged, Cassidy gasped, and Joanna clapped her hands.

"That's so cool! Can I come visit?"

I placed my hands on her shoulders. "You can do more than that. You can come live with me on holidays and school breaks, in the summer. You'll have your own room that you get to decorate and— No, honey! Why are you crying?"

Her big blue eyes were overflowing with huge teardrops. It broke my damn heart.

"Joanna?"

"I've never had my own room before. I never even lived in one place for more than a few months at a time since I was little."

"Joanna, this is why I wanted to be your guardian. I want you to have a home, have a real family."

She wiped at her tears. "Can we decorate for holidays? Like, a Christmas tree? And oh! Can we celebrate Halloween? I always wanted to."

The light within her shone so bright as she bounced in her seat, dreaming of all the possibilities.

"Whatever you want, honey."

She clapped her hands, and I caught Cassidy wiping at a tear. I gave her hand a squeeze and she smiled.

Joanna turned to face her. "And you'll be there, too."

It wasn't a question.

"I...well, of course, I'll be around."

"Joanna—"

"But you guys—"

"Give me a second to ask her, would ya?"

"Oh," Joanna said, covering her mouth. "Sorry. I'm, uh, gonna go grab a spoon for...a few minutes." She jumped up from the table and ran toward the condiment cart, then stopped and turned back to us. She ran for me and gave me a big hug before running away again.

"Oh, the roller coaster that is life with a teenaged girl," Cassidy said.

I took both of her hands in mine. "I want it, I want every minute of it. And I want you to share it with me."

Her eyebrows shot up. "What?"

"Marry me, Cassidy. Please. I know you'll be traveling and in school, but I want to be the home you come back to. I want movie nights, slumber parties, adult happy hour, alone time...I want it all with you, like a real family."

"I...I love you, Jackson, but are you sure about all this?"

"I've never been as sure about anything in my life. You and I make a great team, we have since the start, and I want to spend the rest of my life with you, whatever that means, however that looks."

"We do make a great team," she said, looking at our hands together. "And I kinda like the idea of being a stepmom to that sweet girl."

"So you'll do it? You'll marry me?" I got down on my knee at the exact time that a mariachi band happened to start playing, or so I thought, until I saw Joanna whispering to the bandleader. *I love that little girl.*

Cassidy teared up and started laughing. "You're really doing this?"

"Yup." I reached into my pocket. "I got a ring and everything."

While brightening up my apartment, per Nigel's instructions, I went through a box of my parents' things and found my grandmother's wedding set. My parents hadn't found happiness together, but my grandparents shared a love for the ages. I think that was part of my mother's disappointment with my father. She knew they weren't destined for a love like her own parents, but she made do. Now I had a chance to have what she didn't. If Cassidy said yes.

"All right, under one condition…"

"Name it."

She sighed. "We do it at the courthouse, or in Vegas. I don't want to step foot in another church—"

"Done." I put the ring at the tip of her finger. "May I?"

She gasped. "Oh, Jackson. It's beautiful."

"Did she say yes?" Joanna shouted over the music.

"Yes, she said yes," Cassidy called, then nodded for me to slide the ring on her finger. She gestured for Joanna to come over, and we were tackle-hugged while the entire food court cheered for us.

I hugged my girls tight and knew I'd been blessed. No matter the sins of my past, the people I felt I'd let down, these two loved me and we were going to be a family. Together. Against the world.

"Can we go on the Tower of Terror one more time?"

I groaned but how could I say no?

"Anything for you. We have time for one more ride before we gotta head back to the hotel."

Joanna lit up, clapping her hands at the next part of our adventure. She chatted nonstop on the walk back to the ride about how she couldn't wait to meet her siblings, and I prayed to whoever was listening that I could keep her safe from any harm when it came to her biological family.

I smiled at Cassidy, who was absolutely glowing as she stared at her hand. I was determined to make this marriage a better experience for her than her last one. I'd never let her down, never betray her. I'd be her Superman as long as I had breath in my body.

Which better be a long-ass time. I had a lot of love to give these two women, and I didn't want to waste another minute.

THE END…

ACKNOWLEDGMENTS

Connection has been one of the most difficult books I've ever written. I'd started it in 2012 after I finished the first draft of Healer and then abandoned it until 2020…in the middle of The Great Pause, when creativity and focus were under attack. I couldn't have done it without the help of my brilliant editor, Kelli Collins.

To my family who continue to support me following my dreams. I love you. I promise, I'll take that pile of donations to the drop off.

To my dear friends Chrissy and Vanessa, thank you for sharing your life with me. So glad to have you on my side after all these years.

I also couldn't have survived the past couple of years in my writing life without the support of my writery pals: Marielle, Sera, Eva, the SBC: Shannon, Kilby, Amy, Rebecca, Addie, Jackie, Anne, Elizabeth, and Dafina. The ridiculously talented Emerian Rich, mistress of all things HorrorAddicts.net and Author Babes Loren, Michele, E.M. and Heather. My coach Rachel Herron and the 90 Days Revision cohort who cheered me on. My BAQWA pals Marvin, Liz, Wayne, Rick, Baz, Gar, and Vincent. To Amy, Phyllis, Scott, and Annabeth who are always there when I have a question, I appreciate you! To Avery, thank you for your guidance and for introducing me to PA extraordinaire, Rachel! You totally rock! And to Angela James and my friends in the From Written to Recommended and Book Boss cohort, you are all superstars.

Thanks also to my beta readers Tricia and Wendy, MMU maven

Wanda, and my awesome readers in Ro's Roadies of Romance who have been shouting at me for the past two years to finally get this book out into the world (Agnieszka, I heard you all the way in Poland).

My heart goes out to all of those who have suffered trauma at the hands of folks who use their power and faith to do harm.

Stay Tuned for More of *The Gifted* universe...

ABOUT R.L. MERRILL

Whether she's writing contemporary romance featuring quirky and relatable characters or diving deep into the paranormal and supernatural to give readers a shiver, R.L. Merrill loves creating compelling stories that will stay with readers long after. Winner of the Kathryn Hayes "When Sparks Fly" Best Contemporary award for Hurricane Reese, and a Foreword INDIES finalist for Summer of Hush, Ro spends every spare moment improving her writing craft and striving to find that perfect balance between real-life and happily ever after. She writes diverse and inclusive romance, contributes paranormal hilarity to Robyn Peterman's Magic and Mayhem Universe, and pens horror-inspired music reviews for HorrorAddicts.net. You can find her connecting with readers on social media, advocating for America's youth, raising two brilliant kids, or headbanging at a rock show near her home in the San Francisco Bay Area! Stay Tuned for more…

Visit my website at www.rlmerrillauthor.com. Join Ro's Roadies of Romance for hijinks and hilarity!

COMING NEXT...

And Coming September 2022, I'll be releasing a new supernatural suspense/paranormal romance connected to the Gifted series called *Sundowners*...

I'll also be joining the folks in the Love Is All project to raise funds for the LGBTQ community in June and Book Three in The Miscreants series, part of the Magic and Mayhem Universe, will be out in October 2022.

I'll also be releasing audiobooks for A Match Made in Spain and Healer: Gifted Book One this year! I'm thrilled to finally be joining the audio world.

Follow me on BookBub and sign-up at www.rlmerrillauthor.com for my newsletter for the latest news!

OTHER BOOKS BY R.L. MERRILL

Haunted Series: (Contemporary Romance)

Haunted

Fated

Bated

Jaded – (Coming Soon)

Minded Series: (Paranormal Spinoff of Haunted Series)

Minded

Blossomed

Father F'in' Christmas

A Peculiar Prom Night

Magic and Mayhem Universe: (Funny Paranormal Romance in the universe created by Robyn Peterman)

Shifted

Ghoul Me Once

Gator Me Twice

Magic and Mayhem/Shifted Collection

Fang Me Three Times

Fangtastic Four

Next Installment October 2022

Hollywood Rock 'n' Romance Trilogy: (Contemporary Romance)

Teacher

Teacher: Act Two

Teacher: The Final Act

Contemporary Romance Series:

The Rock Season

Road Trip

You Fell First

The Heart Knows (Re-Release 2022)

A Match Made in Spain

LGBTQ Romance

Pinups and Puppies (Originally in Love Is All Vol. 2)

I Want, More – Bolder Breed Studios #1 (Love Is All Vol. 3)

Love and Pride – Bolder Breed Studios #2 (Love Is All Vol. 4, out solo November 2021)

The Gifted Series: (Supernatural Suspense/Paranormal Romance)

Healer

Connection

Forces of Nature Series: (Gay Contemporary Romance)

Hurricane Reese

Typhoon Toby

Earthquake Ethan (Coming Soon)

Summer of Hush Series: (Gay Contemporary Romance)

Summer of Hush

Brains and Brawn

Book Three (Coming Soon)

Anthologies:

Thanksgiving Day Parade From Hell (Worst Holiday Ever) (Gay Contemporary Romance

Valentine's Day From Hell (Worst Valentine's Day Ever) (Gay Contemporary Romance)

Salty and Sweet (Summer Fair) (Lesbian Contemporary Romance)

The Fourth Man (The Banes of Lake's Crossing) (Historical Horror Romance)

A Piece of Him (Gone With The Dead) (Horror)

Breaking Bread—Dark Divinations from HorrorAddicts.net Press (Horror)

Exchange (Renewal) (Science Fiction)

Tap-Tap-Tap (Impact) (Horror)

Human Sacrifice (Innovation) (Horror)

Joy Is A Phone Call Away – A More Perfect Union (Lesbian Contemporary Romance)

The House Must Fall – Haunts and Hellions from HorrorAddicts.net Press – May 2021 (Horror)

A Kept Woman – BAQWA Presents: Horror Show 2021(Lesbian Horror Romance)

Gods of Rock 'n' Roll (email Ro for a copy at rlmerrillauthor@gmail.com)

How Bittersweet is Karma?

Holiday Romance

A Peace Offering (Re-release)

Love and Pride – Bolder Breed Studios #2

Audiobooks

The Rock Season (Kiss App)

Brains and Brawn (Kiss App)

A Match Made in Spain (Summer 2022)

Healer: Gifted Book One (Fall 2022)

Made in the USA
Columbia, SC
12 March 2024

32519009R00224